PRAISE FOR *HIDDEN*

"[A] thrilling tale of passion and suspense...Realistic characters and a frightening plot will keep readers spellbound with numerous twists and turns...Wraps up with a love scene that's hot enough to make a polar bear sweat."

– Romantic Times Book Review, 4½ stars

"A page-turning blend of romance, thrills, and danger! *Hidden* is a winning debut from a new star in romantic suspense."

– Allison Brennan, *New York Times* bestselling author

"Make room on your keeper shelf! *Hidden* has it all: intricate plotting, engaging characters, a truly twisted villain. I can't wait to see what Kendra Elliot dishes up next!"

– Karen Rose, *New York Times* bestselling author

ALSO BY KENDRA ELLIOT

Hidden

CHILLED

Text copyright ©2012 by Kendra Elliot
All rights reserved.

Printed in the United States of America.

Published by Montlake Romance
P.O. Box 400818
Las Vegas, NV 89140

ISBN-13: 9781612183893
ISBN-10: 1612183891

CHILLED

A BONE SECRETS NOVEL

KENDRA ELLIOT

Montlake
Romance

For Dan, who believed in Fate

CHAPTER ONE

"Here's the plane's last known whereabouts." Sheriff Patrick Collins tapped a finger on the plastic Cascade Mountains map spread across his Suburban's hood and turned a resolute brown gaze on his team. Shivering, Brynn studied the wet map, ignoring a buzzing rush as it dumped a load of adrenaline in her gut.

It felt good.

"A hunter called it in late yesterday. He'd seen a plane flying low through the range that sounded like it was in trouble." Collins spoke grimly. A dark, lean man, the deep lines around his mouth reflected his demanding twenty-five years with the sheriff's department. "He said the little plane barely made it over Cougar Ridge, and he swore it had to have hit the trees on the other side of the ridge, but he couldn't see any smoke from his position."

The determined eyes of his three Madison County Search and Rescue team members memorized the spot on the map as icy rain ran off their red hoods. Brynn brushed a drip off her cheek and plunged her hands into the pockets of her winter parka.

"He didn't try to check it out? Give us a clearer location?" Jim Wolf, the SAR team's leader, scowled at the map. Confidence hovered around the stocky man like a mist. "The possible search area is huge."

Collins shook his head. "He was alone and scouting from the forest service road." He drew his finger along a dotted line on the map. "From that road—actually it's more like a muddy, rut-crammed path—Cougar Ridge is over a thousand feet straight up before it drops to form a deep valley in the Cascades. There's no way he could have hiked up there."

Brynn eyed the distance from Collins's finger to their present location on the map. "We're miles away," she muttered. From the spot where a small plane *may have* crashed in a huge forest.

"This is the quickest way into that valley," Collins stated. "It's gonna be a harsh run. You guys are the most experienced, and that's why I want you out there. You're the best hasty team I've got."

As the hasty team, their mission was to get in to the emergency site first and fast, and assess the location. The sheriff's department had nicknamed them "hard chargers." After appraising the situation, they communicated their needs to the sheriff, requesting specific help or conveying bad news.

Brynn watched as Collins traced a route from the trailhead where they stood. The route left a groomed wilderness trail and pushed through one of the densest forests in the Cascades. The path wasn't flat. There were ups and downs all the way to the site. Mostly ups.

It was going to be a tough one.

Bring it on.

Two wavy blue lines crossed their projected path on the map, and Brynn's stomach gave an acid twinge. Rivers. And they'd be deadly fast and high from the five inches of Oregon rain in the last twenty-four hours. She glanced at the three men. Sheriff Collins and the biggest member of the team, Thomas Todoroff, were studying the route, discussing elevation. Jim wasn't looking at the map. His concerned gaze rested on her; he knew her hatred of river crossings. She gave him the tiniest shake of her head.

"So we don't know for sure if the plane even went down? And we're guessing where it might've crashed?" Steam hovered in the frosty air from Brynn's quick questions. She'd wanted to distract Jim, get his piercing eyes off her. "What about its emergency locator transmitter? Can't they pinpoint it?"

Collins shook his head. "The plane didn't make its scheduled landing at the Hillsdale airport last night. Calls to other airports confirmed it hadn't landed anywhere within two hundred miles. And as for the ELT, no one can pick up anything. You've got to be in line of sight to pick up the signal, and the crappy weather is keeping away the search planes. Or it's possible the ELT is damaged and not working."

"Not working? I thought those things were indestructible." The words tripped out of Brynn's mouth as she stared at the sheriff.

"They run on batteries," was the dour reply. "Or can be turned off."

The group grumbled in unison at the information.

"No luck with the radar?" Jim asked.

The sheriff grimaced. "Apparently, there are several radar gaps going over the Cascades. The hunter's visual spot was farther north than where the plane last appeared on radar. That valley's the best place we've got to start, and this weather isn't going to let up, so we've got to go in on foot." Collins paused. "One more thing." Three gazes locked onto his, and Brynn tensed at the heavy discomfort in his eyes.

What worse news could he tell us?

Collins rubbed his lips together.

"What?" Jim asked sharply. "What is it?"

"I got a call from the US Marshals' office early this morning. Looks like the plane's one of their transports."

Transport? A plane packed full of convicts?

"I thought they flew the big stuff. You said this plane was small." Brynn's stomach twisted.

Collins shook his head. "This was a lease. They were moving a single prisoner back to Portland. The caller also told me there were two pilots and a marshal on board."

Brynn's stomach relaxed the littlest bit. *Only one convict.*

"What kind of prisoner? What'd he do?" Thomas cut to the chase. The dark man didn't usually say much, but when he did, it was direct and to the point. The huge Alaskan hoarded words like thousand-dollar bills.

"'Extremely dangerous' was the phrase the marshal used to describe him." Collins's brown eyes glanced at Brynn. "He didn't get more specific, but I could tell he was uncomfortable with the idea that the guy might be loose. Even in this freezing wilderness."

Brynn looked steadily at the sheriff. He wanted to suggest she sit this search out, but he didn't dare say the words. Her team's first instinct was to keep her out of harm's way. She was a nurse, not a cop. Thomas and Jim were both deputies with the Madison County sheriff's office, and she was the only one without a gun or two hidden on her body. Her job as a death investigator with the medical examiner's office didn't require firepower. Her role on the team was strictly medical support and investigation.

She glanced around the dreary clearing.

"Where's Ryan? He's going in with us, right?" Brynn asked Collins.

Ryan Sheridan made up the fourth and final member of their SAR team. The young, energetic cowboy of a cop worked for the city of Salem and volunteered for the rescue team. Just like the rest of them. No bonus pay here.

Collins's cell phone rang. He glanced at its face as he answered Brynn's question. "Ryan should be here any second. I called him at six this morning. Same as you guys. I gotta take this call. It's the marshals' office again. Hang tight for a minute." He stepped away from the truck.

Brynn glanced at the other two men. "Marshals? Like in *The Fugitive*? Or *Con Air*?" Images of Tommy Lee Jones and John Cusack dashed through her mind.

"Extremely dangerous? What the hell does that mean?" muttered Jim. "A fucked-up felon, probably. A damn rapist who likes little girls or a murderer who likes to feed his victims their fingers before he finishes them off. A piece of shit I don't want to waste my time on in this fucking weather."

"Jesus, Jim. Thanks for the lovely images." Brynn swallowed the lump in her throat and took another look at the dark sky. *A rapist? Murderer?*

Jim clomped his waterproof boot in a puddle, sending muddy water shooting in all directions. "Hate the rain. Classic March in Oregon."

"Beats hiking in during a snowstorm," Thomas spoke up. He'd removed the hood from his parka, pulled the collar up around his neck, and put on a red cap with the Madison County SAR logo. Thomas never wore hoods. Brynn felt the icy breeze touch her cheeks and wondered how he put up with the bitter cold on his neck.

"We're gonna get snow. Weather report shows temps dropping. We'll have snow tonight and tomorrow." Both men swore at Brynn's words. This wasn't a one-day, quickie in-and-out rescue. They'd be in the freezing wild for at least two nights.

The weather didn't bother her. She welcomed the rescue trip for the chance to get out of town and put some space between herself and Liam. She guiltily fingered the cell phone in her pocket. Liam had been asleep when she got the call for the mission. She'd left him a note.

She flipped open her phone and held down the end key until the screen shut off.

"Hey." Jim pulled her aside two steps and lowered his voice, his blue eyes probing. "Any chance you're pregnant?"

"What?" She shot out the word as her lungs stopped functioning. *Pregnant? Where the fuck did that question come from?*

Jim had the decency to blush, an odd sight on the rugged man. "Liam was pretty pissed about what happened to you on our last rescue mission. He claimed he was gonna get you knocked up to keep you out of the woods."

"Liam said *what?*" Brynn's throat choked out the words. Knocked up? Was this a movie? Just because Jim had known her since she was fifteen didn't give him the right to stick his nose in her private life. Blinking rapidly in the misting rain, Brynn opened her mouth and then closed it, coughed, glared at Jim, and then tried again. "First of all, it's none of your damned business."

"As field team leader—"

She cut off his words with a sharp swipe of her hand in the air. "You need to think twice about the crap spilling out of your mouth, Jim. Liam doesn't decide if I'm getting pregnant." *And then tell* you *about it.*

"He was furious when you got caught in that rockfall last time. You were lucky to walk away with a concussion and broken collarbone," Jim argued, leaning closer.

Her face heated, she glanced at Thomas, who was blatantly following the conversation with mild amusement. "That could've happened to anyone. I'm gonna pretend you never brought up this subject. If Anna knew you were talking to me like this you'd be sleeping on the couch for a month."

She wanted to smack Jim on the back of the head. His wife, Anna, would cheer her on. Jim pressed his lips together.

Brynn seethed, her vision tunneling. Was Liam trying to ruin her volunteer job? And why in hell was Liam discussing private things with Jim? *Jesus Christ. Pregnant?* She blew out a breath. She'd been right to sneak out this morning.

Jim shouldn't listen to Liam. Liam was the one who'd been sleeping on the couch for a month at his brother's house. There was no possibility she was pregnant. The only reason Liam had stayed in her spare room last night was because they'd argued late into the evening. She bit her tongue. She didn't have the energy to explain their issues to Jim. He thought Liam and she were still living together and skipping down the contented road to marriage.

Wasn't. Going. To. Happen.

At the sound of sharp barking, she turned toward the forest. Her gray-and-white dog bounded out of the trees, leaping over puddles as it sped toward the group.

"Kiana!" Brynn held her arms straight out from her sides and then brought her hands together at her stomach. "Come 'ere, girl!"

At a second hand command, the dog skidded to a stop directly in front of Brynn. Brynn jumped and ducked back, knowing what was coming. Kiana shook, drenching Jim, and then she sat, her eager blue gaze on her master. Jim cursed at the unexpected soaking.

Good dog.

"I think you're waterproof. It's just a little more rain." She scratched the dog under the chin, smiling as Jim gave Kiana a rough head rub with both hands. The dog pressed her nose against Jim's leg, asking for more attention. Seeing her dog soak Jim cheered Brynn immensely, and their spat was forgotten. Almost.

"Rain doesn't fall upward." Jim brushed the dirty water off his cheeks.

An old Ford truck roared into the clearing and parked behind Brynn's Nissan. Brynn watched Ryan Sheridan toss his battered cowboy hat on the seat, yank up his jacket's hood, grab his backpack, and jog over to join their group, holding the forty-pound pack like it was a sack lunch.

He slung on his pack. "Sorry. Traffic sucked. Are we ready?" He nodded at the three waiting team members, his gaze eager. Enthusiasm radiated from Ryan. He was pumped for the mission. As usual.

Thomas shook his head, tipping it at the sheriff. "Collins hasn't given the OK yet."

Jim updated the late member on what they knew about the plane and its occupants.

Ryan's eyes lit up. "A felon? Someone's ass to haul back in cuffs. Excellent."

Collins slapped his phone shut and marched back to the wet clique. Brynn eyed the tight muscle in his jaw and stiff set to his neck and knew he was furious.

"OK. Listen up. We've got a fed coming in from the marshals' office. They say he'll be here any minute, and he's going out on the search and rescue with you guys."

"What?" Brynn blinked.

"Bull-shee-it." Ryan drew out the word into three syllables.

"Forget it." Jim shook his head. "We don't need some idiot who doesn't know what the hell he's doing out here. I won't compromise my team's safety or speed with a suit."

Collins went on as if he hadn't heard, "We are to extend every courtesy…"

"Courtesy? It's not a fucking tea party. Do we have to take this guy on the mission? What if he can't keep up?" Thomas's angry voice packed the intensity of a lion.

Collins firmly met the livid man's gaze. "I told them this wasn't how we did things out here. But he insisted. That was the head honcho at the Oregon US Marshals' office, and if he says he wants a man on our team, then he'll get a man on our team." Collins blew out a harsh breath. "I'm outranked here. He says the marshal is physically fit and won't have a problem keeping up. Claims the marshal competes in triathlons. I don't have a sufficient reason to turn him down."

The search and rescue quartet stood silent.

Jim spoke first. "You know there's more than just fitness involved out there, Collins. It can be a mental nightmare. Especially if the crash site is an ugly one. You're telling me I'm taking a rookie into this shitty weather to find a plane crash that has a convicted criminal on board? Maybe a murderer?"

At the word *convicted,* Ryan's gaze met Brynn's and an eager grin stretched across his face. *Adrenaline junkie.* She narrowed her eyes at him and he winked back with those damned gorgeous lashes. He had a face high school girls would pin on their walls. Adult women too.

"Marshals aren't wimps. I think he can handle whatever gets thrown at him. And that plane's carrying a pair of blameless pilots and at least one other agent who deserve our damnedest effort." Collins spotted Ryan's grin. "No hotdog stuff. You'll probably be disappointed anyway."

Translation: a plane crash in the Oregon Cascades meant death.

"This is a big-ass waste of time," Thomas said evenly. "No one can survive a crash out there, and chances are we won't find the plane until we get some air support. It's going to be like hiking in circles in the Arctic."

"Fine. You sit on your big ass." Brynn glowered at him, her voice sharp. "I won't wait around when there's a chance that someone's hurt out there and my help could determine whether or not they live. That's not how I'm programmed. If there's a chance I can help, then damn it, I'm going in. And I don't care if it's a convict or your grandma. It makes no difference to me."

The plinking sound of rain on their outdoor gear was the only noise in the forest clearing. Thomas had looked down at Brynn's words, his boots shifting in the mud.

She softened her tone but maintained the urgency. "We won't know till we get in there. We have to try. The marshal on the plane and those pilots might still be alive." The men all nodded, purpose spreading across their faces.

Jim looked to Collins. "So where's our fed at?"

Alex Kinton pulled his SUV to a lurching stop, choosing the smallest puddle to park in, and then sat and absorbed the gloomy tableau before him. Wet, foggy, cold, and wet. A close-knit circle of red parkas turned his way. Even from fifty feet away he could see and feel the tension in the postures.

He wasn't welcome.

He didn't blame them, but he also didn't care.

He had a plane to get to.

Alex forced himself to open the door and step into the bitterly cold air. *Christ. Fucking weather.* No turning back. He ran a restless hand through his hair and pulled up his hood as goose bumps spread across his arms.

One of the red parkas stepped out from the circle as Alex worked his way across the mud and muck. His lungs contracted at the stabbing chill in the wet air. It smelled like snow. That fresh-scrubbed, icy smell that came before the skies let loose with the white stuff. Had to be close to freezing. He couldn't stop a full-body shudder and shiver and hoped the onlookers hadn't noticed. Why hadn't the crash happened in the middle of August? When it was hot enough to wear shorts?

The man in the parka approached, holding out a hand in greeting, but his brown eyes were cautious. The dark man looked to be in his fifties; an air of natural leadership emanated from him.

"Alex Kinton?"

Alex nodded. "You must be Collins. The boss said you'd have a pack and equipment ready for me."

Collins's chin jerked at the curt tone, and Alex levelly met his gaze. He didn't have the time or patience for how-do-you-do chitchat. His stomach abruptly cramped, reminding him he'd skipped breakfast. The gut pain coordinated with his growing headache from ignoring his medication last night and this morning. He'd wanted a clear head to meet the plane so he'd deliberately left the small orange pill bottle on the shelf.

Now he had a clear, pounding head.

Collins nodded slowly, his gaze plainly assessing. As if he'd decided something, his expression suddenly cooled and his lips thinned. "I'll get you a pack. This is the team that's going in. Jim's in charge." Collins tilted his head at the four remaining men, turned his back, and strode to his Suburban.

Alex let his spine relax a millimeter. Collins had recognized the persona Alex had presented. A soldier reporting for duty. No opinion on the task ahead, a simple acceptance of what was thrown on his plate. Locked, loaded, and ready for action.

He turned toward the others, sucking in a deep breath to fill his lungs. Wondering which red parka was Jim, Alex solidly met each man's stare. *Whoops.* The last person was a woman. Her mouth twitched and her dark eyes danced in amusement and confidence at his obvious surprise.

Alex froze. His vision tunneled on her face, and her eyes widened a fraction. Their eye contact splintered his carefully constructed wall of indifference. For a split second Alex didn't feel the cold, his concern about the missing plane evaporated, and his mind became refreshingly clear. She bit her lip and glanced away, breaking the connection.

Alex's brain slammed back to the task at hand and the muddy woods.

With her height, hood, and bulky parka, she'd blended in neatly with the men. A big gray-and-white dog sat at her feet, studying him with a keen blue gaze, its tail happily wagging. Alex's gaze went back to the other men, and he blinked at the hostility that'd crept into their faces as he'd stared at the woman. He stiffened.

At least the dog didn't seem to mind his presence.

"Alex Kinton." He gave a stiff nod and fought the urge to salute.

They rattled off their names, and Alex's mind snagged on the woman's unusual one. *Brynn.* Different. Her warm brown eyes were now curious, and her mouth spread in a tenuous smile as she bent down to rub the dog. Blonde hair peeked from under her hood. Clear features and a long elegant neck reminded him of a ballet dancer. Could she keep up? Collins had argued long and hard against Alex's presence on the hasty team. Claimed it was a physical and mental effort most people couldn't do.

Jim turned out to be the shortest guy. His experienced gaze probed and traveled over Alex from his brand-spanking-new hiking boots to the hood of his Columbia Sportswear Titanium jacket. Alex had ripped off the coat's tag just before stepping out of his SUV.

His new boss spoke, "What you got on under your rain pants?"

Alex's mouth tightened at the direct question. He had to answer to this guy?

"Clothes."

With one step, Jim was in his face, rain dripping off his nose. "We're going out into a bone-chilling, goddamned wet environment. If you get pissed and tired because you're cold and damp because you wore the wrong fucking clothes, I ain't gonna slow my team to babysit you." Jim's blue eyes sparked dangerously.

Point taken.

"Under Armour, then fatigues. Two pairs of socks. No cotton. My boots are waterproof, and my damned gloves cost more than this platinum jacket." Alex held up a navy gloved hand, still amazed at the ridiculous price. "Either I'm perfectly dressed for shitty mountain weather or the clerk at the outdoor store saw me coming from a mile away and pocketed a commission big enough to buy a plasma TV." He spoke directly to Jim, gaze locked on his leader, forcing himself to accord the man respect. He'd made a mistake. This wasn't someone he wanted as an enemy.

"Good." Jim backed up two steps and snorted, still assessing him, still obviously ticked at having a stranger in their midst.

"Titanium," Brynn stated.

Alex turned to her. "Huh?"

"Your jacket's line is called Titanium, not platinum." Her lips curved up on one side and her eyes smiled.

"For as much as it cost it should be made of platinum. I spent more money on clothing this morning than most people make in a month." Those lively dark eyes sparkled at his reply. She wasn't beautiful. Her mouth was wide and her chin a little too stubborn. She was more interesting looking, but probably caught her share of double takes from men. Men like him.

One of the guys coughed, clumsily covering a laugh. Ryan, maybe? Alex scanned the men coolly, aware he'd been caught a second time looking longer than was polite. He studied his "team."

Ryan was biting his cheek, a weak attempt to stop his grin. Sun-bleached hair lazily covered his forehead, reminding Alex of a surfer. Ryan looked like he belonged in a different kind of wet environment. Jim had a manner of natural leadership and sharp, focused eyes that swore to keep tabs on Alex. The third man had stayed silent, his face expressionless. His black hair and tanned skin hinted at a Native American background. Thomas was the biggest of the bunch, and Alex's neck muscles contracted as Thomas's deep eyes considered him.

One to watch.

Brynn was still silently laughing at him. After the dog's wagging tail, Brynn's brown eyes were the only cheerful objects in the gloom. Almost sunny, Alex decided. *If brown eyes could be called sunny.* His chest warmed at the sight.

"Here." Collins appeared and roughly shoved a heavy pack into Alex's startled hands. "That's my own seventy-two-hour pack." He eyed Alex's height. "Extra clothes in there should fit all right. You got a cell phone?"

"Yes."

"GPS?"

"Uh…in my phone." He had no idea how the thing worked.

There were snorts from the team. Collins mashed his lips together. "You're not looking up directions to a party downtown. That's gonna be useless out there. I meant a GPS unit with an altimeter and US Geological Survey maps."

Alex lifted his chin. "Don't have one." He felt like he'd been caught with his pants down.

"Won't matter, I guess. Everyone else has one." The sheriff stood motionless for five seconds, his stare digging into Alex's personal thoughts. "Your boss wouldn't tell me much about that plane. I know it's a Piper Cheyenne."

Alex steadied his breathing, his fists tightening, and didn't volunteer any extra information. "Are we ready now?" He needed to get to that plane ASAP. Away from this man who looked at him with the eyes of a psychic, digging deep into the darkest corners of his brain and finding him lacking.

Collins coolly nodded. "Jim will bring you up to speed." Curiosity touched his features. "Damn, you look familiar. Name doesn't ring a bell though."

"I've got one of those faces." He turned from the older man and lifted a brow at Jim. "I'm ready."

Thomas and Ryan were already headed up a dirt—make that mud—trail. Jim grudgingly waved Alex on and then brought up the rear with Brynn pacing ahead of him.

"Kiana, go," Brynn spoke. Her dog shot past Alex and out of sight between the trees.

Alex blew out a breath, wishing he cared as little about the rain as the dog did. To him, trekking in the great outdoors was as much fun as getting a prostate exam. And trekking in the *rainy* great outdoors was something he avoided like bad meat. But here he was, biting off more than he suspected he could chew. He stepped heavily in his new boots, splashing water onto his rain pants. He watched the drips roll down the waterproof surface. He could stomach a little rain for a while. Maybe this wouldn't be too bad.

He glanced over his shoulder at the woman trudging ten feet behind him and tossed a question back to her. "Did Collins say seventy-two-hour pack? What's that mean?"

"It means your pack is supplied to last for three days."

"Three days?" He stumbled over nothing and her laugh echoed off the skyscraping firs.

"This isn't TV. Did you think we'd find the plane before the first commercial break?"

He wished he'd packed that pill bottle.

CHAPTER TWO

Darrin Besand's head hurt as if a grenade had exploded nearby. He shifted in his seat, trying to reposition his left shoulder so it didn't ache like it'd been stabbed with a dull blade. He slowly turned his head to the right and tried to open his eyes, but they felt sticky. Like melted ice cream was gluing his lashes shut. Using his right hand, he brushed at his face. Because he was still cuffed, his left arm had to move with the right and he groaned at the pain. The goop on his eyes was warm and thick—definitely not ice cream. But why was he so cold?

Snow.

He forced his eyes open and stared at the ceiling above the seat in front of him. It'd been ripped wide open, giving him a view of a dark gray sky, its light barely illuminating the interior of the plane. A half-inch dusting of snow over the seat backs and on the floor told him he'd missed a snowfall. He sat up straight in the wrecked plane, ignoring the scream of pain from his shoulder as memories of the crash rushed through him.

The ride had been rough. Wind and rain and ice had pelted the little plane, making the pilots double-check that everyone was belted up as they headed for the nearest airport. Forget the landing site in Granton. They were going to find whatever was closest. The original filed flight plan had been to land in Hillsdale just west of Portland. The undisclosed real plan was to land at the tiny airstrip in Granton, thirty miles south of Portland. That plan had been scuttled for whatever airstrip or airport was closest, as the weather whipped in with a blow strong enough to make the two pilots sweat.

During the wild turbulence, the US marshal across the aisle from Darrin had held his armrests with a death grip. Sweat had formed on his temples as his lips had moved in a silent prayer.

Darrin had been fascinated with the strength of the storm and the effort of the small airplane and pilots. It'd turned into a life-and-death contest, and he'd found himself siding with the weather. The thought of death didn't bother him. Anything was better than returning to prison. He'd struggled to survive in prison. The dreary walls and rules and suffocating atmosphere had been slowly killing him. A fast death in a storm was preferable to a lifetime of slow rot behind bars.

He'd been a country boy growing up. He hadn't realized until he went to prison that he needed access to nature to thrive. All those years he'd lived in big cities trying to forget his rustic roots had been a joke. He was a man who could castrate a bull, spend the day throwing hundred-pound hay bales into a truck, or camp for a week in the dry flatlands of eastern Oregon with only a knife and a sleeping bag. When the plane had taken off he'd felt a surge of pure energy. Being able to see nature from the skies had powered fuel into his soul. Fuel he'd been starved of in prison. And the air had smelled a million times better.

He inhaled a deep breath of icy clean air and studied the silent marshal across the aisle. The agent's skin was gray and his head sat twisted at an odd angle on his shoulders. Darrin couldn't see any blood, but the man was obviously dead. Apparently, the marshal's God had ignored his whispered prayers.

Darrin leaned into the aisle to look around the high seat in front of him to see into the cockpit. He caught his breath as ice stabbed his lungs. No cockpit. Just trees and snow.

There wasn't just a hole in the ceiling of the plane; the entire front end was gone.

Where's the cockpit? Where are the pilots?

His shoulder throbbed as he clumsily undid his seat buckle with cuffed, frozen hands. Standard operating procedure said he was to be transported in leg irons, waist chains, and cuffs. And with two marshals as escorts. But Darrin Besand wasn't a standard transport. Cuffs and a single marshal were all he needed. And the cuffs were just a show for the pilots.

He stiffly straightened his body and stood in the aisle, swaying slightly. He stamped his feet to get some feeling back and swore as needles pricked his toes.

That pain's a good sign, right?

He stared at the dead body. Odd to be looking over a dead body when he wasn't the cause. He dug in the marshal's inside jacket pocket for the key to unlock the cuffs. The agent was cold.

How long have we been down?

Darrin blew out a breath of air. The cloud of fog he created hung heavy before dissolving into the cold air. He fumbled with the key, dropping it several times and ineptly scrambling for it on the floor in the crowded cabin. His damned fingers were numb. The pinky fingers useless. Finally the cuffs dropped from his wrists and he relaxed as he rubbed at his wrists and hands. He threw the cuffs on the floor and roughly kicked them away. A rush of heat filled his veins as the cuffs slid across the aisle and out of sight under a seat.

Freedom.

With new strength, he opened the marshal's suit jacket again and slipped the gun from the agent's shoulder holster. He tucked it into his waistband and immediately hated the foreign feeling. It felt like the gun would drop down his pants. He wrestled the agent's jacket off and removed the shoulder harness, buckling and adjusting the straps on himself, and hissing at the pain in his arm until the fit was good. He squared his shoulders, feeling the straps of the holster touch in odd places. He'd never worn one before.

He touched the butt of the gun at his side and practiced quickly drawing it out, annoyed at his clumsiness. He wasn't real familiar with handguns. The only firearms he'd handled were shotguns as a teen on his dad's farm. A shotgun didn't take a lot of talent. To hit an offending crow or coyote he'd simply point it in the right direction and count on the wide spray of shot and loud noise to scare them off. Other than being on the wrong end of a handgun while being arrested, he hadn't dealt with the smaller weapons. He preferred to use his bare hands on a victim.

Less mess. More personal.

Guns were impersonal. Darrin didn't get pleasure from instant results. He liked his tight hands wrapped around a neck and staring into the fading eyes. Then easing off and watching light and comprehension ooze back into their sight. Tightening the grip and watching them panic and fade again.

Darrin breathed deep and his eyes drifted closed as a narcotic-like lightness touched his brain. *The rush.* He lived for the rush.

But an impersonal handgun might come in handy out here.

He took the cell phone from the marshal's belt and turned it on.

No service.

He mashed his lips together as he stared at the small screen. The phone was fully charged. Maybe he could find a pocket of service outside somewhere. A better clearing or up on a peak or something.

He stepped out of the ruptured plane and his boots sank into the powder. Utter stillness and silence. He glanced back into the plane and eyed the small drifts of snow that had formed on the floor and again wondered how long the plane had sat in the snow. He squinted in the direction of the sun. The sky was completely overcast, but a faint glow pushing through the gray over the high mountain range to the east indicated the sun's low position. Early morning. The plane went down yesterday evening, maybe ten hours ago. He glanced at the roof of the plane and blinked.

Four inches of fresh snow sat on top of the plane.

Why didn't the cold kill me?

Darrin rubbed a hand down the stomach of his bright orange jumpsuit with *prisoner* stamped on the back. He had on a full set of clothes underneath the baggy suit. Probably the fact that he was wearing a wool sweater and had yanked on a Blazers knit cap to annoy the Lakers-loving marshal had saved him from freezing to death. The marshal had brought Darrin's favorite Timberland boots to wear along with crispy new Levi's. In the clothing he'd felt like a real man again. But then he'd had to cover it up with the orange suit. The damned jumpsuits were like wearing a plastic bag that itched and they'd made him sweat like crazy in his prison cell. In this case the synthetic blend material had done him a favor by trapping his body heat.

The marshal had been worried the pilots would notice the boots, but Darrin had no fears. He'd flown enough to know the only attention he'd get from the pilots would be sneers.

He brushed a thin layer of snow from a window, took off his cap, and studied his reflection, carefully touching the gash on his forehead and the drying river of blood it had left on his face. He rubbed at the blood on his eyebrows and eyelids with the hat. There'd been a padded seat in front of him. It wouldn't have created this bloody gash no matter how hard he'd hit his head. Something loose in the cabin must have hit him. His fingers moved through his hair and he hissed as he touched a tender spot above his ear.

His eyes fought to stay open as a wave of dizziness smacked him.

Shit. Something had nailed him in two different spots on his head. Not good.

What if he had a concussion or bleeding in his head? What would happen next? Could it kill him? Would it be painful?

He took a deep breath, letting the cold air pierce his lungs and drag him back to full alertness. He continued his trek around the plane. They'd landed at the beginnings of a dense forest in a huge clearing on the side of a steep hill. Glancing behind him and across the clearing he saw a group of firs with their tops sheared off. He blinked. Apparently, that was the way they had come. The impact with the old growth must have ripped off the cockpit. Some of those trees had to be six feet in diameter.

Besides the missing cockpit, one of the engines had also vanished, along with most of a wing. The little plane had been ripped along an odd diagonal that'd stolen one of the seven cushy chairs from the passenger area. If Darrin hadn't been seated as far from the cockpit as possible, he might have vanished along with the pilots.

He stared up the mountain at the steep expanse of pristine snow that seemed to climb for several thousand feet. No help that way. He checked the cell phone. Still no service.

He walked around to the downhill side of the plane and spotted the cockpit several hundred feet below him. Eagerly he stepped in that direction and plunged up to a knee in the snow.

"Fuck!"

He pulled out his leg and cautiously stepped to his right. That was better. The snow was very deep, but when he walked closer to the forest's edge he found it had formed a hard crust under about six or eight inches of powder. He broke a very slow path down to the cockpit, sinking into the snow five or six more times. He pulled the marshal's gun out of the shoulder holster, his finger on the trigger. As he neared the cockpit, he exhaled in fast pants from the snowy exercise and the tension rose in his chest. His ears strained for any sort of noise, but the forest was eerily silent. As was the cockpit.

The cockpit had broken off in one big awkward piece along with the missing wing and engine. The rough edges looked like a giant child had ripped it from the rest of the plane in a fit of temper.

The gun in his right hand, he reached with his left to touch the sheared metal edges and pain shot from his shoulder to his brain. He rotated the shoulder very slowly. Nothing seemed broken and there'd been no blood or gash. Maybe he'd pulled a muscle or tendon.

He could see the backs of the pilots' heads. Both were still in their seats. Immobile. The copilot sat in a pool of blood that had spilled onto the floor below him. Stepping closer, Darrin saw his left thigh had been sliced open. He'd bled out. Probably in under two or three minutes.

Darrin wondered if the copilot had known he was dying. Had he tried to stop the bleeding knowing he only had minutes to live before his heart pumped all his blood onto the floor? His gaze went to the copilot's hands. Spotless. No blood. He hadn't applied pressure to his leg. He must have been unconscious as his life spilled out.

A pity.

The other pilot breathed deep, a gurgling rattle erupting from his chest. Darrin whirled in his direction, heart throbbing, gun pointed at the man's head. The pilot's eyes met his. There was no fear.

"Asshole," said the pilot.

Darrin's lips turned up on one side. The man was half-dead but still had the strength to mouth off. He remembered meeting the pilot's gaze as he'd boarded the plane. As expected, the pilot had glared with disdain and then distinctly told the copilot how he hated doing these convict flights for the government. As the marshal had double-checked his cuffs, Darrin had grinned impudently at the pilot, flashing his straight, white teeth. The pilot had nearly hissed.

"I might be an asshole, but I'm an asshole with two good legs." Darrin let his gaze slide down the pilot's legs to where they intertwined with metal and wire. The man's hands were bloody, and Darrin eyed the gory mess of his metallic bindings where the pilot had desperately tried to free his legs. He relaxed and holstered his gun. The pilot was an interesting shade of gray, and Darrin wondered how he'd mustered up the energy to cuss at him. The man was very near death.

A kind person would put the pilot out of his misery.

Darrin wasn't kind.

"Does the radio work?"

The pilot dropped his gaze. "No. Believe me, I've tried," he muttered.

"What about a locator device?"

"It's in the tail of the plane. I can't tell if it's working or not." The pilot clumsily pointed at a switch and breathed deep for air. "I've got no electrical. Normally that would be flashing if the locator was armed."

Darrin stared at the tiny, dark LED light. *Is someone coming for me or not?*

He snagged the two pilots' duffel bags and took a close look around the remains of the cockpit, searching for anything useful for survival until help came. The copilot was wearing a wonderfully thick coat. One of those cowboy-looking suede coats with the lamb's wool lining. He set down the bags and wrestled the copilot out of the coat. Rigor was just settling in his limbs.

"Fuck you." The pilot spit the words.

Darrin kept his back to the man as he slipped on the copilot's coat. Strangely, it was still the tiniest bit warm from the dead man's evaporated body heat. Good coat. He turned back to the dying man and made a show of modeling the coat, turning up the collar, and tucking his hands in the pockets.

If looks could kill, Darrin would be prime rib. Well done.

Darrin scooped up the bags with one hand and gave the pilot a painful salute. "Later, dude."

He trudged back to the other piece of the plane, an uncontrollable smile his face.

Blasted, fucking media.

Sheriff Patrick Collins had established a perimeter just in time to keep out the wildlife.

Satellite trucks, cameras, microphones. How'd the word about the plane crash get out so fast? He spotted a few reporters writing down the license plate numbers of his hasty team members' vehicles and cursed. He hadn't thought of covering them. Wasn't like his team members' names were any big secret, but the media had a fascination with heroic sacrifice and his team was definitely sacrificing today. He glanced at the dark gray sky and caught a giant drop of icy rain in his eye.

At least he could sit in his truck. His team had to be freezing their asses off. And probably for nothing. Patrick had commanded two other remote plane crash rescues that had turned into recovery missions. One of the planes had ended up in a lake. Upside down and intact. The two bodies had still been buckled in their seats.

He prayed for better results this time.

"Any word?" Patrick asked as Deputy Tim Reid stopped beside him. The deputy was enjoying the excitement; his wide baby face lit up with adrenaline. Reid shook his head and his eyes dimmed a degree. Patrick knew the deputy would have immediately mentioned if the team had called in, but he couldn't stop from asking anyway. The waiting was feeding the growing rock in his stomach. The last contact had been two hours ago. Jim had called in with their coordinates and asked for an updated weather report. Patrick told him to expect snow or ice, just like they'd known when they'd started their mission. The call had been scratchy, fading in and out. With the spotty to nonexistent cell and radio coverage in the Cascades, he might not hear from his team again until they were headed back and nearly to the base camp. Their radios would be useless to contact the base. They could probably talk to each other, but the immense peaks and deep valleys would ruin any outside contact.

On how many missions had he anxiously waited and waited for word from a team? Patrick missed being out with the group, deep in the action, the buzz of the search in his veins, feeling like he was *doing* something. Now he was the brain and mouthpiece for Madison County SAR. And he was good at it.

But he missed being in on the battle.

He looked at his maps for the millionth time, guessing where the team might be at that second. Depended on terrain. He wouldn't be a bit surprised to hear they'd found mudslides or a washed-out trail. And then there were the water crossings. He'd almost suggested Brynn sit this rescue out, but she would have fried his ass for breakfast if he'd said it.

He'd never met anyone so stubborn. Brynn had legitimate, horrifying water fears but didn't let them slow her down.

Another vehicle pulled into the clearing and Patrick sighed, glancing at the black Suburban. Two men stepped out, and he did a double take at the long overcoats and suits. Definitely not reporters.

Federal marshals?

His theory was confirmed as the taller man held out his ID to a deputy posted at the perimeter. The deputy turned and pointed at Patrick. The two men tracked toward him, swerving around puddles. The second popped out an umbrella that he held over both their heads. He was the younger of the two men. The first and obviously senior agent was silver haired. As he drew closer, Patrick noticed he didn't have the facial lines of an older man. Patrick revised his mental age estimate of the agent down ten years, closer to his own fifty, maybe even younger. The man lifted his ID as he approached, meeting Patrick's gaze with razor-sharp intensity. His eyes were pale blue, nearly color-less. Patrick couldn't look away.

"Paul Whittenhall. I'm with the United States Marshals, and this is Deputy Marshal Stewart. That's my plane out there. You find it yet?"

Patrick grimaced at the marshal's directness. This was the fast-talking, persuasive agent from the phone call. "Patrick Collins. There's been no word on the plane." He paused. "Good to finally meet you," he added politely.

Whittenhall's eyebrows lifted. "You were expecting us?"

Patrick frowned at his tone. "I assumed you'd arrive some-time today."

The marshals exchanged a confused look.

"Who told you we were coming?" Whittenhall asked.

Collins blinked. "No one said you were coming. After we talked on the phone this morning, I expected someone from your office would show up."

"Phone? This morning?" The sharp eyes narrowed. "You talked to someone at my office?"

"Yeah. You." An odd sense of dread crept up Collins's spine. "You're Whittenhall, right? You called me and said the plane was a private lease hired to transport a prisoner back to Portland. You said it never arrived at its destination last night, and its flight path would have taken it over the Cascades at about the same point. Your plane's description matched the description the eyewitness gave. Until I talked to you, all I knew was we had a small plane down. You filled in the blanks." Patrick's speech slowed as he watched Whittenhall's pale eyes. No recognition.

Whittenhall stiffened. Confusion and something else Patrick didn't like crossed the agent's face. "I didn't talk to you."

"Then who…who called? Someone from your office called to say there was a marshal on that plane, and he insisted that one of your men be on my hasty team."

The other marshal muttered under his breath and pulled out a cell phone. He handed the umbrella off to his supervisor and stepped away to make a call.

Whittenhall was staring at Patrick. "You've got one of my agents out there? Looking for that wreck?"

Patrick nodded. "Isn't that what you wanted?"

What the fuck is going on? Patrick's temper was fluctuating back and forth. Switching from anger at the abrupt marshal to anxiety for his team.

"What time was this phone call? When did your team head out?" Whittenhall snapped.

"You…someone called at the crack of dawn. The team headed out at eight o'clock this morning right after your agent got here." Patrick forced the words out between clenched teeth. He didn't like the growing red hue of Whittenhall's face. Looked like he was about to blow an artery. Patrick glanced at the wet crowd of reporters. They all had pointed their noses his way. They could sense something was up. As Patrick watched, one reporter approached the deputy who'd let the two agents inside the perimeter, his digital recorder ready.

"I didn't send any marshal, and no one from my office called you. I wasn't informed that plane was missing *until* eight o'clock this morning. At that point, no one could tell me what had happened. It was midmorning when I found out a search and rescue was already in gear and they were sure it was my missing plane. I immediately drove down from Portland when I confirmed the news." Whittenhall spit the words, his face contorted with anger.

Patrick's throat closed. "So who the fuck is out with my team?"

CHAPTER THREE

They'd been in the forest for five hours, and Alex was ready to go home. It had never stopped raining. He'd slipped twice, tripped over countless roots, and stepped in mud up to his ankles. So much for the new boots. An hour ago, his right leg had started to cramp. A physical reminder that he was there for only one reason. Get to the plane ASAP. Not to get distracted by a woman. Not to enjoy a chat in the rain.

There could be danger on that plane that he needed to meet face-to-face. He had to be mentally ready.

Alex's leg was still aching, but there was no way he was gonna mention it. He wasn't going to slow the team's pace even if he thought he might be wasting his time. No one could have survived that plane crash. If someone did, he was going to drown in all this fucking rain.

Kiana chose that moment to rocket back to Brynn from some point far ahead on the trail. The dog's gorgeous fur was soaked, and her feet looked like she'd been dancing in chocolate sauce. She galloped by him, and Alex's gaze followed her to Brynn as she greeted the dog at the end of the line.

"Good-looking dog. What is she?" he asked Ryan.

"Mostly Alaskan malamute. Brynn says her blue eyes show there's crossbreeding somewhere in her line."

The slight twang in Ryan's voice made Alex think of the old television show *Hee Haw*. Ryan was an interesting blend of surfer, country cop, and polite mama's boy. The guy seemed to genuinely like the outdoors. Always smiling, rarely griping about the rain and muck. Just like Brynn.

"Brynn usually do trips like this?"

Ryan shrugged. "We all do a couple dozen a year. Most aren't as involved as this. Some last half a day."

"How do you fit in a job with a crazy schedule like that?"

Ryan dropped back to walk beside Alex. Earlier the younger man had been helpful, pointing out various animal signs and identifying plants even though Alex had never asked. Alex was more than ready for a distraction.

"Well, for Thomas and Jim and me, our departments have committed us to when we're needed. Each police department has at least one man in SAR."

"And Brynn? She's not a cop." Alex knew that in his gut.

"Nah, she works for the medical examiner's office. She's a forensic nurse. Death investigator. Comes out to our scenes when there is a suspicious death and we need an investigator with medical knowledge. She's good."

"Like *CSI?*" Alex would have never connected the sunny woman with such a grisly job.

Ryan choked out a laugh. "Don't let her hear you say that. She hates that show. No high heels for that woman."

Brynn in heels and a smile popped into Alex's mind. The image looked good to him. Real good.

"Where've you competed in triathlons?" Ryan asked with eager interest. "Hawaii?"

Alex pressed his lips together and glanced away. He'd never entered a triathlon in his life. "What? What makes you think I did triathlons?"

Ryan's blue eyes widened. "On the phone. Your boss told Collins you did triathlons. That's how he convinced him you were fit enough to join our team."

Alex snorted. "He exaggerated. Wanted to get me on your team. He knew I'd keep up. Mentioning triathlons was probably the fastest way to convince the sheriff."

Ryan paused to absorb that reason then laughed. "Shit. That was cocky."

"Yeah, he's been known to say whatever it takes to get the job done."

"By the way, are you armed?" Ryan's eyes scanned Alex like he could see through his jacket to the gun below his arm, the second gun he'd discreetly tucked in his borrowed pack, and the knife in his pocket. The backpack was rubbing at odd spots on his shoulder holster and he wished he hadn't worn the heavy 9 mm Beretta. When he had a chance, he'd switch it with the lighter SIG and belt holster in his pack.

"Yeah. Why?"

Ryan shrugged. "Never know if we might meet up with a bear or cougar."

Fuck. "Aren't they hibernating or something? It's only March." Alex had never shot an animal in his life. When he'd packed his weapons that morning he hadn't been thinking of bears. Maybe he'd keep the Beretta out.

"Never know. I've seen black bears in January out here."

"Hungry?" Alex scanned the forest. He couldn't see deeper than twenty feet in most places. How many animals were lurking, watching them?

Ryan grinned at the higher pitch of Alex's question. "Nah, usually more curious or scared of us. Just wave your arms at them. Make a lot of noise."

"I thought you're supposed to play dead."

"That's when you're caught by a grizzly. You won't see grizzly around here."

Alex winced. Could he tell a black bear from a grizzly? He hadn't been to the zoo in thirty years.

Ryan tipped his head at Thomas. "Thomas has met up with grizzlies. He's originally from Alaska." Ryan's blue eyes lit up. "He's got this great .44 Magnum Ruger Redhawk. Huge revolver that he carried up there in case of a grizzly encounter."

Alex pictured the big man hiking past a bear, ignoring the angry animal the same way he ignored Alex. As far as Alex had seen, nothing fazed Thomas Todoroff.

"Aim for the brain," Ryan added helpfully.

"Thanks a lot," Alex muttered.

"Take a break, guys." Jim's words carried over Ryan and Alex and up to Thomas, who immediately halted and slung off his pack, hooking it on a nearby sturdy branch. The big guy squatted on his heels, pulled out some sort of energy bar, and began eating.

Jim held up a huge, oatmealy looking bar wrapped in plastic and cocked his eyebrows in question to the other team members. Alex, Thomas, and Brynn shook their heads, but Ryan nodded and Jim tossed him the bar. Ryan unwrapped it and crammed half in his mouth.

"Why're we stopping again already?" Alex's feet itched to keep moving, lost cause or not. They'd already taken several breaks and he wasn't hungry, thirsty, or too tired, but his stomach was slightly nauseous and a little shaky. He just wanted to push through the symptoms and get this trip over with. He left his pack on, confronting Jim in even tones.

Brynn and Jim had removed their packs. Ryan stood next to Alex, his pack still on, mouth full, his attention flitting between Jim and Alex.

"It's just for ten minutes," Jim stated.

Alex scanned the group, taking a hard look at Brynn, who was speaking to the dog, her back to Alex. Was she the reason Jim wasn't picking up the pace? "No one looks tired."

"We rest *before* we get tired. And even though you're soaking wet, drink something." Jim's tone sharpened, his voice belying the calm gaze that met Alex's.

"We're moving too damned slow."

"It's called pacing. Ever heard of it? Should be key in triathlons."

"He never did triathlons." Ryan grinned around the words and popped the rest of his bar in his mouth. Apparently, the younger man liked to push Jim's buttons a little.

Jim narrowed his eyes at Ryan then swung his gaze to Alex. "What? Your boss said—"

"Am I slacking? Am I having trouble keeping up?" Alex felt new sweat start on his forehead.

Jim shook his head, eyes angry.

"Then it's not important."

"The only reason Collins let you on the team was because your boss insisted you were in some incredible physical shape."

"Doesn't matter now, does it? It's a moot point." Alex glanced at his watch. "How long we sitting here?"

"Until I'm done taking a piss." Jim spun around and stomped into the thick trees, letting the wet branches fling water back at the waiting group. Brynn's forehead wrinkled as she watched Jim vanish in the deep brush and her brown eyes turned to scrutinize Alex.

Alex calmly met the three stares as his mouth went dry. He'd stepped over an invisible line. "Is there a problem?"

"Any other lies we need to know about?" Brynn simply looked curious.

"Wasn't my lie. How was I to know my boss would say something like that?" Uncomfortable with his words, Alex looked away from Brynn into Thomas's deep eyes. The man was regarding Alex like a lion spying its prey.

"You didn't answer her question," the big man stated.

Alex met his stare. "There's nothing else you need to know."

"This is a team. If there's something we need to know that could affect the safety and the results of this operation, let's hear it now," Thomas rumbled.

Alex said nothing. What could he tell them? It was too early to open that can of worms. When they got closer to the crash site, he'd pull Jim aside and tell him the truth.

Well, part of the truth.

"Alex?" Brynn prompted.

Her brown eyes had lost the dancing luster he'd seen at the trailhead and it depressed him. So far, watching her had been keeping him sane. Her enthusiasm for the outdoors and her affection for her dog were engrossing. Not quite distracting enough to ignore the rain and icy wind, but every little bit helped.

He bit his tongue and looked away, his mind scrambling for words to change their focus. "Sorry. I'm in a hurry to get in there. Linus, the marshal on this flight, was a good friend. I need to know…" It was the first time Alex had mentioned the name of the marshal from the missing plane. He used to consider Linus Carlson one of his closest friends. Their families had even been together for a Christmas or two. Before.

Brynn nodded, sympathy warming her eyes and making him feel like a piece of shit for exaggerating and lying. Jim emerged from the dripping, wet woods, still scowling.

"Hey," Alex spoke up, knowing a public apology was due. "Jim, I didn't mean to question your decision. I'm just in a hurry."

"He knew the marshal on board," Brynn added quietly, watching Jim. Their eyes connected and some sort of silent message passed between them. Alex frowned, glancing from one to the other, feeling out of the loop.

Jim pinned Alex with a stare. "I'd appreciate having a better idea of what we might find at that plane. I don't like going in blind."

"I don't know a lot," Alex replied slowly. *How much can I tell him?* "I would say be prepared for the worst." He hated keeping Jim in the dark.

A brief wave of understanding crossed Jim's sharp eyes. He'd caught the warning and knew Alex wasn't referring to possible gore at the crash. Jim didn't ask any more questions.

Jim glanced at his watch. "OK, let's go."

"Shit." Ryan froze, his pack half on. "Jim, what was in that oatmeal thing you gave me?"

Jim frowned as he slung on his own pack. "I don't know. My wife made them. Why?"

Ryan stuck a finger in his mouth and scratched at the roof of his mouth. "Walnuts?"

"Maybe. But I didn't taste any."

Ryan stretched his lips and rubbed inside his cheek with his tongue. Annoyance flashed across his face.

"You allergic to walnuts?" Brynn asked rapidly.

"No." Ryan scratched at his lips. "Just extra sensitive. Make my mouth and throat itch and tickle like crazy."

"Here." Brynn tossed Ryan a small bottle. His eyes lit up as he spotted the label, and he grinned like he'd caught a bottle of Grey Goose.

"Let's hear it for the nurse. Prepared for everything." Ryan turned the bottle to show the Benadryl label to Alex. "Thank God. The itch was going to drive me batshit."

Alex stared at Brynn's pack. "You got a complete pharmacy in there?"

She tucked away the clear bag. "No. I always carry Benadryl, some ibuprofen, and local anesthetic. That's about it."

"Ibuprofen?" He sounded pathetic.

Questioning dark eyes met his. "Need some?"

"Please," he nearly begged.

When the little brown pills hit his palm, he knew how relieved Ryan had felt. Alex greedily swallowed all three and studied his watch. Twenty minutes. In twenty minutes relief should start. If the pain in his head and knee vanished, he might become as cheerful as Brynn. Might.

The others wrestled on their packs and restarted the march. Jim fell in beside Alex, slowing his strides with a hand on Alex's arm until they'd dropped twenty feet behind the others. "Next time, keep your mouth shut if you don't like how things are going. I've got twelve years of search and rescue under my belt. I know how this particular group thinks, and I know what they need. If you have a problem, you take it up with me in private." Jim's words were low and grim, his eyes hard.

Alex nodded. Jim was right. He'd questioned Jim's authority in front of his crew. Major mistake. Alex would've punched any asshole who'd pulled it on him. "Won't happen again. My mouth is shut."

"Damn right." Jim sped up to join Brynn and left Alex alone to bring up the rear.

Alex plodded on. It was fucking cold and it'd immediately started to snow after the break. Steadily. Not nice, soft snowflakes, but the little ice balls that stung every bit of exposed flesh. Maybe it was a good thing that his face was numb. He knew his nose was dripping even though he couldn't feel the damn thing. He just kept wiping at it. He probably looked like Rudolph's closest relative.

Feet were numb too.

He hated the forest. He hated snow.

He had a hand warmer on in each pocket and the heat was doing absolutely nothing other than making him wish for a six-foot-tall warmer that he could wrap around his naked body. If anything, the damned molecule-sized warmers were making him more miserable.

Kiana shot by him, a gray blur. Her speed nearly knocked him off balance, and he hated the dog for her enthusiasm. Anyone who was happy in this weather was now his enemy. They were being happy simply to spite him. Simply to harass him because he was a nature hater.

He'd been relegated to the end of the line. He didn't know if he should be insulted or pleased that they weren't worried about him keeping up. Or maybe they didn't care if he fell behind and got lost in the haze. He glanced at his watch. The ibuprofen should be taking effect any minute. He concentrated on his knee. Seemed a little better. Each step wasn't—

The ground slipped out from under him. With a shout of surprise, he fell and slipped down the slope. After a split second of pure terror and air rushing past his ears, he slammed to a stop in a puddle of mud. Make that a lake of mud. Nearly freezing mud.

He was on his ass, his hands and feet sunken six inches into the crap. He gasped to catch his breath and slow his hammering heart. He looked up the bank he'd slid down like a Slip 'n Slide. Thomas stood there, humor flashing in his dark eyes.

"Gotta watch your step."

The other three appeared at Thomas's side, surprise and fear on their faces. He wrenched a hand out of the muck, staring at the brown goo.

Good gloves. His hands were dry.

"Thomas, you didn't point out the slide to him?" Brynn was furious.

Thomas shrugged. "I figured he'd see it. Wasn't a bad one. I knew if he fell, he wouldn't go far."

"What?" Brynn gasped as the other two men muttered and glared at Thomas.

"He needs to learn to watch out for himself." His face didn't show it, but Alex heard the smugness in Thomas's tone.

With a superhuman effort, Alex pulled the rest of his body from the mud with a squishing, sucking sound. He stared at his pants. How was he supposed to get the crap off? He brushed a hand at the stuff. Not just mud, sticky mud.

He hated nature.

"Here." Ryan had stepped down the embankment and held out a hand. His other hand was securely attached to the limb of a tree behind him. "Grab on."

Alex wanted to tell him to go to hell, but grabbed his hand. With some effort, the two of them got back up to the trail. Brynn scooped up a handful of snow and rubbed at Alex's pants with it. The mud washed off with the ice crystals. He batted her hand away.

"I'll do it," he said. She said nothing as she stepped back, but he saw brief annoyance flash in her eyes. "Thanks," Alex muttered. He glanced at Thomas. Complete innocence gazed back. He refocused on his pants.

"Jesus Christ, Thomas. What if he'd broken an arm or leg?" Brynn was angry. "You'd be the one hauling his butt back to camp."

"Todoroff, use some common sense!" Jim crossed his arms on his chest and eyed the silent man. "Kinton doesn't know what to look for out here."

"Forget it," Alex snapped. He didn't want people talking about him like he was a helpless wimp. Brynn trying to clean off his pants was bad enough. "Let's just go." He pulled off his expensive gloves and glared at the mud, wondering if he should use some of his drinking water to clean them up. He liked his gloves. That morning he'd choked when he saw the price tag, but now he understood the value of good gear in this freezing hell.

The others started up the path. Alex glanced up to find Thomas waiting for him, a bottle of water in his hand. He held it out to Alex. "Mud should rinse off. They're waterproof."

"I know," Alex mumbled. He took the bottle, feeling no guilt for using Thomas's drinking water as he rinsed his gloves.

He mentally cursed at his shaking hands. Alex turned slightly, moving his hands from Thomas's view. He used more water than was necessary and handed the bottle back. Thomas silently tucked it in his pack and moved out after the others. Alex followed.

Alex figured that was as much of an apology as he'd get. Considering the source, it wasn't a bad one.

Brynn heard the river before anyone else. No one else had had his ears pricked for the last two hours, waiting for the sounds of white water. Her boots moved one in front of the other. Step after step. It'd been quiet and tense since Alex slid down the embankment. She didn't like the tension among the men, but she'd learned that getting them to talk it out wasn't a solution. These men did things their own way. They glared, mashed their lips together, and shot dirty looks without using a word. Eventually it'd be over. She glanced at the wide shoulders trudging in front of her. Even from the back, Alex looked annoyed.

Thomas had been out of line, unfairly testing Alex like that. She'd wanted to tell him so, but she knew it'd do no good. He'd simply tune her out. She, Ryan, Thomas, and Jim had done at least a dozen missions together in the past three years. They worked well together. No major personality clashes. Everyone respected each other's expertise. Jim was leader, Ryan was navigation, she was medical, and Thomas was... well, everything else. He knew stuff from mountain climbing to extreme survival skills. He could have had his own TV show on the Discovery channel if not for his glaring lack of personality.

Ryan turned and looked past Alex to meet Brynn's eyes, his gaze dead serious. He'd heard the water. She gave him a half smile, her heart in her throat. She wouldn't reveal the terror pounding through her chest.

They'd been descending for thirty minutes. The trail was slick and covered with broken boughs from the last windstorm. At least there was a trail. Once they crossed the river, they'd leave the trail and head north, breaking their own path.

She just had to get across the river.

Then she'd be fine until the next water crossing.

The snow paused and Brynn pushed off her hood, feeling the icy breeze nip at her neck. The sky was still dark gray. She tipped back her head, inhaled the fresh air, and watched the wind push the layers of multicolored clouds across the bleak sky. They ranged from pure white to slate gray to a deep, dark gray that was heavy with snow. She estimated ten minutes before the next cloud ruptured. For the moment, there were no towering firs blocking the sky, and the forest released its hold on the group for a few seconds.

Kiana shot out of the brush to her right and fell in beside Brynn, matching her quick doggy pace to Brynn's steps. She whined softly and brushed her muzzle against Brynn's leg. Surprised, Brynn glanced down and met sympathetic, devoted blue eyes.

Did the dog know?

Throat tightening, she ran a hand over Kiana's furry ears, tugging at them lightly.

"Good dog," she whispered.

"Water ahead," Jim spoke behind her, his voice flat.

She tossed him a nod and smile over her shoulder, rubbing at Kiana's back.

They entered another large copse of trees, darkening their surroundings, making the time seem later than four o'clock. The sound of fast water grew louder, closer.

They trudged out of the trees into the light and stopped on a ridge, looking down at the river.

Ryan gawked. "Holy crap. I've never seen it so high."

Jim shot him a black look. "It's not so bad."

Brynn stared at the rush of muddy-colored water. Jim could play it down all he wanted, but the river was at least six feet higher than it should be. The fallen tree that had been converted into a footbridge was a measly six inches above the swirling, loud water. Green fir branches and thick sticks floated by, some catching on the tree bridge before dislodging and swirling downstream. She eyed the far bank. Half-moon craters bit into the bank where the fast water had washed out the support and giant chunks of land had slid into the river. It looked like a massive monster had taken bites right out of the dirt.

In a way, it had.

"Look at that!" Alex pointed downstream.

Brynn watched three fir trees, still upright, slide down the steep bank and into the stream. The water sucked them away in a whirl of green and brown, leaving a new bite-shaped crater, water dripping down its steep banks.

"What if that'd fallen in upriver from the bridge?" Alex exclaimed. "It'd create a dam. Probably loosen the bridge with the pressure from all the debris it'd trap."

"Let's cross. Now." Thomas spoke as he started down the bank to where the tree bridge bared a big dirty knot of straggly roots. He climbed up the roots and yanked at the ropes the forest service had rigged, testing them for balance. The ropes paralleled the footbridge at waist height. They looped through eyes on metal rods jammed deep into the tree every ten feet. "Seems secure."

Seems.

Brynn didn't move.

Jim stopped beside her, studying her face. "I'll hold on to you," he said quietly.

She grinned feebly. "So I can pull you into the water with me?" Her gaze went back to Thomas who was halfway across. She gasped as he stopped mid-span and jumped, slamming his weight into the log, checking out the sturdiness of the natural crossing. Something sharp stabbed deep in her gut.

Thomas jogged to the other side and waved at Alex to cross.

Alex's face was studious as he sought footholds in the roots, climbing to the bridge. He imitated Thomas, tugging on the ropes then stepping carefully onto the big log. The tree had to be three feet in diameter, spanning the thirty-foot-wide crossing that took up two-thirds of the tree's length. Alex slowed as he stepped around the first metal rod. Brynn watched his foot slide in the thick layer of snow and felt her heart slip into her stomach. Alex grimaced, but kept his balance.

Brynn wanted to vomit.

Squeezing her eyes shut, Brynn saw a girl crossing a shorter tree bridge with no ropes for balance. It was hot and sunny with skies the color of Hawaiian oceans. The girl's bare foot slipped on a slick section and the child flung out her arms, wavering on one foot.

"He's over. No problem." Brynn heard the forced cheeriness in Jim's tone. Her eyes flew open and the girl in her mind vanished as she watched Ryan scamper up the roots. He paused and looked back to Brynn, his gaze going from her face to Jim's.

"Go. We're coming." Now she sounded as falsely cheery as Jim. Who could guess her feet felt as agile as blocks of ice? "Kiana, go." She motioned the dog ahead of her and Kiana darted nimbly up the roots and trotted onto the bridge after Ryan. No fear.

Brynn forced her feet to move, climbing slowly up the roots. She reached the top in time to see Ryan leap off the end and hold up his hand for a high five from Alex. Alex gave a rare grin and met his palm. She saw his lips move but couldn't hear his words over the roar of the water. Jim came up behind her.

"Let's go, Brynn." His tone was firm, but kind. "I'll be right behind you, honey."

She pulled the gloves off her hands and crammed them in her pockets, eyeing the ropes. The ropes were so narrow, so thin.

She couldn't lift her feet. The river was too loud. It was too fast. Too brown. Too everything. She saw Alex do a double take as he noticed the two of them on the bridge. His lips moved again, questioning Ryan, his eyebrows narrowing. Ryan spoke, and Alex's face filled with concern. He stepped in their direction, but Ryan stopped him with a hand on his sleeve, speaking urgently. Alex knocked Ryan's hand off his sleeve, but moved no farther, his gaze locked on her. Thomas stood a few feet behind the two men, his arms crossed on his chest, watching everything.

She wouldn't make a fool of herself. The three guys had practically skipped across the tree. She was being ridiculous.

"Want me in front?" Jim met her eyes, his gaze probing deep.

"No. I'm ready." She grasped the ropes and stepped out over the water.

She'd known it would be bad. But she'd never guessed it would be this bad. Her gaze locked on the swirling brown muck, so close to the bottom of the log. Flashes of sticks and debris flew by. From the log, the floating crud appeared to move faster than from the view on the bank. She swayed.

"For God's sake, breathe, Brynn!"

Jim's irate tone made her lungs inflate. She hadn't noticed she'd been holding her breath. She moved her left foot in front of her right and repeated. The shuffle step felt steadier than regular walking and her hands slid along the rope as she awkwardly scooted her feet one after the other. The log vibrated with the power of the river.

"Good girl. Almost halfway already."

She pulled her gaze from her feet and looked to the far end. Jim was right. She could do this. Alex had moved onto the log and was waiting, gripping the ropes, his jaw hard as he watched their progress.

She felt like a little kid under the weight of his concern.

Her shuffle continued. Her gaze back on her feet, trying to ignore the swirl of brown on both sides of the log.

"Closer. We're getting real close, Brynn. No sweat." Jim sounded relieved.

Someone shouted, echoed by two other sharp shouts.

She looked up. The three men at the end were staring upstream. Ryan's jaw hung open, his eyes panicking. She followed his gaze and froze.

Up the river, a fallen tree was speeding toward the bridge. The fast current was propelling the wooden missile down the river straight toward where she stood. It was huge, and it wouldn't fit under the bridge. Jim gasped.

"Go, Brynn! Get moving!" He shoved at her pack.

She couldn't move. The tree would ram the bridge and knock the two of them into the water. She'd hit her head or get a foot caught in the freezing water and it'd be over.

Jim shoved again at her pack, pushing her forward. She stumbled a step and slipped, hanging on to the ropes with every ounce of her strength. She regained her footing and froze again, staring upstream.

"C'mon, Brynn!" Ryan's desperate yell carried over the water.

She watched the tree move closer, its distance to the bridge had halved already. Her head whipped around at a rough jerk on her jacket front. Alex's hands were on her coat, his steel eyes furious.

"Move!" He turned, hauling her behind him with one gloved hand, her feet tripping to keep up. Her hands were ripped from the ropes and they were running. She didn't look down. She no longer heard the river. She heard only Ryan's shouts and Alex's curses. They reached the end of the log, and Alex hurled her into the outstretched arms of Ryan and Thomas. He and Jim leaped.

It sounded like a car crash. The log bridge shuddered from the impact of the giant projectile. The bridge held in place then shuddered again as the tree in the water turned ninety degrees and slammed parallel into it, creating a dam by plugging the small space below the bridge. The tree was almost the same length as the bridge. Water could barely get by both ends and the river's level rapidly rose and washed over the top of the bridge. No one could cross now.

If they'd been ten minutes later, they'd be stuck on the other side. If Brynn had stalled longer at the edge, the river would have separated the two groups. Or she and Jim would be on their way downstream.

"Jesus Christ! Are you nuts? What the hell were you doing out there? You almost got the both of you killed!" Alex shouted in her face, his clenched hands shook her shoulders. Anger rolled off him.

Her throat closed as she stared at his wild eyes.

He was right. Her Achilles' heel had nearly killed Jim.

"Back off!" Thomas yanked him away, pushing him to one side. Alex tripped over a root and went down. He swore at Thomas.

"What was *she* thinking?" Jim shouted at Alex. "What were *you* thinking, running out there? That stupid stunt could have killed all three of us!" Jim wrapped an arm around Brynn's shaking shoulders. She couldn't stop shivering, and her stomach felt dangerously close to losing her last protein bar.

Ryan held out a hand, pulled Alex to his feet, and turned a furious glare on Jim. "If he hadn't run out there you'd both be downriver. I was too fucking scared to do it."

"Rule number one. You take care of your own safety first. Teammates second. You all know that." Jim's arm tightened around Brynn as he spoke. His voice was calmer but still too loud. Every few seconds Brynn felt a quake rattle through Jim's body. Anger and testosterone hung heavily in the cold air as waves of fury and fear shot between the team members.

"Then Brynn should've been crossing alone. Not with you. That's a double standard. You bend the rules to suit yourself." Alex took a step toward Jim.

Jim was silent for a second. "Yeah, for her I do."

Brynn stared at Jim.

Steady eyes turned to meet hers. "You're like a sister to Anna. It'd kill me and her if something happened to you."

The roar of the rushing water whirled in her ears, and the rage in the air evaporated.

She swallowed, her throat still tight. "That's not how it works out here, Jim. You know that. No heroes." She paused. "But thank you. And you too, Alex." Alex nodded shortly, his angry gaze on the water behind her.

Thomas spoke evenly, "We can't have a liability like this. Brynn crosses alone from now on." Ryan and Jim started to protest, but Thomas held up a hand. "You know I'm right." He eyed the water covering the footbridge. "When we leave we're going to have to go out a different way. Isn't there a railroad crossing a few miles downriver? Is that the closest crossing?"

Ryan nodded. "Yeah, that's the only other way out. Gonna take longer though."

Brynn studied Alex out of the corner of her eye. He'd stayed silent during Thomas's statement, not protesting like Ryan and Jim. Alex probably had no issues with her crossing alone. She stepped away from Jim, pushing off his arm and taking a deep breath. "We're wasting time. This is where we leave the trail, right? Which way do we go?" It took a Herculean effort to keep her voice from shaking as four sets of male eyes blinked at her.

Could they tell her knees were about to give out?

Ryan gave a grim smile, slowly shaking his head. "I don't know how you do it, Brynn." He blew out a tense sigh and dug his GPS out of his pocket.

Alex had been quiet since the river, but Brynn had caught him staring at her a few times. Sometimes with confusion, sometimes with anger. Understandable after what she'd put her team through. She was still vacillating between terror and disgust herself.

But his confusion told her Alex wasn't the unfeeling, silent soldier who'd first joined their team. His emotions had been thrust out in the open along with everyone else's.

He'd acted without thinking of his own life.

She briefly closed her eyes and saw his determined, furious expression as he yanked at her jacket on the bridge. He'd literally shocked her into moving. She'd already accepted that she was headed for the water. Why had he risked so much for two people he barely knew?

And he'd demonstrated no aftershocks. No unsteady legs or breathlessness from adrenaline. An untypical reaction to nearly dying. Was it his marshal's training? Or didn't he care that he'd nearly become a Popsicle? He'd been more upset that she'd turned into a statue.

Alex's hair was black and his skin was a light tan color that came from genes, not the sun. Under his jacket and layers of pants, she couldn't get a look at his body, but something told her the physique was rock solid. She'd heard marshals had to work out daily and meet rigorous physical requirements. She watched the lean muscle flex in his neck and jaw as he turned his head toward her and guessed he was older than her twenty-eight years. Ten, maybe even fifteen years older. About the same as Jim.

"I still don't get why anyone volunteers for this shit."

Brynn didn't think Alex meant anyone to hear him as they trudged through the trees.

She dug deep for a lighthearted tone to answer his rhetorical question.

"For the fun and games."

He looked over his shoulder and gave her a pointed look. "No, really. What keeps you going out time after time?" His eyes were a cool gray that made her cheeks heat oddly as he looked at her. He'd rattled her during their introduction that morning. The pleasant rush of blood in her head during his stare had surprised her. In a good way. The other men had fumed at the length of Alex's look, and she'd rolled her eyes at their protective testosterone. They had done a dozen rescue trips together, and now her team had become surrogate fathers.

She let her thoughts wander over the rescues she'd done, grateful for the distraction. Nothing glorious. Nothing newsworthy. Not like those two men who found the seventy-year-old grandmother who'd been lost in the wilderness for ten days. Everyone had assumed she was dead. But the men had wanted to look one more time. On their own time. And found her.

But that incident reflected the heart of her own motivation.

She could make a difference in an impossible situation.

Convincing Alex Kinton that she liked what she did wasn't going to be easy. Contempt for the outdoors oozed from him. He'd been keeping his mouth shut about the weather and woods, but everyone could read it in his eyes.

"People need help. I like to do it, and I believe I do it well. I might be the reason somebody survives. That is incentive enough for me to put up with any weather or discomfort. And sometimes we have a lot of fun."

"Like today?" More sarcasm.

"It hasn't been so bad."

His stunned gaze shot to her eyes, the water incident clearly in his mind.

She ignored him and continued, "There's something about being out here with these guys. There's an adrenaline rush and camaraderie that you can't find anywhere else. Getting tired just makes us goofy. We rely on each other to stay sane and that leads to ridiculous games, stories, and challenges. Trying to keep each other from total boredom and worry is a challenge. What do you do for fun?"

He was quiet for a second. "I write software in my spare time. Some computer games. Some security programs. I have a knack for it, and it's a good side business."

She waited for him to continue, but he said nothing else.

"That appeals to me about as much as cross-country skiing probably would to you."

He gave her a half smile. "Cross-country skiing? You mean jogging on skis? I'll pass. I like to downhill ski. I don't mind a little snow for that, the rush and speed is totally worth it. And I like to run, but not in the rain or snow."

"And you live in Oregon?"

"My gym has an indoor track."

"Running around in circles, staring at the same plain walls. Joy," she teased. She liked the light banter with him. It lightened his cheerless eyes.

"Gives me time to think. Develop game programs in my head."

She rolled her eyes. "Dear Lord. You're lucky you ended up out here. This adventure is going to show you how much is missing in your life."

His eyes almost twinkled. "Adventure is *Pirates of the Caribbean.* This is more like watching an endless documentary on making concrete while I'm tied to the chair."

Ryan and Jim looked back as her laugh rang through the snow.

"Alex Kinton."

"Alex Kinton? He's out with your team? And he told you I sent him?"

At Whittenhall's shout, Patrick worried about the marshal's blood pressure again.

Stewart, the younger agent, whipped his head in their direction, his cell conversation arrested at Kinton's name. Whittenhall glanced at Stewart and roughly gestured for him to wrap up the call. Stewart nodded and refocused on the cell. Patrick saw Stewart swallow hard as his eyes darted from the media to the perimeter of sheriff's deputies.

"If you didn't send him, then who is he?" he asked Whittenhall.

Whittenhall was dialing his own phone. He wiped at a drip of sweat on his forehead; Patrick blinked at seeing the marshal sweat in the near-freezing temps.

"Who's Kinton?" he repeated louder. His stomach was starting to churn. Who'd he sent out with his team?

"Former marshal," Whittenhall muttered as he concentrated on his phone. "I don't know how the fuck he heard about that plane." Patrick caught a glimpse of widening eyes and dilating pupils as Whittenhall glanced at the reporters and lifted his phone to his ear.

Former marshal?

"Hey." Patrick grabbed at Whittenhall's phone arm. "Is my team in danger? Why isn't he a marshal anymore?" His voice rose as Whittenhall ignored him. "Why would he go out in this shitty weather to get to that plane?"

Whittenhall shook off Patrick's grip and stepped away, his gaze on the ground. Temper expanded in Patrick's chest. He wanted some damned answers. Now. He stepped into the marshal's view and fought the urge to knock the damned phone from his ear.

"Who's on that fucking plane?"

CHAPTER FOUR

Brynn leaned against a fir, watching the curtain of white fall from the sky. From under the boughs the view was utterly gorgeous.

"Remember the dude with the glasses?" Ryan took a long swallow from his water bottle during their brief break. He squatted on his haunches with his pack in the snow beside him. The group huddled under a group of firs, hiding out from the snow while grabbing a bite to eat and catching their breath.

Jim shook his head in exasperation at Ryan's question, and Brynn saw Thomas crack the smallest smile. *Oh, yeah. How could any of us forget?*

Alex studied Ryan's big grin, but directed his question at Brynn. "Bad story?"

"One of those rescues where everything is going against you."

Alex gestured at the snow. "More than this?"

"This is just Mother Nature. Try working against human nature."

"It wasn't his fault. The guy couldn't help what happened," Jim argued.

Ryan hooted, and Thomas shook his head.

Ignoring them, Alex raised a patient eyebrow at Brynn. "Could this be one of those stories to help me stay sane?"

She grinned. "Could be." His eyes begged for a distraction.

"Then get on with it."

She took a deep breath, enjoying the shock of cool air in her lungs as she thought back to that search. She closed her eyes and could almost see the blue sky. "It was almost two years ago. Summertime. Gorgeous weather. Must have been in the nineties that day." She heard Alex grumble, and she hid a smile. "It was real hot that day. Wasn't it, Ryan?"

"I don't remember it being hot."

She rolled her eyes. Ryan had totally missed her gibe at Alex. Spoilsport.

"Well, it wasn't raining. Or snowing." She watched Alex's lips twist. He knew the heat remarks were meant to harass him. "Anyway, we were called out for a hiker who got separated from his group, and we had a huge area to cover. There were about thirty of us looking on foot. Thankfully we had helicopter help."

Everyone glanced up at the low clouds. They knew the weather was supposed to clear sometime in the next forty-eight hours, but it wasn't showing any sign of it. Until then there was no chance of support. It was simply too stormy.

"Two of the search groups had found single human tracks, but they were over a mile apart. Each group followed a set."

"How'd they spot the tracks?" Alex raised a brow. Kiana had taken up residence at his feet, and he rubbed an occasional hand through her wet fur.

"There'd been a light snowfall the night before."

"You said it wasn't snowing." He glowered.

"It wasn't snowing during the day. It *was* sunny. And we were really high up. In the summer there's usually snow on the ground all the time up there. Anyway, these tracks seemed to lead all over the place, no rhyme or reason to them. They trailed through valleys and around giant rock formations. Up and down and around in circles."

"Two different people? Or was someone drunk?" Alex cut in.

"Neither." Brynn raised one arched brow to admonish him for the interruption. "One team followed their set of tracks down to a creek where the hiker had apparently crossed the river within thirty feet of a footbridge."

"He didn't take the bridge? Why wouldn't he cross on the bridge? Was he trying to throw searchers off his tracks?"

She continued as if she hadn't heard him, enjoying his focused attention. "Then one of the teams heard someone responding to their shouts and whistles. But they were having a hard time locating him. The rough terrain was making it difficult with dead spots and echoes. But they could hear a human voice shouting back replies to their calls. They kept searching, expecting to find him just over a ridge or on the other side of the next peak, but no luck. They'd yell for him to tell them where he was, but he kept saying he didn't know."

"What the hell? He *was* drunk," Alex stated.

"We had the chopper fly over the area. The lost man would shout that he could hear it and said he was waving his arms, but he couldn't see the chopper. And no one in the chopper could spot him. Then no one on the ground could hear him anymore because the chopper was so loud. The chopper was nearly out of fuel and ready to turn around when they spotted him."

"So what was his problem?" The marshal was impatient.

"He couldn't see," she said simply.

"What?"

"He'd lost his glasses. He couldn't see a thing. That was why he didn't take the bridge over the first creek. He didn't know it was there. And he couldn't describe his surroundings to searchers because it was all a big blur."

"Jesus Christ. Something so simple…And it made your search a dozen times more difficult." Wonder rattled Alex's voice.

"But we found him. That's all that mattered."

Ryan coughed, giving his opinion of that statement. She saw him exchange a smirk with Alex.

"Let's move out." Jim slung on his pack and motioned for Brynn to take the point. Alex lifted her pack, motioned for her to turn around, and held it in place as she slipped in her arms. She nodded her thanks, briefly meeting his gray gaze. His eyes reflected a measure of relaxation she hadn't seen before. She hid a smile, pleased she'd cracked that cold shell again.

Getting him to loosen up was a challenge. And she liked it.

She stepped out from the shelter of trees and caught a gust of snowy wind in her face. Her lungs shivered, protesting the icy air. At least it looked like the snow was easing up a little. It wasn't falling nearly as thickly as when they started their break.

Her boots sank into six inches of snow. She glanced back at Ryan to get a heading. He'd already consulted his GPS and pointed toward two o'clock. The men fell into line behind her.

Along the makeshift trail, Ryan continued complaining about the blind hiker, telling Alex more details of the problems the man had created for the search teams. Brynn tried to tune Ryan out but soon glanced over her shoulder in irritation at the weird blowing noises he was making.

The noise wasn't coming from Ryan. Ryan was looking backward over his own shoulder. Jim and Thomas had pulled out their guns and were pointing them to the left, at a dense area of rhododendrons.

"Brynn." Jim's voice was urgent. "Get back here."

Heart speeding, Brynn spun around and darted the fifteen feet back to the group, her gaze trying to penetrate the dark of the underbrush. She knew that rough sound. It blew harder and louder.

Where is Kiana? She sucked in a breath and scanned for her dog, thankful for the dog's absence. Hopefully, Kiana was hot on the trail of a rabbit or squirrel.

"What is making that fucking noise?" Alex's voice was low, his gun and Ryan's had joined the other two. Now four men had handguns trained on the bush.

"Bear. Black bear," Ryan spoke from the side of his mouth.

"I can't see anything." Alex's voice was a forced whisper

"It's definitely out there." Ryan's trigger finger lifted from the side of his gun.

Brynn grabbed two snow-covered rocks near her feet and hurled them into the brush. "Oh, for God's sake. Yell, damn it! Don't shoot the thing. Just make a lot of noise and yell." She let out a holler that made Alex's eyebrows jump. The male team members let out piercing whoops, and she was rewarded with the sound of crackling brush and blowing as the bear ran in the opposite direction.

The men let out a collective sigh as their gun barrels drifted down. Except one.

"Fuck." Alex stared into the brush, arms stiff.

"He's gone."

"How can you be sure?" His gaze didn't leave the woods.

"He was just curious. They don't usually attack."

"Usually," Alex said flatly.

Jim slapped Alex on the shoulder. "Put it away. We'll hear him if he decides to come back."

Alex slowly lowered the gun but didn't tuck it back in his shoulder holster. "I can't believe this." He shook his head, his stunned gaze traveling from one searcher to another and then darting back to the forest, disbelief distorting his forehead.

Brynn sympathized with his shock, remembering the first time she'd come across a black bear while camping. She couldn't have been more than six. The bear snatched the fish her dad had just caught and promptly ran off. She could still see the black, furry tush darting down the gravel road, a huge steelhead flopping in its mouth.

"I couldn't see its brain," Alex muttered.

Brain? Brynn cautiously eyed him. *What in the hell is he talking about?*

Ryan shouted with laughter, bent over, scooped a handful of snow, and nailed Alex with a snowball. "Next time I'll tell it to hold real still so you can line up your shot."

The second dose of ibuprofen was working on Alex's head and leg as they pushed through the forest. His stomach had settled and the shakes in his hands seemed to have subsided. The relief felt as good as a heated blanket tossed over his shoulders. Could the ibuprofen be helping his withdrawal? Hopefully, Brynn had enough to medicate him for three days. *Three days?* He shook his head in wonder. Was he going to be in the mountain snow for three days?

Would the results of this mission help him sleep better at night?

He had his doubts.

He absently touched his coat pocket. He'd placed his Beretta in the pocket because earlier he'd fumbled away precious seconds as he'd wrestled off his gloves and thrashed under his coat for the gun. He wouldn't be caught unprepared again. He stared hard into the trees.

"Hey! Look at that!" Ryan's shout brought Alex out of his mental bear-encounter preparations.

The line halted as four sets of eyes followed the direction of Ryan's hand pointing up into the trees. Something pale billowed and fluttered thirty feet above their heads. Alex's feet froze in midstep. *A parachute?*

"Is that a parachute?" Brynn voiced his thoughts.

His Beretta instantly in hand, Alex quickly scanned their surroundings for signs of life, his heart in his throat. Nothing. All was quiet as microscopic flakes fell with silent speed. He raised his gaze again. Next to the white of the snow the parachute was yellowed and dirty. Ripped.

"It's old," Thomas muttered. "It's not from our plane."

Not from our plane.

Alex slipped his handgun back in his pocket and felt his lungs contract in regret and relief. Then pity. Who'd used the parachute? How long ago?

He concentrated on watching Brynn as she searched the ground, making a roundabout pattern that circled out from the trunk of the tree.

"I can't see anything under all this snow," she complained.

"Who'd it belong to?" Ryan whispered.

"Lots of people have gone missing in these woods," Thomas said quietly. "Planes too."

Alex couldn't speak; he was nauseous. Had someone hung up there? Waiting for days on end? Waiting for a rescue that never came? Or had they died on impact? He glanced at Brynn. What was she thinking? She was still kicking at the snow, scowling and muttering to herself.

His ex-wife would have been near tears and frantic with shock and sympathy.

Brynn was looking for answers.

"Note the coordinates, Ryan."

"Already done." The deputy was scowling at his GPS. "This doesn't seem right."

Thomas glanced at Ryan's screen then back at the screen of the GPS he'd pulled out. "Mine's different. Way different."

His forehead wrinkling, Jim studied the two units the men held out. He reached in his pocket and checked his GPS. Alex felt like a useless idiot. It was a foreign feeling.

"Mine's different too."

"What?" Brynn stopped and looked up in surprise. "How can that be? I could understand one unit malfunctioning, but how can we get three different readings?"

Alex blinked as suspicion crept up his spine.

"Something magnetic? Maybe there's a meteor buried nearby." Ryan sounded as confident as if he'd suggested fairy mischief.

"Could that cause it?" Brynn murmured. Everyone looked blank.

"I have no fucking idea what would affect them," Jim admitted. "They get their readings from a group of several satellites. Maybe the storm's interfering. But it shouldn't be. These things are supposed to get accurate readings in deep chasms and through bad weather."

Alex watched Thomas. The Alaskan's face was expressionless as he studied his GPS and then the others'. Mistrust knotted Alex's stomach. Could someone have tampered with the units?

His gaze went to each face, studying and assessing as his jaw tightened. He was starting to like these people and it was affecting his objectivity. Not good.

In Brynn's stooped search position, a lock of hair came loose from her ponytail and she tucked it behind her ear. The woman genuinely cared about the people for whom she went on missions. It couldn't be her. She wouldn't put anyone at risk for any reason. More likely it was one of the men. Or someone at base camp.

Who'd want to keep us from finding that plane?

US Marshal Paul Whittenhall pulled Stewart aside, out of hearing range of that interfering sheriff. "Who's available? Who can do this outdoor kind of snowstorm shit?" His heartbeat was doing double time and blood was pressuring the walls of the veins in his head.

Alex Kinton.

The name ricocheted through his brain like a Super Ball.

How in the hell had Kinton gotten out there?

Gary Stewart licked his lips. "Uh…Matt Boyles does this sort of thing, I think. He's always going climbing or snow caving. He's in Eugene right now, not too far away. I could call…"

"Call him." Paul's fist tightened on Stewart's arm. "And tell him not to breathe a word to anyone else or he's out of a job. It's gonna be just the two of you going in after that search team."

"Me?" Stewart's eyes widened. "I can't…" His dismayed gaze met Paul's and he visibly fought down his panicked reaction. "Uh…Only two of us going after them? Don't you think one more person—"

"No more. I want as few people as possible knowing about this. Get a hold of Boyles. I don't care what he's working on. He's to drop it and get his ass up here. Then go to town and get your camping shit together. Collins said that team will be out there for two or three nights. That gives you plenty of time to get to Kinton."

Stewart blinked. "But Boyles was—"

"Boyles is on a need-to-know basis. Just tell him Kinton's cracked again and we're worried about the safety of the crew out there. He'll accept that." Paul glared at the younger man, eyes burning. "And then I'll have to trust your judgment on the best way to take Kinton down."

Patrick Collins was being shut out and it was royally pissing him off.

The two federal agents had held a whispered conversation and then Deputy Marshal Stewart had jumped in the black Suburban and vanished while Whittenhall vented on his cell phone, waving Patrick off every time he'd approached.

Patrick didn't know anything about Alex Kinton. He didn't know who was on that plane. He didn't know why Whittenhall appeared to be one symptom away from a stroke.

Anger simmered and smoldered in his chest. Patrick had way too many questions without answers. He chewed on his cheek. *What is the best way to get Whittenhall to talk?* Good thing Patrick had bucket loads of patience. With a little time, he'd figure out what made Whittenhall tick. He'd caught the nervous glances the marshal had cast toward him. A nervous man was usually a guilty man. Patrick just needed to find out why.

Tim Reid stopped beside Patrick. "Still not talking to you?" Reid's gaze followed the marshal. Even Reid was picking up the nervous vibes Whittenhall shot out like ammo.

Patrick shook his head, lips tight.

"Why're they all fired up about that Kinton guy?"

Patrick shrugged and didn't answer. During their initial meeting, Kinton had been terse, direct, and determined to get to that crash. Not bad things to be, Patrick believed. That was the kind of person he needed on his hasty team.

But obviously Kinton had made the early morning phone calls to Patrick. He'd talked himself onto Patrick's team by posing as his boss. Ex-boss. All the facts and logic pointed to Kinton as a manipulative liar. That was *not* the type of person he needed on his hasty team.

Heat shot up Patrick's throat.

Why? Why did Kinton need to get to that plane?

Patrick glared at Whittenhall still yapping on his cell phone. That asshole knew why. And he wasn't telling.

"So what if Kinton's an ex-agent? What'd he do, kill someone?" Reid was muttering to himself, not expecting answers.

"He can't hurt anyone out there. Everyone on that plane is gonna be dead. No one survives that sort of shit."

"Shut up," Patrick snapped.

Patrick hated that kind of pessimism. It was too early in the game. People survived out in the elements when no one should have. Patrick cut out the amazing stories and kept them in a notebook. Especially the plane crash stories. Children who lived even when their parents didn't. Seniors with broken bones who survived nights of subzero temperatures. The human spirit was amazing. It drove people to achieve the impossible.

Patrick never said never.

It was his duty to hope for the best. He'd be letting down the people on that plane if he didn't. They deserved every effort he had to give.

Reid hadn't flinched when Patrick told him to shut up. The easygoing deputy was the type who let everything roll off his back. Sort of like the soggy snow was doing right now. The rain had turned to snow exactly at noon. Already the puddles were showing thin sheets of ice forming at their edges as the temperature dropped. The promised cold front had blown in with a vengeance.

Patrick glanced guiltily at the Madison County RV pulling into the clearing. His new headquarters. He was going to have a roof over his head while his team struggled in that icy shit.

"Hey, Gentry!" Reid hollered, and Patrick's gut clenched as he turned to see a tall man shake hands with a perimeter deputy and then stride confidently toward him and Reid, lifting a hand in greeting.

Shit. Not now.

Patrick didn't want this guy in the base camp. The newcomer was a helicopter pilot for the nearby air force rescue squadron and had assisted several times when Madison County Search and Rescue needed air support. Obviously, no flying could be done today. The wind and weather were creating near whiteout conditions in the Cascades and all helicopters were grounded back at the air force base. A pilot who couldn't fly was a bundle of energy that Patrick didn't need bouncing in his face today. Especially a pilot with a vested interest in the safety of the search team. Gentry would go ballistic when he heard about the suspicious circumstances with the ex-marshal. He'd immediately assume the worst for the security of the team.

Patrick pasted on a smile and greeted Brynn's boyfriend.

CHAPTER FIVE

"What do you know about that plane?" Liam's forehead wrinkled in concern, nearly touching his dark crew cut as he questioned Patrick.

The pilot wouldn't stop peppering Patrick with questions. When did the team leave? How long did he expect the search to take? Had he heard from Brynn?

Patrick shot a black glare in the direction of the US marshal. "I don't know fucking enough about that plane."

"I heard Darrin Besand is the escorted prisoner." Liam dropped his voice.

Patrick's eyebrows shot up. *Darrin Besand?*

His skin crawled.

Besand had been sentenced to life in prison for a string of killings that went back twenty years. Raping and strangling women had been his favorite pastime. And he'd had no preference for age or race. No one had linked Besand to two-thirds of the killings until he'd confessed after his first trial. The killings were too varied. Detectives in eight counties and three states hadn't realized they were looking for the same man.

After his arrest, the killer had become a media sensation when he'd started communicating with a Portland television reporter via mail. He'd made her his confidant, offering her exclusives in exchange for getting his stories on TV. Regan Simmons was young, beautiful, and searching for her big break to get out of the Portland television market and into something bigger, more glamorous, like LA or New York. The serial killer's story had been huge, and Darrin Besand had offered her the opportunity for national exposure on a silver platter. She'd eagerly grabbed for it with both hands.

Turned out, Besand had been sending Regan Simmons mail for five years prior to his arrest. She'd kept the letters but brushed them off as coming from a nutcase who'd simply wanted attention. If only she'd taken his letters to the police back then… maybe there would have been fewer victims. Investigators had been furious to discover she'd had direct information from a killer with details about what he'd done to his victims, and she'd said nothing. She hadn't believed they'd been true. Patrick slowly shook his head. *What had the woman been thinking?*

"Where'd you hear Besand's name?"

"The name's flying around the media corral over there." Liam jerked his head at the cameras.

Could it be true? Is Besand the prisoner on the plane?

No wonder Whittenhall was about to have a stroke. A serial killer in his custody let loose in the woods. Patrick caught his breath.

My team. When will I be able to update them?

Reid was in charge of maintaining contact with the team. All efforts at phone and radio contact had failed since an hour after the team had left, but that didn't surprise Patrick one bit. That was to be expected in this forest.

Patrick tried to relax. Jim had his head on straight. They'd known there was a felon on board, possibly a murderer. The men were all law enforcement and appropriately armed. Jim would take every precaution out there. Patrick didn't have a better team leader than Jim.

Patrick glared in Whittenhall's direction, furious the press knew the prisoner's identity before him. And he was in charge! Who'd leaked the name? Whittenhall had seemed determined not to let the prisoner's name surface.

Patrick spotted Regan Simmons in the crowd of media, filming a piece for her news station, the bright light from the camera highlighting her hair, which swirled out artfully from under her hat. Even from this distance, Patrick swore he could see the greedy gleam in her eye. She was still hustling for that break into the big time. She'd ruined her chances after the Besand story broke about her withholding information and two married state senators had admitted to affairs with her. She'd lost her job due to an ethics clause but rebounded two weeks later with a less discerning television station. *Is she the one putting out Besand's name?* She was the most likely suspect. She had the right contacts to know what was going on in Besand's life.

"How many did he kill? Twenty-two? Twenty-three?"

Liam nodded. "Something like that. At least that's how many the police suspect. So far, he's only been prosecuted for one murder, but they gave him life in prison. I think he's being tried in other states too."

"Shit."

"Maybe this plane wreck is a good way to save the state some money. Save on room and board for the rest of the guy's life."

Patrick snorted. "But then why is Whittenhall so uptight?"

"What do you mean?"

"He's got steaming high blood pressure because an ex-marshal of his is out there with my crew." Patrick chewed his lip and studied the marshal across the clearing. A thought formed in his mind and he voiced it slowly. "The more I think about it, I don't think it's the prisoner who's worrying him. It's Kinton."

Liam's nose wrinkled. "You didn't tell me anyone else went out with Brynn's team. Who's Kinton?"

"Alex Kinton used to be a marshal. I don't know if they fired him or he quit or retired. But when I told Whittenhall that Kinton showed up this morning to go out with my team, Whittenhall nearly had a stroke at my feet."

"There's a guy out there impersonating a marshal? And you were told he was supposed to go?" Liam's expression was getting darker by the second.

"I got a phone call this morning from someone I thought was Whittenhall. But Whittenhall swears no one from his office called, and I believe him. You can't fake shock like that. I'm thinking Kinton made the calls himself before he got here, clearing his way to get on my team and out to that plane."

Liam turned toward the older marshal, who was finally slipping his phone into his pocket. "Hey!" Liam marched toward

Whittenhall as Patrick grabbed his arm. Liam shook him off. "What's the deal with the marshal who went out with the team?"

Whittenhall wiped at his forehead as he studied the younger man who'd aggressively stepped up in his face and fisted his hands at his sides. Whittenhall's gaze stabbed at Patrick over Liam's shoulder. Patrick shrugged. Maybe Liam could succeed where he hadn't. The pilot had a directness about him that was hard to ignore. Liam said what he thought, rarely believed he was wrong, and could boss people around without their knowing it. Frankly, Patrick didn't know how Brynn put up with him. Patrick could handle Liam's company for only a few minutes at a time before Liam said something to piss him off.

"Alex Kinton is no longer a marshal."

"Then why the hell is he out there?"

"I didn't send him."

"Who did?"

Whittenhall rubbed his lips together. "I don't know. I don't know how he found out about the plane wreck with this prisoner on board."

"Darrin Besand?" Liam asked.

Whittenhall blinked in surprise and nodded. Annoyance and anger flashed across his face.

Score one for Liam. Patrick wanted to whistle.

"Why would Kinton care about that plane?" Liam was direct.

Whittenhall said nothing, pulling out his cell phone and ignoring the pilot. Liam stepped closer, and Patrick held his breath. Liam was getting more information out of the asshole than Patrick had so he'd let him push a few more buttons.

Whittenhall looked up at Liam. "This doesn't concern you." He scowled. "Who are you anyway?" He glanced over Liam's shoulder again at Patrick, who kept his mouth shut and his arms crossed on his chest.

Liam's chin shot up. "Major Liam Gentry, pilot, 304th Air Force Rescue Squadron. I would be flying air support today if the weather wasn't so crappy. My girlfriend is on the Madison County SAR team, and if she's in danger because of Kinton, I want to know about it."

Patrick silently cheered.

Whittenhall got an odd look on his face. He opened his mouth twice to answer Liam, and then closed it. Finally, the marshal leaned toward the young man, his voice sharp.

"Kinton had a nervous breakdown a year ago and physically attacked one of his supervisors. Put the man in the hospital. Kinton was let go from the US Marshals because of it. He is obsessed with Darrin Besand and will stop at nothing to see him get a lethal injection. If Kinton's out there with your girlfriend, she's going to simply be a stepping-stone for him to get to Besand. He'll trample anything in his path to get his hands around that murdering creep's neck." Whittenhall raised a brow at Patrick. "He blatantly lied to Collins to get to that plane. I believe he would've taken more drastic physical measures if Collins hadn't cooperated."

Patrick's spine stiffened, and Liam's head jerked back in shock.

Whittenhall looked intently at Liam. "There're two dangerous men out there, *Major* Gentry. Not just one. I'd say your girlfriend's in a shitload of danger."

"Anyone see anything?"

A chorus of dejected no's answered Jim. They'd been kicking the snow under the parachute for a good twenty minutes. Brynn had found a frayed piece of strapping. Nothing else. Alex stole a quick look at Brynn. She'd efficiently directed the group in a circular search pattern as if looking for human remains was something she did every day. Maybe she did.

Death was a big part of the woman's life.

How does she sleep at night?

Five years ago, Alex had arrived on the scene of a freeway auto accident, and the sight had given him nightmares for weeks. One driver had been beheaded, his neck a bloody stump, his tie and suit jacket still neatly in place. Alex hadn't looked to see where the guy's head ended up. The other driver had been thrown from his car and hit by other cars. His legs had looked deflated with the skin resembling an empty balloon. The flesh from his legs spilled out in bloody red piles and smears on the pavement.

Alex hadn't known the human body could look like that.

He swallowed the bile that surged in the back of his throat and concentrated on scanning the snow at his feet.

How did Brynn do it every day? She probably saw dead kids. Babies, even. Seniors who slipped and fell and weren't found until neighbors called the police because the newspapers had piled up.

What kind of devastation would they find at the plane wreckage?

One corpse. That was all Alex needed to see. One very specific dead corpse. He didn't care if the guy was beheaded or burned to a crisp with blackened flesh and stiffened limbs that looked like he was reaching out for help. Alex would sleep better for the rest of his life once he found out what happened to the plane.

Alex's younger brother, Samuel, had been the only family member he'd seen after death. It had been on a table at the medical examiner's office—after the ME had cleaned him up, but before he'd made that first Y incision. It had ached deep in Alex's chest, allowing Samuel to be cut open like that, but the death had been highly suspicious, possibly suicide: an indication for autopsy.

The original theory was that Alex's brother had been despondent over the death of a friend and decided to drown himself in the pool where she'd died.

But Alex had known it wasn't suicide the moment the police called and told him they'd found his brother in the pool. Samuel wouldn't kill himself. If only Alex had listened to Samuel's sudden ramblings and complaints about one of his caretakers. If only Alex had followed up and double-checked Samuel's statements with the owner of the facility where he'd lived. If only. If only.

Alex's boot suddenly kicked something long and white out of the snow. His heart stopped and tried to leap up into his mouth. He halted his systematic tracking and stared, gaze immobile. Next to the white snow, the bone looked a dingy, old yellow.

"Brynn." His voice came out as whisper, so he repeated with more strength, "Brynn!"

Everyone's head jerked in his direction.

"Whatcha got?" Ryan bounded over in a flash, his interested eyes focused on the remains by Alex's boot. Alex fought an impulse to cover up the bone, hide it from sight. Ryan's eagerness seemed disrespectful. Almost wrong.

Ryan squatted, using his gloved hand to paw all the snow off the bone as the others walked up. They were silent, their quiet manner more appropriate for lost bones. Ryan snickered, and Alex wanted to kick him in the head.

"It's a stick." He lifted the *stick* and waved it at Alex. "You discovered a stick, dude. Nice job."

Alex studied the pale stick that Ryan tossed to Brynn. It was smooth and as long as his thigh. Knobby on one end, but the other end showed a frayed break where it had clearly separated from a tree.

Brynn shot Alex a sympathetic glance as she tried to cover her amusement. "Reminds me of the human mandible you found one time, Ryan." She tapped the stick against her palm and cast an assessing look at Ryan, a grin pulling at the corners of her lips.

Jim hooted and slung an arm around Ryan's shoulders. "I remember that. Rocks can take amazing shapes. Alex's stick looks a hell of a lot more human than your rock jaw did." Ryan genuinely laughed, but he shoved Jim away. Jim winked at Brynn, who covered her mouth with a gloved hand.

"OK. I don't think we're going to find anything. Anything more, that is." Brynn gave Alex a half smile. "Which way are we headed now? This way, right?" She gestured to the west.

"Only if you're headed to the beach, darlin'." Jim put his gloved hands on Brynn's shoulders and turned her east. "This is the way. I thought you were going to have that problem looked at."

Thomas snorted.

"What problem?" Alex watched Jim pat Brynn affectionately on the back.

"Brynn has no sense of direction. Even a compass or GPS can't straighten her out." Ryan hugged her and gave her a smacking kiss on one cheek. "But we love her anyway."

Brynn blushed at the kiss and deftly stepped out of Ryan's arms with a one-handed shove to his chest. Her brown eyes met Alex's for the briefest second.

Had she pointed in the wrong direction to get the attention off his bone blunder?

Brynn was the mediator of the group. Always negotiating, getting between the others when the slightest argument started to surface. Like she couldn't stand the littlest confrontation among the friends. But she definitely wasn't scared to stand up for what she thought. She'd voiced her opinions without a qualm throughout the trip. But for some reason she didn't like to see the men argue. Didn't she know that was part of how men communicated?

"How much daylight do we have left?" she asked Thomas.

Thomas shrugged, squinting at the cloudy sky. "Three, four hours. Plenty of time to get in some yardage before looking for a place to sleep."

Sleep? In the snow? Alex glanced around and shuddered. Tonight was clearly going to suck. "I don't suppose you know of a Motel 6 up ahead?"

Thomas gave a short laugh, more like a bark. "Motel 6? Ha! Good one." He flashed a rare grin.

"Motel 6 below," Alex grumbled to himself at the next break. The temps were dropping along with the light. The sky had been slowly dimming for the past hour and he was starting to wonder where they'd make camp for the night. He used the break to take inventory of his borrowed pack. Along the hike, he hadn't done more than locate the protein bars and water bottles. He stared into the pack and he realized he'd been a walking sporting goods store.

Thank you, Sheriff Collins.

Alex felt like an idiot as he found the sheriff's stash of aspirin and Advil. He'd been carrying his own relief all morning while he suffered. Shaking his head, he dug out what looked like a kid's belt with an odd circular triple pattern on the buckle. His hands were trembling slightly again, but he ignored them. He slid the adjustment straps back and forth. What in the hell was it for?

"It's a headlamp," Ryan spoke.

Alex blinked and stared at the "buckle," finally realizing he was looking at three tiny LED bulbs. His fingers found a switch and he turned it on only to blink again as he blinded himself.

"Shit. Sucker's bright."

"Those lights will last for hundreds of hours." Ryan grinned at his surprise.

Alex glanced around in the dimming daylight, noticing Jim and Thomas had slipped on their headlamps but hadn't turned them on yet. He did the same, tightening the strap that he'd loosened enough to fit over Goliath's head. He also found dry clothing, two types of Leatherman tools, wire, pliers, needles, thread (which he hoped was for clothing repair, not skin), water purification tablets, duct tape, carabiners, and nylon rope. He stared at the heat sheets crammed into bags the size of his fist, remembering that in certain situations the millimeter-thin silver blankets could make the difference between life and death. He snorted at the sunscreen and was tickled to find a package of baby wipes. He ripped one out and washed his face in relief, then rubbed at the ground-in mud on his pants.

Now he smelled like a baby. But in a good way.

What he didn't find was a tent.

Did they plan to sleep exposed to the elements? He examined the sleeping bag. It was down filled and appeared it would come up around his head like a mummy. He'd briefly scanned the sleeping bags that morning at the sporting goods store, but knew there would be a bag waiting for him at the base camp. Alex had been in and out of the store in twenty minutes. He'd told the way-too-young salesclerk where he was going and what he'd be doing and the kid led him on a lightning-fast trek around the store, throwing clothing in a basket. Alex put on the stuff in the changing room, slapped down a credit card, and then paled at the total.

He'd been glad he didn't need to buy a bag. He'd seen one for $600.

He hefted the sleeping bag from his pack. It couldn't weigh more than five pounds. He rooted some more and found a pad to go under the sleeping bag. Was this the extent of his nighttime gear?

"Hey, Ryan."

The other man had his mouth full but managed an inquiring mumble.

"Am I supposed to have a tent?"

Ryan swallowed and twisted up his lips. "I've got one. We usually only pack one for every two or three people. We worked it out before we left. Brynn sleeps with Jim and her dog. The rest of us will fit in my tent."

Alex exhaled. Thank God. At least he'd have a roof over his head.

"Did ya think we'd sleep out in the snow?"

Alex snorted. "I didn't know what to think. I was hoping not to get a lesson in snow caving."

"Not enough snow at this level." The other man's eyes danced at Alex's obvious discomfort. "Snow caving's not that bad. Especially with these sleeping bags. You're gonna be amazed at how toasty they are. If it weren't snowing, I'd consider sleeping under the stars. Nothing better than being in a warm bag as you study the sky at night."

"No thanks," Alex said wryly. "When this trip is over I'm headed somewhere warm for a week. Hawaii, or maybe Mexico. I don't care where as long as it's warm. I'll check out the stars when I get there."

Alex pulled a compass out of a side pack pocket. It was set into a rectangle of clear plastic with ruler marks and an arrow.

"Ever use one before?" Ryan sounded politely curious. He had to have seen the completely blank look on Alex's face as he studied the compass. The only navigation Alex had ever done was with a GPS system in a rental car. He doubted the compass would speak graciously to him and recalculate his route when he made a wrong turn.

"No." He'd seen Ryan check their route several times with a compass and map. Every time the weather briefly cleared or they had a good view of their surroundings, Ryan double-checked their progress. He seemed to be the main navigator. Both Jim and Thomas deferred to the younger man and clearly trusted his guidance. The GPS units were still giving different readings and Alex had been surprised when the other men shrugged off this obstacle. They had confidence in Ryan's skill with a compass.

Ryan was a smart kid behind all the cockiness and chatter. But he'd been quieter as evening approached, coughing and occasionally rubbing at his gut. Alex hoped Ryan wasn't coming down with the flu. This wasn't the environment to get sick. Alex frowned as he felt sweat trickle down his back. They'd been resting for ten minutes, so he shouldn't be sweating. Was he catching something too? *Shit.*

"You feeling OK?" Alex thought Ryan looked too pale.

The younger man shrugged. "Seem to be picking up a cough. Stomach's not feeling so great. Almost feels like I need to—"

"Hey. What was the deal with Brynn freezing over that river? She doesn't seem like the kind of person who'd do that." Alex rapidly changed the subject, not wanting to hear details about Ryan's digestive tract. He nervously rubbed at the sweat on his temples as he glanced around for Brynn. She was practicing hand commands with Kiana thirty yards away. Too far to overhear his questions.

And he'd been wondering since the incident. After the crossing, the rest of the crew had exchanged words and looks that spoke of a deeper understanding of what happened to her. Alex had felt left out and figured it was none of his business. He'd told himself he shouldn't be interested, because what went on with these people had nothing to do with him and his goal. These people were simply a means to an end.

But now he felt a little more connected, sucked into their lives. He knew Ryan the best. He had helped Alex out of the mud, talked his ear off, and teasingly harassed him about the fake bone.

He felt comfortable asking Ryan about Brynn because he seemed like one of those guys who was impossible to offend. The guy would talk about anything. Unlike Thomas. Alex had yet to hear him get chatty, but that was all right. Ryan was chatty enough for the whole group. Alex usually didn't say a word; Ryan carried both sides of a conversation just fine.

Surprisingly, Ryan bit his lip and hesitated at the question about Brynn.

"Hey, if it's private…"

"Nah, it's not like that. Everyone knows what happened. I was thinking it's her story to tell, but I know it rips her gut every time she has to talk about it."

"Oh." A twinge of guilt made Alex sit back and reconsider. It was none of his business. But for some reason the thought of that confident woman having a painful past made his chest hurt. Maybe hearing about the state of Ryan's digestive system would be better.

"I think she was eight or nine years old when it happened."

"It?"

Ryan rubbed at his reddened nose.

"Her best friend died after slipping off a makeshift log bridge. A lot like what we crossed today. Nothing to hang on to for balance though. And it was summertime."

"Shit. Brynn was there?"

"Yeah. Right behind her friend on the bridge. Brynn fell too, but managed to hang on somehow." He sniffed, casting a quick glance at Brynn, who was in deep conversation with Jim. "A search team found her clinging to the log, nearly unconscious. They figured she'd been in the water for hours. Luckily the water wasn't cold that time of year. Her friend was found several miles down the river."

Alex was silent.

"Brynn swears that's when she knew she wanted to do search and rescue. She wanted to save people like she'd been saved. I guess that's why she became a nurse too." Ryan studied the compass in his hands, his mouth tight.

How does she stomach working with more death?

Alex's heart was pounding, and he wiped at his forehead. Why'd he feel like he'd been running for ten minutes instead of resting? He took a series of deep breaths. Ryan noticed.

"Hey. You OK?" Ryan frowned. "You look kinda rattled."

Alex *felt* rattled. His heart rate wouldn't slow, and his shakes were getting more frequent. "Bad story."

"Yeah. It is." Ryan looked unconvinced. "You feeling all right? Want me to grab Brynn?"

"No!" Alex snapped and felt instant guilt. "I'm fine, just need to relax."

Suddenly he knew what it was. Withdrawal. He'd been without his anxiety medication for twenty-four hours, and his body was protesting. He took the stuff only at night to help him sleep, but apparently, his body was really missing the habit. He'd had no idea those tiny pills could affect him this way. Hopefully, he'd be through the worst of it soon. And he was done taking the damn things. If he still had problems sleeping, he'd invest in some boring books. He floundered for a question to distract Ryan.

"So Brynn shares Jim's tent, huh?" The words tumbled out of Alex's mouth, and he mentally kicked himself in the head. Not the way to find out more about Brynn. Without thinking, he'd rudely stuck his foot in his mouth. Real smooth.

Ryan's eyes narrowed a bit. "It's not like that. Jim's wife and Brynn are really close. And she's as good as married."

"As *good* as married?" *What'd that mean?*

"She and Liam have been together for nearly two years."

"Then why aren't they married?"

Ryan paused, and Alex watched a flash of confusion cross his face. "Brynn's not really the marrying kind," he said slowly.

Alex raised a brow and waited. *It's none of my business.*

But he wanted to know more.

The other man coughed and frowned. "That didn't come out right. Her parents...well, her dad anyway..."

He was putting Ryan on the spot. Alex cut him off with a sharp hand gesture. "You don't need to give some big explanation. That kind of complex commitment isn't the right path for some people."

Relief relaxed Ryan's face. "That's kinda what I meant. How about you? Are you married?" His eagerness to change the subject was obvious.

Alex shook his head and wryly twisted his lips. "Divorced. Commitment wasn't the right path for her either."

"Sorry, man. That sucks."

Alex nodded, deliberately dropping his gaze, and Ryan turned back to his own pack.

Their conversation over, Alex took a deep breath, closed his eyes, and concentrated on slowing his pounding heart. How long was he going to have withdrawal symptoms? They weren't going to get worse, were they?

CHAPTER SIX

"I've got to get out there." Liam's honest face contorted as he ran a hand through his tightly cropped hair and paced in circles.

"You're not flying in this weather." Patrick placed a restraining hand on the pilot's shoulder.

"You don't even know where they are. They haven't been able to check in. He might have done something..."

Patrick grabbed both Liam's shoulders and turned him to stare eye to eye. "Done what? If Whittenhall is right and Kinton wants to get his hands on Besand, his best bet is going to be sticking with an experienced crew. He doesn't know squat about getting around out there. He needs those guys to survive."

"What about Brynn? Maybe he sees her as expendable?"

Patrick mentally rolled his eyes.

"Kinton's not stupid." Patrick thought back to their first meeting. He hadn't met an unbalanced man. He'd met a determined one. A man with his wits about him. He was having a hard time reconciling the unstable image Whittenhall painted of Kinton with the resolute soldier he'd met that morning. Something in Patrick's gut didn't like Whittenhall. The marshal was shifty, pompous, and condescending. Maybe that was optimistically skewing Patrick's view of Kinton.

But his gut was usually right. Usually.

"They need air support. They're not going to stumble across a wreck in that forest. It's the old needle in a haystack comparison," Liam said.

"There might be a good window of weather tomorrow."

"Tomorrow?" Liam kicked at a rock, sending a splatter of mud over Patrick's boots. Patrick bit his lip and ignored it because Liam was a good pilot who'd frequently helped Madison County with SAR, and he belonged to Brynn. But that didn't mean Patrick had to hold Liam's hand because he was rattled about his girlfriend's safety.

"You need to stop stressing over Brynn and give her a little more credit. She's tough and smart."

Liam scowled, looking away.

"When she broke her collarbone in that rockslide last year she toughed it out. Finished the search even though she couldn't move her arm. She's pretty good at taking care of herself."

Patrick decided not to mention the obnoxious fit of temper Liam had thrown when he'd found her in the hospital with her arm in a sling. Judging by Liam's tight lips, he remembered clearly.

"No one's going to let your unit fly today. You know that. Don't try to make me out to be the bad guy. Your own CO won't let you up today. Besides, it's almost dark."

Liam was silent, his head pointed in the direction of the trailhead as if he expected to see the team come traipsing back out. He muttered under his breath.

"What was that?" Patrick leaned toward Liam, his neck stiffening at the rebellious look on the pilot's face.

"I won't be taking an Air Force bird out today."

"That's right." He watched the young man closely. "Don't get any ideas."

"I gotta go." Liam abruptly turned and jogged in the direction of his truck before Patrick could say another word.

Fuck. What was Liam going to do? Patrick silently repeated Liam's words, *No Air Force bird.* Surely Liam didn't know of a civilian crazy enough to try to fly in this weather. It'd be a death mission. Patrick mentally rattled through a list of local pilots with their own copters and caught his breath.

"Oh, shit." He did know of one pilot crazy enough to try a stunt like that. Liam's older brother, Tyrone, had his own helicopter.

He turned to shout after Liam, but his truck was already gone.

Patrick glanced at the dark sky, reassured that Liam wouldn't be going anywhere tonight. He'd worry about the pilot tomorrow. Patrick's watch beeped softly, and he cursed as he saw the time. The evening press conference was in ten minutes. He put Brynn's boyfriend out of his mind and concentrated on what useless facts he could toss to the vultures with the microphones.

He winced at the analogy. Vultures circled the dying.

Alex's first twenty-degree night in a tent was over.

Thank God.

He lowered his head and trudged on. They'd gotten a good six inches of snow overnight, and eventually he'd slept like a log. Around midnight, he'd raided Ryan's backpack and swallowed a hefty dose of Benadryl to get to sleep. Maybe a little too much. Thomas had had to roughly shake Alex awake that morning.

He'd had to resort to the sneaky Benadryl measure after realizing his two tent mates snored like trains. Ryan especially. This morning Ryan had been coughing heavily and had a pallor that caused Brynn to question his health. He'd brushed her off, saying he believed he was catching a cold but felt good enough to push on. Alex thought he looked like shit, but he kept his mouth shut.

He followed Thomas's footsteps automatically, but kept a careful watch for any more slides, stepping carefully with the homemade snowshoes Thomas had rigged for him with branches, rope, wire, and tiny bungee cords. Everyone else had lightweight aluminum snowshoes in their packs. Thomas had whipped together the makeshift snowshoes in under a half hour while Alex had watched every move with fascination.

"Don't know why Collins didn't have snowshoes in there." Jim had shaken his head, watching Thomas's hands wrap cording around the pliable tree branches.

"When's the last time the sheriff actually went out on search? He's always stuck coordinating," Brynn had said as she ran a brush over Kiana's thick fur while they waited. Alex could have sworn he saw the dog smile.

Thomas had hooked the bungee cords around Alex's boots and secured the rough frames to his feet. Intrigued, Alex had immediately tried them out. He'd stepped one shoe on the heel of the other and then fallen. Thomas had grinned. Smiling ruefully, Alex had tried again; he was too absorbed in the results of Thomas's talent to get embarrassed. He'd shuffled in circles until he'd caught a rhythm.

The snowfall stopped after the first break and gave them several hours without precipitation. The noon sky was dark and dismal and thick clouds hung low, but the wind seemed to have let up slightly. Contact with base camp had been impossible since early yesterday.

"I don't think this is the window of good weather they were talking about," Jim said. "I don't think they'd risk any flights just yet. Besides, it's not snowing here right now but might be back at camp. We'll try calling again once we get a little higher, but I knew coming in there was a chance we wouldn't be able to talk to base camp at all this mission."

They settled into the protection of a small rocky ridge, out of the wind, and stopped for lunch. Ryan immediately plopped down in the snow after slinging his pack off. He looked miserable. His breathing was labored and sweat dripped from his forehead. Brynn tried to get him to eat, but he shook his head.

"My stomach doesn't feel so hot."

He drank some water, but Alex noticed it wasn't very much.

Jim gestured at the sky behind them. "Looks like I was right about weather back at camp." The sky to the west was black. From their small clearing, they had an unobstructed view of sloping dark forests with snowy frosting.

"I didn't realize we'd climbed so high." Alex squinted down the side of the mountain. The trek had so many ups and downs he'd honestly felt like they were at the same altitude as where they'd started. Only the depth of the snow told him differently

Thomas nodded. "We're probably around four thousand feet."

Jim immediately disagreed, and Alex tuned out their argument. He kept half an eye on Brynn, waiting for her to jump in and mediate, but she was focused on Ryan. The younger man was shaking his head at her inaudible questions. She put a hand to his forehead, but he pushed it away. Her eyes narrowed at him, and Alex couldn't hear her retort. It must have been a sharp one, because Ryan's shoulders slumped and his head dropped.

Suddenly Ryan jumped to his feet and turned. He took four lunging steps away from the group and then started to heave and vomit. Brynn was holding his head and murmuring to him before Alex could even stand.

The concern on her face touched him. He remembered his mother holding his head like that when he was ill as a child. The nasty crap spewing into the snow didn't gross out Brynn; her focus was on the condition of the man. Ryan leaned away from her, gesturing for her to move back.

Alex caught her arm as she stepped back to the group, hurt and disappointment on her face. Seeing her upset, and with worry in her eyes, drove him to speak. "Ignore him. No man wants a woman to witness his weakness."

"I know that. But he's..." She tucked a strand of hair behind her ear, frowning.

"Give him some privacy," Alex suggested. Thomas and Jim were still eating, apparently giving Ryan his space, but Alex spotted Jim's concerned questioning glance at Brynn. She shrugged at him, walked a few yards off, and called for her dog.

Kiana gave an answering bark and came tearing out of the trees. Snow flew up from her feet, leaving a white cloud in her wake. Tongue lolling, ears perked, and tail happy. Just seeing the dog made Alex feel better. He'd never had a dog but had always wanted one. Monica hadn't liked them, and his job took him away from home so much he figured a pet wouldn't get enough attention.

Brynn broke off a branch, stripped it of needles, and threw it hard in the opposite direction. Kiana cranked up her speed and raced after it. A gray-and-white blur.

Brynn's jaw was set. She'd probably prefer to use the stick to beat a little sense into Ryan.

"Hey," the sick man croaked. They all looked in his direction. He'd moved farther away from the group to the top of the rocks. He was pointing down the slope, south from their view. "Plane."

They scrambled up to Ryan's view. White-faced and weak, Ryan braced his hands on his thighs as he stared down the slope. Sure enough. Alex squinted and saw white metal with some orange striping at the edge of a small clearing. Several hundred yards down in almost the same direction they'd come from. They'd probably passed within a hundred feet of it, but hadn't seen it for the density of the forest between their path and the clearing. If Ryan hadn't puked, they would have continued southeast, away from the wreckage.

Jim slapped the sick man on the back. "Nice work. Let's get down there."

Thomas and Jim turned to go grab their packs, but Brynn didn't move. Alex followed her gaze to the puddle of vomit between Ryan's feet.

It was red with fresh blood.

How sick is Ryan? Brynn's heart had nearly stopped when she'd spotted blood in his vomit. Ryan was actively bleeding somewhere in his digestive tract. The possibility of an ulcer popped into her mind first, but Ryan had never mentioned an ulcer before. From what she'd seen, he ate whatever the hell he wanted and how much he wanted. He didn't have the eating habits of someone babying an ulcer. And he was the picture of health; he easily burned off every calorie with his good exercise regimen. He didn't smoke or drink. She didn't think he had a daily ibuprofen or similar habit that could mess with the lining of his stomach.

She'd have to ask him about an ulcer. Another differential diagnosis for the blood was something he'd eaten. Maybe something poisonous or incredibly sharp. Where would he get something poisonous? And surely he would have noticed swallowing something sharp enough to cause that much damage.

Ryan had been fighting a cough, and his forehead had been unbearably hot as she'd held his head when he'd vomited. His health problem was probably systemic, like the flu or some sort of gastrointestinal virus or bacteria.

But those shouldn't cause the bleeding.

Some ulcers were caused by bacteria. Weren't they?

She snorted. Some nurse she was. It'd been too many years since nursing school. Most of those years she'd dealt with dead people, not living people and their various ailments. Her continuing education requirements were fulfilled in the classroom or online. A nurse learned a lot more when she worked with ill people day in and day out. An experienced ER nurse could probably look at Ryan, ask three questions, and have him accurately diagnosed before the doctor entered the room.

But could that nurse take the liver temperature on a corpse?

Before they'd taken a single step down the steep slope to the plane, Jim had looked up the mountain behind them and waved a hand at the wide expanse of snow. "Heavy snow. A lot of wet snow has fallen up here. I want everyone to follow the edge of the woods. Stick to the trees and out of the clearing as much as possible. This place is ripe for an avalanche."

Brynn took one look at the tall slope behind them, dotted with rocky outcroppings where the slope was nearly vertical, and agreed. She'd come across avalanches after the fact. She'd never been around one when it occurred, and she wanted to keep it that way. She knew Jim had lost a good friend to a Canadian avalanche.

Ryan waved them on. "I'll come down once I feel a little better. Leave your cell phones. Maybe someone's will work up here. I'll try to get a hold of base camp since we've got some clear views."

"Take a look at all the GPS units too." Jim handed over his unit, frowning. "One of them has got to be right. We need to let Collins know where we are. At least the radios seem to work among the five of us. I'll let you know what we find down there."

They'd left Ryan resting with a couple of thousand dollars of technology in the snow beside him and a low-tech compass in his hand.

Brynn glanced over her shoulder. They'd descended a good distance. Ryan was becoming a red spot against the snow. At least he could keep the group in sight all the way down to the plane. She'd examine him more closely after they checked the plane, and she wouldn't take any more flak from him. He'd insisted he was fine and brushed her off earlier. She hadn't pushed the issue.

Her objective was to get to the plane and see if medical help was needed. Ryan could wait.

The slope was steep, and they moved slowly. It took a good forty minutes to get within fifty feet of the plane. Kiana had bounded down, leaping from side to side like a skier working his way down a steep slope of powder, and was already nosing about the wreckage.

"Hellooo!" Jim's subdued shout was met with silence. Brynn cast back a nervous glance at the mountain of snow. It was doubtful Jim's level of volume would dislodge the snow. But she couldn't stop herself from checking.

Dread was quickly replacing the energizing thrill from spotting the plane.

Could someone survive that?

The wreckage was bad. As they drew closer and saw the damage, her chest felt like it'd been hollowed out with a dull spoon. The plane had been ripped into two ragged pieces, the rear two-thirds had ended up against a stand of firs, and the cockpit had landed several hundred feet down the slope. Looking at the tall firs on the far side of the clearing, she could see where the plane had blown through the forest, leaving a swath of broken treetops and shattered limbs in its wake. Brynn shuddered. How had the cockpit ended up so far away from the body of the plane?

It was a small plane. The larger body piece still had the tail and one wing attached. The wing was barely visible in the powder, its engine a gentle snow-covered bump with its propeller still in place. Orange and brown stripes ran along the side of the fuselage and colored the tail.

Both pieces appeared to have landed right side up, and several inches of snow covered them. The scene was peaceful, pieces of the plane delicately covered with white fluff. How much more snow would completely hide the plane? She glanced at the sky and doubted the plane could be easily spotted from above. Already the snow obscured too much.

They were lucky Ryan had become ill.

She bit a lip. Ryan probably didn't see it that way. If they got some air support today she was sending him back immediately. Unless there was someone wounded on the plane. That would take first priority.

"Hellooo!" Jim called again.

All quiet.

"Thomas and I will check the cockpit. You two check the rest," Jim ordered. He lifted a brow at Alex, held his gaze, and motioned to his side. Alex nodded. Brynn frowned.

What was that about?

She watched as Alex removed a glove and slipped a hand in his pocket as he carefully stepped down the slope in his home-made snowshoes. She'd hid her laughter at his fascination during their construction process. He'd watched every move and asked a dozen questions that Thomas had answered with an absolute minimum of words. The marshal who hated the outdoors sure seemed to like his snowshoes. But now his face was tight, his lips pressed together, and she remembered what he'd said about the marshal on board. *A good friend.* Brynn studied his serious face. She had a hunch this quiet marshal didn't let many people get close to him. When Ryan had mentioned Alex was divorced, she'd blinked, more surprised that Ryan had pried the information out of Alex than by the divorce.

Ryan had a way of talking to everyone like they were his best friends. She'd never known anyone who could put people at ease as fast as Ryan. Apparently, his skills had worked on Alex. Alex was proving to be a commendable member of the group. What he lacked in outdoor skills he made up for in simple persistence. He hadn't let Thomas get the best of him with that slide trick. He'd let Ryan talk his ear off without coming to blows. He deferred to Jim in all decisions. *Well, since that first decision anyway.* And he didn't treat her as a helpless female like some of the other SAR team members she'd worked with.

Except when he'd hauled her frozen ass off that log bridge. But she *had been* a helpless female at that point.

And he liked her dog; that gave him lots of points.

Kiana liked him back. Of course, Kiana liked everybody. She gave Thomas a wide berth for reasons unknown, but she joyfully accepted everyone else.

Brynn's heart contracted painfully. What was Alex thinking as he worked his way down the mountain? With no answers to Jim's calls, he had to know his friend probably hadn't survived. All odds were against them finding a survivor in the wreck. Especially if it had gone down as roughly as it looked.

She watched Alex wipe at the sweat on his brow and saw his hand shake.

"Hey." She surprised herself by speaking and laying a hand on his arm. "Why don't you stay back until I check the wreckage?"

His brows went up. "It's all right. I'm good with it."

"No, seriously. Why don't you hang back for a few minutes?" When he'd first told them about his friend on the plane, he'd briefly revealed a soul-deep ache in his eyes that still echoed in her memory. Obviously there'd been a tight bond between him and the other agent.

"He's a good friend, right?"

Alex seemed confused for a split second. "Oh. Yeah, he *was* a good friend." Brynn couldn't identify the emotion that flashed on his face, and it stabbed at her soul that he'd already referred to the marshal in past tense.

Jim and Thomas were nearly to the cockpit. She watched as they both drew their weapons. She shook her head.

"They're doing the right thing." Alex's face showed no emotion as he watched the men. He imitated them and drew his gun from his pocket. "Are you armed?"

"No."

"Then stay behind me."

She let him take the lead and rolled her eyes at his back.

"And don't roll your eyes at me." He looked over his shoulder at her, his eyes sharp. "There was a dangerous killer on this plane. You won't think this is funny if he's sitting inside waiting for us with a gun in his hand."

"Wait!" She grabbed at his coat. "You know who was on the plane? You said you didn't."

He blew out a harsh breath. "No one needed to know who it was. The mission's the same whether you know his name or not."

Icy fear crept up her spine for the first time since the log crossing. "Who?"

Alex swallowed, paused, and looked back at the plane, speaking away from her. "Darrin Besand."

Brynn halted. "The serial killer?"

Alex nodded as he stepped closer to the plane.

Brynn glanced around, studying the trees and big rocks cropping up out of the snow. An overwhelming urge to hide and get out of sight ripped through every nerve ending. Besand was ruthless. She felt like hundreds of eyes spied on her from behind the trees. She moved closer to Alex's back.

For the first time in her life, she wished she had a gun.

Darrin Besand rubbed at his eyes and stared harder through the binoculars he'd found in the pilot's bag. He lowered them and looked over the top of the binoculars, but he was too far away. Without the magnification he could only see bright bits of red against the snow. And one man in blue. He brought the binoculars to his eyes and focused again.

I'm seeing things.

But it sure looked like Alex Kinton cautiously stepping toward the plane wreck with his gun drawn and his other hand moving protectively at the woman behind him. At first glance, Darrin had thought the woman was a man. She was definitely tall enough. But long, dark blonde hair peeked out of the hood around her face and she moved with a feminine grace. He'd studied her for a few moments, enjoying the view before moving his sights to the person in front of her; his stomach had dropped in shock.

Darrin's heart sped into a steady double-time beat as he stared through the binoculars. He was fortunate. First he'd survived a plane crash that had killed three men, and now Alex Kinton was strolling across his path.

The first time he'd met Alex three years ago, Darrin had never sensed so much pain and suffering emanating from a single person. And Darrin had never laid a hand on him. Usually that powerful and strong emotion was a type he'd only felt from his victims. Alex had been in mourning for his younger brother, seeking answers and someone to blame for Samuel's death. Seeing the grief and torment in Alex's eyes had been like a hit of pure meth. Darrin had wanted more.

Later on in prison, Darrin had rehearsed his words, ready to prod the federal marshal during their scheduled monthly meetings, to cause that flash of fire and rage that gave Darrin the high he could no longer coax from his victims. Alex's prison visits were the only interesting events in Darrin's life. All other days were gray and dull. To experience that blast of fear, sorrow, and rage from another person was better than sex. To say he looked forward to his conversations with Alex was putting it mildly. But there was a price for Alex's visits. Darrin had to reveal facts about some of his previous kills; otherwise, Alex would leave. That was the unwritten rule for the meetings to continue. Facts detectives couldn't figure out on their own. Alex hand delivered the information to the various police departments who wanted to solve their cases. Darrin refused to talk to anyone else.

Darrin watched Alex through the binoculars and felt a spiking rush of power in his veins.

Alex's personal investigating had been what landed him in prison in the first place. Simply because Alex had caught him on a minute piece of evidence.

Alex had been lucky; Darrin's capture had been pure chance. Darrin had left police departments in three states scratching their heads.

Now here was his chance to prove to Kinton that his capture had been a fluke. Alex thought he was so clever, trekking into the forest to find Darrin. It only showed he was scared shitless. Scared that Darrin might still be alive to haunt him.

Now they were on even turf. There were no bars between them.

Darrin tentatively rolled his sore shoulder. It was feeling better after taking the aspirin he'd found in the pilot's duffel bag. His head still hurt, but as long as he didn't touch the spot over his ear, he'd survive.

He focused on the gun in Alex's hand and felt the weight of the gun at his own side. They were even in that regard too. But what thrill was there in killing from a distance? Darrin relished being up close to his victims, studying their eyes, watching their awareness of his actions.

Alex Kinton deserved much more than an impersonal shot in the back.

Darrin could see Alex's death in slow motion. It would be drawn out and painful. Alex would know exactly who was hurting him and why. Then he'd realize Darrin was the shrewder, sharper man.

Darrin smiled in anticipation.

This might be the most rewarding kill of his life.

Alex locked his gaze on the plane as he and Brynn drew closer. The wreck looked as if someone had left a beheaded metal carcass lying on the snow in the clearing. He wasn't interested in the cockpit. The person he wanted to see would have been seated in the passenger area of the plane. He moved cautiously, waving Brynn down behind him.

"Brynn!"

Both of them jumped at the sound of Jim's hoarse shout. Alex glanced down the slope to see Jim waving at her to come to the cockpit.

Good. Get her out of here.

Jim wouldn't be calling her if there was danger.

His respect for Jim Wolf had grown every hour for the last two days. Jim watched out for the safety of his team and had excellent people skills, knowing exactly how to get the best out of each person. He also treated Alex with consideration and kept his suggestions for improving Alex's trek between the two of them.

Brynn gave Alex a questioning look, and he nodded toward Jim. She scurried away, ducking low like someone was watching her from the trees. He frowned. Her reaction to Darrin Besand's name had been shock, then fear. It took a lot to scare a tough girl like Brynn. Bears didn't do it. Snowstorms didn't do it. But the name Darrin Besand caused fear in a lot of women's eyes. He just hadn't expected to see it in Brynn's.

Another good reason to hate Darrin Besand.

Alex watched Jim usher her into the cockpit and wondered what they'd found. Surely no one could have lived through this wreck. But Brynn was a nurse. Why else would Jim holler for her unless someone needed medical help?

Alex turned his attention back to the body of the plane and resolutely pushed on. He had his own mission to complete. He followed his gun around the edge of the plane and saw instantly that it was empty. Except for the corpse in the second row. Alex put his gun away and stepped toward Linus Carlson.

"Damn it, Linus." Alex squatted in the aisle beside him. Linus's head was bent over, nearly in his lap, but Alex had known who it was at once. He'd recognize that bald spot and those stupid clunky shoes anywhere. Alex swallowed and ripped off his other glove, holding his fingertips to Linus's cold neck. Nothing. Gently, he pushed him back to a sitting position; the rigor had relaxed. Linus had been dead a long time. Hopefully, he'd died directly on impact. Alex blinked hard a few times and glared at the dead man.

Alex and Monica had spent their last Christmas as a married couple at Linus's home with his wife and two kids.

Aw, shit. Those cute kids.

Alex thought hard, hating himself because he couldn't remember their names. A boy and a girl. They had to be about ten and twelve now. Alex vowed to be the person to inform Linus's wife.

Bile threatened in the back of his throat, and he pulled his gaze away, letting it roam and rest on the sports jacket on the floor. He stared at the brown coat and then whipped his gaze up to Linus's shirt, blinking at the blue button-down dress shirt.

Linus wasn't wearing his holster.

Alex grabbed at the coat on the floor, felt its lack of weight and immediately dropped it, whipped out his gun, and spun to face the front of the plane. Silent snow greeted him.

For a full minute, he'd forgotten about the killer. Alex glanced at the seat across the aisle where Besand had most likely sat. There was blood on the armrests.

He had to warn Jim.

Alex started out of the plane, but halted with one hand on the ripped metal. He looked back and studied the person who'd once been a close friend. Linus was gone. All that was left now was a cold and empty shell with no resemblance to the warm and funny man he'd been.

Alex shuffled in his snowshoes down the slope to the cockpit, rubbing at the fresh dampness on his cheeks, his eyes constantly scanning the forests.

"He's still fucking warm!" Jim bounced from one foot to the other and impatiently hovered over Brynn as she examined the body of the pilot.

Brynn nodded. "I wouldn't call it warm, but he's not ice-cold like the other pilot. Rigor's just setting in. He's been dead for at least twelve hours."

She studied the mass of twisted metal that'd trapped and pierced the pilot's legs, slowly bleeding him out to death. His bloody hands told the story of his struggle to free himself. It wouldn't have helped. He would have probably died sooner from more rapid blood loss if he'd managed to extricate his legs.

Maybe that would have been better. She squeezed her eyes shut against the agony and mental terror the pilot must have gone through, knowing he was dying. This death would stick with her. This one she would see in her dreams at night. Along with the four-year-old boy hit by the Jeep. And the grandmother on the floor in her bathroom who no one had missed for a week.

"Brynn."

She glanced at Jim, who stared back. "What?"

"I asked about the other guy."

Brynn firmly put the others out of her mind and flexed one of the copilot's arms. "Rigor's come and gone. I'd guess he died on impact or was knocked unconscious and died soon after. He didn't try to help his leg where he bled out." She held up his clean, cold palm for Jim to see. Jim nodded.

"You think the other pilot suffered?" Thomas asked quietly.

She nodded and gestured at his bloody hands. Blood had soaked the pilot's shirt up to the elbows. He'd fought hard for his life. Thomas abruptly turned and left the crowded cockpit.

"Let's see if Alex found anything." Jim gestured with his gun for her to follow Thomas.

"Don't point that thing at me," she snapped.

"Sorry." Jim's apology was clipped. She took a deep breath. Everyone was on edge. She couldn't blame them. They'd worked so hard to get to this point only to be met with horror and disappointment. Why had she kept her hopes up against the odds?

Alex had arrived at the cockpit and was speaking with Thomas as she and Jim stepped out into the freshly falling snow. For once Brynn couldn't appreciate its beauty. She couldn't get the pilot's lonely fight for life out of her mind. She turned a hopeful gaze to Alex, praying he'd had better luck. But his somber face told his story. Their gazes met and held.

"What'd you find?" Jim asked.

Alex split a glance between her and Jim. "One dead. The marshal."

"Oh, Alex. I'm so sorry." Her throat tightened.

"Darrin Besand is missing," Thomas stated.

"You knew?" Brynn whirled on the big man. "You knew who was being transported in that plane?"

Thomas held up his hands in a surrender position. "Alex told me five seconds ago."

"Darrin Besand. That's the prisoner? You've known all along it was a dangerous, psychotic piece of shit like that and didn't tell me?" Jim words got louder and his face grew black as he moved toward Alex. "Did Brynn know?"

"Alex told me just before you hollered me over to the cockpit, Jim." Brynn subtly placed her body between Jim and Alex.

Alex met Jim's stare directly. "I didn't see the need to reveal the name before. But I think you need to know the type of person we're dealing with now."

"Dealing with? We're not dealing with him. We're getting out of here as fast as we can. There are no victims to help, and we don't hang around to rescue serial killers who walk away from plane crashes."

"He must have known the one pilot survived," Brynn spoke.

"One lived?" Alex's voice lifted, his dark eyes brightened.

Brynn touched his arm, shaking her head. Her heart cracked at the hope in his gaze. "He didn't make it. He survived the crash and hung on for a long time, but he's gone now."

Alex stepped past them and ducked into the cockpit.

Jim eyed the hulk of metal. "I can't believe Darrin Besand survived this crash. And I can't believe Alex didn't tell us until now. Anyone see any footprints?"

Thomas and Brynn shook their heads. It was a useless question. Too much snow had fallen overnight.

"Maybe he parachuted out."

"Linus's gun and holster were gone. I didn't find a cell phone either." Alex spoke behind them as he stepped out of the plane, his face emotionless. "Besand was here when the plane went down. He might have lifted weapons off the pilots too. I can't tell. But he's definitely armed." Alex took a deep breath. "I'm sure Besand's left the area, trying to hike out on his own. He knows his way around the wilderness and isn't about to hang out waiting for a rescue team who'll throw him back in jail. I'm going to suggest you guys get Ryan and head back to camp. I need to stay and try to track Besand." Alex paused. Then he slowly but firmly stated, "I can't let him walk out of this wilderness."

Brynn lost her breath at the vengeance in his eyes.

CHAPTER SEVEN

Sheriff Patrick Collins was outside enjoying his morning coffee and scone and watching the media reassemble in their corral when a small helicopter buzzed his base camp. The copter swung in low and thundered in Patrick's ears before making a beeline up and over the forest in the same direction that had been taken by the hasty team. Patrick swore at the retreating metal, his appetite evaporating.

"Goddamn stupid bastards. They're gonna get themselves killed."

Tim Reid jogged over. "Who the fuck was that? Was that a media bird?"

Patrick shook his head. "Liam Gentry and that cocky brother of his."

"Liam? He convinced Tyrone to take him out in this shit?" Reid stared in the direction the copter had disappeared. Patrick gripped his coffee tighter as a strong gust of wind tried to blow the paper cup out of his hand.

"They're gonna get blown out of the sky."

"Are you sure that was Liam?" Reid's forehead creased as he tried to comprehend the airman's foolishness.

"I know it was." The two men had waved directly at Patrick before flying into the Cascades. "That was his brother's helicopter. We've used him before on searches." Patrick had used Liam's brother as little as possible. Tyrone had a nasty habit of taking unnecessary risks. Both brothers were brash pilots, but Liam exercised a little control. Liam knew if he wanted to continue flying the expensive, taxpayer-purchased birds, then he had to know when to pull back.

Patrick took a sip of rapidly cooling coffee and wondered what Liam's commander would say about this stupid stunt. Patrick glanced at the crowd of media, speculating who would be the first to identify the helicopter and owner and then get the information on the air. One night had doubled the size of the crowd, and they were getting arrogant in their questioning. Patrick had held a brief press conference at seven o'clock last night, deliberately after the early evening news, and given as little information as possible.

He rubbed at his eyes. Three hours of sleep was taking its toll. So was the silence from his hasty team.

They're a smart crew. No one knows the outdoors better.

But why had Alex Kinton gone to so much trouble to tag along with the team?

The question was giving Patrick a headache.

Paul Whittenhall strode up. The marshal had retreated to a hotel room for the night, and had now reappeared with two men outfitted for the wilderness. Patrick recognized one as the younger agent from yesterday.

"Who was in that helicopter? Did you finally get one off the ground? Have you heard from your team?" Whittenhall stopped directly in front of Patrick, rolling out his list of questions. Patrick coolly stared him down.

"That wasn't one of my copters. Probably a media copter. You left strict instructions that you were to be notified when I heard from my team, so obviously I haven't heard from them." He struggled to keep his tone calm. He nodded at the two men behind Whittenhall. "Where are they going?"

"I'm sending in my own team. I've got a marshal and a felon out there. I want people with experience on the site."

Patrick bristled. "You're only sending two men? You need at least one more to go out in shit like this. I'll find another—"

"No others. These guys know what they're doing."

Patrick watched the younger marshal's Adam's apple bob. His partner looked competent and prepared, but this guy looked scared to death. The agent had no idea what the fuck he was walking into. He'd probably never taken a sunny day hike in an open field.

"I can't let you send—" Patrick started.

"You can't stop me." Whittenhall turned his back on Patrick to instruct his team. Patrick opened his mouth then clamped it shut. He'd said his piece and Whittenhall rejected his offer. Reid had witnessed it. If Whittenhall came begging for help later, Patrick wasn't going to waste taxpayer money on this jerk's screwup.

"You're on your own," he muttered at the big man's back. The young marshal's eyes briefly widened at Patrick's words, but Whittenhall ignored him.

Patrick put some distance between himself and the marshals. He needed breathing room. Reid caught up with him as he stopped at a sheltered table with coffee urns, scones, and doughnuts where Patrick warmed up his drink.

"Why's he need to send in a team?" Reid complained. "We don't even know where that plane went down. His guys are gonna be cut off from communication just like ours. It's stupid to have two groups wandering around blind out there."

Patrick nodded. His cell buzzed against his waist, and he glanced at the screen. He shot a look at Whittenhall, but he was deep into instructions with his own men. Patrick cocked his head at Reid, and they stepped around to the other side of the table.

"It's Ryan," he told Reid and spoke into his cell. "Collins."

The connection was horrid.

"...found plane...coordinates...all different..." Ryan rattled off several sets of numbers that made no sense to Patrick as he scribbled them down on a napkin he'd snagged from under the doughnuts.

"Did you say you don't know which coordinates are accurate?"

"...GPS...fucked up...all different...one of them should be right...three dead but almost..."

Patrick swore. "Who's dead?"

"...can't find..."

"Is everyone all right?"

"...sick...almost didn't make it..."

"Ryan. The agent who's with you. Kinton. He's not a US marshal. He lied. No one sent him out there."

"...what? Kinton, what?" The crackling through the cell made Ryan's voice nearly indecipherable.

"Kinton's not a marshal. We don't know why he insisted on going with you."

The line went silent. Patrick looked at his screen as it flashed the length of the short call. How much had Ryan understood? He tried to call the man back. No luck.

Patrick studied the napkin, disappointment swirling in his chest. If these were coordinates, they were crap. They were all over the place and missing numbers. Ryan was the best navigator he knew. The call must have dropped half of what he'd said.

"What'd he say?" Reid stared at the numbers with a scowl.

"They found the plane, but he seemed unable to get readings from their GPS units. For some reason the units are giving different readings."

"One of them's got to be right. Any survivors?"

"I don't know. He said 'three dead.' He didn't use the words 'made it' or 'survived.' He did say someone was sick."

"Who?"

Patrick shook his head, hating the powerless chill that had crept up his spine during the call. "I don't know what the hell's happening out there."

"You gonna tell Whittenhall?"

"Fuck, no."

Paul Whittenhall thought Gary Stewart was going to vomit.

The deputy marshal's lips were pressed together as if he was keeping his breakfast down. His gaze was all over the place, and he wasn't focusing on Paul or listening to his instructions. Paul itched to smack some backbone into the agent.

Damn it. Why wasn't there someone else he could send out there with Matt Boyles? Stewart was more a pencil pusher than outdoorsman, but Paul needed someone who could keep his mouth shut and knew the stakes of the success of this mission. Boyles could be kept in the dark, but Paul needed Stewart out there in the woods calling the shots.

Boyles frowned at the map. "That's a huge area to search for a plane. Why don't we wait to hear from the other team? We don't want to duplicate any area they've already covered."

"Can you track the team? Can you just try to meet up with them?"

Boyles furrowed his brow, his eyes curious. "I can try, but the snow makes it nearly impossible."

"I just want you to connect with the group that's out there. Kinton's a wild card. I don't know what the fuck is going through his head. If he runs into Darrin Besand, he's gonna kill him with no questions asked. And I don't want to even think about the danger Kinton poses to the members of that hasty team. He'd risk their safety to get his hands on Besand."

Boyles nodded slowly. "You think he's that focused?"

Paul gave a rehearsed look of surprise. "You need to ask? You wanna see the scar he left on my stomach? Back then, Kinton lost every shred of common sense over one of Besand's transports and took it out on me. Now he's lost it again and I don't want anyone else getting hurt. He's a walking time bomb, and those searchers are completely expendable to him. It's our duty to get Darrin Besand safely to his next trial in Portland. I'm not going to let a hothead ruin the plan."

Darrin stamped his feet. The copilot's coat made him feel heavenly warm, but his damned feet were cold. He'd hoped to find an extra pair of socks in one of the pilots' duffel bags but no luck. He did find sweatpants that he'd put on over his jeans and under his jumpsuit. The sweats were a little too short and tight. Darrin was tall and definitely not skinny, with a wide chest and shoulders. Before he'd gone to prison, he'd had a hard time getting clothes that fit properly.

That was one of the reasons he'd liked his job as a caregiver. Scrubs fit him easily. They came in all sorts of roomy sizes. He'd also liked the open access to a wide range of patients and medical personnel. Drugs too.

Darrin gently touched his left shoulder. In one pilot's bag he'd found a bottle of Vicodin, which no sane pilot should be taking while flying. Darrin had immediately popped two in his mouth and washed them down with bottled water. Now the shoulder was feeling much better. His head too. As long as he didn't move it abruptly.

When is the rescue group going to leave?

He was ready to get out of the woods. He'd follow them back, figure out a strategy for dealing with Alex Kinton, implement it, and then vanish before they reached their base camp. Had the plane wreck created much attention? There had to be media and cameras hanging around, waiting for their heroes to return. Briefly, he considered strolling out in front of the press. Being on TV was a head rush. And what a sensation it would cause if the lone survivor of the plane crash walked out of the woods.

No. He had to leave. He had a new life and money waiting for him in Mexico.

He'd take care of Alex Kinton and then move on.

Darrin raised the binoculars. The group didn't look like they were in a hurry to leave. In fact, they appeared to be having quite the argument. The three in the red SAR parkas were shaking their heads and disagreeing vehemently with whatever Kinton had suggested. Darrin grinned broadly. Kinton was a stubborn bastard when he put his mind to something.

Who'd told Kinton about the plane crash?

Darrin wouldn't have been surprised to see a US marshal on the search and rescue team. After all, there had been an agent on board and the marshals were responsible for the transport. But there were no marshals in the group. Instead, here was a guy who hadn't been an agent for over a year. Kinton shouldn't know a thing about the plane.

Kinton should be standing at the airport in Hillsdale. As usual, waiting to glare at Darrin as he stepped off the plane. Alex Kinton had appeared in the airport every time Darrin had been transported by plane. Darrin had flown several times because three different states were building murder cases against him. Somehow, Kinton always knew when and where Darrin would be returning home, and he'd appear outside the security checkpoint, saying nothing, doing nothing. Simply watching with hard eyes and a face full of hatred. Like an angry superhero with his hands tied.

Darrin had started expecting the familiar face every time he landed back in the Portland area. Darrin would grin and nod, sometimes even greet Alex. He'd looked forward to seeing the A-man.

Not Batman or Superman. The A-man.

Whose special power was to entertain Darrin.

How did Kinton get here so fast? There was no way he could have found out about the flight plan change to the Granton airport. A tiny airport. With virtually no security. Darrin had been looking forward to separating from his federal escort in Granton and hopping into the car waiting to whisk him south through California and across the border.

Darrin ground his back teeth and kicked at the snow.

Fucking snowstorm. It'd messed up his perfect plan.

Darrin's brows shot up as Kinton stepped in front of the female as if to protect her from the words of the shorter SAR volunteer.

Interesting.

The Alex Kinton that Darrin knew had no use for women. The man had been badly burned by his ex-wife and hadn't dated since his divorce. Darrin knew all about Kinton's personal life. He believed in keeping his enemies close. His contacts on the outside had kept tabs on the former marshal.

What else was a guy supposed to do in prison for amusement except plan for Kinton's quarterly visits? When Kinton visited his parents' graves, Darrin knew. When Kinton shut himself away in a cabin at the beach for three months, Darrin knew.

Darrin wished the female in the SAR group would push back her hood. His earlier views of her had been quite pleasant.

She put her hand on Kinton's arm to move him aside and joined the argument. She waved one sassy finger in the shorter man's face as she angrily spoke.

Darrin sucked in a breath as he pressed his eyes against his binoculars. He'd never put up with that type of attitude from a woman. The new LPN at his second nursing home had learned that lesson the hard way.

The search and rescue woman turned, giving him a perfect view of her face. *Lovely.* Dark, direct eyes, strong cheekbones, and a wide mouth that made his heart jump.

Ohh. She had to have an effect on Kinton. How could anyone spend time in her company without falling madly in lust? Darrin's lips turned up in a half smile. *Kinton in lust?* He'd like to see that. Kinton was always a walking, emotionless rock except when it came to his dead brother.

Darrin moved his binoculars to Kinton.

Sure enough. The A-man was wearing his usual stone mask.

Do I know this guy or what?

Darrin's gaze swung back to the female. *Now there is some passion.* What was she arguing about? The determination in her expression would be enough to convince Darrin to follow her. Wherever the fuck she might lead.

Maybe she was already paired up with one of the men? He frowned. She didn't act attached. The shorter rescuer had visibly cringed at her tongue-lashing, and the big guy had barely spoken to her at all. Neither acted like a boyfriend or husband.

The argument continued. The female kept gesturing up the hill in the direction they'd come and then back to the plane. The shorter guy pointed toward the faint sunlight. Darrin glanced at his watch. Three o'clock. Surely they weren't considering making camp at the crash site? Why weren't they heading out? Was the trip back too long?

The female dropped her pack and made tracks back up the hill, leaving a snowy wake of attitude. The rest of the men stared after her, the shorter shaking his head. Kinton stood silent and then dropped his pack. The other men did the same.

Darrin slowly lowered the binoculars.

Alex tried not to stare at Brynn as she hiked away to check on Ryan. Even under the thick coat, she pulled his attention. It was the way she carried herself, the way she moved smoothly like she'd been walking though the outdoors all her life. She always showed confidence and a clear head, and he liked to watch her whether she was throwing a stick for her dog or standing her ground with Jim and Thomas. And himself.

He wondered what her boyfriend was like.

"I guess she told us," Jim muttered. He too was watching Brynn hike back up the hill, but Alex knew he watched her with the eyes of an older brother. A stab of jealousy hit Alex in his chest at the closeness of the relationship even though he knew it was platonic. The idea of Jim sharing her tent heated his blood, and not in a good way.

Stupid. Alex shook his head at his reaction.

"What?" Jim caught the movement and regarded him with questioning eyes. "Still don't think I should've let her hike up there alone? You're the one who said Besand probably left the area. You really think he'd risk death in the wilderness over going back to prison?"

Alex nodded, relieved Jim had misunderstood his shaking head. "I know he would. Besand was dying inside those walls. He'd do whatever it takes to never go back."

Jim's gaze probed deep. "I don't know what put the idea in your head we'd ever consider leaving you alone out here to find the guy. Especially considering you don't know shit about the outdoors. Why don't you just ask me to sign your death certificate?" A curious light entered his eyes. "You seem to know this asshole real well. Better than most armed escorts would."

Alex met his frank gaze. Jim was an honest, up-front sort of guy. The type of guy Alex would have considered a friend before his life had crumbled to pieces. Alex looked up the hill, following Brynn, a tiny red figure against the snow. His guts ached to be honest with *someone*. He abruptly decided to take the plunge.

"I've made it my business to know everything about Darrin Besand. He murdered my brother."

Jim stood silent, his gaze hard on Alex. His blue eyes flickered, his focus speeding from one of Alex's eyes to the other. Alex held his breath, hearing his blood pound an erratic beat in his ears.

Would Jim shut him out or help? It wasn't every day someone told you his brother had been murdered.

Jim's gaze went up the hill to Brynn and Ryan, and then he turned to check on Thomas, who'd disappeared into the cockpit.

It'd felt good to unload on Jim. Alex's shoulders felt lighter, his brain less clouded. Deep down he'd always known Besand was going to face death at his hands.

Jim looked Alex directly in the eye again. "You're here to kill the guy."

Alex nodded.

Jim's lips tightened and he glanced up the hill. "My objective is to search for survivors and maintain the safety of my team. Do you see a conflict here?" His voice was stiff, words clipped.

Alex shook his head.

"I'm here to protect life, not take it away," Jim stated firmly.

"If he gets out of this mountain range alive, more people will die. I'm protecting life. I don't see a conflict." Alex kept his voice even as he ran a hand through his hair. He was losing Jim. His mind raced for explanations to prove his cause.

Jim gave a rigid nod. "That's for the courts to decide. I've never believed in vigilante justice."

Alex hesitated. "There's more…"

"More what?"

"There's a flaw somewhere. Yeah, the courts sentenced him, but someone's been trying to get him out of prison."

"Get him out…What the fuck are you talking about?" Jim eyed him cautiously. He was carefully dissecting every word out of Alex's mouth.

Alex shifted his feet, speaking slowly. "The security details on Besand are always too light. He nearly killed a marshal because only one agent was assigned to him when there should've been at least two. He's one of the most violent offenders, but treated as a white collar. And this flight—"

Alex stopped abruptly. He hadn't put all the pieces together yet. He'd been thinking and concentrating the entire hike, but there were holes in his theory. He blew out a tense breath.

"What about this flight?" Jim snapped.

"Someone closed the flight plan after the takeoff. It was canceled."

"How do you know?"

"I asked. I was waiting for Besand at the Hillsdale airport. The landing time came and went." Alex pounded his fist in his palm in time with his words. "I knew when and where that plane was scheduled to land. When it didn't, I asked at the airport and they told me the flight plan had been closed. When I asked what time it'd been closed, they said it'd happened soon after takeoff. And there weren't any other marshals at the airport to meet the plane like there should have been. They knew the plane wasn't going to land."

"Wait a second." Jim's eyes narrowed. "Why didn't you call your boss to find out where the plane was supposed to land?"

Alex twisted up one side of his mouth. "'Cause he's not my boss anymore. I haven't worked for the US Marshals' office in over a year." He waited, watching Jim.

Jim's face reddened. "But…" He closed his mouth and his nostrils flared as he stared at Alex.

Alex counted off three seconds in his head.

"You're impersonating a fed," Jim said quietly.

Alex smiled wryly. "It's not hard."

Brynn stamped her way up the hill, keeping to the side of the steep slope.

Idiots. Alex was stupid if he believed they'd even consider leaving him behind to attempt a manhunt on his own. And Jim was crazy to believe Ryan could fast-track back to base camp. She'd set him straight on that idea. Everyone would sit tight until tomorrow morning. There was no other logical option. If they were lucky maybe they'd get some air support and evacuate Ryan. Or maybe he'd feel good enough to head out.

She wasn't leaving Alex behind. He was utterly lost in the woods. He didn't know a thing about the GPS units and compasses. Maybe he had a criminal to catch, but then what would he do? It wasn't like they could leave him a trail of bread crumbs. She fought a smile. With her lovely navigational skills, if she and Alex stayed behind together they'd be as lost as Hansel and Gretel.

Ryan waved. The hike up the slope was longer than she'd remembered. And steeper. She was huffing good when she plopped down beside him.

"What'd you find?" Ryan wrinkled his forehead. "Jim radioed that there was three dead."

"There's a body missing."

"Missing?"

She frowned. "Turns out Darrin Besand was on that plane. And he's the one missing. Alex wants to stay behind to look for him while we head back."

"Besand?" Concentration skittered across Ryan's face as he tried to place the name.

"Killed a bunch of people in Portland. Idaho too. Mostly nurses and nursing home patients. Claimed he was being merciful."

"Oh! I remember that. Nasty dude." Disgust filled Ryan's tone. "So he was being merciful by killing the nurses after he raped them?" His face suddenly blanked and Brynn knew he'd remembered she was a nurse.

"How you feeling?" She changed the subject.

His smile was wan. None of his usual sparkle. "Not bad."

"Bullshit."

"Yeah, you're right." He gingerly touched his abdomen. "My stomach feels like I swallowed acid. Lungs are tight."

Brynn laid a hand on his forehead. He seemed pretty hot, but her fingers were half-numb. "You don't smoke, do you?"

His chin jerked. "You know I don't. What kind of question is that?"

"Any chronic pain problems you dose daily with ibuprofen or something else?"

His brows came together and he shook his head.

"No ulcers, right?"

He started to shake his head but stopped. His eyes narrowed. "I've had chronic heartburn for a couple of weeks. I've been dosing it a lot with the pink liquid stuff."

"That could signal an ulcer. And that pink stuff has salicylic acid in it. Could be thinning your blood, making you bleed easier. You're not supposed to use it over and over for weeks on end." She took a quick glance at the roughed-up snow to his far left. Faint hints of red showed in two spots.

"Still bloody?"

His eyes dropped. "Yeah. And I feel like I've run a marathon. Not the kind of tired I get from doing these missions, more like everything hurts and I've used up every resource in my body."

"Muscles and joints hurt?"

He nodded.

"Can you think of anything you ate that could make you throw up?"

"I've been running over everything I ate in the last twenty-four hours or so. Nothing new or odd. Couldn't it just be a virus?"

"Not with blood. Either something's torn the lining of your stomach or esophagus or you've got an ulcer you've not known about or…"

"Or what?"

Her gaze went down to the group of men far below them on the mountain. "Poison's the only other thing I can think of that causes that kind of bleeding."

"Poison! Fuck that. I'd have to have eaten a cup of lye or something to do this. I think I'd notice if I ate something like that."

Brynn shrugged. She didn't know much about poisoning. She automatically associated it with bloody vomiting just like ulcers but didn't know the hows or whys. "Anybody give you something to eat?"

"Oh, Jesus Christ! No one's trying to kill me!" His eyes wavered between disgust and amusement. "*You're* the one who gave me the Benadryl. You must be trying to off me. Or Jim's wife. She made the cookies he gave me. Maybe Anna's trying to get rid of Jim because she's banging someone else."

Brynn had to grin. Ryan was right.

"I think you've got the flu and a bad ulcer. That's my diagnosis," she stated firmly.

"So now what?" Ryan screwed up his forehead.

"Rest and fluids."

Ryan picked up a handful of snow, squeezing it into a small hard ball. "Plenty of fluids available out here. Don't know about getting any rest. Oh, I got a hold of Collins. Well, kind of got a hold of him after Jim radioed me about the deaths." He grimaced. "The connection royally sucked, and I haven't been able to get him back."

"Did you tell him we'd found the plane?"

"Yeah, but telling him where we found it was a problem. I gave him all the coordinates to check from each GPS. One's got to be right. Someone would have to fly them to check them out. Maybe he can get a bird in the air today."

Brynn scanned the sky. Clouds were whizzing by at different levels. It wasn't too windy on the ground, but apparently, higher up the wind was blasting away. And the snow was getting heavier.

She wasn't holding her breath for the sound of a chopper.

"I hope he got all the coordinates. I was only getting about every fourth word from him so I probably sounded just as bad." Ryan paused and gazed at the group below with a frown. "What do you think of Alex?"

"Uh…" Brynn tried to arrange her thoughts at the quick change of topic. "He's OK. Quiet. He's kept up even though I think he'd rather get a root canal." She closed her mouth, not wanting to say she thought Alex kept a lot below his smooth surface. Still waters and all that. Several times she'd seen things start to boil in his expression like he had a lot to say or felt strongly about something, but Alex had kept his opinions under wraps. From the moment Jim had verbally ripped the marshal to shreds at the base camp, she'd wondered what made him tick. Alex had kept his temper and responded with a gut load of self-assurance. Not an easy task in front of Jim.

Ryan snorted. "My thoughts exactly. He hates every minute of it out here. Something is driving him to put up with this."

"It's his job. Besand's a murderer. He wants to make sure Besand's either dead or put back in prison." Brynn shuddered as she glanced at their surroundings. "Alex thinks Besand is trying to hike out of the woods. Armed. I guess a gun is missing from the dead marshal."

"Jesus! And they let you hike back up that hill alone?" Ryan's gaze swirled in all directions, and he threw an arm around her shoulder to press her down. "We shouldn't be sitting out here in the open."

"Stop it!" She shoved off his arm. "He's not here. Don't you think he would have waited with the plane if he wanted to be rescued? I think he started walking out. Alex says this guy hated prison, and he believes Besand's taking this chance to get away. Besand knows if a rescue crew found him, he'd be back in prison within hours. So he's gonna do everything to avoid us. I already had this argument with the other guys below. We don't need to go through it again."

Ryan sat still. "What did Alex want to do?"

"He wants us to get out of here. But I knew you weren't up to hiking out right now and vetoed that. Alex wants to go after Besand after we leave. Like we would even consider leaving him alone out here." She frowned. "He seems to think Besand has some big plan for getting out of the country. How could he have a plan? He didn't know his plane was going down or that he'd live through it."

"Maybe he's always had a backup plan. Just in case the opportunity arose to escape from prison. I know I would."

She smiled. "You'd be a lousy criminal. You're too damned honest."

Ryan rubbed at his nose. "Collins said something that I didn't understand. Something about Alex."

Brynn's stomach tightened. "What'd he say?"

"It sounded like 'Kinton's not a marshal.'"

They both were silent for five full seconds.

Brynn slowly shook her head back and forth. "That's not right. I've worked around you law enforcement types for years. Alex has 'cop' tattooed on his forehead."

"I'm with you. There's law enforcement in there somewhere."

"Maybe you misunderstood. Maybe Collins was saying…" She scrambled for words. "Kinton isn't…I don't know." Her hands went up in exasperation. "You said the connection sucked. Maybe he didn't say 'Kinton' maybe he said 'kitchen' or…or 'kitten.'"

Ryan laughed, but sobered rapidly. "You're right. But it's bugging me. Collins said it twice, but neither time was clear.

I want to talk to Jim about it, see what he thinks." He grimaced. "But I guess it doesn't make much difference. Let's say Alex isn't a marshal. That's fine. He's pulled his weight on this mission, and we've done our job. He seems to be a decent person, and I kinda like him. After this we can all go home and laugh about the guy who was dumb enough to fake being a marshal to go along on the rescue from hell."

"But Alex isn't going home. He's going to hunt down and kill Besand. I saw it in his eyes." Brynn's voice broke as she shuddered, remembering Alex's cold gaze and wondering what had knocked him down to such a low point.

CHAPTER EIGHT

Alex leaned his back against the plane as he watched Brynn climb the hill. He ran a freezing glove over his eyes. It was partially Monica's fault he was here. If she had only agreed seven years ago to accept Samuel, Alex wouldn't be in this position. And Samuel wouldn't be dead.

Stop it. He should have known he could never change Monica. Rule one of marriage: don't go into it assuming the other person will change for you.

Monica had been five and half feet of black-haired, brown-eyed spitfire. A corporate attorney, his wife could argue any opinion until she had Alex agreeing that blue was red. When he'd ask her to come with him to visit Samuel, she'd refuse. Every time.

Alex would leave the house convinced Monica didn't need to see his brother. But by the time he'd parked in front of the care home he'd realize she'd bowled him over again. She always managed to finagle her way out of visiting Samuel.

So it wasn't a surprise that she'd also refused his requests to let his brother come live with them.

Alex had understood, but he didn't want to. Her arguments had made sense. How could their marriage grow with his brother in the house? How could they have any privacy or intimacy living with a mentally handicapped man who didn't know what those words meant?

His brother was a twelve-year-old in a man's body, and Alex had known he was asking too much of Monica by suggesting Samuel live with them. Samuel had been pretty independent, but he'd been known to get lost on the bus system or wander out of the house at two in the morning.

Alex had loved his brother fiercely. The age difference of seven years didn't matter. All his life he'd been his little brother's protector. First against the teasing kids of the neighborhood; then the kids at school; and then, after their parents died, Alex protected Samuel from the system. Samuel was one of those kids who kept falling through the cracks. Too advanced for full-time care, but needing more than part-time supervision. Alex had resorted to private care for his brother, looking for homes that would treat him like a family member. It wasn't easy. Care for the mentally handicapped didn't pay well and often attracted some of the dregs of society without skills. He was between a rock and a hard place. Samuel didn't need people with advanced degrees taking care of him. He just needed a helping hand, some love and affection. Something Alex could have done if his wife hadn't given him an ultimatum.

Live with her or his brother. Not both.

He'd sworn before God to make his marriage work.

So he'd chosen his wife and found the best care home possible for his brother and visited every weekend.

It was a relief that Samuel had liked the group home. He'd been more independent than several of the patients, and the owners often gave him responsibilities that included helping with other patients, odd jobs, organizing crafts, working in the gardens, and even cooking. Samuel had been thriving. Each visit he'd drag Alex from one end of the Maxwells' group home to the other, reintroducing him to people Alex had met dozens of times over the years and showing off his latest artwork or the blooming rosebushes.

The guilt never went away. Samuel was Alex's responsibility. But he'd known he couldn't provide him with the stimulation and socialization Samuel found in the home. It had ripped at his heart. Kathy Maxwell had patted Alex's shoulder as he left each weekend and said her usual mantra. "He's happy here. Stop beating yourself up."

Alex would smile and nod at the kind woman. And ignore the spasms that squeezed his lungs.

He'd never forget his last visit with his brother.

Samuel's greeting hadn't packed his usual enthusiasm. He'd looked away when Alex held out his fist for Samuel to bump.

"Hey, Buddy. What's wrong?" He tousled Samuel's dark hair and made a mental note to remind Kathy that he needed a haircut.

"Don't call me Buddy." He knocked Alex's hand off his head and scowled out the window.

Ouch.

He'd called Samuel "Buddy" since he was born. Their father had started the nickname when Samuel was an infant. When he was young, Samuel had informed people his name was Buddy, not Samuel.

Alex studied his brother carefully. Samuel looked thinner, and his eyes had dark circles under them. Usually Samuel sparkled. He had an infectious grin and a rolling, low laugh that pulled everyone's attention to him. Alex had often wondered what Samuel would have been like with a normal birth, where he hadn't been deprived of oxygen for so long. He had Alex's height and coloring, but he was softer, rounder in the face and build. If Samuel had Alex's obsession for running and weight-lifting, they would have been twins. Now with the shadows and weight loss, Samuel looked more like Alex than ever.

Something was definitely wrong. Alex glanced around for Kathy, wondering if the grandmotherly caretaker knew what was bothering Samuel. When Samuel was in a cranky mood, Alex could rarely get him to talk. The woman wasn't in sight so Alex settled back into the old flowered couch and tried to relax his brother.

"Want to watch some TV? I'll see if *SpongeBob* is on."

"No."

Okaaay. SpongeBob was a favorite. Alex looked out the window of the cramped living room. Pouring rain. He couldn't ask Samuel to take him on a tour of the garden. Maybe…

"Rosa's gone."

Alex blinked, trying to remember Rosa. He pictured a woman with black hair who carried around a little dog that could fit in a teacup.

"Where'd she go?"

Samuel shrugged.

"Did she go home for a visit? Or just shopping?" Had his little brother developed a crush on the young resident?

"She's gone. And she's not coming back." Samuel's voice cracked, and Alex worried he was about to cry. Samuel never cried.

"Did she take her dog with her?" It was possible Samuel was more upset about the dog than Rosa.

He nodded and rubbed at his eyes. Alex wrapped an arm around his shoulder, and Samuel leaned into his chest. He'd always been an affectionate kid who'd responded to a comforting touch. "What was the dog's name?"

"Hero."

Hero had been a tiny little mutt, but the name was fitting with the dog's big heart. "That's too bad. He was a cute little guy."

"He was mean to Hero."

"Who was mean?"

"That man. The new one. He doesn't like dogs, and he was mean to Hero. I hate him. I was going to tell on him."

"Is that why Rosa left?" Alex mentally flipped through the newer patients, trying to remember one who didn't like dogs. Would that be enough to make a patient move out?

Samuel shrugged again. "I don't like him. It's all his fault Rosa is gone. He threw Hero in the pool. I saw him do it. It hurt Rosa. I hate him."

He could picture Rosa's fury at her little dog getting thrown in the pool. It must have taken ten minutes for the itty-bitty dog to paddle his way to the pool's edge. Rosa must have been angry enough to move out.

Alex wondered how to cheer him up. Or should he let it go? In a few days, Samuel would have completely forgotten about the girl and her dog. Maybe Samuel would like his own dog? The two of them had always wanted a dog when they were kids. He pondered the idea, picturing Samuel romping with a big golden retriever. Maybe that wasn't a good idea if there was a dog hater in the group home. Kathy Maxwell might not go for it either. Rosa's little dog had been more like a hamster.

"I'm still going to tell on him for hurting Hero, but right now I'm tired." Samuel stood and left the room, leaving Alex on the couch in silence.

Alex rubbed at his thighs and stood, feeling guilty and abandoned in the little living room. Once Samuel stated he was tired, he wouldn't speak for hours. Samuel would come out of his bedroom when he was ready, no earlier. No amount of talking, ice cream, or potato chips would make a difference. Alex had just slipped on his jacket when Kathy Maxwell stepped in from the garage, her arms loaded with groceries. She looked like the perfect grandma in her old-fashioned housedress. Alex always expected her to offer him chocolate chip cookies and milk.

She usually did.

"Oh. Hello, Alex. I thought that was your truck out front." She glanced behind him at the empty space. "Where's Samuel?"

Alex twisted his lips and took both bags of groceries from her arms. "He's pretty upset about Rosa and Hero. He went to his room."

Kathy's sweet face fell. "It's so awful. He's doing much better, but he seems so sad and angry all the time. He keeps picking arguments with the residents and my new assistant. I've brought in extra therapists this week to help everyone deal with it, but Samuel's been tougher to handle since he's the one who found the body."

Alex's stomach dropped. "The body?"

Kathy gave a confused look over her shoulder as she led him into the kitchen. "Rosa's. Isn't that what you were talking about?"

"I thought she moved out. Are you saying she's dead and Samuel found her? Why wasn't I told?" He dropped the bags on the counter as his voice rose.

"I told your wife on Tuesday. I had a long talk with her just after it happened. I assumed she'd told you." Kathy paused, tilting her head at him. "I did wonder why you didn't come out right away. Samuel could have used the support."

He squeezed his eyes shut as his stomach churned.

Monica.

Why? Why would she not tell him? Did she think Samuel would forget by the following day? Or did she not want Alex running to the rescue and instead stay home with her?

Bile rose in his throat.

"Jesus Christ. He was the one to find the body? What happened to the woman?" Alex ran a hand through his hair.

"Samuel saw Rosa in the pool next door. Spotted her through the fence. I don't know how she got over there. Our gate is locked, and the neighbors have always been so good about keeping their gate locked too. We've talked about it many times. And both gates were still locked when your brother spotted the body."

"In the pool? He saw her in the pool?" Alex whispered as he stared at a scratch on the countertop. Icy chills were swirling around his spine. "Where was the dog?"

Kathy's face fell. "It's so sad. Hero was in the pool too. We don't know if Rosa went in the pool to rescue him or if little Hero jumped in after Rosa. Either way it's too sad to think about."

"Who threw the dog in the pool?"

"What?" Confusion covered Kathy's face, and she halted in the act of lifting cans of soup out of the sack.

"Samuel said the new guy threw Hero in the pool. Said he didn't like dogs."

"I never heard about Hero being deliberately thrown in the pool before. When was this?" She set down the cans, her tone bewildered.

Alex shrugged, meeting her eyes. Time was relative to Samuel. "Who didn't like Hero?"

"Everybody liked Hero. He was the cutest little thing. I don't usually allow dogs, but Hero barely qualified as a dog. Rosa carried him everywhere like a doll."

"Who's the new guy Samuel was talking about?"

"I don't have any new residents…"

"You said you had a new assistant."

"Oh, yes. Darrin. He's been just wonderful. I don't know how I got along without him. And he loved Rosa's dog. He was always offering to hold Hero."

Four days later Alex's brother was dead.

Alex had sat silently in the pew after his brother's funeral. It had been a small service. Kathy Maxwell had arranged for everyone from the group home to come, and most of the agents Alex worked with had shown up. But they'd come alone for the most part. A few brought their wives. No one from Monica's side of the family came. He wondered if she'd even told her parents that her husband's brother had died.

Alex's family was simply him and his brother. Their parents were dead. No uncles, no aunts. It'd been just the two of them for a long time. Maybe that was why he'd tried so hard to take care of Samuel. He was his only real family. Now Alex was alone.

Except for Monica.

He'd been furious after discovering she'd not told him about Samuel finding Rosa's body. It'd developed into one of their hottest fights. She'd claimed she'd forgotten.

"How on earth could you have forgotten to tell me something like that? Who can forget a death? Especially one that Samuel discovered? He must have been going crazy unable to see me."

The tendons in Alex's neck felt like they were about to snap.

"I forgot! I tried to call you on your cell and couldn't get through. And then I had to get ready for dinner! I just forgot!" Her spine stiffened, but he'd seen the fear in her eyes. She'd known she'd messed up.

He'd balled up his suit jacket and thrown it across the bedroom, wanting to throw something harder, heavier. "It just shows where your priorities lie."

"Samuel is your priority, not mine!" she'd shouted, tears welling in her eyes. "He's all you think about."

"If you really loved me, he'd be your priority too." His gaze had been fierce. He was giving her one last chance. It was an unfair chance, he knew that. He also knew exactly how she'd answer. Maybe it was his way of admitting he couldn't fight for their marriage anymore.

She'd pressed her lips closed and stared helplessly at him. Then she'd spun into the bathroom and slammed the door.

It was the end.

When Samuel had drowned in the neighbor's pool days later, the coincidence had been too much for Alex to handle, but all he had to go on was Samuel's rambling statement about

Darrin being mean to the dog. The police were calling both deaths accidental, but Alex's gut wouldn't accept it. Alex picked up a cigarette of Darrin's and took it to a friend at the Oregon State Police lab. That single cigarette yielded a DNA sample that eventually linked Darrin to the multistate deaths of six nursing home patients and four nurse rape/murder scenes.

Much later Besand confessed to a dozen more.

Alex had led the police to a killer, but this particular DNA evidence didn't link Darrin Besand to Samuel's or Rosa's murders. The police ruled the deaths accidental because there simply hadn't been any evidence of foul play. Samuel had water in his lungs, indicating he'd died in the pool, but no bruising on his face or neck to indicate a struggle. Just like Rosa. Darrin Besand refused to admit he'd killed Alex's brother and Rosa.

But Alex knew better.

Paul Whittenhall wandered too close to the media corral, and they stuck their microphones in his face.

"Sir, any word on survivors of the plane crash?"

"Have you heard from the search team?"

"I'm hearing that Darrin Besand is now confirmed to be on that plane. Do you care to comment, sir?"

Paul jerked at the last question and locked gazes with the female who'd thrown it at him. Regan Simmons. The television reporter from Channel 5. The rest of the media looked cold, tired, and irritated. Many of them had spent the night in their cars. But Regan looked energetic and raring to go. She and Paul had spent the night at the same hotel. He knew because she'd shared his room and bed.

He'd confirmed Besand's presence to her last night with the understanding she'd keep it to herself until he gave the go-ahead to release the information. Now she stared at him, microphone thrust forward, a knowing smile on her lips and a reckless challenge in her blue eyes.

Paul knew he'd been screwed.

Regan had attached herself to him in the bar last night. All perky boobs and shiny hair and perfect teeth. She'd laughed at his jokes and tossed their respective jobs out the window, whispering that she needed to blow off some steam and she thought he looked like he needed to do the same. She'd been right.

The talk had been kept to a minimum. She hadn't pried into the case, and he'd only dropped Besand's name as she got dressed to leave. For some odd reason he hadn't wanted her to leave just yet and had offered her a lead if she'd agree to stay another hour. Under the condition of keeping it to herself for now.

Traitorous bitch.

Now in the freezing snow, she stretched out a smile, subtly licked her lips, and winked. Paul hated his body for responding. Her arched, perfectly plucked right eyebrow slowly rose in unison with his cock as she silently informed him she knew he was hard.

Yesterday he'd tried to quash the rumor of Besand. Giving the usual line of needing to inform family before press. He'd tried to point the media's nose in a different direction, hinting that the plane had already made its transport and was simply returning home.

He'd only put off the inevitable. If Regan's station ran the story, everyone else would do the same.

"Darrin Besand?" One reporter nearly swallowed his gum. "When we asked yesterday, you said that was a rumor."

"Is there confirmation or not?"

"Did she say Besand? The serial killer? Is that true, sir?"

The pack erupted into a chorus of more eager questions, excitement in their eyes. Some broke away to make calls.

"No comment."

Paul stomped away, crossing paths with Sheriff Collins. "You can answer their damned questions."

Paul rubbed a hand across his cold face. He'd fucked up getting into bed with that female viper and needed to step more carefully. His thoughts turned to Stewart and Boyles, wondering if the two men would have any success. Surely Boyles was as good in the snow as any of the men the sheriff had sent out. The tiniest flicker of guilt touched him as he studied the tall firs at the trailhead. The trees were barely visible behind the sheets of falling snow. Maybe he should have sent one more man with them…

No. Too many people already knew about Besand. And knew about Kinton. He should have locked Kinton up when he'd had the chance. But there'd been too many eyes on the marshal.

Paul's shoulders twitched. He could still see the raw anger on Kinton's face when he'd stormed into Paul's office. Kinton had already been on leave several times, taking personal time to deal with the shrinking tatters of his marriage. Alex had been obsessed with Darrin Besand since he'd murdered his brother the year before. The police had been unable to prove that Besand killed Samuel, and that made Kinton furious.

Paul had tried to reason with him. "Besand's been linked to several murders in three states. The guy is eventually gonna fry. Isn't that good enough? You believe he killed your brother. Do you really need to hear it from Besand's mouth? Can't you see the guy is playing with you? He's jacking off every time you talk to him. He loves jerking your chain and watching you blow a fuse. He's never gonna admit to Samuel's death because he's having too much fun watching you get upset."

Kinton hadn't heard a word as he'd paced in Paul's office and ranted. "Why is Besand being transported each time with only one agent as escort? The guy is solid muscle and smart, and he's proved he's dangerous. You know he's gonna try to escape again. Haven't you figured that out yet?" Kinton had pointed an accusing finger at Paul's face. "Besand wants out and will use every opportunity to try. One agent isn't enough for a psychotic prisoner like him. When we moved him to Salt Lake he nearly killed Cal Berry. Put another agent on him!"

"I'm trying," Paul had answered. "We're shorthanded right now. I've had to make some difficult staffing decisions of where to assign people. Besand hasn't been as high a priority as some of our other transports."

Paul had waved him off but had seen the suspicion in Kinton's eyes as he stomped out of his office and slammed the door. It was SOP to put at least two agents with a transported prisoner and extra agents on the prisoners considered dangerous. Now Kinton had started to wonder why Paul always transported Darrin Besand with just one agent. Usually one of the newer agents, the smaller ones.

Damn you, Darrin.

Paul hadn't dreamed the situation could blow up until Kinton had stabbed him with his own letter opener.

That sucker had been sharp.

To give Kinton credit, Paul didn't believe he'd meant to stab him. Just intimidate him. Use the opener as an exclamation mark on his tirade.

Two days after the last rant, Kinton had shoved Paul's office door open with his shoulder and raged into the room, primed for a new confrontation. "You fucking asshole."

Paul had jumped up from his computer, where he'd been playing Angry Birds; he'd had enough wits about him to exit out of the computer screen. With the blinds closed and the office door shut, he hadn't seen Kinton coming. *Jesus Christ.* Everyone knew to knock and wait when his door was shut. Only Kinton had the habit of knocking then walking in without a pause. This time he hadn't even knocked.

"Why is Fitzpatrick the only agent on Besand today? First you move him with just Berry and nearly get the marshal killed, and then you moved him with just Danielson. At least Danielson kept Besand under control when he tried to grab at his gun." Kinton's shoulders were twitching in anger. "You need *at least* two people on this guy. Are you fucking stupid?"

"Watch your mouth." Paul had shot a nervous look over Kinton's shoulder. Two female office workers with dropped jaws were watching the scene through the open door. *Why don't they call security?* Paul had reached for his phone.

"Don't move!" Kinton had pounded a fist on the desk. "Answer my question! Why do you insist on transporting one of the deadliest serial killers we've ever had with a minimum amount of security? Even that idiot bank robber had three guards last time we moved him."

"Steele shot four people during holdups. And I didn't have the manpower to put another guy with Besand today." Paul had pulled his hand back from his phone.

"Steele was stupid! He got lucky waving his gun around. Besand's sharp! He can disarm someone as fast as lightning and have their throat cut before they can say 'uncle.'" Kinton had leaned both hands on Whittenhall's desk. Paul's heart had stuttered for two beats and then started to race, his tongue drying up.

One of Kinton's fists had tightened around the letter opener as he leaned. Paul eyes had widened and blinked fast as he caught the movement, but Kinton hadn't seemed to notice what was in his hand. He'd raved on about Besand and numbers and death, but Paul no longer followed his words. He'd never seen Kinton so angry. Paul had always known a temper simmered under Kinton's surface, but this was his first real look at it. Apparently, Kinton had a long fuse before his temper lit. That day it'd been on fire.

Paul had touched the button under the lip of his desk. He'd never used it before and hoped it worked. Kinton had continued to rage, pacing back and forth with the letter opener in his hand, slapping it from palm to palm, never looking at it.

Over Kinton's shoulder, Paul had spotted two armed security guards step out of the elevator and scan the floor. The two office women had vanished and been replaced with a small group of staring marshals. Linus Carlson had stepped in the office behind Kinton.

"Alex. What the fuck…" Carlson had been the closest thing Kinton had to a friend left in the office. Since the death of his brother a year earlier, Kinton had successfully ostracized himself from the other agents.

"Stay out of this, Linus. Whittenhall has got some explaining to do and I'm not leaving until he says why Besand's getting sloppy details. He's doing it on purpose, and I want to know why." Kinton hadn't even turned around when Linus spoke.

Paul had pointed at Kinton. "He's a raving lunatic, and I don't know what the fuck he's talking about. Linus, get out of the way before he stabs somebody with that thing."

At Paul's words, Kinton had stared at the letter opener in his hands, seeing it for the first time. His eyes had rolled in disgust.

"Oh, for Christ's sake..." Kinton had started to say.

Over the past year, Paul had relived the next three seconds a hundred times. He still wasn't certain what had happened. But Kinton had made a move as if to throw the opener back on the desk at the same time that Linus put out a hand to stop his arm. Paul had lunged to the right, believing Kinton was aiming for him and Linus's arm had guided Kinton's hand directly into Paul's right side. He'd felt the blade skitter off his ribs and sink deep.

The three men had stared at the blood on Paul's white shirt as the security guards pushed through the doorway and tackled Kinton from behind. The little office had turned into a melee of shouting men and blood. Paul had passed out.

Kinton hadn't defended his actions at his behavior hearing and was fired a week later. He hadn't apologized either.

Paul hadn't pressed charges. He'd wanted the entire matter dropped as quickly as possible. No telling where an investigation might have led. Thank God, no one else had the balls to ask questions about Besand's details except Kinton. If the other agents noticed, they'd kept it to themselves. What he didn't need was an internal investigation into what had set Kinton off. Luckily, Kinton never showed his face around the office again. Paul managed to keep single men on Besand's details, knowing the right opportunity would eventually present itself to take care of Besand's private demand.

Glancing over his shoulder, Paul watched Sheriff Collins hold up both his hands, gesturing in a "quiet down" movement to the crowd of media. Paul was relieved he'd handed it off to the sheriff. Right now Paul was agitated enough to say something he shouldn't. He was definitely going to have a private talk with Regan Simmons tonight. He spotted her blonde head in the crowd, her lips moving as she shouted a question at the sheriff. *What if she pushed for a repeat performance of last night?* He pondered the dilemma for a split second. He could handle her for one more night, but this time he'd keep his secrets to himself.

Hopefully, the search and rescue team was finding a blackened, charred wreck full of crispy skeletons. That would take care of his biggest problem. That would be a perfect end to the huge thorn in his foot, and everything could return to normal. All secrets would be secure. No loose ends floating around. Surely Darrin's attorney wouldn't see a plane crash as a suspicious death. Planes went down in bad weather all the time. An attorney wouldn't suspect anything unusual about that.

Would he?

CHAPTER NINE

The female moved up the hill and out of his sight. Darrin sighed and turned the binoculars back on the three men below, wondering what she was up to. She'd left her pack behind, so she wasn't going far. The other men stared at each other for a few seconds, then the biggest one ducked into the cockpit while Kinton and the short guy talked.

It still bugged him. How had Kinton known where to find him? Maybe he'd been unconscious longer than he realized after the crash.

No. He hadn't lost a complete day. He could tell by how hungry he felt and how much he'd pissed.

Stubborn. That was the only word to describe Alex Kinton. Alex's brother, Samuel, had been stubborn too. Not nearly as bad as Alex, but enough to drive Darrin into action. Darrin had been sloppy with Samuel. And it'd been Darrin's undoing. But he'd learned his lesson: don't kill the brother of a federal agent.

Darrin smirked. He pictured himself wrapping his hands around the neck of a grandma in a nursing home. "Oh, by the way, any relation to government agents?"

He nearly dropped the binoculars as he slapped his hand over his mouth, stopping the laugh, knowing how easily sounds could carry over the snow.

He hadn't asked any questions of Samuel.

Samuel had kept following him, harassing him, whining about Rosa and her dog. He'd seemed more upset about the dog than the woman. Darrin hadn't realized Samuel had seen him kill Rosa until Samuel accused him of throwing Hero in the pool. He'd drowned Rosa first. The yippy little dog had been next. Sort of like the cherry on top of the sundae.

Darrin had tried to bribe Samuel. Usually with the retards it didn't take much to distract or convince them they'd seen something incorrectly. A little chocolate or a soda usually did the trick. He should know. He'd been dealing with frail-minded seniors and retarded adults for two decades. But Samuel was persistent.

Nursing homes. Group care homes. He'd worked in several. They were rife with easy kills and vulnerable victims who'd finished their necessary roles in society.

He'd wanted to be a doctor. That had been his original plan. He'd done what he could at the community college and transferred his credits to a state school where he could get a real degree. Then he'd planned to apply to medical school, driven by a fascination with life and death. He'd wanted to feel that power that doctors exercise when their patients are close to death. Like on the television show *ER*. To be an emergency room doctor was his long-term goal. But first he'd move to a big city like New York or Chicago. Someplace more violent. The doctors at his local emergency room dealt with a lot of sore throats and ear infections. He wanted the big stuff. Shootings and car accidents.

Death.

But Dad had lost his job and spent his time drinking instead of looking for a new one. Mom had held down two jobs, but it was never enough. Darrin had to work and pay for his own tuition. Not easy at minimum wage. So he'd left home. Why give money to Mom to pay her bills when he could simply pay his own bills? He'd become a certified nursing assistant and found work in a nursing home. Everyone else had hated working there. He'd loved it.

In a nursing home he'd been as powerful as a doctor. His hands had determined who lived and who died. As they died, he would study the fading light in his victims' eyes and wonder what they saw. Some looked happy; some looked scared. And then he'd watch the families as he drank in the range of emotions at the news of the death of a loved one. Some relief, some sorrow.

It was delicious.

Darrin swallowed hard, new anger burning his throat. Would he ever get another chance to play God?

Switching to the group homes for the mentally challenged from the nursing homes had been a good move. The victims had more emotions, posed greater risks and bigger challenges. Silent kills took more creativity. One time he'd set up an accidental overdose, slyly letting a patient get into another patient's medications. Another time it'd been a fateful slip in the shower.

He used to spend hours plotting a kill; that was part of the fun. But with Rosa and the two women before her, he'd hardly planned at all. He'd seen and he'd reacted. The kills had stopped being about the control. He'd killed for the thrill and instant gratification. It became his undoing.

Darrin's breaths sped up, creating a heavy minicloud around the binoculars.

Samuel had been an overreaction. If the guy hadn't pissed him off so bad with his relentless questions and whining he would've let it go. It'd been simple to get Samuel to follow him to the pool on the pretext of talking about Rosa. Because the retard had been highly distraught over the woman's and dog's deaths, Darrin had figured he could play up the suicide card if anyone questioned him. And then Alex had shown up, never believing that his brother had committed suicide. Samuel's and Rosa's deaths had been perfectly clean with absolutely no connection to Darrin, but Alex's pure tenacity had managed to put him in prison.

His hands gripped the binoculars, trembling as he focused on Alex.

The superhero A-man was trying to catch him again.

Both Jim and Thomas weren't speaking to Alex. Jim had walked away and joined Thomas in the plane after Alex had admitted he wasn't a marshal. Now he felt like he'd let Jim down. Alex picked up a handful of snow, packed it into a ball, and hurled it at the plane's tail. It wasn't like he'd deceived Jim personally. And what did it matter? After they left these woods, he'd never see Jim again. Wasn't like they were gonna meet up for beers afterward.

He needed to focus on his objective. Alex packed another snowball, then crushed it between his fingers, letting the pieces fall. Things around him were cluttering his concentration.

The team had come to a compromise. Everyone was staying until morning and then they'd reassess. No one was hiking out that day. They made plans to move Linus's body to the cockpit of the plane with the pilots and then they'd sleep in the larger piece of plane. Thomas suggested building a snow wall to close the open end of the plane. Should be warmer than tents, and the plane's seats were more comfortable to sleep on than the frozen ground. The plan had sounded good to Alex. Maybe Ryan and Thomas wouldn't snore so much if they slept upright. After helping Thomas and Jim move Linus, Alex headed up the hill to help Brynn move Ryan and his gear down to the plane.

Why hadn't Jim told Thomas yet that he wasn't a marshal?

Not a marshal. The words still hurt.

Alex had loved his job and had known he did it well. He'd spent several years on the judicial security branch of the service, protecting federal judges and securing federal courthouses. When he'd needed a change he'd gone to prisoner services, moving prisoners between institutions, some clear across the country, and deporting others back to their country of residence. He'd spent a lot of time on little planes just like the one sitting in pieces on the snow. He'd missed the judicial security work, where his supervisor hadn't been an incompetent ass like Paul Whittenhall.

If it hadn't been for Whittenhall, he'd probably still have a job.

Alex breathed hard as he worked his way up the hill. One thing about being in the marshals was that he couldn't afford to let his physical condition slide. Daily workouts were a part of the job to keep prepared for any situation that might arise. Now he was lucky if he made it to his gym once a week. He sucked in the icy air.

Promise number one to self. Restart daily workouts.

Actually it was promise number two. The first was no more chemical dependency.

Like he could forget. His shaking hands and upset stomach reminded him every hour. He'd had no idea that his body had been so used to the tranquilizers. It wasn't like he walked around in a drugged-out daze every day. He just took a few milligrams each night to help him sleep and keep away the nightmares. Sometimes a shot or two of whiskey to relax in the evening. He would have never believed he was addicted until his body started telling him yesterday. Looked like part of this trip was becoming a blessing in disguise. Intervention and treatment at the same time.

Alex still had a couple of hundred feet before he reached Ryan and Brynn. Hopefully, the tension at the top of the slope would be lighter than at the bottom. He could relax around Ryan and Brynn. He pushed his legs a little harder. He wanted to see the sparkle in Brynn's brown eyes and hear her laugh. Another promise started to enter his mind, but he pushed it away, shaking his head. He wasn't ready for a woman in his life. Although Brynn was definitely the type he would look for second time around. Alex couldn't keep his eyes off her whenever she was near. Something about her pulled him to her, drew him in. Several times he'd wanted to simply touch her, feel her hair.

Instead, he'd crammed his hands in his coat pockets and felt like a kid in high school.

Alex could faintly see the outline of her and Ryan up the hill. He blinked. It was like looking through a steamy bathroom. The snowfall was so fine and light it was like mist. Was it time to tell Brynn and Ryan the truth too? No doubt Jim would tell them pretty soon. Alex would rather they heard it from his own mouth. Was it so bad pretending to still be a marshal? To make sure a killer was dead?

Wasn't like Alex was hurting anyone on the team. So far the only one who'd been hurt was him. Sliding down that mud had reinjured his knee. If not for the constant doses of ibuprofen it would be killing him, slowing down him and the team. His headache was being kept at bay, but he could feel it pressuring the gate. What he wouldn't give for a quick shot of good whiskey.

No more. That's past. That's over.

The nights he couldn't sleep he'd pored over the casebooks from Besand's murders, making copious notes. The detectives on each case hated him for his constant pestering. He'd stopped phoning them once he'd realized they wouldn't answer when they saw his number on the caller ID. He'd switched to e-mail and tried to keep the number of those to a minimum.

He'd told Brynn he created computer games and security software. Truthfully, Alex had been blocked for three months. His mind wouldn't cooperate when he sat down to work, and he hadn't sold a new game in a year. At least the money from his last three games was more than enough to see him through his retirement.

A far off *wump-wump* sound entered his consciousness, and Alex scanned the hazy sky. He'd bet his last dose of ibuprofen that was a helicopter. But in this weather? With no visibility? It couldn't be. The trees were keeping the team out of most of the wind, but above that it was whipping real good. How could anyone fly?

He stopped his climb. The sounds were growing louder, but he still couldn't see the chopper. Far above him on the ridge, Brynn and Ryan stood up, looking in all directions. They couldn't see it either.

Damn, it had to be close. The sucker was loud, and Alex felt like he was standing outside a rocking nightclub. Any second it should break through the haze. Alex trudged to the center of the slope and started to wave his arms in anticipation of flagging down the helicopter. In his bright blue coat, he should be easy to see against the snow.

Against the background of the rhythmic thumps, he heard faint yelling. Glancing behind him, he saw Jim and Thomas awkwardly running from the plane to the trees. *Have they spotted the chopper?* He glanced up the slope at Brynn and Ryan. More yelling and hands waving, but they were facing him. He scanned again for the helicopter. The chopper sounds were now a roar, the sound as intense as a freight train.

His gaze shot back to Brynn and Ryan, his stomach curdling. They were waving at *him*. Ryan was pointing over and up the slope at the white cloud that was rolling and pounding down the hill.

Avalanche.

His blood hammering in his brain, Alex ran for the closest trees, knowing he'd never make it in time. The sounds of the savior helicopter had triggered a death trap that was rushing directly at him.

They'd heard it at the same time. On top of the ridge, Ryan turned his head in unison with Brynn's, searching through the curtain of the snowfall for the helicopter.

"No fucking way," Ryan exclaimed. He pushed out of his snowy seat and spun in all directions, eyes wide. "Who's stupid enough to fly in this shit?"

Brynn's chest had shrunk in on itself. *No, Liam. Even you can't be this dense.* But she couldn't stop her eyes from searching as eagerly as Ryan's. The wind whipped her hair into her mouth, and she brushed it away with an impatient hand.

"Where is it?"

The beating sounds of the blades came closer. Any second she expected to see the outline of a chopper through the snow. Would it be the Pave Hawk of the air force rescue squadron? Or a local? Someone who donated his time and gas to help the SAR team?

The vibrations rattled in her brain, and she knew the chopper was close. So close.

"He's gotta be right over the far ridge," Ryan shouted over the racket.

She nodded and focused her gaze in that direction. Next to her, Kiana started to bark, backing away from the sounds. Brynn ran a gloved hand over her fur. The barking sounded more upset than excited.

Abruptly the thumping volume started to decrease.

"No!" Both shrieked and frantically waved their arms, spinning in all directions, even though no chopper was in sight. *It can't leave.*

"Holy shit!" Ryan froze, pointing.

Brynn whirled his way, heart sprinting, expecting to see a helicopter rising over the ridge. Instead she saw a cloud sliding down the mountain. Kiana lunged at the moving sea of snow as Brynn grabbed at her collar.

"The chopper set it off."

She clutched Ryan's arm, holding him tight like Kiana. He'd tried to move in the direction of the smashed plane below as if he could beat the avalanche and get the other three men away in time. "No!"

The avalanche would miss her and Ryan. It would sweep by, eating everything in its path. She stared down the mountain and spotted two red parkas tearing toward the tree line at their right. Jim tripped and went down. As she watched, Thomas bent over and dragged him back to his feet without breaking stride. Her gaze flew back to the thundering snow to measure the distance before it reached the men. But her eye was caught by a royal blue figure striding up the hill.

Alex.

Brynn's heart stopped.

Shrieking, she waved her arms, gesturing him to the right as if she could physically move him. Alex froze, looking behind him then back at Brynn. He broke to the right and tried to run through the fluff. He was moving too slowly.

"Aw, fuck." Through the roar of the avalanche and fading sounds of the helicopter she heard Ryan's curse.

Brynn couldn't breathe; she'd never felt so utterly powerless. She dropped to her knees and watched as the cloud overtook Alex, swept past the large piece of plane, and then buried the cockpit.

CHAPTER TEN

"Oh, God. Oh, God. Oh, God."

Brynn squeezed her eyes shut and dug her knuckles into her eyelids, but it didn't hide the image burned on her retinas. Alex vanishing under that snow.

It was quiet on the hill, but her ears were still ringing from the roar of the avalanche. She slowly lowered her hands, hoping to see Alex climbing up the hill. The unseen helicopter had flown away, and a tank brigade of snow had ripped down the mountain, leaving a jumbled wake of white fluff. Ryan pulled on her arm.

"Let's go."

She hated the determination in his voice. In her gut she knew all was lost. No one could live through that. Ryan yanked harder.

"Brynn. Get moving. We've got to hurry." Her feet started to follow, concrete weights tied to her ankles. *He's dead. Alex is dead.*

No. No. No! Silent words hammered her brain. *I don't believe it.*

She couldn't give up without trying. She couldn't give up on Alex.

She wrenched her arm out of Ryan's grasp and started to run down the side of the slope. Kiana raced ahead, while far below Thomas and Jim dashed from the trees. Thomas was pointing in one direction, but Jim was shaking his head.

"Where is he? Did you see where he went?" she screamed at the two men.

Jim pointed to a spot twenty yards away from a spot Thomas was indicating.

Brynn stumbled and fell. Ryan stopped to help her up and roughly pushed her ahead. "Go, go!"

Minutes. They only had minutes to find Alex before he suffocated.

Death's clock clanged in her brain.

It took too long for them to get down the slope. It felt like hours before they met up with the men. Thomas and Jim were frantically scooping snow, yelling Alex's name.

"Is this the spot? Did you see him go under?" Brynn fell to her knees and pawed at the snow like a dog. Ryan did the same. Kiana sniffed at the snow by Brynn's hands, ran in a circle around the group, and barked.

Thomas and Jim exchanged a glance, Jim nodded.

"I think he's over there." Thomas gestured to his left.

Were they digging in the wrong spot? Brynn froze at the possibility. She turned wide eyes to Jim. He angrily shook his head. "I don't know. I swear he should be about here." He stood and gestured. "Thomas, take Ryan. Go dig over there."

Brynn's breath shot out. By splitting up they'd lose speed at this dig site. "Jim—"

"I know. I know! What else can I do? Thomas is as positive about what he saw as I am."

Tears stung. "Dig faster," she begged and doubled her speed.

Darrin was on his feet, mouth open, binoculars pressed hard enough to leave rings around his eyes as he watched the diggers.

Holy shit.

He'd never seen an avalanche except on TV, and he didn't want to ever see one again. The power of that thing! It'd been like a hungry monster, devouring everything in its path. How had silent snow made so much noise?

It had smacked directly into Alex Kinton. Darrin had watched him pump his arms like a swimmer. Was Kinton dead?

Darrin ran his binoculars over the snow. Kinton had to be dead. It was like getting sucked under in the ocean, only you wouldn't float to the top.

Wow.

His shoulders twitched, waiting for Kinton to appear. Besides Alex, the snow had scooped up and eaten the cockpit of the plane like it was a tasty snack. How could they expect to find a person under the snow when they couldn't even see a piece of the plane?

Darrin zoomed in on the woman and watched tears flow down her face. He could see her lips moving as she shouted at the other men, but he couldn't hear the words. His eyes widened.

Now there were three men in red. *Where did the third guy come from?* He'd been so focused on the damage down the slope Darrin hadn't watched the woman come back down. She must have brought the third man.

The nutty dog was running in circles. Going from one set of diggers to the next. It finally decided to dig next to the woman and sent the snow flying from between its legs. Handy animal.

Darrin straightened as the new guy stopped digging, leaned to one side, vomited, and then immediately started digging again.

Adrenaline. Darrin understood that effect on the stomach. *They must be utterly freaked.*

The new guy dug slower than the others, but all their faces reflected the same determination to find Kinton. The woman didn't even stop to wipe at her cheeks.

Paul Whittenhall couldn't believe it.

The two-man team he'd sent to tail Kinton was trudging out of the woods and back into his base camp. A chorus of questions and excitement rose out of the media corral. The team had been gone only half the day.

"What the fuck?" Paul muttered and jogged to meet them. That asshole Sheriff Collins moved faster. He beat Paul to the team and started peppering them with questions. Good men. They were ignoring the sheriff. Gary Stewart locked eyes with his boss. He looked defeated.

What kind of cowards would be back so fast?

"What happened?" Paul reached the men and cut his question in over the sheriff's.

Stewart glanced at the sheriff then back to his boss, his brown eyes tired.

"Footbridge over the river is under water. We tried, but there's no way to get across the water that way. Boyles says there's a train trestle or something farther south that crosses the river."

Collins nodded. "There is a train trestle a few miles from here. But it's gonna add a lot of time to getting in there."

Paul turned on the sheriff. "How'd your team get across? I thought they went in the same way." Had Collins been lying to him?

Collins shrugged. "Maybe it wasn't underwater when they went over. As far as I know it's the only way to get across up that way."

Boyles nodded. "It looked like a tree floated down the river and wedged itself under the bridge, plugging the free space, making the water flow over the bridge. Maybe that happened after your guys went through."

"My guys…" An odd look passed over Collins's face.

Instantly suspicious, Paul jumped on it. "What? What about your guys?"

Collins mouth went up on one side as amusement darkened his eyes. "It's nothing. One's a woman; they're not all guys. That's all." The amusement vanished. "She's not fond of crossing water."

Paul saw Gary Stewart straighten, his face covered with surprise. He read Stewart's thoughts. *A woman went out in that shit?*

Paul smirked at the look on his man's face. Maybe Stewart would stop being such a whiner about the weather. Being shown up by a woman. *Ha!*

"OK, where's this train trestle?"

Goddamn, he was cold. Had someone left the tent flap open?

Alex tried to peer through the dark, but his eyes weren't working right. He was too tired. For once Ryan and Thomas weren't snoring in unison. He sighed and tried to relax, shift deeper into his sleeping bag.

Icy-hot pain shot through his knee, forcing his eyes wide open. Shit, what had he done to his leg? The pain was nearly as tortuous as when he'd first caught a bullet with it. He tried to move it into a better position.

He couldn't move his leg.

Snow. Avalanche.

Alex's breath shot out.

He was underground. *Under the snow.* He thrashed in instant panic.

Breathing hard, he managed to unstick an arm from the packed snow and reach for the cold ceiling above his face. His frantic thrashing was halted by shock as he found the snow-packed roof. *It was so close.*

It was ten inches from his nose to the ice. And even less between his chest and the ice. He remembered clawing, waving his arms as he was tossed inside the avalanche. A faint thought from a very tiny part of his brain had screamed, "Swim!"

Those arm movements had probably kept the snow from settling on his face and immediately smothering him.

At least he faced upright. Gravity was telling him that much.

He breathed slowly and purposefully didn't think about how little oxygen there must be in his snowy coffin.

Alex tugged his other arm free and used both hands to dig at the ceiling of snow above his face. Ice crystals trickled into his eyes, so he moved his hands lower, digging above his chest, moving slowly, not wanting to overexert and use too much oxygen.

Was he close to the surface?

What about the others?

Brynn was safe. She and Ryan had been out of the avalanche's path. But what about Jim and Thomas? Alex dug faster. The men might be in the exact position as him. They would need help.

An image of Brynn trying to find all three of them physically hurt his brain. She and Jim were so close. He grit his teeth as he pawed at his ceiling.

Why did Jim and Brynn's closeness irritate him?

Alex barely knew the woman.

And if he didn't get out of here he wasn't going to know her any better.

His hands dug faster.

A dog barked faintly. *Kiana.*

"Hey!" he hollered, hurting his own ears. "I'm down here!"

Nothing. He swallowed hard and yelled again.

Still nothing.

Maybe he'd imagined the dog. Was he oxygen deprived already? Tiny sharp lights danced in his eyes and he sucked in a deep breath to send more oxygen to his brain. But it didn't help. His lungs burned and he inhaled again, forgetting his previous caution to pace his breathing. He must have been unconscious for quite a while because he was nearly out of air. He felt light-headed and dizzy. Not good signs.

He settled his hands at his sides and closed his eyes.

There wasn't any point in fighting anymore.

He exhaled and relaxed. It'd be easy. He'd simply fall asleep.

Then he heard her voice, and his eyes flew open. Brynn's brown eyes were looking down at him, laughing at him. "Are you trying to make this hard for us?"

He smiled back as relief filled his throat and kept him from speaking. Brynn looked great. From the minute he'd met her, he'd felt she was special. The animation and energy in her face set her apart from other women. One of those people whose spirit illuminates them from the inside, giving them a special glow. One of those people your eye always comes back to, but you don't know why. You just can't look away.

He couldn't look away now.

She seemed to have eyes only for him. Dark brown, expressive, dancing eyes. He'd never met anyone with such communicative eyes. Damn. If he wasn't careful...

"You need to tell us where you are, Alex. We can't find you if you don't tell us."

She smiled patiently at him and waited, her gaze losing a small degree of its joy.

He tried to speak. And couldn't.

Her face fell and her eyes pleaded with him. "Come on, Alex. Where are you?"

He wanted to please her, he wanted that brightness back in her gaze, but he still couldn't speak and he didn't know where he was. His eyes closed in frustration as his brain silently screamed.

He was so fucked.

Brynn couldn't feel her hands anymore. The cold of the snow was making them numb. *I won't stop. I won't stop.* She dug, ignoring the splinters of pain from her upper arms. A picture of Alex, lifeless and gray, flooded her brain and she shoved it away.

Not. Going. To. Happen.

"Good girl, Kiana. Where is he? Dig him out!"

Kiana paused to shove her nose into the deep hole she'd dug and started digging again. Kiana was like a little snowblower, shooting snow in an arc behind her. The dog's determination calmed Brynn. Surely Kiana wouldn't be digging if nothing were down there.

Jim sat back on his heels and huffed. His face was red, and he wouldn't meet Brynn's eyes. "Just catching my breath."

She nodded and kept digging. A second later she jumped to her feet, scanning the area. "I'm so stupid. Where are the packs? Why in the hell aren't we using the shovels?" A small collapsible shovel was standard equipment in their packs.

Jim grimaced. "Already thought about it. Don't know where they are. The avalanche spun the body of the plane in place, but it sucked up the packs that were beside it."

Brynn stood still. "No packs?" Their lives were in their packs. They weren't going to survive out here if they didn't have them. She looked at the hole at her feet. Was she digging Alex out to die in the elements? She glanced over at the big piece of the plane where she'd dropped her pack before hiking up to Ryan. Sure enough. The avalanche had caught the edge of the plane and rotated it ninety degrees.

And stolen their backpacks.

"Thomas, did you see where the packs went?" she called over to the other diggers. The big man simply shook his head, his face grim. He didn't lose a beat in his digging rhythm. Ryan did.

"What? No packs?" Ryan worriedly looked around, his eyes wide as they stared at the plane. "Mine's still up top," he said slowly.

"Better than none," Thomas stated.

"Shit." Ryan attacked the snow with fresh vigor, and Brynn imitated him.

Her gloved hands hit a hard patch, and she punched the snow with her fist to break through. Blue. She could see blue through a layer of snow. Kiana barked.

"I've got him!" she shrieked and attacked the snow. Jim lunged closer.

"Which way's his head?"

"I can't tell. Hang on."

Ryan and Thomas were instantly at her side, digging faster. The blue haze under the snow grew larger and she touched the fabric. *Thank you, God. Thank you.*

"That's not him." Thomas spoke just as the realization punched Brynn in the gut.

It was one of the packs. The four of them sat back, utterly drained. Kiana barked and dug at the blue fabric.

"It's mine," Brynn whispered. "It's got Kiana's food in it." Tears traced hot paths down her cheeks. They'd been wasting time and muscle power digging in the wrong place. Thomas stood, strode back to his hole, and began to dig. Ryan followed.

"Brynn, get your shovel out of the pack and get over there." Jim's voice was tired. "I must have seen the blue of your pack getting tossed in the avalanche. So maybe Thomas saw the blue of his coat. Fuck!" He rubbed his palms over his eyes. "I screwed up."

"No, you didn't. Look how accurate you were in locating this. We're gonna need it." Her voice was calm as she located the collapsible shovel, but her heart was crying. "This shovel might be what we needed to find him. Go on." She gestured for him to join the others. "I'll be right there." She forced her breaths to stay even.

Jim pushed to his feet and jogged over. Ryan slapped him on the shoulder and made room for him to dig beside him. The agony on their faces broke her heart.

Brynn maneuvered her shovel out of her pack, and her fingers brushed Kiana's sack of food. She wrenched it out of the half-buried pack and held a handful out to her dog. "Here you go. Good girl." Kiana wagged her tail and attacked the food.

Brynn grabbed the shovel and headed over to the men. She held the shovel out to Thomas, who silently accepted it and attacked the growing hole. Brynn fell to her knees and started to dig. Her back ached in protest.

"Alex! Can you hear us?" Ryan shouted and the others held still, listening. "Alex!"

Silence.

"Call him again," Brynn whispered. Her throat felt too swollen to yell. *Come on Alex. Where are you?*

"Alex!" Ryan yelled and then froze. "Call him...shit. Anyone know his cell phone number? Maybe we'd hear that."

"There's no coverage up here." Thomas kept digging.

"There's some. I got through to Collins a little while ago."

"But you were higher." Brynn's heart lifted a fraction.

"It's worth a try! Jim, do you have his number?"

Jim shook his head. Ryan turned hopefully to Brynn. "Brynn?"

She shook her head, and Ryan's face fell as he tentatively looked at Thomas. Ryan didn't bother to ask.

"Wait. Collins gave me the number for Alex's boss before Alex even showed up at base camp yesterday morning." Jim had an odd look on his face.

"You want to try to reach him and ask for Alex's number?" Brynn asked hopefully.

"No." Jim paused, brushing at the snow on his pants. "I think its Alex's number I have. Alex was the one who called Collins and talked his way onto our team yesterday morning. Not someone at the US Marshals' office."

Brynn stared. "Why would he do that?"

Jim had already pulled out his cell phone and was dialing. He ignored her question. "It's showing a weak signal. One bar. Quiet."

Brynn shut her eyes and tried to stretch her hearing. She heard Kiana's tail swishing and the crunch of her kibble, but she didn't hear a cell phone ring.

"Knowing him, it's probably on vibrate," Ryan mumbled. His face was long, his eyes red.

"Shhh." Brynn heard the wind blow snow out of the firs, but she didn't hear a ring.

Jim slapped his phone shut with a crack.

"Try again," she urged.

He started to shake his head, but faltered as they made eye contact. She pleaded with her eyes, and he hit send again.

Thomas coughed. Brynn wanted to smack him for the noise.

Jim stood still, holding the phone to his ear, his face as blank as the snow.

Come on, Alex. Tell us where you are. This time she kept her eyes open, scanning the snow for any movement, any color.

"Damn it, Alex, answer your frigging cell," Jim said into his phone.

Without looking at the others, Jim snapped the phone closed and dropped to his knees to dig. "I reached a voice mail, but it didn't say who it belonged to." Jim's throat sounded tight. Kiana padded over and enthusiastically dug beside him.

"No food this time, girl." He ruffled the dog's fur.

CHAPTER ELEVEN

Darrin's stomach tied in knots as he watched the team dig. When they'd rushed the hole next to the woman and pulled out a backpack he'd been strangely disappointed.

Shouldn't he be pleased to get that pain-in-the-ass ex-agent off his back?

Instead, he found himself pulling for the team.

He wanted another day to challenge Alex Kinton.

Another day to piss him off, watch the rage in Kinton's eyes and the pain in the lines on his face. Darrin swore Kinton had twice as many lines around his mouth as when they first met.

He'd glimpsed Alex a time or two before the "accidents" at the group home. The resemblance between Alex and his retard brother had been startling. It was like the retard had suddenly been injected with brains, pounded by a personal trainer, and had his hair trimmed. But it wasn't until after Samuel's incident that Darrin got to know, really know, Alex Kinton.

After Samuel's death, Alex had raged through the group home, upsetting all the residents and making the owner cry. He'd been something to see. Those gray eyes had become a shade of steel that burned, and the tendons in his neck had looked like taut bungee cords. He questioned every resident and employee multiple times, and he had harassed the homicide detective until the cop had ordered him escorted out of the home by a couple of uniforms.

When Alex cornered Darrin for questioning the first time, he'd felt the heated rush of Kinton's rage flow across his chest. Heavenly. When he'd stopped Darrin in the hallway, nearly face-to-face in the narrow corridor, Alex had smelled like clean sweat and hot anger. The two men weren't all that different. They were about the same height, but Darrin had ten years on the agent and Alex had a lot more hair.

"Where were you last night after nine o'clock?" Those steel eyes had been dagger sharp.

Darrin had put on his best worried face, rubbing a hand across the back of his neck. "In my room. I always watch TV after the residents go to bed in the evening." He'd inhaled slowly through his nose to get more of Kinton's scent. All pissed-off male.

"What'd you watch?" The question was like a whip.

"Uh. That guy in the jungle. The reality show where the army guy survives wherever the show decides to dump him. Then the local news."

"Did you see Samuel go to his room that night?"

"Of course. I'm usually the one to get everyone moving in that direction. Kathy doesn't care to supervise bedtime, and I don't mind. I saw Samuel leave the bathroom and close the door to his room."

Kinton had worked his jaw as Darrin watched in fascination and decided to throw him a little piece of bait. "I did hear someone's door open around eleven or so. I figured someone was using the bathroom again." Darrin scrunched his forehead. "The sound did come in the direction of Samuel's room. I can't say for sure that it was his door."

Kinton's jaw had grown harder. "Did you hear the door close?"

Darrin had twisted his mouth. "No...I can't say I did. I was only paying attention to the TV."

"Why didn't you get up to check? Why didn't you make sure that person was back in their room?" Alex had leaned forward an inch, somehow seeming taller at that second.

Darrin had blinked and stepped back a little, his spine touching the hallway wall. "Well, usually the residents are great about returning to their rooms. Kathy has never had a problem with wanderers before." He'd injected a small quiver in his voice and licked his lips. He hadn't thought Kinton's eyes could get any hotter, but they did.

Darrin had started to sweat. In a good way.

"Rosa died the other day and you're not watching the residents? You don't get up to check late-night noises? Two people from this home are dead. Don't you think you should've stepped it up a little?"

Darrin had thought his spine would melt. Kinton had been physically pumping testosterone into the air. Darrin had sniffed and dropped his gaze. "I guess I wasn't thinking."

"Thinking is what you're paid to do! These people need extra attention," the man had said with clenched teeth.

Darrin had squeezed his eyes shut, afraid he wouldn't project the right level of sorrow. He'd been luxuriating in the hot rush. The whole confrontation had turned into an emotional heat wave Darrin had never experienced before.

Darrin had an empty chasm deep inside him. He felt nothing. All the time. Other people were born with something in their brains that Darrin was missing. An important chemical or hormone or synapse. Even as a child, he'd known something was wrong.

The antidote had appeared the first time he'd watched his young cousin die. He been in the pool with her and simply watched. The rush that'd rolled over him as her last breaths left her lungs had addicted him. He'd sought more from other victims over the years, needing his fix, feeding hungrily on their terror as he physically squeezed out their life's essence. But Alex Kinton was giving him the same dizzying rush in his brain and Darrin hadn't laid a hand on him.

"I'm so sorry. It's all my fault. Maybe if I hadn't been so tired your brother would still be alive." He'd slowly let his eyes open, gradually dragging his gaze up from the floor, aching for the next reaction.

All color had rocketed out of Alex's face, and his bloodless lips clamped together. His eyelids had widened the tiniest bit, and Darrin had held his breath. Alex had looked ready to collapse. Instead, the agent had turned, made tracks down the hallway, and strode out the front door. Pushing past two residents, Darrin had darted to watch from the living room window. Outside in the hot sun, Alex had leaned on his palms on the hood of his truck and stared down at the asphalt between his arms. He'd looked like a man resting from a hard run or someone waiting to vomit. He didn't move as Darrin had slowly counted to ten.

Then Alex had abruptly straightened and taken a hard look at the group home over his shoulder. Darrin had darted one step to the right, hiding behind the curtain. Had Kinton seen him staring? Kinton's gaze had slid to the gate to the backyard and pool of the house next door and his shoulders sagged. With a rough yank, he'd opened his truck door, climbed in, and left.

Darrin had exhaled, suddenly exhausted.

Alex Kinton had just led him on a roller coaster of adrenaline that rivaled Space Mountain. No, better than that. Faster, higher. And Darrin wanted another ride.

He'd figured surely Alex would be back soon.

Instead, Alex had returned and snatched Darrin's discarded cigarette butt for DNA.

Darrin hadn't left any DNA with Samuel or Rosa. But he had with Kimberly Brock, Susan Mannon, Claire Hines, and others. He'd known it was virtually impossible to avoid leaving DNA behind. He tried his best. He'd always figured the best way to protect himself was not let himself be tested, therefore avoiding any connections. Thanks to a computer database and a cigarette, suddenly he'd been linked to several of his victims.

So simple. He'd been brought down by evidence any *CSI* television show addict could have spotted. How had he been so stupid? Twenty years he'd slipped away from the police and then was brought down by something so trivial.

Him and Al Capone.

The day Darrin had been arrested had started like any other normal day. Until the swarm of police that showed up before breakfast. Alex had been there. Silent and watching. Staying back out of the cops' way under the tree by the driveway.

Darrin had winked at Alex as the police pulled him down the driveway in handcuffs.

At least Alex had visited him in prison. It'd been Darrin's idea. He'd reached out to the marshal, hinted that meeting with him in prison could be of benefit to other victims' families. Alex had come, probably hoping that one day Darrin would confess to killing Samuel. Thanks to modern technology, he'd been linked to a lot of his crimes. But there'd been others the police didn't know about. To keep Alex coming back he'd given names, dates, and locations, which Alex passed on to detectives. But never more than one tidbit a visit.

Alex had hounded Darrin, who soaked up every minute of it, getting off on the agent's ragged grief and anger. In a way Darrin became Alex's private therapist. Darrin wanted to know what made Alex tick. So he'd made Alex speak, telling Darrin about every shitty thing in his life in exchange for facts on Darrin's victims. Now Darrin knew how it hurt to grow up with a retarded brother. Darrin knew about the selfish wife who made Alex choose between her and his brother. Darrin knew all too well about Alex's asshole of a boss.

Quid pro quo.

He'd visit every few months. Sometimes every month. Each visit he seemed thinner and paler than the last. Like something was eating him from the inside out.

Alex had only crumbs of information to show for all the meat he'd sliced off his psyche and handed to Darrin. Alex's visiting days were Darrin's best prison days. He'd live for weeks off the buzz from being in the man's potent presence.

Darrin rubbed his gloved hands together, annoyed with the bitter cold. It had been several months since he'd last seen Alex, and it'd made him irritable. Even with his pending escape, Darrin had been short-tempered. He'd known he'd have to give up the visits from Alex once he entered his new world in Mexico with a different identity, but that glorious future hadn't kept away his irritation about permanently severing the bond with Alex.

There was some freaky compulsion that had pushed the two of them together. One angry man searching for answers and one empty man searching for emotion.

Brynn was past tears. Her face had dried as she dug, and she ignored the other men. She didn't miss their furtive glances at her and at each other. She knew exactly what was on their minds.

How long do we dig?

She glanced at her watch. It'd been about twenty minutes since they'd started to dig. That wasn't too bad. Surely Alex had ended up with some sort of oxygen cushion. He might still be breathing. *I won't give up, I won't give up.* She got a small burst of energy and bit her lip as she pushed her frozen hands deeper into the snow. Ryan rested on his knees and breathed hard.

"Take a break. You're not a hundred percent," Jim ordered.

"Just for a second." He was out of breath and looked paler than Brynn liked. She figured she looked pale too. Every member of the team had shadows under their eyes.

Thomas paused and leaned on the shovel. "Maybe we should look somewhere else."

"Where?" snapped Brynn. "You pointed here. You got another spot where you think you saw something?"

Thomas shook his head. "I'm just sayin'."

"Well, unless you saw something, I vote we stay with this spot. There was a reason you led us here. Don't start doubting yourself."

It was the wrong thing to say. Skepticism and uncertainty swept Thomas's face and he dropped his gaze. She'd put too much pressure on him. Now he'd feel responsible if they didn't find Alex.

"No one else saw anything. This is our best spot," she amended.

Thomas nodded without looking at her and started to shovel.

"Wait. Did you hear that?" Ryan held his hands out for silence.

Everyone froze and strained their ears. Brynn closed her eyes and heard silence.

"I don't hear anything." Jim's gaze was searching in all directions. "What'd it sound like?"

"A soft ding. Like a chime."

Brynn's eyebrows shot up. "A chime? From what? Are you sure you heard something?"

Ryan's face was tight with concentration. "I heard it. I know I did."

"From where?"

Ryan glanced into the hole. "From there?"

"You don't sound very certain." Brynn pushed her hair over her shoulder. *Had he heard something?*

"Keep digging," was Jim's advice.

The group was silent as they dug. Everyone's ears stretched to the limit. A minute later Thomas jerked. "Was that it?"

"I didn't hear anything!" Brynn cried. How could she miss it?

"Yeah." Ryan was nodding. "It did come from below us." He attacked the hole with the strength of a healthy man. Thomas did the same, an excited light in his eyes.

"What'd it sound like?" Brynn asked between hard breaths, digging faster. The others' excitement was contagious. *Please. Please. Please.*

"Just like he said. A soft chime." Thomas plunged the shovel in hard and halted. "There's something here. Ryan! Dig right here!" He loosened the snow, and Brynn helped get the excess out of the way. They'd dug nearly four feet down.

She saw blue.

Please don't be a backpack.

"It's him! I know it's him." Ryan's words were strangled as he fought back tears. Both he and Jim were in the hole, digging frantically. More blue was exposed, then the black of Alex's pants. Thomas moved to dig at the other end of the blue parka.

"Oh, thank God. Thank God." Brynn's face was wet again. *Please be all right.* "Hang on, Alex, we're almost there."

Thomas uncovered Alex's face. His white face. His eyes were shut, and he was so still.

"Is he breathing?" Brynn whispered. She felt nauseous; her arms and legs shook with exhaustion. Thomas shook his head as he brushed the snow away from Alex's nose and mouth.

"Get him out, now!" Jim shoveled the last of the snow off Alex's boots and gestured for Thomas and Ryan to grab his shoulders. Brynn grabbed a leg while Jim grabbed his belt. "On three. One, two, three. Out!" They all heaved at the same time. Alex's left shoulder got hung up on the hole's wall halfway up, and Brynn moved from his leg to free the shoulder. It was tight maneuvering in the hole. They hadn't prepared a big enough space for several working bodies, but Thomas and Ryan yanked Alex out with sheer brute force.

"He's not breathing. Jim, get the mask from my pack. Left top pocket." Brynn ripped off a glove and put two fingers below Alex's jaw. Her arms shook, and her fingers were nearly numb. She couldn't feel a thing except the pounding of her own heart.

"Can you feel it?"

"Shhh!" She hushed them and slowed her breaths to concentrate on feeling the ends of her fingertips. Alex's chest wasn't moving. "Get his airway going." She closed her eyes to concentrate as Jim pulled Alex's jaw upward and slapped the safety mask for resuscitative breathing over Alex's nose and mouth.

There.

She felt a single beat at her fingertips. Then another. Very slow, but strong. His heart hadn't stopped; he hadn't been without air for too long.

"He's got a pulse. Get him breathing." Thomas and Ryan exhaled at her words.

Jim was already working at it.

"Come on, Alex." Brynn watched Alex's chest move with Jim's powerful breaths. The beat under her fingertips increased slightly in speed and she nearly cried in relief.

He's going to make it.

Behind her Ryan sat hard into the snow, and she studied his exhausted face. He'd overdone it. He'd been ill to start with, and now he'd pushed too hard.

But not too hard if it saved Alex's life.

At that moment she heard a rasping breath from Alex. Jim pulled the mask off, and the two of them rolled Alex to his side as he coughed and took rough breaths. She met Jim's eyes.

We did it. He mouthed the words at her as his eyes filled.

Brynn brushed at her own wet eyes.

Ryan let out a whoop and pounded Alex on a shoulder. "Goddamn it, Kinton, you scared the crap out of us!" Ryan threw an arm around Brynn and laid his head on her shoulder, rubbing his eyes on her coat. She felt him sway with fatigue.

"Holy shit," Alex said as he hacked and coughed and looked at the team with blurry eyes. He had snow frozen to his hair and eyebrows. Next to his icy, pale skin his lips now looked unusually red and flushed.

"Thanks." He spit the word out with a gasping breath. Brynn brushed some of the snow out of his face and laid her cold hands on his cheeks to warm him. Compared to him, her skin was on fire. He blinked unsteadily at her, and she couldn't breathe. The way Alex stared was setting off sparks in her brain.

"Hey." She swallowed hard, unable to pull her gaze away. "I thought...We thought..." Her thoughts evaporated in the heat generated by the pounding heart in her chest.

Those steel-gray eyes of his turned sharp as razors. "I know. Me too. God, you look gorgeous." Shivering lips pulled into a lopsided grin. "My lips are numb. So's everything else."

"We'll get you warmed up." She turned to the men and rattled off directions.

Alex sat wrapped in a space blanket in the cargo area of the plane and huddled over the tiniest portable stove he'd ever seen. He'd tucked everyone's hand warmers into his armpits and into his pants, but he still shivered. He wanted to pick up the stove, wrap his coat around it, and hold it against his chest. Damn chills wouldn't stop. His hand shook as he took a sip of the hot broth that Brynn had heated for him. It blissfully burned its way down his esophagus. He sipped again and sighed.

"Good stuff?" Ryan poked his head in through the open end of the airplane. When the avalanche had spun the body of the plane like a toy, it'd left the open end half-buried in a snowbank. A person could just squeeze through. They'd already decided to pack snow into the space to close it and use the hatch toward the rear of the plane for exiting and entering. After they looked for the packs.

Ryan's shaggy hair poked out around his hood and his eyes looked like he'd pulled an all-nighter studying for college finals.

"Like single malt whiskey."

Ryan's gaze went to the little stove, and Alex wondered if he wanted to tuck it under his coat too.

"Got your pack from the top of the hill?"

Ryan nodded. "Two packs for the five of us. That's not good numbers."

"Someone will come in after us."

Ryan shook his head. "I think we've had our window of good weather. The weather on my GPS is showing nothing but storms for the next two days."

"We won't starve in three days." Alex watched Ryan pale and swallow hard. "Stomach still a wreck?"

"Let's not talk about food." His smile was feeble.

"GPS working?"

Ryan nodded. "They're all showing the same readings now. I don't know what the fuck was wrong with them earlier."

Alex took a sip of salty broth as Ryan stepped all the way into the plane and held his hands out to the little stove. He studied Alex from head to toe. Alex raised a brow. "Surprised to see me breathing?"

"Yes."

"Me too." Alex stared at the stove and its glowing flame.

"What do you remember?"

Alex was silent for a moment. His stomach knotted as he pulled up the memory. "I remember seeing you and Brynn waving at me. I remember looking up the hill and seeing a wall of white rushing at me." He took another sip. "I remember thinking I was a dead man and tried to run." He rubbed at his leg. Brynn had shoved three Advil in his hand along with the broth, but his knee still felt like he'd been hit by a truck. Or an avalanche.

"You didn't get very far," Ryan spoke softly.

"It was loud; I remember that. And then my ears were plugged with snow, but I could still hear the roar. Maybe the sound was in my head."

Ryan shook his head. "No. It sounded like a train or tornado coming. That sucker was loud."

"It reminded me of being tossed in the ocean while body-surfing. You know, when you can't tell up from down? That absolute panic that makes you pump your arms and legs and hope you're headed toward the surface. That was my only thought. For some reason I knew I needed to move like I was swimming. I don't know how I got lucky enough to end up on my back. I could have ended up head down. That would have been a hard target for you diggers to hit."

Alex clamped his jaw as a full-body shudder rocked him. *God, I was lucky. So damned lucky.*

"Nah, your feet probably would've been sticking out of the snow. Might've been easier to find." Ryan forced a smile.

Alex let an answering smile spread across his face. His smile wasn't forced. He was aboveground, and that was all that mattered. He could smile forever.

"I was awake for a while under there."

"Fuck. I can't imagine..." Ryan's eyes widened.

"Looking back, I'm surprised how calm I was. At first I wanted to scream and dig out and fight. But then after the first panic I just accepted it. I knew there was nothing I could do. And I was OK with that. Peaceful almost."

He met Ryan's curious gaze and kept quiet about his dream of Brynn. He'd thought about her a lot since he'd been dug out of the ground. When he'd first seen her above him, she'd looked so damned scared, and then relief had shot through her eyes.

At the same moment, something had shot through him, bonding him with her. Some sort of freaky cosmic thing. He'd heard that rescuers would forever carry a piece of the soul of the people they'd saved. He didn't know he'd physically feel it when it happened to him.

"Thomas knew where you were. He saw you get tossed in the avalanche."

Alex bit his lip. What if the big guy hadn't seen him?

"Jim thought he knew where you were. We started digging in two different spots, but Jim's spot turned up Brynn's pack." Ryan cleared his throat. "I thought Brynn was going to lose it when she realized it wasn't you under all that snow. We were all about to give up after that."

"I'm glad you didn't."

"Maybe it was my ears. I don't know what I heard, but when we were digging at the hole where we finally found you, I swear a sound was coming up from under the snow."

"What kind of sound?" *Screams? Moans?*

"A chime. Just a single quiet chime." He studied Alex.

Alex blinked. A chime? Like his...he reached in his coat pocket and pulled out his cell phone. The screen showed two

missed calls and a voice mail. The chime would sound occasionally until he checked his voice mail. He dialed.

"It's from Jim." He stared at a grinning Ryan. "He's cursing
at me to answer my phone."

Both men burst out laughing.

"You tried to call me? Did you think I could tell you where I
was?" Alex gasped between laughs. "I can't believe the call went
through."

Ryan snorted. "We were trying to hear the ring. I'd gotten
through to Collins earlier. It was worth a shot."

"Fuck. I keep it on vibrate."

"I knew it!" Ryan exclaimed and clutched at his stomach as
if he could stop the pain from laughing too hard.

"The only sound it ever makes is that damned chime every
five minutes when I've got a voice mail. Do you know how
many times I've tried to get that annoying noise turned off? You
can't do it on this phone." Alex's voice choked as he fought to
control another laugh.

Ryan's shoulders shook. "That damned chime might've saved
your life. We might've given up if I hadn't heard it. Everyone
thought I was hearing things."

Alex's nose began to run from laughing. He wiped at it.
Another sign he was thawing out. He closed his eyes and smiled.
Damn, it felt good to laugh and shoot the shit with someone. He
hadn't done this since…he couldn't think of the last time. A subtle pounding in his head reminded him why. He'd cut himself
off from everyone.

He had to start living again. Doing something with his life.
Not hiding.

He'd been given a second chance. If it hadn't been for the
determination of this team… He shivered as a chill rocketed

through his nerves and Brynn's smiling image crossed his mind. She was the type of person who touched lives and made them brighter, lighter. She and all the guys had potential to make big differences in the world.

Alex stared at the tiny stove, chest tightening.

He still had to figure out what to do if he found Darrin Besand. If Darrin was in these woods, Alex might get a chance he never would have had out in the real world. He could meet the man face-to-face, no guards, no bars.

What would he do? His goal suddenly wasn't as clear as it had been. Could he truly kill a man in cold blood?

Doubt wrapped around him like a cold coat.

Is that Alex *laughing?*

Brynn stopped and cocked her head. She recognized Ryan's laughter, and the lower-pitched laugh had to be Alex. Turning, she spotted Thomas and Jim digging in various places, still searching for the missing packs. They'd already partly dug out the cockpit. It had ended up a couple of hundred feet down the mountain, the pilots still strapped in their seats. The marshal had been tossed out, but they found him nearby and moved him back in with the pilots. They'd thought the cockpit was twenty feet under until Thomas had spotted some white metal sticking up out of the snow. Why couldn't their packs have a strap or two poking up out of the snow to see?

She paced a grid pattern, studying the snow for any signs of their packs. She'd sent Ryan in to rest and to keep an eye on Alex. Hopefully they'd keep an eye on each other. Ryan was a walking ghost. He'd insisted on climbing to the ridge to retrieve his own pack, and it'd taken him three times as long as it should have. The vomiting seemed to have stopped, but she'd seen him frequently touch his abdomen like something still burned. He refused to eat. Could he hike out tomorrow? If they went slowly?

She kicked a fir branch out of her path.

Their walk out of the forest was going to be twice as long if they went down to the railroad river crossing. Maybe they should go back and check on the river footbridge. Maybe the river level had dropped enough. But would the footbridge be stable? It had been slammed with the force of a runaway semi. A shallow wave of dizziness swept through her brain, bringing back the image of the raging water. She breathed deeply and focused on the snow, putting one foot in front of the other. Water didn't have to be raging to do damage. She knew that all too well.

She dropped to her knees and dug at a shadow under the snow.

A stick.

She continued her rhythmic steps, mentally inventorying their supplies and needs. Her pack held enough food for her. Ryan's pack held three times as much, but he ate three times as much. Usually. Their food situation was pretty good. The human body could go for weeks without food. Not very efficiently, but well enough for their purposes. Water was abundant. Everyone was dressed for freezing temperatures. And the plane made an excellent shelter for the night. Too bad they couldn't drag it with them for the next few nights. Now everyone just needed to stay healthy.

Alex looked like he was going to be fine. He'd said he had awoke underground and found breathable room around his face. He'd said he didn't know how long he was conscious while below the snow. He'd looked away as he said the words, and she had a hunch he knew all too well.

A shudder rippled through Brynn's chest.

Could she have handled that terror? She'd been above-ground during the avalanche and was going to have nightmares for weeks. She snorted. Alex would have nightmares for the rest of his life. What if they hadn't found…She firmly placed the thought out of her head.

Kiana's frustrated barking startled her, and she glanced around for her dog. Out of sight. Probably spotted some small prey that'd darted up a tree and out of reach. As the dog had dug beside her on that first hole of Jim's, Brynn had been so certain Kiana believed there was a person below the snow. She'd never done any formal rescue training with the dog. Maybe she should. Maybe they would've found Alex sooner.

Thank God he was OK.

A rush of confusion and relief swamped her. The same feelings that overpowered her every time she thought about him. She twisted her lips and glanced up the hill at the piece of plane that still sounded with bellows of male laughter at odd intervals. A sort of zing had rattled through her nerves when Alex had made eye contact for the first time at base camp. A warmth had started in her stomach.

He'd been so silent, so serious during the first part of their trip, but she'd felt his eyes on her. And she was more aware of him than she should have been. She'd noticed when he'd start to limp then fight to hide it. She'd noticed his eyes light up as Kiana would tear off in pursuit of something only she could hear.

The other men didn't pull her attention like that.

And when he'd looked at her after they'd pulled him out of the snow…Brynn stopped and closed her eyes, breathing deep. She'd never felt better in her life than she had at that moment. It wasn't just the adrenaline from the save. It was the person. If they'd never found him it would have been like part of her had lost something precious, but something unknown. Like losing the sparkling center diamond from a ring before she'd ever put it on her finger.

She shook herself and continued her steps.

Alex made her palms sweat when he turned that serious gray gaze on her. He made her wish she wasn't in the forest with three other men around. That she could sit across from him at dinner and huddle together in front of the TV. Simply talk and...

Shit. She stopped her pattern and stared at nothing, blinking rapidly.

She and Liam had been together for years, but it hadn't started with an instant rush of attraction and curiosity. They'd been together because they were so similar; they liked the same things. They were an outdoorsy couple with mountain bikes and a dog. But when was the last time they'd biked together? Liam had changed. Over the past year he'd grown increasingly paranoid and protective of her.

He made her feel like she couldn't breathe.

They'd had the latest version of an old argument the night before this rescue. He'd wanted her home, not in the woods. Why didn't she find a regular job in a hospital? Why did she work at a job that took her to bloody car accidents in the middle of the night? Why did she insist on doing search and rescue when she could get hurt?

These questions from the pilot who flew a helicopter for his country into unknown situations on a moment's notice.

She kicked at another shadow in the snow. Another stick. She sighed and moved on. The snowfall was picking up again. The entire day had alternated between showers of heavy snow and light icy pellets.

Brynn frowned as she scanned the ground. Until that rock-slide last year she'd never been injured while out on a SAR mission. She'd always felt in control when out in the wilderness, but that time she'd ended up with a broken collarbone and concussion. At the emergency room, Liam had been furious. He'd stated the first ultimatum then.

Give up search and rescue or give up him.

She didn't care for ultimatums.

Their argument had echoed through the emergency room. A doctor had interrupted, glaring from Liam to Brynn, asking if she needed to call the police. Brynn had shaken her head, and Liam had stomped out of the hospital. Later the same doctor had a well-intentioned but misguided talk with Brynn about abusive men.

Liam would never lay a hand on her. If he did he'd be the one in the emergency room and he knew it.

She'd ignored his ultimatum and he'd kept his mouth shut for a while.

The next one had come a few months later. He wanted kids and he wanted marriage.

Brynn had wanted to panic.

Not learning his lesson from the first provocation, Liam had begged her to agree to an engagement or he'd move out.

He rescinded his words the next day.

But it was too late. Tension had ratcheted between them, and Liam started sleeping on the couch. Then she'd asked him to move out. He'd moved in with his brother and waited a week before speaking to her again. Over the last two months they'd slowly talked about what each of them wanted from the other.

Their needs didn't match. They were both utterly stubborn. She wouldn't change, and he wouldn't listen to her refusals to change. They were so over. And now she was attracted to another man.

CHAPTER TWELVE

Where is the team?

Liam Gentry's eyes burned from staring into the blinding white stuff for hours. And that was with his protective eyewear. His brother, Tyrone, hadn't said a word in over thirty minutes. Liam knew Tyrone wanted to head back. The winds were rattling the copter like crazy, and visual range was incredibly short. He glanced at Tyrone, who bounced his gaze from the window to his controls every three seconds. The muscle twitching at his jaw told Liam he'd pushed his brother's limits.

They were both stupid.

Liam's commander would ground him for six months if he knew he'd convinced his brother to take him out in such

188 • KENDRA ELLIOT

high-risk weather. Liam wouldn't survive the grounding; he had to fly.

He had the job of his dreams, flying million-dollar equipment bought on someone else's dime, and he had the perfect woman.

Now he just had to convince Brynn to marry him and have some kids. He wanted the rest of his dream. The 2.3 kids, the picket fence, the smiling wife at the door as he came home from work. But Brynn didn't see it that way.

Would being married to him be so awful? Liam grabbed at the handle above his door as the copter jumped in the wind.

When she'd been in that rockfall, he'd been certain she'd see the danger of her SAR missions and cut back. But it was like she flung herself at them with more enthusiasm, determined to prove him wrong. He was terrified of the day he got the phone call that she'd been killed in a stupid accident. Yesterday morning had been bad enough when he'd read her note. Her very brief note.

Plane down in the Cascades. Gonna be a long one.
B

That was all she wrote.

He'd checked the location and checked the weather and nearly punched his computer screen in frustration. Could the plane have crashed anywhere worse? Brynn knew he'd be pissed about the danger of this particular job. That's why she'd slipped out of the house without waking him. If he hadn't crashed on her couch after their three-hour discussion the previous night, he wouldn't have known for days that she'd gone on a mission.

And top it off with a serial killer on the damned plane.

No one could have survived the crash. The odds were against that. But, shit, why was there a killer on this particular plane? Did Brynn know? And go anyway?

She would go. It wouldn't make any difference to her who was on the plane.

Liam cursed colorfully. Tyrone glanced at him but stayed silent, his mouth tight.

The little copter bounced, dipped, and jerked roughly in the wind. Liam ignored it. The sensations were so different between this baby bird and the mammoths he flew. Sort of like a Winnebago and a Miata.

"Fuck! Hang on!"

Liam's gaze flew to his brother's tense face, and then he read the controls. His heart skipped several beats; sweat instantly covered his forehead. Grabbing his seat, he looked out the window and estimated the distance before they smashed into the trees.

Daylight was fading as Brynn and Kiana entered the plane. Jim had hollered that he and Thomas would be in soon. They weren't ready to quit searching for the packs yet. Brynn figured the missing packs weren't going to go anywhere overnight, so she'd search again in the morning. In the light. The three of them hadn't found a thing and she was ready to drop.

What a day.

Alex opened his eyes from where he'd stretched out on the cargo area floor, his arms tucked under his head. Ryan snored quietly on one of the thickly padded leather seats that looked like they belonged in a CEO's office. She kept her gaze on Ryan, assessing. He looked comfortable but exhausted. The temperature inside the plane felt heavenly, and Brynn threw back her hood, running a hand over her low ponytail. To be inside an enclosure with hard walls and out of the wind and constant snow felt like she was at the Hilton. It just needed a hot bath. The men had closed in the ripped plane's front end with packed snow. It looked like the inside of a kid's snow fort. With luxury seating.

She felt Alex study her closely, his gaze heavy on her back. She finally turned his way and met his eyes. The lines of his face were taut and drawn, but she'd never seen him so relaxed and at peace. Amazing for a man who'd faced death hours ago. She felt her lips curve and her own worries lifted from her shoulders. They'd been very lucky today.

Kiana sniffed at Ryan's boot and trotted over to Alex. He sat up and rubbed her head, a genuine smile crossing his face. Brynn swore the dog smiled in return. She also noticed Alex's hand shaking slightly as he petted her dog.

"How do you feel?"

Amusement entered his eyes. "Alive."

She cocked a brow at him, waiting. "Cold?"

"My toes are cold. That's good. It means I can feel them. I feel bruised up and down my body like a tanker hit me. I think I reinjured my knee. And I'm hungry." He smiled again, and she felt her skin heat under her coat.

He didn't look like he minded the pain or hunger. "What did you do to your knee?"

"Now or originally?"

"I think I know what happened to it today. How about originally?" She kneeled beside him, pushing her dog out of the way and laying her hands on the leg he rubbed.

He froze.

Brynn jerked her hands back, eyes widening. "Did I hurt you?" She squinted in the bad light, checking his leg for blood. It looked OK.

"Ah, no. I think you shocked me." He shifted on the floor and frowned at his leg. "Old hole from a bullet."

"You were shot? How long ago?"

"A few years. Nearly destroyed my knee joint."

"Work related?" she asked.

"Yes. It happens sometimes in my line of work."

She waited for an explanation but none came. *Who'd shot him?*

"Do you want me to look at it?"

He met her eyes and grinned as her cheeks painfully flushed. *Wrong thing to say.*

"There's no blood. I think I just overstrained a weak area. It's gonna ache like hell for several days." His smile stayed strong.

"Everything else OK?" Relief flooded her. Getting Alex out of those pants wasn't something she could handle at the moment. "Are you cold?"

He raised a brow and shook his head. "Just my toes."

"That's right. You said that," she mumbled, embarrassed she was repeating questions. She retrieved her pack from one of the seats and unzipped a side pocket. "Protein bar?"

"Please."

"More ibuprofen?"

"Pretty please."

She snorted but kept her gaze inside her pack. "Charming, aren't you?"

"When I want to be."

"And when is that?" Their light banter relaxed her as she continued to dig through her pack, looking for her little bag of drugs.

He didn't answer.

She glanced at him, her hands buried. He was looking at her, his gaze serious…and something else. She looked closer at his eyes. *Had he hit his head?* In the plane the light was dim, and his pupils were dilated, nearly filled his irises, making his gaze dark and heavy. Warm.

His eyes weren't dilated from a head injury.

She drew a fast breath, unable to pull away. It felt like he'd buried her in warm honey.

"Brynn. I really owe you for today." His voice was low, those eyes locked with hers.

"I didn't do anything."

"Bullshit."

"It was a team effort." Her heart thudded in her chest.

He waved that aside. "I know. Always the team, but Ryan told me how upset you were when you dug up your pack."

She nodded.

"You kept going."

"Everyone did. Ryan pushed himself beyond healthy limits digging for you. Thomas was like a backhoe with the shovel. None of these guys were going to stop until we'd found you. Neither was I." Her tone was fierce as she felt the terrified determination flow through her bones again. Just like when she was digging.

"Ryan said he nearly gave up a dozen times, but seeing you attack the snow inspired him."

She glanced at the sleeping man. "I felt the same way watching him. All three of those guys. We'd still be out there digging if we hadn't found you." She pressed her lips and felt her eyes sting. Alex would be dead, long dead.

"Still. I'd like to think…" He reached out a hand as if to touch her cheek. She couldn't move away; she wanted to feel his touch. Her lips opened slightly, and she inhaled softly. He'd touched her before on the trail, helping each other along, but they'd both worn gloves. Now his fingers hesitated an inch from her jawline, and he held her eyes with his as she knelt beside him. Her hands tried to strangle the protein bar. He was so close she could feel the heat from his fingertips on her skin. His gaze dropped to her mouth as his hand touched her. The energy from his palm made her lips open, and he shifted closer.

"When I was buried I thought I saw…"

Pounding rattled the door before it flew open. Jim and Thomas tromped in, brushing the snow off their jackets. In a single fluid movement, Alex pulled back, his hands at his sides, and the sudden cold stung her face.

"Ahhh." Jim breathed out in pleasure, throwing back his hood. "It's got to be twenty degrees warmer in here. Nearly a sauna." His grin was contagious.

Thomas pulled off his gloves and sat heavily in a seat to work off the snowshoes. "No packs."

"That's all right. I think we'll be just fine," Brynn stated quietly. She stood, feeling her legs tremble slightly as she handed Alex his squished protein bar and his hand brushed her fingers. His gaze met hers again, something stirring in the depths, promising her they weren't done. The intense look on his face had vanished at the sight of the two men. But its aftereffects lingered in her blood, tingling, warming.

"I owe you my life," Alex said to the men.

"That's right," Jim quipped. "I expect five years of free car washes and I like my lawn mowed twice a week." His grin didn't fade as he stepped forward and slapped Alex's shoulder.

"Done," Alex said.

Jim's grin faded. "I was joking."

"I'm not." Alex's lips twitched. "But I'm not doing any manual labor for you. Would you settle for car wash tickets and a yard service?"

Jim's hand lay still on Alex's shoulder as he blinked. Brynn had never seen Jim speechless before.

"If Jim doesn't want 'em, I'll take 'em." Ryan stretched and yawned. Brynn jerked her head in his direction. How long had Ryan been awake?

"Except I don't need a yard service. How about a subscription to a Beer of the Month Club?"

Alex nodded. "Thomas?" He turned toward the quiet man who'd been closely following the conversation.

Thomas shook his head. "Don't need anything. Didn't do it for a reward."

"I know that, but it'll make me feel rotten if…"

Thomas grinned. "Perfect. If it bothers you then I'm happy."

Alex stared then laughed. "There's a sick sense of logic there."

"What about Brynn? What are you gonna give her?" Ryan smiled and turned innocent eyes on Brynn. She felt her cheeks flush.

"I don't…"

"Don't tell me you want me to be miserable like Thomas does," Alex prodded.

"No, of course not, but…"

"Aw, come on, Brynn. Give the guy some slack. Tell him you'll settle for a big ol' diamond and he'll be happy." Pure devilry shone out of Ryan's eyes.

Now she knew he'd been awake as she kneeled near Alex.

"No diamonds. No car washes." She threw a protein bar at Ryan's head, which he handily snatched just before it nailed him in the mouth.

"Come on, you can think of something. He's not going to give up until you name something. You don't want him stalking you, do ya?" Ryan caught his breath as his face fell. "Shit."

Brynn's mouth dried up.

"Sorry," he muttered.

Silence filled the broken plane.

Alex looked at each teammate, but the men were all looking at the ground and Brynn was trying to get her lungs to work properly.

"Did I miss something?" Alex asked.

Brynn's heart felt as heavy as the plane as she turned to Alex. Curious concern shone from his eyes.

Jim spoke first. "Brynn had a stalker last year. This dipshit let his mouth flap without thinking." He whacked Ryan's head with a glove.

"A stalker?" Unease replaced the concern in Alex's eyes, and he frowned at her.

Brynn wanted to tell him, but didn't know why. She hadn't spoken of the incident in months because it'd seriously freaked her at the time.

"Awhile back..."

"You don't have to say anything." Alex popped three ibuprofen in his mouth and swallowed them dry. "Forget it."

"No. I don't mind talking about it. Really." And she didn't. She forced her stomach to relax as she sat back in one of the cushy chairs and tried to figure out where to start.

"Last year I was called to a suspicious death of a teenager. It was plainly suicide. The boy had locked himself in his room, left a long, rambling good-bye note, and shot himself in the mouth. He'd attempted suicide twice before, he'd been treated for depression, and there wasn't a shred of evidence that anyone else could've been in the room."

"Window?" Alex was following her story closely, his eyes intense.

"No window. And the door was locked with a bolt from the inside. His mother heard the shot and was at that door within seconds. No one else could have gone in or out of that room."

"So what was the problem?" Alex raised a brow.

"The problem was the dad. He lived in Tennessee and believed his son had been murdered," Brynn explained.

"Stupid asshole," Thomas swore. He chomped into a protein bar.

"The father stalked you?" Lines creased Alex's forehead. "From Tennessee?"

Brynn nodded. Her lungs were working normally now, and she breathed steadily. The father had been a big man—a big, determined man. And he'd scared the crap out of her.

"He harassed me by phone for a week. Swearing, cursing, calling me every name in the book, and threatening to get my license taken away. He threatened to shoot me and see if some idiot death investigator thought it looked like a suicide. The medical examiner and I had determined an autopsy wasn't needed in this case, and the father was livid. He wouldn't accept that his son had committed suicide. He had my cell number and wouldn't stop calling."

Alex's brows shot together; he looked furious. "How'd he get your cell number?"

"I don't know." She suspected someone at the ME's office had given it out, but no one had ever admitted it. "Then he showed up at the office. He'd flown across the damned country to yell at me in person. I'm not at the office that much because I'm usually out in the field. The secretary told him that and he left. My boss called me at home to warn me, and I got Jim to park his squad car in my driveway and sleep on my couch."

"Liam was out of town," Jim added.

"Did he come to your home?" Alex's voice was tight. He looked ready to kick the man's ass. Brynn tried not to smile at the sight.

"No. I don't think he was able to figure out where I lived."

"If someone had given out your home number, he could've easily found you."

Brynn nodded. That fact had haunted her. "I persuaded the examiner to do a partial autopsy a week after the death and all his findings supported suicide. The dad went back to Tennessee, and I got a new cell number." And she removed her home number from every source at the ME's office except her boss's phone contacts.

"I was just waiting for that guy to show up. I wished he had." Jim automatically moved his right hand to his waist where he usually kept his service semiautomatic.

"Sorry, Brynn," Ryan muttered again. She met his gaze and smiled to let him know he was forgiven. Sometimes she felt twenty years older than him instead of two.

"You carry enough weight to say when an autopsy should be done?" Alex was still watching her intently.

"I can make recommendations. The final decision is up to the ME."

"You don't do the autopsies though."

She shook her head. "I try to go and watch if it's my case."

"I've seen enough of them." Jim's nostrils widened a fraction as if he smelled something bad.

Both Thomas and Ryan agreed. Brynn knew the two younger men hadn't been to more than a few. It wasn't for everyone.

"Attended any?" Ryan asked Alex.

"Just one. I left. Couldn't make it through." Alex's face was suddenly strangely blank, like he'd exited his body and left a shell.

"After the first one I saw, I was off mac and cheese for months. It looks just like adipose tissue." Brynn watched the men react to her comment. Ryan looked ready to vomit again, and Thomas had developed the same blank look as Alex.

"Exactly like mac and cheese," Jim chortled.

"Stop it, Jim. Ryan's gonna lose the tiny piece of protein bar he finally ate." Brynn bit her lip.

"How can you eat after watching something like that?" Alex muttered.

She shrugged. "I don't. I always seemed to lose a pound or two after each autopsy. I usually don't feel like eating for a while."

"Can we talk about something else?" Ryan pleaded.

Brynn glanced at the windows of the plane. It was full dark outside. The plane was downright cozy with the hot bodies of the four men and Kiana.

Her heart sank as she remembered the cold corpses in the cockpit. "Should we...I don't know. Take the men out of the cockpit or take in some snow to pack around them? Are they going to attract animals?"

"What if we buried them several feet deep? Could a cougar or bear smell through that?" Ryan looked to Thomas, the wildlife expert. Thomas lifted a hand in an "I don't know" gesture and finished his bar.

"I know a good hole," Alex managed to say before he broke into gasping laughs.

Brynn's eyebrows shot up as her jaw dropped. Incredulously, she scanned the men. They all had the same shocked expression. Ryan laughed first, breaking the astonishment. Then the other three joined, even Thomas.

A big portion of the stress of the day evaporated with their laughter.

Alex jerked awake, his shoulder immobile and his feet freezing.

For a moment he was back underground and terror rocketed through his nerves. Then he realized the weight on his shoulder was Brynn's head as she slept next to him on the floor of the cargo area. He blew out a frazzled breath and commanded his limbs to relax. Heat spread from where she touched him, making him feel secure and safe. The plane rumbled with the snores of sleeping men, not the silence of his snowy grave. He closed his eyes and waited for his heart to slow as he enjoyed the sound. The sounds of the living.

He drank in the sight of Brynn in the indirect light from a headlamp. Last he remembered she'd been sitting in one of the comfy chairs talking quietly to Jim. Alex craned his neck and saw that Jim was stretched out on the other side of Brynn.

Thomas and Ryan were sleeping upright in two of the chairs, heads leaning against the walls of the plane.

Alex wished he'd been awake when she moved next to him. Her mouth was open the slightest bit, breath softly puffing. He felt it touch his neck. Her eyelashes lay still against her cheeks. He could see the faintest movement of her eyes behind her lids.

He'd nearly kissed her last night. When she'd first touched his leg it had been a shock. He hadn't lied. It'd been a shock that raced up his thigh, stunned his groin, and then nailed him in the chest. And all she'd done was lay her hand on him.

In the gold light from the tiny camp stove, with her kneeling beside him, and the unstable, emotional set of his mind, he'd ached to touch her. The light had bronzed the skin on her face, and her pupils had dilated. He'd felt that if he didn't touch her he'd explode. And he was damned certain she'd felt it too. He'd been about to tell her that she'd spoken to him underground when Thomas and Jim had walked in and the moment had vanished. He'd never gotten it back.

His hand reached over and traced her cheekbone. He wanted to touch the dense lashes or soft lips, but was afraid he'd tickle her and she'd wake. Then his moment would be gone again. He slid two fingers through the hair that'd come loose from her ponytail. Silky. Just like he'd known it would be.

He silently swore and pulled his hand away.

I have no right. He squeezed his eyes shut.

She was living with someone. But she hadn't pulled away last night, and behind the initial confusion in her eyes when he reached for her he'd seen...something. And it wasn't rejection. It was warm.

He wanted her. In a bad way.

Maybe he was just overreacting after nearly dying. Seeking the ultimate affirmation of life, wanting to mark it with a female, show that he was alive. And Brynn was simply the closest woman. Showing up in his death dream didn't mean squat. Simply because he'd felt something in his dreams didn't mean it existed in real life.

He gazed back at her face and felt his heart speed up.

Who am I trying to fool?

In forty-eight hours he'd fallen head over frozen heels for Brynn. She was smart and strong and feisty. Life radiated from her and had touched the part of him that had felt dead for so long, slowly bringing him back to life. It was like that allergy drug commercial where the scene is fuzzy until the person pops a pill and suddenly everything is crystal clear. She'd shaken something awake inside him. No wonder he'd fallen hard.

Shit. The first woman to catch his eye and his heart, and she was already taken.

Or was she? She hadn't uttered a single word about her boyfriend. Don't most women mention them every other sentence? She hadn't said she couldn't wait until she got back home, or talked about what the two of them would do, or said she hoped her boyfriend wasn't worrying about her. If Alex's girlfriend was out in this hell, he'd be worried. The only mention he'd heard of her boyfriend was from Ryan. And there'd been an odd tone when Ryan talked about—what was his name?—Liam.

Liam. Alex mouthed the name. He didn't like the feel of it. Felt foreign on his tongue.

His jaw tightened. There could be an age issue in Brynn's mind.

Well, maybe for her. He doubted she'd hit thirty yet and he'd passed forty a few years ago. It didn't bother him, but she might see him in a more…fatherly light. He cringed, his chest tightening. Ugh. She looked at Jim like that. There was true friendship and caring there, but there was also a respect from Brynn that one gave to their elders.

Did she see Alex like that?

Ryan coughed, paused, and resumed snoring. Startled out of his thoughts of Brynn, Alex studied the sleeping man. Would Ryan be strong enough to hike out? He'd looked like hell the night before. At least Alex felt nearly fully recovered. He'd be able to hike out fine.

His body jerked as he remembered the purpose of his mission. Every muscle tensed. How could he have gone for hours without thinking of the killer?

Darrin Besand. After the avalanche, he had nearly been wiped out of Alex's mind. Alex had been distracted by Brynn and his newfound interest in doing something with his life. Besand couldn't wait. He had to find the asshole now. He had to know.

Alex closed his eyes and thought. If he'd been a convicted murderer hurt in a plane crash who didn't want to go back to prison and saw a rescue crew come in, what would he do?

Hide.

But then what?

Wait and follow them out.

He knew Besand would choose death over going back to prison. That was one fact he'd learned about him. Even if he were bleeding to death, Besand wouldn't make himself known to the group. So was he close by? Or had he already tried to hike out before they arrived? That was the theory he and Jim had arrived at yesterday, but now Alex wasn't so sure.

The only place Besand could have survived the nights would have been in the other piece of the plane. Alex shifted on the floor, forcing himself to not dash out and check the cockpit. His mind raced. There were no other possibilities. This little plane wouldn't have carried a tent, so Besand was either dead in the woods or taking cover from the elements in the cockpit while they slept.

The bloodstains on the plane seat across from Linus's weren't that big. Besand probably hadn't been hurt too badly. Internal injuries were a possibility. Alex felt a hot rage stir in his belly.

I hope you died in the snow, you fucker, with icy pellets hammering your face as your body shut down. And I hope you were awake for every minute of it.

Next to Brynn, Jim sat up abruptly, scanning his surroundings, his eyes clearing as he remembered where he was. He took in Brynn with her head still on Alex's shoulder. His eyes narrowed as he met Alex's stare.

Go ahead, Jim. Say something. Anything.

Jim quietly cleared his throat as his gaze slid away and he peered toward the window. Light was dim. Alex estimated the time to be around six o'clock.

"What's your plan?" Alex whispered.

Jim turned back to him, deliberately not looking at Brynn. "We need to talk."

Alex nodded. "Not now."

"Later. Alone." Jim's voice was hard.

"I want to go take another look at the cockpit," Alex said. He also needed to take a piss, but couldn't bear to move Brynn's head just yet.

"The cockpit? Why—" Jim stopped speaking, and understanding crossed his face. "You think Besand is still here?"

Alex shrugged his unoccupied shoulder. "Either he's dead under a layer of snow or he decided to hike out, and I doubt he would have survived the night without a tent or tarp. He's dead or he slept in that cockpit last night." He took a breath. "Until I see his dead body I have to believe he's alive."

Her eyes still closed, Brynn lifted her head, turned it, and curled her body away from him.

Alex's shoulder was suddenly cold. And very empty.

He watched her, silently begging her to move back. She slept.

Jim's eyes showed an odd mix of sympathy and annoyance. Alex wondered how much his own face revealed of his feelings for the woman. Judging by Jim's reaction, just about everything.

Jim jerked his head toward the cargo door, opened it, and stepped out of the plane. Alex heard Jim's knee pop as he walked. Sitting up, Alex's spine creaked and his head ached like hell. He'd talk to Jim, then get some ibuprofen before checking out the cockpit.

He wasn't aware of his hand instinctively checking his gun at his side.

CHAPTER THIRTEEN

Sheriff Patrick Collins stepped out of his four-wheel drive and surveyed the base camp in the morning light. He'd sped home, showered, changed, kissed his wife, hit Starbucks, and returned in under two hours. The number of media vehicles had increased again as word had spread that Darrin Besand was on the plane. CNN had arrived overnight. At first CNN had used the feed of a local network, but when the time frame of the missing plane lengthened and Besand's name came to light, they'd sent in their own people.

Patrick had dealt with national media before. Twice, missing mountain climbers had caught the rapt attention of the nation. And then there were the two middle school girls who vanished as they walked to school. On different days. In the same neighborhood. Again the national media came calling and camped on his doorstep. The girls turned up buried in the backyard of their friend's father's house. The same man who'd given interviews to the media, sobbing about his daughter's missing friends.

That case had nearly driven Patrick to retire.

RVs clogged the small clearing at the trailhead. The only local hotel was booked solid, so the media was making do with whatever sleeping arrangements they could find. He'd seen Regan Simmons arrive from the motel all perky and ready to sling some mud. She'd pissed him off yesterday by complaining on air about the lack of information from the sheriff's department. Claimed they weren't sharing with the media and were withholding information from the public and families.

Bullshit.

The families of both pilots and the missing marshal had been in constant contact with him. He'd assigned a deputy to do nothing else but see to their needs and make sure they could reach him whenever they needed to. None of the three families were willing to go on the air. With Patrick's encouragement they'd asked the media to respect their privacy, and that had got Regan Simmons's goat. She didn't have a single tearful spouse to put on the air.

She'd tried to get Patrick to change their minds.

He'd threatened to arrest her if she didn't stay out of his face.

He'd met with the three spouses and privately told them all he knew. Which wasn't much. He'd passed on his spotty conversation with Ryan Sheridan about "three dead." The looks on the women's faces had sunk in despair, then shot up in hope, then down in despair again. When four men were on a plane, "three dead" weren't good odds.

Patrick had fielded more questions about the damned helicopter too. The reporters had all talked among themselves, and no one confessed to sending up a copter.

Patrick had claimed no knowledge of the copter's source.

Why did it feel like that denial was going to come back and kick him in the ass?

Deputy Tim Reid jogged over, his cell phone in hand. "Dispatch has been trying to reach you."

Patrick pulled his own cell off his belt. The damned screen was blank. Dead battery. "Shit." He never let his cell completely die. Especially on a mission like this. At least he had a charger in his truck. He held his hand out for Reid's phone.

"Collins."

"Morning, Sheriff. I trust you got some caffeine this morning?" The grandmotherly voice of his favorite dispatcher came across the line.

"I'd be doing a disservice to Madison County if I skipped it, Marilyn."

"I'm well aware of that, sir." She gently cleared her throat. "I've got Al Rice at the tower from the Springton airfield on the other line, sir. He says Tyrone Gentry never returned with his helicopter yesterday. He talked to Tyrone personally, sir. Tyrone had told him he and his brother would be back before dark. He's already tried calling both the Gentry boys' homes and no one is answering."

Patrick closed his eyes and felt his heart land on his toes. Only Marilyn would call thirty-year-olds "boys." "Has he checked any other airfields?"

208 • KENDRA ELLIOT

"Yes, he did, sir. Within the last hour he called every place he could think of. He tried both boys' cell phones too. He's very worried, sir. Knows that family real well."

Patrick did too. Was he going to add Liam and Tyrone Gentry's mama to his list of grieving women? "Thank you, Marilyn. Tell Al I'll take care of it from here."

There was a pause.

"Do you want me to send someone over to Shirley Gentry's home, sir?"

"No, not yet, Marilyn. I'm gonna get a hold of Liam's commander. He's officially their boy, not ours."

Marilyn paused again. "You're right, Sheriff. Anything else I can do?"

"Yeah, keep it quiet for now."

"Of course, sir." She huffed.

"I know you will, but I have to say it, Marilyn."

"Stay warm, sir." The line clicked in his ear.

His mouth in a grim line, he handed the phone back to Tim. "Gentrys."

"I'd guessed, sir."

They both hazarded a look toward the media camp. Several faces and one camera were pointed their way. Patrick wondered if any of them could read lips. That'd be a handy skill for a snoopy reporter to have. "Keep it under wraps for now."

Tim nodded.

"Tell them there will be a briefing in…" He checked his watch. "Five hours."

Tim grinned and jogged over to the engrossed reporters.

Patrick sighed and rubbed both hands on his face, stretching the skin. What the fuck had happened to the Gentrys? Their helicopter must have gone down in the arctic weather. He had one team in the field and he really hated to send in another without knowing what was going on in the forest. One of his deputies had been instructed to try the team's cell phones every hour, hoping they'd move into a pocket of cell reception. He hadn't heard a word from the deputy so he knew there wasn't any good news.

Patrick suddenly felt very old.

How many more people would die because of Darrin Besand?

Alex ducked out through the cargo door and nearly ran into Jim as he sat strapping on his snowshoes. They had exited as quietly as possible as the other three in the plane slept.

"Sorry." Alex took two steps and sank to mid-calf.

They must have had eight inches overnight. They were going to need those snowshoes. He yanked up the hood to his parka and took a good look around. The snow was heavy. Visibility was shitty. At least the wind had eased up. Snow was coming down at a soft twenty-degree angle instead of the face-biting ninety degrees.

With all this snow, how would last night have been in a tent? Alex patted the body of the plane affectionately. Wherever they slept tonight was going to suck.

"You think Besand slept in the cockpit last night?" Jim kept his voice low.

"I would have."

"If he's still here."

"If he's still here," Alex agreed. "Yesterday…"

"What about yesterday?"

Alex wiped at his nose and stared into the snow. "I kept getting that hinky feeling. You know? Where you turn around because you think someone's behind you? But no one's ever there? I felt...watched all day. Until...you know."

Any cop understood that feeling. That rise of the hair on the back of the neck feeling. Jim's gaze darted around. "It's 'cause we're in the woods. You hear soft sounds sometimes from snow or rain or leaves and you think someone's there." His tone didn't match the surety of his words. "I feel that all the time out here. Get your snowshoes on. Let's go look. You carrying?" Jim placed a palm on his side.

Alex nodded, imitated the gesture, and grabbed his home-made snowshoes from just inside the plane. He awkwardly wrapped the bungee cords around his boots. Jim grinned at Thomas's work. "That boy knows snow."

"How long's he been in Oregon?" Alex stamped his feet, checking the cords. Jim was right. Thomas had whipped up some solid snowshoes.

"About three years, maybe four."

"And he's originally from Alaska?"

Jim nodded. "Was a cop and in the reserves. Did several tours in Iraq. Wife divorced him while he was over there."

"No shit. What a bitch." Immediate sympathy flooded Alex. And he'd thought *his* wife was unsupportive.

"I don't think Thomas was the same guy when he came back. He'd seen a lot of action and spent some time in hot situations. He and two others were held hostage for two weeks."

"Shit." Alex couldn't think of anything else to say. Nothing was adequate.

"Yeah. He's had a lot of treatment for PTSD."

"I don't think anyone fully gets over that," Alex said quietly. He knew two agents who struggled daily with post-traumatic stress disorder. Some days were better than others.

"You notice his parka doesn't have a hood?"

Alex nodded. Thomas wore a high, thick neck cover under his jacket, but Alex had always wondered how the guy could stand the cold, wet weather on the exposed areas below his cap.

"They had their heads covered with hoods nearly the entire time he was held captive. Even to eat they only lifted the hood enough to expose their mouths."

"Shit."

Jim led the way down the hill, Alex trudging behind. Both men had slipped off their gloves and held their guns in a pocket out of the snow.

"He only started wearing caps about a year ago. He says he doesn't truly get cold. Says he's experienced the coldest a person can be and everything else is just annoying."

"So this is nothing to him."

"Yep."

The men plodded through the snow. Jim was right. Alex kept hearing the soft, floaty thumps of clumps of snow falling out of the trees. Each time he'd turn his head in that direction, expecting to see Besand. His gun was out of his pocket now and his fingers were getting frozen. He transferred the gun from hand to hand, wiggling his fingers back into warmth.

"What's going on with Brynn?" Jim sliced him with the surprise question, and Alex stumbled. He'd been so focused on Besand and Thomas he'd nearly forgotten his pleasant surprise upon waking that morning.

"Nothing." Truth.

Jim stopped and turned to face him; his brows were together and the lines around his mouth creased deeper. He carefully pondered his next words. "She's seeing someone. They live together."

"I know that."

"Leave her alone."

"I haven't touched her. What's it to you?"

"She's practically my wife's little sister."

"So you're the overprotective big brother. Can't she think for herself?"

"Yeah. But I've seen the way she looks at you. She admires you for some stupid reason and was beside herself with grief when we couldn't find you yesterday."

"She would've been like that for any of you."

Jim nodded, then angrily shook his head. "No. It's different. She doesn't know who or what you are. Maybe I should say what you *aren't*."

"You mean I'm lying to her. You don't think I deserve her sympathy."

"Just don't be twisting her sympathy around into something else."

"I can't make her do anything. She's a big girl, Jim, and I think she's got her head on pretty straight."

"No, she doesn't." Jim clamped his mouth shut, and a guilty flush touched his cheeks. Alex's eyebrows rose.

"What the hell does that mean? She's as sharp a woman as I've ever met."

Jim started to speak, paused, and started again. "She comes from a messed-up family situation. Her parents completely ignored her. They didn't even protest when the state placed her in foster care due to neglect."

"When she was sixteen, she was placed with my wife's parents for foster care. These are good people. She'd been bounced from home to home before that. Me and Anna had been married about five years at that time, and Anna adored Brynn. Even though Anna no longer lived at home, Brynn was like the little sister Anna always wanted. I think Anna was easier for Brynn to bond with at first. It took her awhile to warm up to Anna's parents."

"That's understandable. So her childhood pretty much sucked?"

Jim snorted. "What childhood? Brynn was the adult in her real family. Her mom was like a spoiled little kid, and both parents were alcoholics. Anna says Brynn told her she was packing her lunch and getting herself to school in the morning as far back as she can remember, because her mom was always still sleeping off her drunk. Brynn would ask the neighbors for bread to make sandwiches for her lunch or she'd ask if she could pick apples from their tree. Some weeks she lived off what she scavenged from the next-door neighbor's garden. Do you think the neighbors knew that girl wasn't getting fed?"

"No other relatives she could've gone to?" Alex asked slowly. He was feeling sick to his stomach. He'd lost his parents in his midtwenties, but before they'd died there'd been lots of happy times.

"None. No one wanted a thirteen-year-old. I don't know if any of them tried to get to know her. They probably worried that she was a rebellious, out-of-control kid. But they were so wrong. She was the adult in that family. She paid the bills and went to the grocery store on her bike. They never bothered to take her to get her driver's license. Her foster parents did that. They told me she was a perfect driver from day one."

"She probably wasn't using just her bike to go grocery shopping," Alex said dryly. His brain was trying to absorb Jim's story.

His mental hard drive was struggling to process all the data. How could someone do that to their kid?

"She had perfect grades in high school. Valedictorian. Full ride to college. Could have picked any school, but wanted to stay in Oregon and do nursing. Said she didn't want to be too far from Anna's parents. By the end of high school, she was a true member of that family. Anna has three brothers and one sister, all older. They gave Brynn the big family she'd always wanted.

"But Brynn's got a pretty bad track record when it comes to men. I think her upbringing gave her a slightly distorted view of marriage. Most men she dates have walked all over her, and they've all been older than her. She seems to lean toward older men." Jim looked at him sideways.

A touch of relief went through his head. Maybe he wasn't too old in her eyes. But he didn't want to be a father figure. Alex scowled.

"Liam is closer to her age and treats her like a queen."

"I don't see a ring on her finger."

"Liam says it's just a matter of time. They're already talking about getting pregnant."

"She might be pregnant?" Alex's toe caught in the snow and he tripped again, barely catching his balance.

"She says she's not."

"Jesus, you asked her? You outright asked her if she's pregnant? When?"

Jim looked uncomfortable. "Day before yesterday. I wasn't going to let her come on this mission if she was pregnant."

Alex studied his face. "I bet that conversation went well."

"I think she was about to skin me. I'm glad she doesn't carry a gun."

They were walking just inside the tree line, moving quietly from tree to tree as they talked. Jim cut off the conversation as they drew within a hundred feet of the cockpit. Alex continuously scanned the area, seeking any movement. He didn't like the constant prickle in his spine. He couldn't see a reason for it. The avalanche had slammed the cockpit against a bank of firs and covered two-thirds of the metal. Alex couldn't make out where Jim and Thomas had dug their way in yesterday. The men had hoped to find some extra supplies. Flashlights or tarps or even something to eat, but they found nothing.

Had someone beaten them to it?

The snow turned everything an innocent white. But tension hung in the air around the cockpit. Maybe it was simply from knowing there were two dead men still sitting in their seats and a third laid out on the floor. They'd argued about putting the men in better positions. Courtesy to the remains of a fellow human. But the pilot's legs were horribly mangled in with the wreckage. Getting him loose would have been a messy chore. They'd reluctantly decided to leave them as they were.

Jim motioned Alex behind him and took the lead as they neared the plane. Alex wanted to argue, but he let him lead. He was part of Jim's team, and Jim had impressed him several times with his leadership skills. And Jim was a cop. Not unemployed, *former* law enforcement like Alex.

The path Jim and Thomas had made yesterday was gone, buried in the fresh snow. Alex strained his eyes trying to see a new path made by different feet that had entered or left the plane. Blue shadows were everywhere in the snow, making him see footprints where there were none. His breathing seemed too loud in the quiet Christmas card setting; inside his head he sounded like a train struggling to make it up a long, steep hill.

Jim looked over his shoulder. Alex nodded and stepped to cover Jim as he turned the corner and pointed his gun into the open back of the cockpit. Every fiber of Alex's being strained to hear. The inside of the cockpit was silent. Jim motioned him in. The two men studied the interior. Linus was still stretched out on the floor where Jim and Thomas had placed him yesterday after he'd been tossed out by the avalanche.

"Has anything been moved?" Alex asked.

Jim continued to examine the inside, his gaze constantly moving and sweeping. "I can't tell. The wind's blown some snow in. But I would think there would be more. You know how windy it got last night."

Alex nodded. Three-quarters of the ripped entry to the cockpit was blocked by a bank of snow. It had been totally blocked until Jim and Thomas dug it out. His neck prickled again and he swung around, his gaze tracking the tree line.

Nothing.

"Fuck this. There's no one here. There wasn't anyone here last night. If Besand was on that plane—" Jim started to say.

"He *was* on it. He took Linus's gun."

"Well he's gone now. He left before we got here yesterday. And unless he found a tent or tarp to sleep in overnight, we're going to stumble across a human Popsicle on our way out. More likely a hunter or hiker will find him this summer." Jim kicked at the snow. "Let's get back and get packed. We need to head out too."

"You think Ryan is ready?"

Jim frowned. "He seemed better last night. I'll see how he feels this morning." A myriad of emotions flickered on Jim's face. Concern, determination, and exhaustion. "One more thing."

"Yeah?"

"Brynn still believes you're a marshal."

Alex didn't say anything.

"She might suspect something though. I nearly told her."

"I'll tell her." Alex had never felt the loss of his job so keenly as at this exact moment. He had nothing but an inner burn to stand face-to-face with his brother's killer.

When that was accomplished he'd start his life over. Concentrate on his computer game development. It had always been a hobby. An excellent-paying hobby. He had no worries about retirement, and he'd always enjoyed it better than the security programs he wrote. Could he stick to it as a career?

Most definitely. He stood straighter.

His life wasn't completely about Darrin Besand. Not quite.

But Besand had been his primary focus for two years. Especially the last year. That couldn't be healthy, so much negativity flowing through his brain and heart. He'd spent the last year getting as close as possible to the scumbag. Visiting him in prison and following him to different states as he stood trial for his crimes. They'd developed a sort of sick repartee. Alex had nearly begged for any crumbs of information Darrin would drop about his crimes that Alex could pass along to detectives. Darrin had always gloated, feeding off Alex's pain.

Darrin had revealed the hiding places of two female bodies in Arizona during one particularly upsetting exchange. For those women Alex had traded stories of his wife's dislike of Samuel, ripping open fresh emotional wounds to bleed all over the prison floor. But Alex's suffering was worth it. If he could alleviate the pain of other families then he'd gladly sacrifice some time being mentally poked at by a killer. It was almost as if he was seeking absolution for not listening to Samuel, for not letting him live in his home. Yes, he was experiencing mental and emotional pain through the process, but helping solve Darrin's other crimes made it worth it.

But each session's aftermath was hard.

Alex had to shower for extended periods of time after being in the same room with the killer. Or swim in his hotel's pool. Lots of chlorine seemed to destroy the stench of Darrin's ego. But nothing had completely helped with the cling of despair that swamped Alex after those meetings.

"Christ. It's not the end of the world." Jim was staring at him, studying his face.

Alex jerked. "My mind's somewhere else."

Alex met Jim's gaze, but there was no pity, only strength.

"Besand's last assumed victim was a male. I remember it. I also remember the vic's brother was instrumental in getting Besand arrested. Something about DNA evidence even though it didn't link Besand to that last murder. You were all over the news for a while. No wonder Sheriff Collins thought you looked familiar when you first met."

"It was nothing." Alex looked away.

"You probably stopped Besand from killing a lot of other people."

I didn't stop him soon enough. His gut wrenched as looked back to Jim, silently transmitting those words.

"I'm sorry about your brother, Alex."

Now pity did flash in Jim's eyes. Alex turned away from him and started back up the hill. He said over his shoulder, "Don't worry. I'll tell Brynn the truth."

"Hang on. I want to get these guys' IDs. There's a chance we might not be back."

Jim ducked back into the cockpit while Alex waited. He could help Jim get the pilots' drivers' licenses, but he really didn't want to go back in there. Breathing was difficult. The cockpit was so tiny and those bodies…

"Alex! Come look at this!"

Jim sounded like he'd been punched in the stomach. Alex's teeth ground as he whirled around and took two leaping steps back to the cockpit.

He knew it would be bad.

Paul Whittenhall's mood was black.

The damn rescue team was unreachable. He hadn't heard a word from his own two-man team, and Regan Simmons had spent the night with the cameraman from CNN.

Paul had been awake most of the night expecting her to call or knock on his door, and she hadn't done either. After the dirty looks he'd shot her at yesterday's press conference because of her comments about Darrin Besand on the plane, what'd he expect? If looks could kill, she'd be slaughtered. And he thought she'd return to his bed?

How stupid was he?

Two new deputy marshals were manning the outpost from Antarctica with him. He didn't know either very well. They were new to Oregon and not men he considered part of his inner circle. He gave them strict instructions not to talk to anyone, especially media, and left them alone. They'd spent most of the time in one of the federal SUVs. They'd tried to hide their DVD player, but Paul had seen it and knew they were watching one of the *Die Hard* movies.

He glanced at the black Suburban. One of the men threw his head back and laughed at something on-screen. Paul wanted to strangle him out of sheer boredom and stress. But there was nothing else for the men to do. Why not watch a movie?

Paul stomped around the vehicles. He'd made a path over the last few hours and continued to stomp down the fresh snow as it fell. Every few laps he'd stop and brush the snow off his own Suburban. And a few other cars. He had too much restless energy. If he were a decade younger and knew the slightest bit about winter survival he would've gone in after Kinton. He had too much to lose if Kinton and Besand crossed paths now.

Besand had to be dead.

"Whittenhall!"

Paul turned at the voice of the sheriff.

Sheriff Collins looked tired. The skin around his eyes was tight, like it was tired of holding open the lids. His mouth was pressed closed so firmly his lips were nearly hidden.

"Sheriff?"

Collins glanced over Paul's shoulder at the Suburban with the two agents inside. "They watching anything good?"

Paul shrugged. "*Die Hard.*"

Collins relaxed slightly. "I wouldn't mind a little John McClane right now. Anything to get my mind off this shit."

Paul nodded. The sheriff wanted to make small talk? He didn't believe it for a second.

"I've just heard about that chopper that flew overhead yesterday. Remember?"

Paul's spine tightened, and he nodded again.

"Was a pair of local boys. Both pilots. One's from the air force rescue squadron up north. His brother flew the two of them out to look for that downed plane."

Paul grew hot in the icy air. "Air force? You knew about that?"

"I know who Liam and his brother, Tyrone, are. We've used them before in rescues. I didn't know that was them in that bird yesterday." Collins's eyes darted to the left and Paul knew he was lying. The sheriff had known exactly who'd flown overhead and why. "The rescue squadron didn't sanction that flight. It was just two boys trying to help out on their own."

"They find anything?"

Paul hadn't thought it was possible, but Collins grew more grim. "They haven't been heard from. They were supposed to return yesterday. No one can raise them.".

Paul stared. "So now you've got two aircraft down in those woods."

Collins met the stare. "Yes, I do."

"Any more aircraft going up today?" He deliberately drew out the words.

Collins shook his head. "Not in this weather. I don't know what got into their heads to try to fly yesterday." His eyes went to the left again and Paul wondered what he was holding back.

"Press know this?"

"No." Collins looked like a beaten dog.

"Gonna mention it in your next conference?"

Collins winced. "Don't know. Their families need to be told first. And those boys weren't part of this process. They were acting on their own."

"Looks like you've got another rescue to organize."

Anger flashed in the sheriff's eyes. "I don't know that they went down for sure. I've got people on the phone trying to find them. They might be holed up in a hotel with a couple of pretty women, waiting out the storm."

Paul almost missed the flicker of skepticism in the sheriff's eyes. Collins was a lousy liar. That could be a good trait or a bad trait in a cop.

In Paul's opinion it was usually bad.

"Let me know what you hear."

"Will do." Collins marched back to his RV.

Paul knew he was lying again. The sheriff wouldn't tell him any information until it was absolutely necessary. He watched the retreating back of Collins's parka, the big Madison County Search and Rescue name and logo clearly visible through the snowfall. Collins hadn't mentioned Darrin Besand or either of the search groups. Everything was in a holding pattern. Until the damned snow and wind let up, no one was finding anything. He rubbed at his frozen nose, thinking of Kinton spending the night in the woods. He hoped he froze his balls off. Paul was still trying to accept the fact that Kinton had attached himself to the search group.

Kinton couldn't have guessed his connection to Darrin. There was no way.

So why the fuck had he gone to such lengths?

Paul grabbed the broom he'd leaned against his truck and swept vigorously at his hood. Powdery snow flew. Kinton was out to get him. He could feel it. He'd heard the rumors. Kinton asking questions. Kinton nosing around, asking about Darrin and his transport coverage. If Darrin had left Kinton's brother alone, they'd never be in this mess. Kinton wouldn't have looked twice at Darrin, but Darrin killed the relative of the one guy who had the tenacity of a hungry dog staring at the last bone in the world.

Damn it.

This transport was supposed to have been Darrin's last flight. But not in a plane crash sort of last flight. It was a last flight to get

Darrin off his back, give him what he needed to walk away and stay out of Paul's life. If Darrin hadn't survived, that was OK. It solved the problem. If Darrin had survived and crossed paths with Kinton...

Paul had warned Darrin, several times, to cool it. He'd known what Darrin was doing. He'd known his tastes and habits. He'd read about the cases in the paper, talked to the detectives. To Paul it was like Darrin had signed his name to his victims.

But Darrin had gotten away with it for so long.

And Darrin knew that he knew.

Paul hadn't needed a reminder to keep his mouth shut.

He valued his wife and his expensive home. He valued his way of life.

Darrin could destroy it all with one sentence.

Alex Kinton could be the person to pull that sentence out of Darrin.

How had he missed *that*?

Alex and Jim hadn't been looking up as they checked the men in the cockpit. And they especially hadn't been looking at the ceiling, but both men stared at it now.

"Could the pilots reach..."

"There's no way." Jim's voice was flat.

Alex already knew that. "Yesterday, did you look—"

"I can't remember. I've been racking my brain since I saw it. I don't know if I looked up there yesterday or not."

"It's gotta be new." Alex reached out to touch the blood on the ceiling. Dry. But dry from twenty-four hours ago or last night? Or this morning?

His hand shook as he slowly lowered his arm.

"He didn't finish writing his words. Maybe we scared him off before he finished."

"It's finished," Alex whispered. He couldn't swallow. His throat was completely dry. But his heartbeat rivaled a rock band.

"'A man'…that part doesn't look finished. What was he going to write after 'A man'?"

"A-man is me."

Jim pulled his startled gaze from the bloody writing on the ceiling. "You?"

"That's what he called me. 'A-man.' *A* is for Alex."

"You had fucking nicknames for each other?" Jim sounded ready to puke.

Alex shot him a level look. "I didn't call him anything but murderer."

"Did he ever say the other part of this sentence?"

Alex read it again. He didn't need to. The second he saw it, he knew exactly what it meant and who it was for. "That's how he referred to his victims. The younger ones, anyway. The nurses. He was particular about their looks. Took pride in his selection."

He watched Jim's Adam's apple bob. His hands were in tight fists, and Alex didn't blame him one bit. Alex was feeling like he'd been sucker punched in the head. Several times.

"He's seen you up here. He wrote this for you. About Brynn. But he can't know that she's a nurse. How could he?"

Alex shook his head. "He doesn't know. He just knows she's beautiful. That's enough for him."

"We've got to get out of here." Jim spoke through clenched teeth, but Alex could hear his panic.

Alex nodded. He didn't know if Jim meant the cockpit or the forest. It didn't matter; they just had to move. The men checked their weapons and turned to leave, but Alex couldn't stop himself from taking one last look at the writing on the ceiling.

Beautiful girl, A-man.

His hand tightened around his gun.

CHAPTER FOURTEEN

She hadn't seen Alex that morning. He and Jim had snuck away before anyone else woke. But when she'd stepped outside to look for the men, she'd seen two sets of footprints heading down toward the cockpit. Together. It didn't surprise her one bit. They were a paranoid pair. How many times had she caught Alex studying the terrain around them? And she'd known he wasn't admiring the trees. He had a haunted look, make that a *hunted* look about him. He might be after someone, but he acted like he was being followed.

She touched Ryan's forehead and flinched. He was hot. When he woke up, she'd see if he could keep down some ibuprofen. It wasn't the fastest for bringing down fevers, but it was all she had. Hopefully, his stomach had settled. She'd watched him carefully last night. He'd only nibbled at the bar she gave him.

Thomas had been awake when she stepped back in the plane. He'd nodded to her and vanished out the door, surprisingly with Kiana at his heels. Usually the dog kept some distance from Thomas. She glanced at her watch. Those two had been gone about five minutes.

She sighed.

They needed to head out today. She wished they had a more accurate idea of how far off the railroad trestle was. She didn't know if Ryan could go. And the plane was so comfortable compared to the tents. *Tent*, she corrected. All five of them and Kiana would be in one tent if they had to camp another night. Not good.

Maybe some of them should stay behind.

She bit her lip. Jim would hate to split the team. But with Ryan ill, they might have no choice. She'd stay behind with Ryan. Wait for a helicopter or better weather for him to hike out. Jim and Thomas moving together could travel fast and tell Collins exactly where to find them. And Alex...

She didn't know what she wanted Alex to do. He was probably strong enough to move out with Thomas and Jim. But it'd be nice to have one more person if she needed help with Ryan. Plus he was armed. She shivered. Ever since Alex had said Besand's name, she just hadn't felt secure.

Alex made her feel safe.

More than Ryan or Jim or Thomas and all their guns. She stared at Ryan awkwardly sleeping upright in the seat. She'd known him for years and Jim for even longer. Why did a deputy marshal that she'd known for two days rate higher than her friends?

She cleared her thoughts, uncomfortable with their direction.

Ryan was going to have a stiff neck when he woke. It was tight, uncomfortable quarters for everybody. No one could stand up straight in the tiny plane.

Jim had stretched his legs as he and Brynn sat in the comfy chairs and talked while everyone drifted off last night. Alex had fallen asleep in the cargo area. He'd said he couldn't sleep in a chair.

"I'm so tired I can't see straight," Jim had muttered.

"It's been a hell of a day. We all need some rest." She'd glanced at Ryan.

"How's he doing?"

"We'll see in the morning."

"Think he'll be up to hiking out?"

Brynn had shrugged.

"You feeling OK?" His tone was too light.

She'd narrowed her eyes at him. "I'm worn out like everyone else. I already told you I'm not pregnant." He'd looked down at his hands.

"Besides…"

He'd waited. "Besides what?"

"It's nothing," she'd mumbled, wishing she'd kept her mouth shut.

"What is it? What's going on with Liam?" Jim knew her too well.

"It's over."

"You guys are over? You broke up?" He'd looked horrified. Jim had always thought Liam was the best guy she'd ever dated. Jim had always been on the lookout for someone he thought could "take care of her." Of course, looking over her dating history, Liam did look pretty good. But that didn't mean she had to settle.

"He's been living with Tyrone for over a month."

"What? I had no idea. Does Anna know about this?"

Brynn had shaken her head. "We haven't told anyone yet. He keeps saying we can work things out. But I know it's over. We just don't want the same things."

"He's crazy about you, Brynn. He'd do anything for you."

She'd turned to him earnestly. "That's what I mean. He absolutely smothers me. I had to sneak out for this job because we'd had a fight about my volunteer rescue work. He didn't want me going on any more missions."

"He's worried for your safety. After last time—"

"That could've happened to anyone. You know me, Jim. You know I can't walk away from this kind of work. It's a part of me. I have to do this stuff. To ask me—let me correct that—to *tell* me I can't go on any more missions simply shows me how much he doesn't know about me. How could you tell someone you love and respect that they're not allowed to do what they love?"

Jim had blinked hard and started to speak several times, but he'd finally given up. He'd slumped in his seat. "You're right. I just didn't want to see it. Even Anna thought he was too controlling for you. But some women like that."

She'd raised a brow and wrinkled her nose. "Do you honestly see me as one of those women?"

"Hell, no. But I saw how worried Anna was when you got hurt last year. I guess I'd hoped Liam could protect you better."

"Liam needs a little woman at home to greet him with a freshly baked apple pie as he comes in the door."

Jim had grinned. "He would love that, wouldn't he? But God, he'll be bored to death. As much as he hates your risk taking, I think it was part of what attracted him to you in the first place. You guys are a lot alike in that manner."

"He wants to get married," Brynn had whispered, her eyes staring into the night.

"Can you blame him? You two have been together for a while now."

"You know I can't."

"Not with him," Jim had stated quietly. "Don't completely write off marriage simply because of what you saw with your parents, Brynn. I never dreamed I'd be the type to settle down, but I thank God for dropping Anna in my path. It just takes the right person to spin your brain around. Then you find yourself doing things you never dreamed possible." He'd shaken his head. "I never thought I'd buy a minivan. But damn it, with two kids that thing is awesome."

"Yeah, but you haven't given up your Mustang."

"I'm saving it for Chris when he gets older."

Brynn had studied him. Jim had a wistful smile on his face, like he was imagining handing over the Mustang's keys to a teenage son. He hadn't looked horrified to be letting go of his most precious possession.

She and Jim had both had trouble keeping their eyes open and decided to lie down in the cargo area. She'd lain awake for a long time, thinking about Liam and about Alex.

Now inside the plane, Brynn suddenly heard Jim and Alex coming back. She could hear panting and running footsteps in the snow. Were they running a race? Uphill in the snow?

Alex shouldn't be running. He'd had a terrible shock to his system. The huffing from the race outside grew louder, and

Brynn jumped at the force with which Jim yanked open the cargo door.

"Get packed up. We're getting out of here." He wildly scanned the plane and spun to look outside. "Where's Thomas?"

Her heart pounded. The determination on Jim's face had a shadow of...fear. Fear? From Jim? Alex appeared beside him; relief flashed on his face as he spotted her. He bent over and rested his hands on his thighs as he panted, his eyes never leaving her. She felt her cheeks pale.

"What's wrong? What happened?" Her hands clutched the back of a seat, her nails digging into the fabric.

"Where's Thomas?" Jim shouted the question.

"Out there!" She gestured at the woods. "He's been gone for a few minutes. Now what in the hell is going on?"

The two men exchanged a glance she didn't like. Not one bit.

"Tell me! What happened?" Her breathing sped up.

Alex licked at his lips and exchanged one more look with Jim. She wanted to slap them both.

"Besand's here somewhere. We need to move out."

"Here? Where? How do you know?"

"We think he spent the night in the cockpit."

"Did you see him?"

Jim shook his head. He wouldn't look her in the eye. Something was dreadfully wrong.

"What made you think he was there?"

Jim bent over and tossed her gloves at her. "Get packed. I want to get out of here."

She caught the gloves and hurled them back at his face. He batted them away. "Answer my question, Jim. I'm not packing up one thing until you tell me what's going on." She was nearly yelling, and Ryan stirred.

"What's going on?" Ryan awkwardly slouched forward in his chair and Brynn stepped over to support his shoulders. "Fuck," he said.

"You look like shit." Jim stated.

"Thanks. I feel that way too." He exhaled roughly and leaned into Brynn's support. "Dizzy."

Jim spun around and stomped out of the plane. Brynn realized he'd been holding his handgun where she couldn't see it as they talked. She shot a questioning gaze to Alex. He had his gun ready too.

"Can he walk out of here?" Alex nodded at Ryan, ignoring the question in her eyes.

"I can hear you, man. Ask me." Ryan was hoarse; his eyes closed halfway as he leaned on Brynn. She touched his forehead. Hot and dry. She gave Alex a small shake of her head.

"I saw that, Brynn. Let me decide what I can and can't do," the sick man muttered. He sat up again and leaned one arm on his thigh. His eyes met hers and she tried not to wince at the effort he put forth.

Ryan was very sick.

"You're burning up with a fever. How's your stomach?"

"Stomach's good. Throat's killer, and my skin hurts everywhere."

Flu? Could he possibly have just a flu bug? His symptoms could be viral. He'd simply started with a nasty stomach virus that ripped him up and probably exasperated a new ulcer. She hoped.

Ryan sat up farther and tried to stand. He sprawled back in the seat, and Brynn helped him sit straight. "I'm not walking today. Ask me tomorrow."

"Where's your weapon?"

Ryan reached down between the seat and fuselage and lifted out his Glock.

Alex looked at Brynn. "You know how to use that?" She nodded. "Give it to her. Keep it on you at all times and keep an eye outside. We'll identify ourselves before we come in. Shoot first. Ask questions later. We're gonna find Thomas." He held her eye contact until she nodded again. He ducked and vanished out the door.

Brynn stared after him, her heart in her throat and an icy cold gun in her numb hand. Shoot first? Could she do that?

A grin split his face as Darrin watched the two men race up the slope. Yep. They'd found his message.

How long had it taken Alex to understand it?

One second? Two?

This felt good. He'd scored a point against the other team and had set the bar. Now to see what their response would be. Would they run out of the woods with their tails between their legs? Or hunt him down?

He shivered, his smile steady.

Alex would never stand idle after the threat he'd made about the woman. It wasn't really a threat. Darrin had simply made an observation, but Alex would see it as a threat. Darrin had always been particular about the nurses he chose. He'd looked for different things when he decided to put patients out of their misery, but for the nurses they had to be beautiful. They had to have that special internal glow that radiated. He'd needed to feel the power that came from destroying that beauty. Even as she'd fought against the hands around her neck that special element shone in her eyes.

234 • KENDRA ELLIOT

It'd made him want to smash it, annihilate it, and then drink it in.

The rush...

He exhaled heavily.

Would they come after him? He fingered the gun in his pocket. It was awkward, bulky, and didn't feel comfortable in his hands. He could use it if he had to, but he'd shot a handgun only twice in his life. It was doubtful his aim would be any good. Maybe he shouldn't have challenged them. He swore under his breath. There were four men. And they were probably all armed.

Suddenly his message on the ceiling of the cockpit didn't seem too smart.

Why had he confronted Alex that way? He should have just let him leave and then followed.

Darrin screwed his eyes shut. He hadn't been able to stop himself. It was like one of their sessions where he'd thrown Kinton scraps of information and watched him grovel for more. He'd loved the power he held over Alex Kinton during those times. Like the session where he'd started talking about Olivia Short. The police hadn't located her body by the time he'd been arrested. Darrin had been grilled by some sharp detectives but hadn't revealed her whereabouts. It'd been one of the factors that he'd used to negotiate his visits with Alex. He'd offered to possibly reveal the resting places of the three women still missing, but only to Alex Kinton. The three women the police knew about, anyway.

Darrin leaned against a tree and sighed.

Alex had still been with the marshals' office at that point of their relationship. At their session, Alex had looked like he hadn't slept in a week. And most surprising, he'd pulled a pack of cigarettes out of his coat pocket that he proceded to chain-smoke through the session.

At first Alex had just sat in the cold little room, his eyes on the table as he fingered his cigarette. It'd been one of those typical interview rooms. A bland box. No windows. Scavenged furniture. A camera in the upper corner. Darrin's demands had been for the camera to be turned off during their sessions. Alex had agreed. The only witness had been a cop who stood directly outside the door and occasionally peeked through the skinny rectangle window. And the cop couldn't hear a thing.

Alex's technique with the cigarettes had been awkward, and Darrin knew the habit was recently formed. His chest had swelled with pleasure. He'd caused that habit.

"What'd you do this week?"

Alex hadn't met his eyes as he flicked ash into an ashtray. "Nothing." He'd sat casually in his hard chair. He'd dressed neatly in jeans and a jacket, but there was a feral look about his eyes that spoke of restless nights.

Darrin had frowned and tried again. "Did you watch *American Idol*?"

Alex had snorted, one side of his mouth lifting. "Fuck, no."

"You should. There are some very talented kids on that show. Some can really sing. Beautiful girls too."

Alex's gaze had flown to meet his.

Gotcha.

"I like the girl from the Philippines. She's got an amazing range."

Alex had inhaled heavily on his cigarette, gaze still locked with Darrin's.

Darrin's heart had slowed. It was like meth rushing through his system, and he'd wanted to stretch out the effects. He'd breathe shallowly and let the high seep through his body. If he kept calm, the buzz would linger.

"It was county music night. I hate country music, but she managed to transcend the twanginess. Truly a great performance by a beautiful girl. She reminded me of Olivia."

Alex's lashes had twitched ever so slightly, but Darrin had been watching closely and spotted it. "Olivia?" Alex's voice had been purposefully casual. Darrin had inhaled and tasted the curiosity that permeated the air between them.

Darrin had swallowed and smiled. "Oh, yes. Olivia. She was from Hawaii or something originally, right? Long black hair, dark eyes, wide smile. Gorgeous."

The room temperature had perked, but Alex hadn't moved. He had charged the air in the room without moving a muscle. Darrin had casually moved his gaze to the small window where he could see the back of the guard's head.

He'd let Alex sweat a little. He'd known better than to ask Darrin any direct questions. He'd known he'd have to wait until Darrin was ready to talk about Olivia. When Darrin had told him of Megan's resting place, he'd drawn the facts out over three sessions.

He'd looked back at Alex. Alex had been acting casual, focusing on a blank spot on the wall, but the fingers holding the cigarette had quivered for a split second. Lovely.

Darrin had rested his chin on one hand and thrummed his fingers on the table. It was an art. If he gave too little, Alex would simply leave. If he gave too much, it would be over too soon. It was a delicate balance to keep Alex sitting across from him. One time he'd said too little and Alex hadn't come back for several months.

Darrin had nearly cried with relief when he did return. And had nearly dumped out every hidden body location on the table between them. Control. He'd had to exercise control. He'd spend hours thinking about how best to string Alex along. What words and phrases he needed to use to push those emotional buttons.

"Looks like I've got your attention now, A-man."

Anger had flashed in Alex's eyes as he avoided Darrin's gaze. He'd crossed an ankle over his knee. "Don't call me that," he'd muttered.

They'd both known Alex had just made a mistake.

One of the unwritten rules of this game had been that Alex didn't lose his temper or verbally react when Darrin prodded him. Darrin had licked his finger and made a score mark in the air.

Alex had shot out of his chair and slapped one hand on the handle of the door as he pounded for the guard to let him out.

Darrin had jumped to his feet. He'd fucked up.

"Alex. Don't…Fuck! I didn't…I'll tell you where Olivia is." Darrin had breathed hard. Alex had been one step away from leaving the room, and Darrin knew he wouldn't come back again for months.

Alex had spun around and nailed him with a direct stare. "Now. Say it now or I'm out of here."

Darrin's throat had tightened and he'd scratched at his neck. "Well—"

"Say it now!"

He'd swallowed. "I'm not really sure—"

"Fuck this. I'm out of here." Alex had turned back to the door and pounded again.

"She's in Forest Park. About twenty feet off one of the bike trails!" Darrin had screeched. Then he'd pressed his lips closed.

The guard had finally opened the door, one hand on his gun as he'd stared in surprise at the two men.

"Get me a map of Forest Park. Now," Alex had snapped at the confused man. He'd turned back to Darrin. "You are going to show me exactly where. The first sign of shitting around or screwing with my head and I'm out of here."

"Yes," Darrin had whispered as he sat. His spine had slumped. He'd lost the battle.

The snowfall started up again. Darrin raised the binoculars to his eyes and rolled his injured shoulder, pleased with the low level of pain. And his head felt a million times better too. The body of the plane looked silent, and he wondered what was going on inside. Were the two men blabbing his written message to the others? Pride expanded his chest. He lowered the glasses, blew out a satisfied breath, and turned to go back to his excellent hiding place. He had to be ready when they decided to leave.

Alex scanned for footprints outside the plane. Thomas's big tracks led upward and to the woods, with paw prints close by. Jim's messier jogging prints followed. Alex started after them. His mind wouldn't slow down.

Beautiful girl. Beautiful girl.

How many times had he heard Besand use those words? The most disgusting, dreamlike happiness would cover Besand's face as he uttered the words. Like he was remembering squeezing the life out of them. Desecrating the beauty.

A profiler had told him Besand had the need to destroy beauty. The profiler couldn't tell him why but had theorized it had something to do with the women in his life from when he was younger. Perhaps someone physically beautiful had emotionally scarred him somehow. Alex had dumped the theory with a laugh. What guy hadn't been shot down by a gorgeous woman? With that logic the world would be crawling with serial killers.

The profiler had shaken her head at him. It wasn't the act itself, she'd explained, it was the act in conjunction with the killer's psychopathic thinking.

Alex made no excuses for Besand. Besand simply liked to kill.

And he had Brynn in his sights.

Alex jogged through the snow. He could hear voices far ahead. Jim must have caught up with Thomas. They were tough men. The three of them should be able to hold off one injured serial killer. Alex pursed his lips. Besand had a gun, but Alex knew he didn't have much history handling weapons. That was a big strike against him. Three against one. Four if you counted Brynn, which he did. She was incredibly tough. Too bad Ryan was on his ass. He was a scrappy kid.

They should have no problem overpowering Besand.

Then why was his skin crawling?

Besand had a good hiding place and was obviously well enough to move back and forth to the cockpit. If he'd been a halfway decent shot he could take them out one at a time like a sniper.

He glanced back and measured the distance from the body of the plane to the closest big trees. Darrin would have to be an excellent shot. And Alex knew he wasn't.

Kiana barked in the distance.

"Jim!" he called out the name before he could see the men. He didn't want the cop drawing on him as he came on them in the woods. They were all a little trigger-happy at the thought of Besand creeping through the trees.

The two men were watching for him, Kiana beside Jim's feet.

"Ryan isn't going anywhere," Alex said. "He can't even stand up. His fever's pretty high."

"Shit. We were just talking about what to do if that was the case." Jim twisted his lips.

"Brynn has Ryan's gun. Announce yourself before you enter the plane."

"Crap. She won't use that thing. She hates guns."

"She said she knows how to use it."

"She does. I taught her. I wouldn't let her on any of my hasty teams without knowing how to shoot first, but she refuses to carry one."

"What now?" Alex calmly asked the question even though his nerves were spiking like he'd been shocked.

Jim and Thomas looked at each other. "Someone needs to hike out," Jim said. "Tell people where we are. I just tried calling Collins. There's no coverage at the moment. I don't know how long this storm is going to last. Whoever hikes out can't go alone though. And obviously Ryan shouldn't be left alone."

"Something tells me he'll see that differently," Thomas muttered.

"Brynn won't leave him. I know her. She's in full nurse mode and won't let him move." Jim gnawed on his lip. "I think the three of us should head out. We can move fast."

Alex pictured himself trying to keep up with the two mountain men.

Jim frowned. "Unless you're not feeling up to it. You had quite a shock yesterday. And I've seen you favoring your knee. Did that happen in the avalanche?"

"No, but it didn't help it. Old injury."

"Can you hike out?"

Alex paused, and Jim didn't let him answer.

"You wouldn't have to stop to think about it if you could. You're staying here."

"I'm good with that. I think one of us should stay."

"Good. It's settled." Jim made a definitive motion with his hand.

He hadn't wanted to leave Brynn. That's what had made Alex pause. He couldn't leave her alone with a serial killer wandering the woods. Especially now that Besand had seen her. She might as well have a big target on her back.

"I'll feel better knowing you're here with her and Ryan anyway. Thomas and I should be able to hike out in under twenty-four hours if we push it. We'll get more supplies and come back on foot or by copter if the weather breaks," Jim stated.

Alex nodded.

Thomas scowled.

"What?" Jim asked.

"Don't like breaking up the team," he said evenly.

Jim exhaled and nodded. "Neither do I. But I don't see any other choice. We could all stay, but what's the point? We'll get help faster if we move out." He glanced at his watch. "As soon as possible." He shifted his attention to Alex. "Can you hold down the fort?"

He nodded. Jim held his gaze for a second longer than was necessary.

"Let's get going."

242 • KENDRA ELLIOT

Silently, eyes scanning, guns at the ready, the three men headed back to the plane. Kiana kept pace next to Alex.

"What happened to your leg?" Thomas asked.

Alex jumped at the sound of Thomas's voice. The man spoke so rarely. "Uh, gunshot wound."

"How long ago?" Apparently, Thomas was feeling chatty.

Alex counted in his head. "Four years or so."

"Judge Braeden?"

Alex nearly tripped. Jim turned from his position at point and raised an eyebrow at Thomas. "You talking about that murdered judge? I remember that." He frowned at Alex. "Were you there?"

Alex could only nod. *How had Thomas put it together?* He'd added one and one and come up with four. Accurately.

Jim stopped their trek and faced Alex. "Two marshals died in that courtroom. You were shot too?"

Alex met his gaze and nodded again.

Jim's brows came together. "The judge and the shooter died too. Wasn't the shooter the wife of some illegal drug importer on trial? She shot the judge and three marshals, but one of them managed to take her down with a shot." He eyed Alex. "You got her, didn't you?"

Alex looked straight ahead, avoiding Jim's penetrating eyes. "Never shot a woman before." And he hoped he never would again. He'd had horrific dreams and weekly counseling for months. Along with physical therapy for his leg. "Don't we need to get back to the plane?" Alex asked in an end-of-topic tone.

Jim was silent for a second and Alex watched the emotions war on his face. Jim was curious about the incident, but obviously didn't want to leave Brynn alone any longer than they had.

He mashed his lips together and spun around, setting a fast pace back to the plane.

Alex silently exhaled. He didn't need the Braeden case rehashed at this minute. His forehead throbbed, and he wished for an evening alone with some Vicodin.

The wind picked that moment to blast up the valley, and he burrowed his nose into the collar of his coat. Kiana bumped against his bad leg, nearly throwing him off balance. Thomas cursed as his hat blew off. He lunged and stomped on it, barely catching it by the brim.

The hike out of the Cascades was going to suck. Alex was glad he wasn't going anywhere for at least the next two days. It was going to be cold and cramped and there wouldn't be much to eat, but he'd have all the time in the world to get to know Brynn better.

And be watching for Besand over his shoulder.

Maybe the hike out would be better.

CHAPTER FIFTEEN

Liam Gentry huddled over his brother, warming him with his body heat. Since he'd piled enough snow up over the broken window to create an icy wall, the temperature inside the helicopter wasn't too bad. Didn't people pay big money to sleep in hotels made of ice? He'd seen that in a magazine somewhere.

Last night had been the worst night of his life. Tyrone had faded in and out of consciousness, sometimes talking to Liam like he was their dad. Other times mistaking Liam for an old army buddy. At least this morning Tyrone knew who Liam was. And he knew how dire their situation was.

They hadn't packed any food. The little chopper had held no basic supplies other than a flashlight, tarp, and lousy first aid kit.

A flare gun was stashed under one of the seats but was useless in this weather. Who'd see a flare?

Who'd be stupid enough to fly in this weather?

He'd be repeating that question the rest of his life. And there was a good chance the rest of his life wouldn't be that long.

He'd survived a helicopter crash. The first one of his career. And he didn't plan to ever be in another one. He hadn't been scared when the copter went down; he'd been angry. Angry at Brynn, himself, and his brother. None of them had exercised the brains God gave them to stay home out of this shitty weather. And now they all were paying for it.

If he ever got out of here...

He was saying "if" a lot.

If he saw Brynn again. If his brother didn't die on him. If he didn't die.

Too many ifs.

He moved closer to his brother. Tyrone's head injury was serious. The broken ribs didn't bother him if he didn't move too much, but Liam worried Tyrone would accidentally puncture a lung.

How Liam had managed to escape the wreck with only a sprained wrist was a miracle. Both brothers should be dead. Only the cushion from the tree branches and then the fall into a deep snowdrift saved their asses.

To die alone.

How many times overnight had he wished they'd both simply died in the wreck? So much faster. Instead of this long, drawn-out, slow death. No one was going to find them. They were working off the clock and had probably been off the radar when they went down. The tower at Springton was probably wondering why they hadn't returned, but whom would they contact? Even when someone did realize they were missing, they wouldn't know where to look.

He didn't have any more tears. He'd silently cried them dry in the night as he'd worried his brother would never wake up. If he ever got out of this mess he was going to stick a ring on Brynn's finger. He'd waited too long. He knew she had doubts about marriage, but after this experience she had to listen to him. She had to let him move back in. He knew she was what he wanted from life. And their kids. He wanted children with that woman, but now it might never happen.

He turned his head so his nose was buried in Tyrone's hair. His brother's breathing was rough, like a virus had been planted in his lungs and was starting to expand.

Aw, shit.

A pounding on the glass made Liam jolt, and Tyrone cried out at the movement against his ribs.

A single big silhouette was visible through the steamed glass, and Liam happily discovered he did have more tears to shed.

Help had arrived.

Brynn sympathized with her dog. Kiana lay in front of the door with her head on her paws, watching the three remaining humans closely. She'd whined as Jim and Thomas left to hike out, even following for a few feet before turning around to wait for her master to follow. Somehow the dog had known Jim was leaving for good. And she'd wanted to go with him, but she wouldn't leave Brynn.

Brynn felt the same way about Ryan.

More than anything she wanted to be hiking out of this hell with Jim and Thomas, but she couldn't leave Ryan. Was it a woman thing? Always left to wait for the man to return? Always the one volunteering to stay with the sick? Was it a gene?

She looked around the cramped plane. No one could stand up straight, and no one could have any privacy. Alex had laid down the law about any outside excursions. She wasn't even allowed to pee alone. A twinge of claustrophobia pricked at her neck. If they were lucky there would be two, maybe three more nights spent in this plane.

They'd buried the pilots and marshal before Jim and Thomas left.

She'd watched Alex's face as they lay the dead marshal in the hole. It had been carefully blank. She'd tried to get him to talk about the agent, but he'd shaken his head.

"Not now."

But would he talk later?

A strange stiffness had settled among the three left behind. She'd found a pack of cards in her backpack. An unnecessary luxury she'd nearly thrown out of her pack many times. She'd never been so thankful to see a useless stack of cards. They'd started with poker, betting with fir needles that Alex had reluctantly agreed to go grab. He'd had Brynn cover him from the cargo door with Ryan's gun as he dashed to the nearest tree. Their plane was like a cave. Every few hours Alex would step outside and make sure their cargo door wasn't pinned closed by a growing snowbank while Brynn covered him with a weapon.

"Do you think he's still here?"

She'd asked the question as they waited for Ryan to make his bet. Alex had told them of the message on the cockpit ceiling, but he hadn't been sure of when it was written, and neither Brynn nor Ryan could recall if they'd glanced at the ceiling when they were in the plane the previous day.

"It could be old," she'd stated.

"It could be fresh," Alex had countered. He hadn't looked her in the eye.

He'd creamed both of them at poker, and then Ryan had headed to the cargo area to stretch out and take a nap. Alex had leaned his head back in one of the big seats and partially closed his eyes. The silence had been heavy. He'd acted tired, but she noticed he kept one eye on the door at all times. Even while they had played. He'd watched Kiana too. When she'd start at a noise, Alex would leap, causing Ryan and Brynn to leap. Finally, Alex had relaxed somewhat, seeming to rely on the dog to give him an early warning if anyone approached.

Brynn had already figured that out. Kiana wasn't a watchdog, but she did have a tendency to perk up when someone approached. Brynn assumed she could hear through the wind. She touched Ryan's gun she'd tucked in her coat pocket. It was slightly assuring. Alex's hyperawareness was more assuring.

She'd tried to return the gun to Ryan. The ibuprofen had lowered his fever and he seemed halfway normal, but he professed to feeling extremely weak. He shook his head at the offer of the gun. "My reflexes are off, and all I want to do is sleep. It's better in your hands."

She'd seriously doubted that, but Alex had backed up Ryan.

Now she and Alex pretended to doze while Ryan snored. She glanced at her watch. Thomas and Jim had been gone for two hours. They'd agreed that when the weather cleared and it seemed fine for flying that one of the bright-blue tarps would be laid out in the snow for searchers to see from the air. Alex had checked the ELT and found it undamaged, so a signal was being put out, but someone had to be in line of sight to pick up the signal. Either in the air above them or up the mountain. Hopefully, the batteries had a strong charge.

As more snow fell, the wind became quieter and the cabin grew warmer. The makeshift wall at the ripped end of the cabin grew thicker as snow piled against it outside. Condensation dripped down the walls. Sort of like snow caving but with luxury seats and metal-framed walls and ceiling.

Brynn wanted to go stretch out in the back by Ryan. But something kept her sitting in the seats with Alex. A peaceful air had descended in the tiny cabin, an intimacy she didn't want to disturb. They sat facing the wall of snow, listening to Ryan snore. The tiny aisle between the two seats seemed to shrink. It could have been a quiet evening at home. The TV off, the dog drowsing at their feet.

"Why did you freeze going over the river?" Alex asked. "Ryan told me a bit, but I'd like to hear it from you."

His question fired the air around Brynn. Any sort of comfort vanished and tension rang in her ears. She turned toward him. His face was grave, a touch of reluctance in his eyes, but there was also concern. Suddenly she wanted to tell him. Wanted him to understand the terror that had racked her core as she stood over water.

"When I was eight, my best friend died crossing the small river near my home."

"You were there." It wasn't a question.

She closed her eyes and felt the sun from that hot day touch her face. "I was following her. It was my idea to cross the water. There was a log bridge similar to what we used the other day, but it had nothing to hang on to. I'd crossed it a hundred times. All the kids in the area used it. But usually the water wasn't anything more than a quiet creek. That day was the first sunny and warm day after several days of rain. There'd been a freak storm in the middle of summer, and we were itching to get out of the house. It'd been three days of pouring rain followed by one hot day of bliss.

"The footbridge was the fastest way back to Sarah's house. I still remember how high and fast the water was. Even though it'd stopped raining during the night, the river hadn't crested. It was still rising from the runoff and other little streams that fed into it."

Brynn's heart was strangely calm, but her chest felt tight, like it was forbidding her heart to speed up. The story was rolling off her tongue with an ease that surprised her. She kept her eyes shut, not wanting to see the expression on Alex's face. She hated pity.

"Sarah crossed first. The log was wet and slimy from the rain. There were many trees right at that spot that kept most of the sunlight off the bridge. It always grew moss that sometimes was helpful for traction during crossings, but that day it was terribly slick.

"I remember we were both barefoot and wore light sundresses with swimming suits underneath to celebrate the return of the sunshine. We were going to set up the Slip 'n Slide in her backyard. But she fell. At first I thought she was fooling around, pretending to be on a balance beam. Her left leg was high in the air and both her arms had flown up like a ballet dancer. Then she slipped. She clung to the log, but her hands couldn't get a grip. I rushed out and knelt on the log and managed to grab one of her hands, but it was slick with slime from grasping at the log."

Brynn paused. She could smell the ripe scent of the fast water and wet log and taste the blood where she'd bitten her tongue while grabbing her friend's hand. She could feel the little hand slip out of hers and hear both their screams. Her scream had lasted longer. Sarah's had been extinguished as her head dropped below the water.

"The water rushed her downriver. I saw her head bob up five times before the river turned. I crawled on all fours, and my knee slipped. I went over one side of the log, but my foot caught on a branch about two feet below the water's surface. It stopped me from going completely under. I balanced on that branch and clung to the slimy log. I couldn't pull myself back up. I hung on and watched as the water moved higher up my body. They say I was in the water for hours. It was so cold. I couldn't feel my feet or legs. The sun managed to break through the trees and shine on my head and back. It probably saved my life."

"Who found you?"

"The sheriff's department. Someone had pulled Sarah's body out of the river. She was immediately identified, because everyone knew everybody in our little town. When the sheriff notified her parents they asked about me. That's when the search started. The footbridge was the first place they checked. Her parents knew we used it to cross back and forth to each other's house even though we'd been told a million times not to. There was a regular bridge and road, but it was at least hundred yards farther downstream. We always went to the footbridge."

Sarah's father had destroyed the footbridge the following day. Brynn hadn't known until weeks after the accident when she'd found herself drawn back to see the place she'd lost her friend. She'd frozen in shock at the sight. Sawdust had still coated both banks where Sarah's father had attacked the log with his chainsaw. She'd cried at the sight, confused by her anger at the loss of

252 • KENDRA ELLIOT

a childhood adventure site and her happiness that someone had taken revenge on the log that killed her friend.

She still felt the bewildering war of emotions.

"Jesus Christ. I don't see how you managed to cross the other day."

"I almost didn't." Her lips smiled, but her eyes didn't. She turned to him, studying his reactions. He showed horror, pity, sadness, and...understanding?

"Do you swim?"

"Only if I have to. I made myself learn about five years ago. I hadn't been in water since that day. I was sick of making excuses not to swim with friends. I even missed birthday parties. One day I was watching a movie on TV about Hawaii and the water was so beautiful. So many shades of electric greens and blues. The movie was about female surfers, and they were so strong and determined. They loved the water. I realized that I'd never get to experience that amazing water if I didn't learn to swim. So I took lessons at the local pool."

"And you went to Hawaii?"

"Not yet." She looked at her hands in her lap. She couldn't bring herself to get on a plane and fly over that much water.

She felt his steely eyes study her face. "How do you feel about flying?" he asked.

Damn, he was perceptive. "Flying's great. Flying over water is a different matter."

He nodded. "I can understand that."

Brynn squirmed, hating his scrutiny. She'd ripped off a big scab, exposing raw and sensitive skin for his examination. She toyed with the deck of cards, nervously shuffling them. "Now you know my greatest fear, what's yours?"

He sat straighter in his seat, gaze guarded. She didn't feel any pity. If she could do it, then turnabout was fair play. It was like playing truth or dare in junior high. How much would Alex reveal?

He rubbed a hand over his mouth and then raked his hair with his fingers. She watched. His black hair was threaded with the smallest touches of gray at his temples. He wore it short, sort of spiky on top. Although three days of hats and hoods had flattened things considerably. A simple run of his hands had things back to normal. She wanted to touch the growth of hair on his cheeks. It was past the harsh stubble stage. It would be soft under her fingers.

Brynn suddenly felt self-conscious. Three days with no shower. Three days of hard exercise in the same clothes. She must stink. She was pretty sure her hair looked OK, because she'd kept it pulled back like always. She rarely wore much makeup because her eyes and eyelashes could hold their own.

"That's hard to say."

"Because you're not scared of anything?"

His eyes pinned her. "No. Because there are too many."

She blinked.

Not the masculine answer she'd expected.

"What are you afraid of?"

He ran his hand through his hair again. "I don't know where to start. But I guess I'm not afraid of dying. Not anymore. Been there, done that."

She studied his face. He was completely serious.

"I'm not afraid of things happening to me. I get more tense, nervous when I think of things happening to the people around me." He glanced over his shoulder toward Ryan. Brynn could see the sleeping man's boots sticking out from under one of the thin blankets. She brought her gaze back to Alex as he spoke. "I'm more afraid of what you and he will suffer if we're never found out here. I don't care about what happens to me."

A subtle look of shock crossed his face, and she realized the words had surprised him as much as her.

The words had stumbled out of Alex's mouth before he'd had time to consider them. But they were true. He didn't want his new friends to suffer. Especially from an incident he might have caused. He wasn't guiding Besand's hand, but the killer had definitely reacted to Alex's presence; therefore, he'd put his friends in danger.

"We're perfectly capable of hiking out of here when the weather clears. We don't have to wait for someone to come find us."

"I know that." And he did. "It's more..." He didn't know how to say it.

Brynn cocked her head in a movement like Kiana. "You're afraid you've brought us into Besand's range of interest."

He exhaled. She'd nailed it. "Yes."

He'd seen firsthand the horrific pain Besand could inflict on a person holding his interest. He'd seen the autopsy photos and heard the descriptions directly from Besand's mouth. He'd told the stories with a calm detachment that scared Alex more than the words themselves. Besand simply liked to hurt people. Alex was an anomaly for him. He could hurt Alex without touching him. Besand simply opened his mouth to speak and Alex felt pain.

He didn't want that for Brynn. Besand would take his time with her, wrench as much pleasure from her physical pain as possible. Alex's chest grew hot and his fingers clenched on his thighs. He remembered how the skin of her face had felt when he'd touched her that morning as she slept. If Alex had his way, Besand would never touch that silkiness.

Possessiveness landed on his back like iron weight.

"You can't control what he does."

"Yes, I can."

Brynn jerked like the words had stung her. "You'd kill him."

Alex looked at his hands; his knuckles were white as he squeezed them together. "I didn't say that." But he wasn't saying he wouldn't. He didn't know what he was going to do. He didn't know if they'd even cross paths. If they did, what would his gut tell him to do? He'd had satisfying dreams where he choked the life out of Besand, but a frail voice in his head told him it wouldn't be the same in real life. Could he attack with intent to kill? On the offensive, not the defensive?

"You don't sound like law enforcement." There was a question in her words, and in her eyes he saw caution, a watchfulness. Like she would bolt if she didn't care for his answer.

"I'm not." He held her gaze. *Don't run from me.*

She nodded slowly, prudence still on her face. She was reserving judgment. For now. "Jim let something slip. And Ryan got a confusing message from base camp. Collins said that you weren't a marshal. We didn't know what to think." Her voice dropped into a whisper. "We didn't want to believe it."

She'd said "we," but he knew she meant "I."

"I was. I was a deputy marshal for fifteen years. I walked away from it."

"Why?"

Meaningless words pushed at his lips, but he bit them back. She didn't need the story softened. She deserved the truth. "I assaulted my boss about a year ago. It was more of an accident really, but I hurt him pretty bad. I'm lucky he didn't press charges."

Brynn blinked a few times and sat a little straighter, but she didn't look too surprised and that disturbed him. Did he seem like someone who would hurt his boss?

"They fired me, but I'd already decided to never go back," he clarified.

"Why did you attack your boss?" Her voice was quieter but not upset. She didn't speak to him like he was the stinking liar he had been since meeting her. She sounded simply curious and her gaze raked his face, searching for something.

Alex tried to swallow. No more lies. Not with her. "Because he was giving Darrin Besand preferential treatment. Not handling him the way a killer should be handled. We'd moved the guy several times. Besand was facing charges in several states for his murders, and my boss would transport him like he was a ninety-eight-pound accountant with sticky fingers. Like he'd wanted the guy to be able to bust out. One time Besand attacked the marshal escorting him and he would've escaped if the pilot hadn't taken him down. The pilot and plane were a private lease, like this one. We were lucky the pilot was a big physical guy with a military background."

"Didn't your boss believe Besand was dangerous?"

Alex paused. "That's what I thought at first."

"But?"

"I don't know." He turned in his chair to look deliberately back at Ryan again. Alex was done with the topic. He didn't want to voice his thoughts on Besand and Paul Whittenhall. He had no proof, just hearsay. And his own gut reaction.

Brynn sat silently for a long moment, still watching him with sharp eyes. "Ryan said you guarded federal judges."

"I did. Then I moved into prisoner transport."

The silence stretched between them. Alex's mind whirled as she waited for him to explain why he'd switched. This had been one of Monica's biggest complaints. He hadn't talked to her. He'd answer her questions, but he'd never let her know what he was *feeling*.

Brynn didn't want to know how he felt, he told himself. She was simply making conversation, finding out about the person she'd been in the wilderness with for the last three days.

Why was it so hard to talk about himself?

"I did prisoner transport for three years. I've ridden in a lot of little planes just like this one. It's a little more physical and more interesting than guarding the judges. I liked it better."

"But you weren't wild about your boss." It was said with a touch of sarcasm and one of her lovely smiles.

He met her brown eyes and felt the room warm a degree. "He was a jerk long before I stabbed him."

"Christ. You stabbed him? When you said you assaulted him I assumed you punched him. What did you stab him with?" Her jaw dropped, her lips opened, showing perfect white teeth as her eyes widened.

"I didn't mean to stab him. It just happened." Even to him the words sounded lame. "And it was with a letter opener."

Her mouth snapped closed. She smiled and then broke into a grin, and he knew she was about to laugh. "A letter opener? Seriously? That's like a bad movie."

He had to smile back. "It was on his desk. I guess I picked it up while I was yelling at him. I don't even remember doing it. Then he sort of walked into it. Well, I'd sort of swung it as he sort of walked into it."

She laughed and the sound was like sunshine in the plane. "How'd that explanation go over with your superiors?"

258 • KENDRA ELLIOT

He grimaced. "I don't know. I never went to the hearing. I just quit instead."

He'd always wondered why Whittenhall let it go. Whittenhall wasn't the type to let someone stab him and walk away. He was more of a hunt-you-down-and-stab-you-in-the-back-for-revenge type of guy. Whittenhall's silence was one more strike against him in Alex's suspicion book.

"So, this is entirely personal. You're not here on behalf of the marshals' office to see to your fellow deputy or recapture an escaped convict. You're here to make sure Darrin Besand doesn't escape."

"Linus was my friend," he stated quietly. "I told the truth about that. And I'm going to see his family when this is through. Besand isn't going to walk out of these woods by himself. Either the forest will stop him or I will be on his back."

"And nothing will stop you from achieving this goal."

Alex paused a half beat. "I thought that at first. Your team was my means to an end. I was going to take everything you guys could give me to reach this plane."

"And now?" Her question was quiet but loaded.

"I feel a responsibility to four people I'd never met before." He held her gaze. "Your safety is now a priority over finding Besand."

"Do you think he'll kill again?"

"I know he will."

"I know he is an evil person," Brynn said slowly. "But your interest in him...seems more personal than someone trying to right a wrong. Several wrongs. Maybe your boss wasn't giving him the correct type of transportation details, but...I don't understand—"

"He killed my brother."

In the poor light he saw her face pale, and she sucked air into her mouth. Her voice quivered slightly. "I knew there was more. From the very beginning you've been so driven. At first I thought you were just intent on doing your job. Then I thought it was because of the marshal on the plane."

Alex felt like he was covered in a thick sheet of slime. He'd used her and the other men. "I was driven. I still am. Samuel was the only family I had left and Besand took that away from me. He killed my brother to cover up his murder of another woman. Samuel had seen the killing but didn't understand."

"What do you mean he didn't understand?"

Alex swallowed hard and held her puzzled gaze. "Samuel was a boy inside a man's body. He was mentally disabled. Something happened at his birth and he didn't get enough oxygen. He had to rely on the help of others to live in society.

"I wanted him to live with me. But my wife refused. She didn't want him in our house."

"That's a lot to ask of someone," Brynn whispered. "You obviously loved him dearly. It must have ripped you apart to realize your wife couldn't do the same."

"You could have done it," he said softly.

Brynn gave a small gasp as her head jerked.

"Forget I said that. That wasn't fair."

She shook her head. "You can't play 'what-if.' I don't know how it would have been and you don't know either." She focused on the wall of ice in front of them as he mentally kicked himself in the ass.

"It was stupid for me to try to blame her when I know that it was my fault he was in the care home where Besand got to him."

"Was it a good home? Was he happy there?" She looked at him closely.

Alex gave a half smile. "It was a good place. They took him on outings and let him tend the roses and garden. It was like living with wonderful grandparents, and Samuel was happy."

"Then you can't be blaming yourself. If he'd lived with you, would you have been home all day to entertain him? Or would you have been at work till late at night? Would you have cooked all his meals and read to him? Stretched his brain and broadened his view of his tiny world? Or would he have been watching TV all day, waiting for you to come home?"

Alex looked down at his hands. She'd said what he'd thought a million times. But it sounded better coming from her mouth. More truthful.

"Sometimes we need to let others do things for us. Because they can do it better. No matter how much it hurts or how accountable you feel." She gave a sad smile. "When I moved in with Jim's in-laws, I was a very independent teen. I was used to doing everything for myself. Cooking, buying clothing, getting myself to school. The first day that Anna's mom packed my school lunch, I nearly cried. I'd been up late studying and overslept and was about to miss the bus. I was going to have to skip lunch, but she saw my need and took care of it. It was so hard to allow myself to lean on them. All my life I'd only had myself to rely on. It took me awhile to realize I could do better in school if I let her parents take care of parts of my life.

"Plus, they liked doing it. At first I couldn't see that. But then I realized they took in foster kids because they knew they had the love to offer. Were the people at Samuel's home good people?"

"The best," Alex said softly. "But I hated them for hiring Besand."

"He *worked* there? That's how he came in contact with your brother?"

Alex nodded, not trusting his voice.

"Oh, how guilty they must have felt."

Alex shut his eyes. He'd heaped a lot of blame on the Maxwells that he shouldn't have. It was easy to focus his anger on them. He'd never accepted their apologies. He could still see Kathy Maxwell's tears at Samuel's funeral. He'd compounded their guilt by hating and blaming them.

Brynn saw his shoulders droop. "You held them responsible."

Alex didn't say anything.

"They knew the pain you were going through, Alex. They couldn't have missed it. It's written all over your damned face. If those people are as wonderful as you say, then they understand."

"I couldn't face them. It was easier to hate them. I'll talk to them when I go back. I can see it differently now. And…" Could he tell her? It took all his energy to turn his gaze to her and meet her eyes. "I couldn't face myself. I hid. I hid in gallons of hard alcohol and antianxiety and pain meds. I used them to avoid thinking, avoid facing what had happened."

She studied his face. "You didn't bring them with you out here."

He shook his head.

"Some days I wanted to take them to meet with Besand too. I couldn't stand to be in the same room with him."

"The same room? You went to see him?" She leaned forward, scanning his face.

"He'd tell me things he wouldn't tell the detectives. He told me where to find missing victims and how he killed some of them."

"In detail?"

"Too much detail."

"Then why'd you do it?"

"For the other families of his victims. I wanted to spare them any pain I could."

"It was your atonement for placing your brother in Besand's path. And in return that murderer filled your heart and brain with his poison," she whispered.

"I can become clean with one stroke." Even he heard the hatred in his voice.

"Do you really believe that?"

Alex wavered. "I used to believe it, but now I don't know."

The cabin was silent. Ryan was in a rare snoreless moment. As Alex stared out a black window, he felt Brynn emotionally draw up inside herself. He wasn't much better than Besand. He'd just told her he could possibly murder the man on sight. What was she thinking? Any second she was going to go lay down in the back with Ryan, put as much distance as possible between the two of them. How could she ever...

Her hand picked up his, and he started at the touch of soft skin. She'd taken off her gloves and leaned over the tiny aisle in the plane. She gripped his hand hard as he turned to her. There was no fear in her dark eyes, only understanding and...

His heart did a double thump.

"You are a good man, Alex Kinton. Nothing you've said can convince me otherwise. I see it in you." Her gaze dropped to his mouth for a fleeting second, and his entire body hardened as if she'd physically touched him there.

"I'm a stupid idiot." Then he proved his words.

Without giving her a second to react, he reached out, slid his hand behind her neck, and pulled her mouth to his. She tensed at his touch then relaxed into the kiss. Elation shot up his spine, and he ran his tongue along the seam of her lips, not asking permission, demanding entrance. She opened for him, and he thought he'd die at the sensation of the silkiness of her mouth.

He'd wanted to do this from the beginning.

He was too far away. He shoved up the armrest of his seat and moved to his knees in the aisle, ripping off his gloves as their mouths fused. Pain shot from his knee, but he ignored it. His hand went back around her neck as he ran his other hand under her coat and up her back, pulling her forward until their chests touched. Through two heavy jackets.

"Damn it." He pulled away, and she gave a quiet protest as his mouth left hers. The temperature in the tiny plane felt like it'd jumped forty degrees. He wanted their coats off. Now. His eyes locked on hers as he tugged at his zipper. She lifted a hand slowly to her lips and pressed against them as if trying to prolong his kiss. His jacket's zipper yielded and he reached out to hers. He slowly opened her coat, holding her gaze, giving her every opportunity to stop him.

Brynn leaned forward, meeting his mouth again. He felt her lips turn up in a smile as she kissed him. The warm softness of her chest molded against him, and Alex forgot he was kneeling in a plane in a snowstorm. This was right. Everything about Brynn was right for him.

He touched her stomach through her shirt and ran his hand up to her breast, thrilled by the feel of the curve against his palm. She pressed into his touch, her mouth opening wider, giving him permission to touch and take. She moved out of her seat, kneeling in the aisle with him. Every inch of his skin went on alert; his nerves shot into a sharp edge of need. Yes, he needed her. He needed her to touch him, needed her to laugh with him, needed her to share with him. Needed her forever.

264 • KENDRA ELLIOT

He kissed her harder and deeper, pushing his body against hers. Every inch of him needed to be in contact with her somehow, someway. Her hands clutched at his shoulders, her thighs pressed against his, her stomach—

Ryan sneezed in his sleep.

Alex froze. Brynn straightened. Her eyes widened as she scooted back into her seat. Away from him. It might have been a mile.

Alex zipped up his coat and backed slowly into his seat. "I'm sorry."

She shook her head. "It's all right. I didn't…"

"I don't know what I was thinking. My brain seems to go on vacation around you." He slumped back in his seat. A headache thundered painfully deep inside his skull. Kiana met his gaze, her chin still on her paws and her eyes full of sympathy.

He knew exactly what'd been on his mind. Ever since he'd been in Brynn's presence he'd been pulled toward her. An invisible rope lashed him tighter and tighter to her as every hour passed. He'd wanted to get a taste of those lips from the first second he saw her. With her so close, every other thought had been driven out of his mind.

"I know what you were thinking. I was thinking the same thing," she whispered. "I wanted it too."

His gaze flew back to her. She didn't look annoyed or pissed. She looked…like someone who was ready to go a couple rounds in bed. With him.

"You're living with someone," he forced the words out.

She looked away. "No, I'm not. I asked him to move out a month ago. He's living with his brother. It's over. It's been over for a long time, but he won't admit it. He keeps saying things will work out."

"Jim said—"

"He didn't tell you I was pregnant, did he?" Her head swung back to him and those gorgeous eyes sparked. Alex feared for Jim.

"God, no. He just said you were living with the perfect guy." She lifted an eyebrow. "When did he say that?"

"Early this morning when we went down to the cockpit."

Brynn pounded a hand on her armrest. "I'm going to kill him. I told him last night Liam had moved out and it was completely over. He lied to you this morning. He's trying to protect me again."

"Protect you from me?" Alex frowned. Jim had a point. A lying ex-marshal wasn't good enough for his little sorta-sister.

"He must have seen something." She looked into his eyes. She didn't explain, but Alex knew she meant the sparks that shot between them every time he looked at her. He didn't tell her where her head had been when he woke up that morning and Jim spotted them. Seeing Brynn with Alex must have really pushed Jim's overprotective buttons.

Brynn dug in her coat pockets, a fierce glare in her eyes. "Where's my phone? I don't care if there's no service. I gotta at least try to chew him out. He's gonna get it. He's pushed his nose in my business for the last time."

Alex bit back a laugh. She was gorgeous in her self-righteousness. He made a mental note to never take anything about her for granted. "You probably won't reach him. Service is spotty."

She snorted. "Won't know until I try." She found her phone and cursed at the screen. "No service." Contemplative eyes looked at Alex. "Let me see your phone." He slid it out of a pocket. It showed one bar of service. Poor Jim. He started to hand her the phone and froze.

"Wait."

Her fingers were on his phone, but she stopped and her eyes flared at what she saw on his face. "What is it?"

"He's got a phone."

"Yeah."

"No, I mean Besand has a phone. He took Linus's phone." Could he call the fucker? Alex's hand shook as he started pulling up his contacts on the screen. Could it be that simple? Could he get a hold of Besand right this minute? *Hey, you dead?*

"You're going to call him? Besand? What...what are you going to say?" Brynn stuttered through the words, shock in her voice. She leaned closer to look at his screen.

Alex inhaled deeply and caught her warm scent. She smelled woodsy. Sort of like campfire and fresh pine needles. His entire body tensed and for a split second he couldn't remember Linus's last name to search his contact list. He hit the *C* key. There it was. Thank God he'd been too preoccupied to buy a new phone in the last two years.

His finger hesitated over the send key. What would he say?

He raised his gaze to Brynn and sunk into the brown depths of her eyes. She looked scared, angry, and curious. Anger shot through his core, and he hit the send key. Alex knew what to say. If he hurt anyone on his team, Besand was a dead man.

His hand shook as he raised the phone to his ear, still staring into those stunning eyes. Warmth raced down his spine. When they got out of here...

The phone at his ear was silent. No rings, no buzz. Alex looked at the screen.

Connected.

He moved the phone back to his ear and heard a click.

"What?" A voice spoke from the phone.

Alex knew the voice. Every neuron in his body fired simultaneously at the sound and intense pain exploded his brain. *Besand.* He lived. He wasn't dead under two feet of snow. All Alex's silent questions from the last three days had just been answered. The back of his mouth suddenly tasted sour, and he closed his eyes. He heard Brynn gasp.

"Besand." Alex's voice was flat.

There was a pause, and Alex swore he could hear Besand smile through the connection.

"A-man! It's my favorite guardian of justice and retards! How's the temperature in that tin can?"

Alex forced himself to exhale. The autonomic muscles that controlled his lungs seemed to have forgotten how to function. They worked only with direct commands. "Where are you?"

Besand laughed. Alex opened his eyes as Brynn made a small sound. Biting her lower lip, she leaned forward and braced a hand on his knee. Was that support for him or her?

"Would you pay me a visit if I told you? I've missed our chats."

Red fury clouded his vision. Brynn's fingers tightened on his leg, and the cloud lessened somewhat.

"Can't be too bad with that hot blonde in there. Wish I had one with me. It'd give me something to do."

Alex swallowed hard and laid his hand on top of Brynn's and gently squeezed. *He's trying to make me react. Rule one. Don't react.* "I'm sure you're staying plenty busy yanking on your dick. No audience out here though. You miss the other prison bitches watching?"

One side of Brynn's mouth fought to pull into a smile, but her eyes looked horrified at his words. Besand always brought out the asshole in him.

"Fuck you! You know I'm not—"

The connection was lost and the screen flashed the short time of the call. Alex felt like he'd rolled in pig shit. He shook his shoulders trying to get rid of the sensation. He turned off the phone; no way was he calling back. He'd found out what he needed to know. The killer still lived and was obviously close enough to know they were still in the plane.

Brynn's other hand slid on top of his, sandwiching his between her two. Her heat gently rolled through him, and he felt the filth dissolve from his skin.

The sound of a throat clearing made her yank her hands back. Both of them turned to the rear of the plane. Ryan sat up in the cargo area, his hair sticking up at all angles, his gaze unfocused. "Who's jacking off?"

"Alex!" A male voice spoke in his dreams.

Kiana barked.

Alex jerked awake in the dark, his hand going for the SIG he'd placed on the floor above his head. Crushed against his back was a soft, warm figure.

Brynn.

After telling Ryan what had happened on the phone, the sick man had fallen back to sleep. After another half hour of talk, Alex and Brynn crawled in the cargo area and stretched out next to Ryan. Alex had lain there for what seemed like forever, listening to Ryan snore, listening for sounds from outside.

"Alex! Ryan!"

Jim's voice.

Alex scrambled to a sitting position with his gun pointed at the door. Neither Brynn nor Ryan had woken. The thick snow covering the plane was distorting the sounds. Then he heard the cargo door shift open against the snow, and Kiana gave a happy whine.

"Down, dog." Affection rang in Jim's tone. A glow from a headlamp lit the plane.

Alex lowered his gun and glanced at his luminous watch face. How long had they slept? Were Jim and Thomas back with help already?

His gut sank as he registered the time. Three in the morning. Something bad must have happened to cause the men to return so soon. He rubbed a hand over his eyes, trying to erase the signs of sleep. "Jim?" He squinted in the direction of the headlamp.

"Everyone OK?"

"Yeah. Ryan's fever is under control. Why're you back so soon?"

"We've got company." Instead of excitement, Jim's voice grew grim.

"Fuck. Besand?" Now Alex was wide-awake. He awkwardly stood, muscles complaining and gun ready. But Jim looked beat, not panicked. He ruffled Kiana's head as he turned exhausted eyes to Alex. His boots and jacket were covered in snow.

"No. Thomas and I came across a helicopter crash about an hour into our trek. We decided to haul the two men back here before they froze to death. We wouldn't make it to the train trestle with them."

"Were they searching for us?"

Jim gave Alex an odd look. "Yeah. I can't believe they went up in this shitty weather. Ryan and Brynn said they heard a chopper right before that avalanche. Chances are the noises from this chopper set it off."

"These are those same guys?"

Jim shrugged. "I don't know anyone else cocky enough to fly yesterday."

"Where are they?"

"Right outside. We rigged a carrier of sorts to drag one of them. Liam was able to walk mostly on his own."

"Liam?" Alex's fingers tingled on his SIG.

Jim had that odd look on his face again. "Yeah. Brynn's Liam."

CHAPTER SIXTEEN

Alex was shaking her, but she didn't want to wake yet. She put a hand on his shoulder and tried to pull him down to her. She didn't work today; why was he waking her?

"Brynn, wake up, damn it."

Damn it? She opened her eyes and stared at Alex. *Snow. Plane.* Right.

"What's wrong?" She blinked at the concerned look on his face. "Ryan?" She rolled to her side to check on the sick man, but he wasn't there. "Where's Ryan?"

"Giving Thomas a hand."

"Thomas?" She sat up. Light from several headlamps filled the plane. There were more bodies in the plane than there should have been. She rubbed at her eyes.

"Brynn? Are you all right?" It was a new voice. One that shouldn't be here.

Jesus Christ. Liam? "*Liam?*" Alex stepped back as a familiar figure kneeled beside her in the cargo area and took her head in his hands as he scanned her from hood to boots. Liam's face was white, but the tip of his nose was bright red. His eyes looked like he'd been in a smoky bar for two nights.

"What...where?"

He pulled her close and buried his icy face in her neck. "Thank God. Brynn. I'd about given up. I was certain I'd seen you for the last time." He pressed his lips in a cold kiss against her neck and worked his way to her mouth like a starving man. She kissed him back for few shocked seconds and then pulled away to meet his eyes.

"We're OK, Liam. We would've hiked out just fine when the weather cleared."

"Not you, Brynn. Tyrone and I crashed his chopper the day before yesterday."

"What? You flew in this? Are you crazy?" She pulled back and ran her hands over his chest. "Are you hurt?" Her hands trembled as they touched his snowy coat. Only Tyrone would dare to fly in this weather. Although Liam probably would have tried if he'd had his own helicopter. The brothers were fearless. Sometimes in a bad way.

"I'm fine. Just a little banged up, but Tyrone..." Liam swallowed hard. "He hit his head pretty bad."

She shoved Liam aside and moved toward the door. "Let me look at him." She abruptly stopped as she met Alex's gaze. His face was blank. He'd been directly behind Liam as she kissed him. Guilt stole her breath.

Then anger gave it back.

She didn't belong to Alex or to Liam. She glared at Alex, furious at herself for allowing the guilt. She'd kissed Alex. So what?

She'd told Alex that she and Liam were finished.

Then she was kissing Liam a few hours later.

Christ. She couldn't deal with this now.

Thomas dipped his head through the cargo door, holding a limp Tyrone in his arms.

"Lay him down." Alex and Liam immediately forgotten, Brynn scooted back to make room as Thomas gently set the injured man on the floor. Tyrone stirred and opened his eyes.

"Hey, handsome. What were you thinking flying in weather like this?" Brynn teased him as she took his pulse. She pulled off Thomas's headlamp and checked Tyrone's pupils with flashes of the lights.

"He had to get to you. No stopping him," Tyrone muttered. "Head hurts."

She nodded, her stomach sinking as she pressed a palm on Tyrone's forehead.

Damn you, Liam.

Alex picked a seat that faced away from the cargo bay. He couldn't watch any longer. For two people who were no longer a couple, Liam hadn't let go of Brynn since they came in. Now they sat on the floor next to Tyrone, heads bent together, talking in hushed voices, looking like a couple having a serious discussion about the state of their mortgage. Brynn had caught Alex's eye several times and minutely shaken her head at him.

Did she mean "Don't tell him about us" or "I made a mistake with you"?

He didn't want to know. He rubbed at his knee. The exertion yesterday had made it hurt worse than it had in years. He could simply grab some pain meds, but he didn't want to. Right now he wanted the pain. Wanted something to distract him from the woman in the plane. Ryan plopped in the seat across the aisle from him, his eyes glassy. The kid had overdone it again.

"Fever under control?"

Ryan grimaced. "Mom back there won't let me miss a dose of ibuprofen. It's like she's got an alarm that goes off when it's time for more."

"You look like shit."

A genuine grin cracked his face. "Thanks. Right back at ya. But I don't think a fever is causing the black shadows under your eyes."

The kid was too observant. "It's three in the morning. And I died yesterday."

"Almost died. But now you look ready to do a little of your own killing."

Alex ignored him, looking at Thomas and Jim deep in conversation in the seats in front of him. Alex had related the news of the phone call with Besand to the two men, and Jim had smacked himself on the forehead. "Why didn't I think of trying to call him?"

But the current stress on Jim's face was new, and he was shaking his head at Thomas.

"What's wrong?" Alex asked sharply.

Both men turned toward him. Jim's gaze went past him to take stock of the cargo area then returned. "How much walking around outside did you do after we left?"

Alex's lungs grew numb. "We've all been using the trio of little trees to the right as a head. About fifteen feet out. Then a rotation to brush the snow away from the door. Haven't done that since the sun went down though. That's all we've done outside." He questioned Ryan with the cock of a brow. Ryan nodded.

Jim and Thomas exchanged a glance.

"There are faint footprints along the edge of the tree line. And one set that comes up to the rear of the plane then heads back to the trees."

Alex closed his eyes. Besand had been right outside the plane. Probably had his ear up against the metal, trying to listen inside. How far away had he been when Alex called? Thomas coughed, and Alex looked at him sharply. "What else?"

"Rabbit," Thomas stated. "Partially skinned. Right beside the tail of the plane. Spread out like it should be nailed on a cross."

"That's fucking twisted." Ryan gagged.

"What do you mean partially skinned?" Alex could barely speak.

"Just skinned the front legs. Must have run out of time."

Vomit crawled up Alex's esophagus, and he forced it back down. Two of the nurses killed by Besand had been found in the same state; Besand had only skinned their arms. He'd later told Alex it was harder work than he'd expected and that he'd only done it out of curiosity and to freak out the investigators. Alex believed him. Once his victims were dead, Besand was finished.

He wasn't into trophies or getting off with dead bodies. It was the thrill of the kill he craved. Once his hunger was satisfied, he usually threw the remains away like garbage.

Besand was sending a message to Alex, reminding him of what he was capable of doing to a woman, payback for his smart mouth during the phone call. *I pissed him off, pushed too hard.*

Alex buried his head in his hands, swallowing hard, trying to get the photos of the two dead nurses out of his mind.

"He did that to a couple of his vics, didn't he?" Jim asked.

Alex nodded, lifting his head. It weighed two thousand pounds. "He's gotta be staying in the cockpit." He couldn't let him near Brynn.

"He wouldn't survive anywhere else," Jim stated.

"Do we need to go down there?" Thomas made a gesture to his jacket. To his gun.

"In the pitch-black night?" Alex countered.

"We've got headlamps," Jim offered.

"You mean targets on our foreheads. We can't get close to him with those things on. For all we know he's also got a little protected place in the woods where he watches every move we make."

"He can't be sitting in the woods. He'd freeze," Ryan said flatly. "He can't be watching us all the time." He shook his head. "The guy can't be dressed for this weather. He couldn't have been prepared for this. How's he doing it?"

"Unless he found one of our packs," Thomas spoke up. "Could be using one of the tents."

Ryan shut his mouth with an audible snap, and the men stared at one another.

"That has to be it," Jim muttered. "It has to be. Now what's he going to do? Will he hide out? Come after us? What's the best way to protect ourselves?" He glanced at Brynn, who was talking in the cargo area to Liam and Tyrone. The three were unaware of the other conversation. And the rabbit.

One man injured and one man sick. And Brynn. Alex leaned his head against the leather headrest. Besand probably had food, extra clothing, and a tent. Alex hoped the tent was freezing and miserable. What now?

"I need to think. I know what makes this guy tick. Just let me think for a few minutes."

The men all sat silently.

Alex couldn't get Brynn out of his mind. "For right now, I think we're OK in here. The dog twitches every time she hears something outside. I don't think Besand will attack the plane. He's blind to what's in here. He's not stupid enough to come through the entrance."

"Would he pick us off as we exit?" Ryan asked quietly.

Alex flattened his lips. "What's the fun in that? That's not his kind of move. He likes to look you in the face, taunt you first. I can't tell you how many times he complained about this one old guy who died from a heart attack or something while Besand was working him over. Made him furious. He gets off on the pain. He hates it when it's over too quick."

"Yeah, I feel safer now," Ryan muttered.

"So what's he going to do next?" Jim's voice dropped. He met Alex's eyes with a look that showed total belief in Alex's opinion about the game in Besand's head. Alex appreciated Jim's confidence. He really wanted Jim's respect.

"He wants me," Alex stated, meeting each of their gazes.

"And Brynn." Jim shifted his feet, glancing to the back of the plane again.

"Maybe. He may have said that just to dig at me." Alex lied. Brynn was just Besand's type. Tall, athletic, natural beauty.

Jim's face said he knew Alex lied.

"I can pull his attention away, get him following me. Then one of you following him." This was met with silence. No one protested; no one shook his head. They all weighed his words.

"Anyone got a better idea?"

Alex felt as obvious as a bright-blue candy wrapper lying in a white field of snow. He left his hood down, wanting to hear the sounds of the forest. The wind had let up overnight and he physically felt the absence of the constant whistling and rustling. It was like his ears were clogged. He pulled on an earlobe and swallowed hard several times, but nothing changed. He wasn't congested; there truly was a lack of sound.

There wasn't a lack of snow. Huge, soggy flakes fell. With the absence of wind they fell perpendicular to the ground, creating a white curtain that offered Alex a false sense of security. It also made studying the area around him difficult.

He'd been out for several hours, checking the terrain farther down the southern slope, knowing Thomas was tailing him far behind, looking for signs that Alex was being followed. Alex had trudged far enough to hear the rush of a river far below the trees. Curious, he'd worked his way down to its banks. It was a different river from the one they'd crossed that first day. This one was farther south. And, of course, they were several thousand feet above the location where they'd crossed the other. Where Brynn was almost hit by a wooden missile.

His chest tightened at the image and his fingers twitched as he headed back toward the plane. He'd almost lost her before he even knew her.

He glanced at his cell and nearly cheered out loud at the two bars of service. He'd checked the phone several times that morning, looking for pockets of service but no luck. He immediately dialed Collins.

"Kinton?" Collins immediately answered.

"Guess you figured out this number doesn't belong to Whittenhall," Alex replied.

"Yeah, that became pretty clear once we met. What's going on up there?"

"We're OK. Could you understand Ryan the other day? The pilots and marshal didn't make it. Besand is still alive here somewhere. We're trying to find him. Also we found Tyrone and Liam Gentry. Tyrone's got a bad head injury. There's no way he's hiking out."

Collins's reply was full of static.

"Crap. I'm gonna talk fast," said Alex. He rattled off what Jim and Ryan had decided were accurate GPS coordinates of the plane. "I need you to look into Whittenhall. I think this flight change was set up to let Besand escape upon landing. I think Whittenhall engineered the whole thing, but I don't know why. It's got to be for money."

"Whittenhall? He's on the take?" Collins's voice was clear.

"You got someone who can do some research? I think Whittenhall was blackmailing Besand or the other way around."

"I know the perfect person to look into that," Collins said. "We're gonna get some birds up there as soon as the weather clears a bit. You guys—"

The call was dropped. All signal bars lost.

Alex groaned and watched his screen for a few moments, walking in circles, holding the phone up. He felt like a cell commercial. He gave up and stayed low, moving silently—make that crunchily—back in the general direction of the plane. He didn't look for Thomas. He had a hunch the man could be invisible whenever he pleased. If he didn't want Alex to see him, then he wouldn't. Knowing the man was watching his back felt right. Stopping behind a fir, he scanned his surroundings.

Nothing.

He could have been the only person for fifty miles.

How rapidly his priorities had changed. He'd butted in on the hasty team with the single goal of hunting Darrin Besand. Now his priority was the safety of six other people.

There had been no tracks outside the plane this morning. No one could have guessed that four men had shown up in the middle of the night with one of them dragged the whole way on a tarp.

It was utterly silent. He wondered if any wildlife was watching him. Like a bear. The thought of a bear possibly close by bothered him more than the presence of Besand. He knew Besand's mind; he didn't know the inner workings of a bear's brain.

Aim for the brain.

He stepped out from the tree, took a deep breath, and pushed through the snow, wishing he was back in the plane exchanging jokes with Ryan.

Alex had spotted Thomas listening a time or two to their banter, an almost wistful expression on his face. What would it take to get that guy to loosen up?

His lips twisted.

Knowing Thomas, he probably had some fantastic repertoire of clever jokes that could knock everyone's socks off, but he'd never share. The Alaskan often sweated inside the little plane, and Alex had realized with a shock that the guy was claustrophobic. How in the hell was he handling so many people in so little space? It was probably a remnant of his capture. Alex had watched Thomas mentally work it off, his lips moving as if in a chant and his eyes focused in the distance. *What did he say to himself?*

Alex had seen Brynn watching the big guy. Assessing, studying, and caring. She'd spoken softly to Thomas a few times. The conversations were too quiet to hear, but Alex knew she was questioning his comfort. Thomas would listen, then shake his head. He didn't like help from others, but there was always a respect for Brynn in his eyes. For Jim too. Ryan usually caught a few glares or eye rolls from Thomas, but Alex felt the big guy genuinely liked the younger man. Maybe even envied his happy-go-lucky attitude.

Alex did.

Alex made a mental addition to his list of self-improvements for when they got back to the real world. *Loosen up. A lot.*

Right now he needed to concentrate on finding a piece of scum in the woods. He ducked under a snow-laden branch, feeling like he was playing cops and robbers in his backyard as a kid. Samuel had always been the robber and Alex the cop. Their fenced backyard had been huge with great trees for hiding and building forts. Alex had wanted to be a cop when he grew up, except for a short period when he was nine and he'd wanted to be a fireman. Then a house caught fire on his street and he'd been traumatized by the absolute destruction and smells. He'd returned to his dreams of being a cop.

He'd always wanted to bring down the bad guy.

Gee. I'm living my dream.

But he'd never dreamed he'd be freezing his ass off while doing it or camping in half a plane that'd run out of protein bars.

His stomach growled. They'd be fine without food for a few days, but he guaranteed everyone was going to get real crabby.

He felt the small disturbance in the air by his face before he heard the crack of the gun. He dropped to his stomach, his mouth filling with snow. His body sank into the snow, but he kept his head up slightly as he scanned around him.

Besand? Thomas? Thomas wouldn't shoot at him, would he?

Alex couldn't tell the direction of the shooter. The crack of the gun had echoed several times through the forest, almost sounding like several shots. His best guess was the shooter was at two o'clock.

Thank God he'd put several hundred yards between him and the plane.

Brynn clutched at Jim's arm as the shot echoed its way to the plane.

"That was a gunshot."

"Yeah, but who shot at who?" Ryan muttered.

"Besand shot," Jim stated. "Alex and Thomas won't shoot unless they can empty their magazines into the prick."

Brynn took two steps for the door and Jim grabbed at her shoulder, holding her gaze with his serious eyes. "No one's going out there. Not till Alex comes back."

But what if he doesn't come back?

Brynn felt the heat wash out of her face and her shoulders sag. She collapsed into one of the chairs. Ryan put an arm around her shoulders. Thomas was out there. He'd help if Alex were in trouble. Alex was consumed with his need to find Besand. He plainly wanted revenge for the death of his brother and all those other victims. Besand had dragged Alex down a graphic path of reliving his killings. Before he'd give up a victim, first he made

Alex listen as he replayed the event. Alex hadn't told her any specific details—she hadn't wanted to hear them. But she'd seen the shift on Alex's face as his humanity disappeared when he talked of Besand's victims.

Her gaze met Jim's. His lips were pressed in a grim line.

How can he just sit here after that gunshot?

She was ready to jump out of her skin.

Jim knew what happened when you took someone's life. He was a trained sniper. The best shot in four counties. For all the times he'd been called on for his expertise, only twice had he fired his gun and killed suspects as they threatened their hostages. One child hostage's throat had been slit a split second before Jim fired. The girl had been saved, but Brynn knew Jim had suffered nightmares for a long time afterward. Dreams where he hit the girl or his shot made the suspect slice deeper.

The glory from the media didn't help. They highlighted each event and dragged it out for days in the newspapers. Each time Jim had spent months in counseling and considered different lines of work. But he was a cop through and through. He couldn't walk away. He knew his shooting skill was a gift for helping others, and he'd learned to deal with his demons. Brynn knew Alex fought his own type of demons. But if Alex were forced to kill Besand, would that wipe them out? Or just add more?

Her mind locked on a question. *Has Alex killed before?*

Deep inside, she knew the answer was yes.

It showed in the shadows in his eyes. The knowledge of taking another life and the emotional torture afterward. He knew exactly what hell he'd face if he were forced to kill Besand, and he would still do it. She rubbed her upper arms with both hands and paced the short aisle between the seats.

Damn it, Alex. Are you OK?

She heard Tyrone stir and mutter and she turned to look back at him, seeing Liam had already responded. Liam's voice soothed as he talked to his brother. Jim joined the two men, as always, checking on those in his charge. Once Tyrone and Liam had entered the plane they'd fallen under Jim's umbrella of supervision; they'd became part of his responsibility.

Tyrone's head injury was beyond her care. His head hurt like hell, and he couldn't stand to be jostled or hear loud noises. He needed a specialist and probably a CAT scan. Brynn ran her hands through her hair, swearing at her uselessness. All she could do was give him ibuprofen and she was nearly out.

Liam had contusions everywhere and had brushed off her offers to examine him.

At each offer he'd snap at her, "I'm fine. I know I'm fine. I don't need you to look." Then he'd turn his attention back to his brother.

She'd backed off.

Surprisingly, Liam had hated Alex on sight. It was almost like Alex had marked her and Liam could smell it.

She snorted. The two men were like dogs. Carefully circling each other, both alpha, neither willing to back down.

She had to set Liam straight. Apparently, kicking him out of her house hadn't been enough of a message for him. In his mind, she still belonged to him. But trapped in half a plane in the middle of a snowstorm with seven people wasn't the time to break up with someone. Again.

Besides, Liam already knew. He had to know. He just didn't want to admit it. Months of sleeping on the couch had to tell him something. Her refusals to set wedding dates or even exchange rings had to tell him something.

Or is he really that dense?

No. He simply ignored it. He ignored everything she'd told him about how she felt. Maybe he thought she'd change her mind if he didn't pressure her.

She sat in one of the seats and leaned her head back. Waiting and waiting. It was all she'd done for almost two days. It'd been nearly forty-eight hours since Ryan had spotted the plane. Twenty-four hours since Jim and Thomas had left to hike out.

Seventy-two hours since Alex had entered her life. And turned her heart and brain upside down.

Is Alex all right? She fought down the need to tear out the door and find him. Jim was sitting on the floor by Tyrone with his head in his hands. If she was stressed, Jim was beyond measure. She strained her ears to hear beyond the plane, but today the woods were silent. No wind, no ice pellets. Simply deliciously soft snowfall.

Alex hadn't changed how she'd felt about Liam. Her feelings for Liam had disintegrated before she'd met Alex. She had been surprised and rather embarrassed how quickly and compellingly she'd responded to another man. A warm flush crawled up her neck as she thought of his gray gaze.

How long had it been since she felt that deep a desire for a man? It was more than lust or simple attraction. She wanted to do things with him. Normal things. Snuggle on the couch watching movies, plant bulbs in the backyard, get coffee at Starbucks. She wanted to know how he liked his coffee. Black? Sugar and cream? She'd bet black. Her eyes watered and she brushed impatiently at her cheeks. He seemed like a no-frills kind of guy.

But how damaged was he inside? Maybe the nurse in her was simply reacting to someone in pain. And Alex had some of the heaviest emotional pain she'd seen since her own.

He might increase her load. He could easily leave her heart in shreds.

Two more gunshots echoed outside. *Alex.* Brynn grabbed at her armrests, sitting straight in her chair. The thumping in her chest beat a drum solo and her lungs refused to draw breath.

Lurching out of his seat, Ryan fumbled at the door. Jim's voice filled the plane. "Ryan! Do not go out there. That is an order." Ryan froze, swaying slightly, his back to Jim, one hand on the door.

"That was a handgun. I think the first shot was a rifle," Ryan said.

Alex ducked from tree trunk to tree trunk, moving in the direction he thought the single shot had come from. It was taking him deeper into the forest, away from both pieces of the plane. No more shots. For now.

He'd heard something else. At first, it'd sounded like a man's voice, but he was too far away to make out words. The sound wasn't directed at him. If Besand had wanted Alex to hear him, he would have. Three times since the single shot, he'd simply heard…noise from this direction.

What was in the woods?

Please, not a bear.

Aim for the brain.

He clenched his Beretta and felt his hand start to numb. He breathed onto his fingers, wiggled them, doing anything he could to keep them from literally freezing. He couldn't risk slow reflexes. Not out here. At least Besand would be suffering the same problem. He'd be an extra-lousy shot.

Did someone just yell?

He blinked and listened hard, holding his noisy feet in place. Arguing. Somebody was arguing strongly. Not Thomas's voice. Not Besand. He knew what Besand sounded like. His voice haunted his sleep and his waking hours. All the time he'd spent in little interview rooms with the killer as he'd recited the horrors he'd inflicted on his victims had imprinted Besand's voice on Alex's brain. Permanently.

Who is out here?

Another voice shouted back. Definitely two men.

Alex felt like he'd fallen through the rabbit hole. Hunters? In this weather? Most likely searchers. His entire spine relaxed. Until he remembered that he'd been shot at.

No one could possibly mistake his New York Giant's colored jacket for a deer or bear.

He'd been shot at on purpose.

Who else wants me dead?

He knew. At that exact second he heard the puzzle pieces click into place in his brain and his legs nearly crumpled. There was one person who had the means and motivation to send men into the forest with orders to shoot him.

Paul Whittenhall.

Alex bent over, hands on his thighs, panting heavily. His ex-boss wanted him dead. Alex knew it as surely as he knew his nose was Rudolph-red from the cold. Alex had probed and poked at Whittenhall, and he must have hit an artery. Whittenhall was dirty.

Why now? Why would he go after me in the middle of a blizzard? Why not take me out in front of my TV?

Besand.

Whittenhall was afraid he'd find Besand.

But Alex had been meeting and talking with Besand on and off for months. What was different out here in the snow?

One of the voices grew louder, yelling orders. Alex's heart stuttered as he recognized the voice, and his feet moved of their own volition. He awkwardly jogged between the trees in his snowshoes, feeling his lungs beg for more oxygen. He didn't know what elevation he was at, but his lungs could tell the difference. Being thrown about in an avalanche might have a little to do with his weakened state too.

He broke into a small clearing and saw two men wrestling in the white fluff. Two backpacks had been thrown to one side and a sniper rifle's butt stuck up out of the snow. He recognized both men immediately. Whittenhall's right hand, Gary Stewart, was blocking blows from Matt Boyles. Stewart was on his back in the snow as Boyles straddled him. Boyles plainly had the upper hand.

Boyles would kick Stewart's ass. Stewart was a pencil-pushing, ass-kissing asshole. Boyles was a Steven Seagal look-alike with the same physical skills. And the soul of a true cop. If this was the team Paul Whittenhall had sent to take Alex out, he'd fucked up royally.

Matt Boyles had been a groomsman at Alex's wedding six years ago.

Out of breath, Alex leaned a hand against a tree as he trained his Beretta on the two men. He wouldn't shoot, but Stewart wouldn't know that. He just needed to distract him.

"Stewart!" Alex shouted hoarsely. He startled Matt, who spun his head to the side and stared at Alex in shock. Stewart flipped Matt off him and onto his back in the snow. Moving to his knees, Stewart drew his Glock and pointed it at Matt's head.

He's going to kill Matt.

Alex fired. Twice.

Gary Stewart fell back in the snow, a stunned look on his face. Through the snowfall Alex spotted the two small holes in his coat near his neck. Alex blew out a breath and his gun hand drooped.

I had no choice. Matt would've been dead.

Matt rolled over to Stewart and slapped a hand over the blood that spurted from the two holes. He looked back at Alex, shock on his face.

Alex jogged over and collapsed next to Stewart. His breath froze in his windpipe as he realized Stewart was still breathing. *Holy shit.* The dying man met Alex's gaze and blinked rapidly.

"Whittenhall," Stewart whispered.

Alex nodded, his heart trying to hammer its way out of his chest. "He told you to take me out."

Stewart's eyelids fell closed, then slowly opened. "He thinks you know."

"Know what?" Alex moved his face closer to the dying man. "What's Whittenhall think I know?"

Surprise crossed Stewart's eyes. "Besand. You know about Besand." He coughed and bloody spittle hit Alex in the face. Alex wiped at his face, knowing he was talking to a dead man.

"Know what about Besand? What do I know?" he yelled.

Stewart's face contorted into a grin, his eyes focused beyond Alex, and his breathing halted. Blood pooled in his mouth.

Alex grabbed the front of Stewart's coat and shouted, "What do I know?" He shook the dead man, froze in horror at his

290 • KENDRA ELLIOT

actions, and then yanked his hands away, dropping Stewart back into the snow. Alex stared at the sightless eyes as he wiped the blood from his hands onto the snow, willing Stewart to say another word. Every nerve in Alex's body screamed the question.

What do I know?

Alex looked up and met Matt's gaze.

The other marshal looked dazed. He kneeled in the snow, his gun drawn too late and resting against his thigh. Matt licked at his chapped lips, breathing hard as his eyes focused. He looked Alex up and down before he spoke.

"Found you."

CHAPTER SEVENTEEN

Alex heaved Stewart's pack onto his back. Matt slung on his own pack, and Alex watched Matt's hands tremble as he fiddled with the straps. They'd covered Stewart with a thick layer of snow and tied a shirt to the nearest tree to mark the area. Matt had noted the location on his GPS. Alex broke the tense silence. "What the fuck is going on? What are you doing out here?"

"You say that like you own this piece of woods. I could ask you the same question." Matt gave him a level look. "Stewart contacted me and said he needed someone with outdoor experience to go in after a plane that'd crashed with Linus on board." He spoke Linus's name with the slightest quiver.

Alex swallowed and nodded for Matt to go on. He'd tell him in a minute about Linus. It wasn't going to be easy. At one time, the three of them had been as close as brothers. Until Alex had stopped all communication.

"When I got to the base camp, the sheriff told me that a marshal had already gone in with his team. You."

Alex didn't say anything.

"Stewart told me you'd manipulated your way onto the team because you wanted to get to Linus. But halfway up here he told me that Darrin Besand had been on the transport, and right then I knew Linus wasn't your only motivation. Hell, Linus might not have been your concern at all." Matt spit the last sentence, his face dark.

"That's not true," Alex stated firmly.

Matt rubbed a hand over his mouth, and Alex knew he didn't believe him. "Then this morning he tells me he has orders to shoot Besand on sight if he survived the crash. I was still trying to wrap my mind around that statement when Stewart spotted you."

Matt shook his head. "It was weird. We'd both spotted you through binoculars, and I was so damned glad to see you in this freezing hellhole that I didn't notice Stewart had put his rifle to his shoulder. I'd told him a hundred times on the hike up here that the AR-15 was too awkward to bring along. Now I know why he insisted on bringing it."

Matt shuddered.

"That shot scared the shit out of me, but I knocked him down and got the rifle out of his hand. What I really wanted to do was beat him over the head with it. We'd been going at it for a few minutes when you came up." He grimaced at Alex. "You startled me when you yelled his name. For a split second you sounded like the big boss man, Whittenhall."

"Did Stewart say why he shot at me?"

Matt shook his head. "I kept asking him why the fuck he'd done that, but he'd only say that he had to." He paused. "Do you know why?"

Alex stood silent. "Yeah, I think I do. I'll fill you in on the way back to the plane." He started off in the direction he'd come, stepping in the footprints he'd made earlier.

"The plane? You found it? Anyone live?" Excitement filled Matt's voice as he stepped along beside Alex, but then he frowned. "How come you're alone?"

"Everyone else is back at the plane. Linus died and the pilots didn't make it." He met Matt's gaze and watched the pain line his face. "I'm really sorry to tell you about Linus. The three of us used to be tight. But it looks like Besand lived."

Matt halted. "Looks like?"

"He wasn't with the plane, and I think he's hiding out nearby, waiting for me. I thought that shot had come from him."

"Then what are you doing wandering around the woods if you think Besand's trying to kill you?"

Alex's lips formed a cold smile. "Trying to draw him out."

"Kinton." A new voice.

Matt whipped around and leveled his gun at Thomas.

"Don't!" Alex lunged and pushed Matt's arms down. "He's with me." Alex glared back at the Alaskan. "About time."

"I've been watching for a while." Thomas's mouth twitched.

CHAPTER EIGHTEEN

Thomas did reconnaissance, covering the area a hundred yards out from the cockpit in a circle as Alex led Matt to the small piece of plane to look for any new signs of Besand. They dropped their packs and approached with weapons drawn. The skin on the back of Alex's neck tingled and pricked as they stopped behind the pilots' seats.

Alex forced his gaze to the ceiling. No new messages. He let his lungs slowly deflate.

"So where is Besand hiding out?"

Alex shrugged. "I've searched the area pretty good. I don't know where he's hiding out during the day. He may have rigged some sort of shelter. We think he might have found one of the packs, which means he'd have a tent and food. He's probably somewhere he can watch the other part of the plane. My gut tells me he's not far away."

Matt's head jerked as he spotted the writing. "Is that blood?"

Alex explained the message.

"God, he's a sick fuck. You think he'll target the woman?"

"I think he's trying to push my buttons."

Matt studied Alex's face, his eyes probing. Matt had a dark brown gaze that could stop a charging bull. "Is it working?"

"Yeah. He's got me wandering around in a blizzard wanting to wrap my hands around his neck. I'd say it's working."

"You said you knew why Whittenhall wants you taken out."

Alex compressed his lips, his eyes on the message. He had a hunch. That was all.

"I think Whittenhall was trying to get Besand out of prison."

Matt stopped short, his jaw dropping for a split second. "Why the fuck would he do that?'

"That's the part I don't know. Besand must have something on him."

"Blackmail? You think he's blackmailing Whittenhall?"

"Possibly. Each time Besand was transported, Whittenhall assigned him a detail made for a kindergartner. Like he was trying to make it easy for the guy to get away."

"Besand's a big dude."

"I know. That's what makes it more suspicious. Besand is a big, physical guy who is willing to kill. Do you remember when he assaulted Berry during the trip to Salt Lake?"

Alex watched comprehension enter Matt's eyes, then anger. "That's right. Berry had a black eye for a week. They didn't beef up the details after that?"

"No, they got worse. Green guys, smaller guys."

296 • KENDRA ELLIOT

"So why would Whittenhall order you shot because you might meet up with Besand out in the woods? What could Besand say to you out here that he hasn't said during all those damned social visits?"

Alex frowned and dropped his gaze, a trickle of guilt running down his spine. "You heard about that?" He silently swore. He'd thought the prison visits to Besand had been kept from the other marshals. The district attorney's office knew, the detectives on the cases knew, but he'd believed that'd been all.

"Everybody knew. They thought you were nuts for seeing that guy. Until the information about his missing vics started trickling in. Besand was telling you, wasn't he? You were the only one he'd talk to, right?"

Matt gets it. Alex's shoulders straightened a little. It was good to have his old friend beside him. He'd missed Matt's straightforward, no bullshit attitude. But that loss was his own fault.

"What did you trade him for that kind of information?" Matt said evenly.

Alex rubbed a glove over his face as every sore muscle in his body begged for rest. He glanced at Matt. "It felt like I gave him a part of my soul every visit. You don't know how filthy I'd feel after listening to that bastard talk for an hour. Inside and out. I wanted to soak in a hot tub of bleach after every episode."

Matt was quiet for a few seconds. "But what's different now? What's got Whittenhall in a panic over you meeting up with Besand? The blackmail?"

"If Besand's got a free ticket out of the country waiting for him somewhere, then he wouldn't have much motivation to keep Whittenhall's secret to himself anymore."

Matt took that in before saying in a stunned voice, "That's a pretty good theory."

"It's all I can think about. I managed to get a call through to the sheriff at the base camp and told him the same thing. I asked him to look into a few things on Whittenhall's background and Besand."

"You got a call through? My cell hasn't worked out here since the first hour we left." Matt slid his phone out of his pocket, looking hopefully at it.

"There're pockets of reception here and there. Not very consistent though."

"What made you stab Whittenhall?"

Alex snorted at the abrupt subject change. "I didn't stab him. That was an accident. He and Linus messed things up and we all scuffled. I was pissed that day, not thinking straight. All those wretched victims of Besand's. And Whittenhall wasn't taking the threat of him seriously."

"You still stabbed him." Alex heard the admiring note in Matt's words. "Had a lot of guys doing high fives behind Whittenhall's back. I think we've all wanted to take a swing at him one time or another."

Alex couldn't stop his tired smile. It *had* felt good to take Whittenhall down a notch. Too bad it'd cost him his job. He mentally shook his head. That move didn't cost him his job; he'd been on the way out for six months. His head hadn't been in the game. He'd been obsessed with his brother's killer to the point nothing else in his life mattered. Not his friends, not his marriage, not his health.

"There were rumors floating around. That Whittenhall could make a convict's life easier for a price," Matt said in a thoughtful voice.

"Easier? What does that mean?"

"I figure it means what you just said about Besand. Light details, maybe get someone switched to a different prison. Like something closer to their home."

"For a felon? Whittenhall couldn't do that."

Matt shrugged. "Maybe he thought he could. Enough to convince people to pay him. Maybe that's the information he's afraid Besand will spill."

"Could be. Besand would need to have some pretty concrete proof though." Alex stared out of the cockpit, faint memories pushing at his brain. "I knew something odd was up. Linus had been sucked into something. He'd said something a couple of years ago after a lot of beer that made me think he was in over his head with…I wasn't sure what."

"I know he got screwed on his mortgage in that lender debacle and was in danger of losing his house. And I think—" Matt abruptly stopped talking, shoving his hands back in his pockets.

"Think what?"

Matt spoke quietly. "I think he had a gambling problem."

Alex thought hard. Linus had always been the one who hit the video poker terminals that sprouted in every bar in Oregon. And he loved to visit Vegas. He'd been going to the Indian casinos when Alex lost touch with him. More affordable. No airfare or hotel bills.

"I can see that." And in hindsight he saw it clearly. Deep in debt with two kids? That would drive a man to do anything. Even something illegal if he needed the money badly enough. What had Whittenhall pulled Linus into?

Alex stopped in the snow. "Do you think Besand was supposed to escape during this particular transfer?"

Matt stopped beside him and their gazes locked. "Are you saying he crashed that plane on purpose? And took his chances in the middle of the Cascades? No one could pull that off."

"No. I mean escape when he landed. If he landed. Hell, do you think Linus was supposed to let him get away? Hopefully, Linus wasn't supposed to be collateral damage in some sort of twisted escape plan set up by Whittenhall and Besand. I wouldn't be surprised if Whittenhall had arranged for Linus to be the fall guy. All I know is someone changed the flight plan for his return flight from Medford. I know because I was waiting at the damned Hillsdale airport because I wanted to check out what kind of detail he had and watch the killer walk by in cuffs."

"That's sick."

Alex shrugged. "Gives my day a purpose."

"Who'd change the flight plan? Who could do that?"

"I'd have to check, but I think anyone could call in a change. That small a plane, flying to smaller airports, no one is going to raise an eyebrow if the flight plan is changed."

"Except the US Marshals' office."

"Not if the flight plan change came from them."

"Maybe it was changed for a different perfectly legitimate reason."

"I called around. I couldn't find another airport in the closest five counties where that plane was scheduled to land."

Matt's brows deepened. "I don't get it. Where were they going to land? They'd be missed eventually."

"That's the part I don't know. But I plan to find out. Let's get Thomas. We should get back to the plane." Alex grimaced. "I'm gonna catch hell for not coming directly back after those shots. They're probably worried sick."

An hour ticked by. With each passing minute, Brynn felt her skin grow thinner, more sensitive, attuned to every word and movement by every man in the crowded plane. She was being stretched to the limit, and it felt like the wrong words could cause her guts to spill out.

Tyrone had been talking a bit. He wasn't confused and had a pretty clear memory of the hours leading up to the crash. Brynn took that as a good sign and gave a silent prayer of thanks. He wouldn't move his head, claiming the slightest movement caused his vision to blur and spikes to be driven into his brain.

She understood completely.

She changed position for the hundredth time on the floor next to Tyrone as he drifted off again, wishing she could fall asleep as easily as he did. Her body was exhausted, her muscles ached, but her mind spun with the high, surging energy of the sun, worrying about Alex.

"Hey, you awake?" Liam spoke softly, ducking into the cargo bay.

"Yeah." How could she sleep?

He lay down next to her and pulled her close, spooning her against him. The way they'd slept a million times. Brynn closed her eyes and relaxed against him, her mind's swirling slowing a bit. The physical intimacy felt good. Right now, she needed a comforting touch.

"I would have never let you go on this rescue." Liam's arm around her waist tightened, his voice a harsh whisper.

"I know." Her semi-relaxed state evaporated.

"You should've woken me that morning."

"So you could've stopped me?" she hissed. *Not now, Liam. Please not now.*

"Yes."

"It was a plane crash, Liam. People could've needed medical help. I know what I'm doing out here. I'm not some idiot wandering lost in the woods," she whispered, worried that Jim and Ryan, who were sitting in the seats, could overhear.

"But last year—"

"Anyone could've been hit in that rockslide. I was simply in the wrong place at the wrong time." *Will he ever let that go?*

"And this trip?" His question hung in the air.

This trip had definitely put her in the wrong place at the worst possible time.

"I can't predict the future."

"We need to talk about this, Brynn. I can't have my wife risking her neck—"

"I'm not your wife," she snapped.

"No. Not yet but—"

"I'm not going to be your wife, Liam." She softened her tone but not the strength behind the words. They were absolutely true. She didn't have any doubts about her decision.

He lay silent.

"I'm sorry, Liam. I've told you before I don't want to marry you. And now...things have been so wrong between us for so long. I can't give up what I do. And you shouldn't ask it of me. I feel like—"

"I love you, Brynn."

Her heart stopped midbeat. *Not fair.* "I love you too, Liam, but not the way I should."

"How do you mean?"

He knew the answer. She heard it in his voice, but he'd asked the question anyway. She was finished with this conversation.

"I want you to move the rest of your things from the house, Liam. You know as well as I that we've been finished for a long time. You're not coming back."

His arm sank heavily on her side as she heard him exhale and felt him press his face into her hair. She squeezed her eyes shut, feeling moisture prick at her lids.

He was silent for a long minute, not moving. His breathing heavy but even.

Brynn waited.

"OK," he spoke slowly. "But first let's get Tyrone out of these damned woods."

Frustration welled up in her throat. He'd said "OK" to mollify her and simply put the inevitable off. Again.

Why doesn't he understand?

Kiana barked, and Brynn jolted out of Liam's arms, propping herself up on one arm to see the door. Ryan and Jim stood abruptly, weapons drawn, moving in the direction of the entry. Ryan was having problems focusing, and he moved slower than Jim. *He shouldn't be holding a gun.*

"Jim? It's Alex. We're coming in."

Brynn's arm buckled and she collapsed to the floor on her back, bringing her hands up to press on her eyes. "Thank God. Oh, thank God. He's OK."

Beside her, Liam sucked in a sharp breath at her words.

A chorus of greetings rose around Kiana's enthusiastic barks. Shaking off Liam's restraining hand, Brynn pushed up from the cargo area and stood, leaning one hand on the wall for balance.

A snowy figure pulled open the door. Steel-gray eyes locked with hers.

Every cell in her body smiled along with her lips. The moisture that had pricked at her eyes earlier spilled over, and she wiped awkwardly at her cheeks, her gaze never leaving his. The men slapped Alex on the back. Brynn saw Jim take a hard look in her direction. She didn't care. Let him think whatever the hell he wanted.

Thomas stepped in behind Alex, and she gasped as a third snowy figure appeared behind Thomas. Her heart stopped as she saw Jim and Ryan whip their weapons back out.

Alex threw up his arms, blocking their view of the other man. "Hang on! It's OK!"

Alex turned, gestured the other man in, and put an arm around his shoulders as he addressed the team. "He's got more protein bars."

They all cheered.

Staring out the window of the county's RV, Sheriff Patrick Collins couldn't stop thinking about his earlier phone call from Kinton. Once he'd gotten over the relief and shock of finally hearing from his team, new concerns set in. Should he share the information with the deputies who'd been running the base camp for four days?

The accusation was too sensitive. What if Kinton was wrong?

Guilt was already sitting heavily on his shoulders about keeping his men in the dark about the new status of the team and airplane. He felt like he was the protective patriarch of a huge family, firmly keeping the closet doors closed. He'd already talked privately with the families whose men were on that plane. They'd deserved to know the truth as soon as he'd found out.

For now, he'd have to keep his mouth shut around any other law enforcement.

Especially Paul Whittenhall.

It was just a matter of sitting tight until the weather cleared and he could get some air support into the woods. According to Kinton, at least one man would need to be airlifted out. Tyrone Gentry. One good thing had come out of this clusterfuck. Patrick should've known the indestructible Gentry boys would land on their feet. He let a broad smile cross his face, drawing a startled look from the deputy manning the radio in the RV. Who other than the Gentrys would survive a helicopter crash in the damned wilderness?

Now Patrick knew where the plane was. Kinton had passed on what the team had agreed were accurate GPS readings. Patrick studied the map on the wall of the base camp's RV. Physical comforts had improved since the initial days of the search, but the number of people was still increasing. A lot of the people were gawkers, not press members and not law enforcement. Just people coming out of the woodwork because of the television coverage. They wanted to be where the action was. Patrick hoped they were getting a good dose of boredom and frozen toes. Nothing exciting about this rescue. Simply the waiting and waiting game. Media numbers were still going up. One of his men had told him the story had gone international.

Especially when the marshals had publicly confirmed Darrin Besand's name.

Patrick placed a finger on the forest service map hanging on his wall, touching the team's location and feeling like he was hiding a classified secret. He studied the surrounding terrain. They weren't camped too far from another river. The water worked its way down the mountain in a serpentine fashion, just like the one the team had originally crossed. The mountain rivers were at their fullest. There'd been flooding in the valleys as the heavy rains and melting snow flowed into the mountain streams and the streams emptied into the valley's wider rivers. He'd heard the governor was surveying via helicopter parts of the flat coastal counties that'd been hit hard with the flooding.

Too bad the weather in the Cascades was keeping his helicopters grounded.

Damn it!

He'd forgotten to tell Kinton about the marshal's team. Probably didn't matter. The chances that those two teams were going to cross paths were slim to none. Patrick bit firmly on the inside of his cheek, thoroughly annoyed with his lapse. The news of the Gentrys had completely distracted him. The first call he'd made after Kinton's had been to Liam Gentry's mama. She hadn't been one bit surprised to hear her boys had survived, claimed Tyrone and Liam each had nine lives and had only used up six. Patrick had hung up his phone, shaking his head at the woman's faith and calm. He could use some of that.

But for right now Patrick had a new mission.

He needed to look for dirt on Whittenhall. Patrick gazed at the snow falling on the media corral. He didn't see the woman he was looking for, but he was confident she'd make an appearance in time for the noon broadcast. He scanned for that blowhard Whittenhall, spotting one of his flunkies, but no Whittenhall. The marshal would crawl out of the woodwork around noon too. He never passed up a chance to get his mug on-screen.

Could Kinton's story and implications be accurate? Too many things rang true for Patrick to doubt it, including his gut reaction to Whittenhall every time they crossed paths.

Patrick couldn't wait until noon to get the wheels in motion. Impatient, he pulled out his cell and smiled as he pictured the shock on Regan Simmons's face when she realized he was calling her.

When their conversation was over, he triple-checked the weather update.

Tomorrow morning. That was their window. The weather forecasters said it'd be a short one. Maybe four hours. But that should be enough time to get a couple of air force rescue choppers up there. Those chopper pilots were pretty stubborn. If they had a chance to get the team out they would push it with all they had. Especially when he told them one of their own was up there.

Hopefully, Regan Simmons was as stubborn and persistent. She'd leaped at the secret lead Collins had offered and decided to skip her live noon television report, letting a stunned junior reporter handle it. She'd appeared at the door to his trailer within two minutes of his request to chat. He'd sent the deputy manning the radio in the trailer on some useless errand. The man had left, raising his brow at the blonde woman impatiently tapping her toe next to the sheriff.

Regan had bargained fiercely. "If I'm going to do this task for you, then I want an update on that team."

"I don't have anything to tell you."

"Bullshit. This lead on Paul Whittenhall didn't come out of your head. You've talked to someone out there who's found something in that plane crash to make them suspicious."

Patrick had been pleasantly surprised. There was a sharp brain under that perfect hair.

"Yes. I've talked to them. They're all doing fine. I can't tell you anything else."

Lake Tahoe–blue eyes had glared at him. "Not good enough. I'm not putting my job on the line by snooping into the history of one of the most powerful men in the state. I need a damned good reason to do this."

Patrick had clenched his back teeth. "I can't give you specifics. But if this story turns out the way I expect it's going to, you're going to be the most popular woman in Portland broadcasting."

Regan had held his gaze, waiting for more.

He'd blown out an exasperated breath. "You get fifteen minutes of solo access to the team when they get back."

"Done." Her eyes had gleamed and she'd stuck out a hand. Patrick had reluctantly shaken it, feeling like he'd been deftly manipulated.

She'd immediately pulled out a BlackBerry and started punching buttons. "I had a related tip two months ago but I kept running into walls at every turn."

"What?" Patrick had blinked.

"This is more specific. This is going to get me somewhere."

"Who? Who told you about this before?"

She'd shaken her head and batted innocent eyes at him. "I can't reveal my sources." She'd made tracks for her car, her cell phone already at her ear, and had promised him an update in two hours.

He glanced at his watch for the fiftieth time. The woman had been gone for fifteen minutes.

A knock on the RV door brought him out of his musing. He pushed it open and immediately wished he hadn't. Paul Whittenhall had tromped up the steps and now was brushing the snow off his sleeves to melt on Patrick's dry floor. Patrick had just watched him on the noon news, answering reporters' questions for sixty seconds and saying exactly nothing. Whittenhall was a pro at blowing hot air.

"Any news?" Whittenhall barked.

Patrick shook his head. "All quiet. Heard from your team?"

"No."

The men silently measured each other. Each knowing the other wasn't being totally truthful.

"We're supposed to get a break in the storm tomorrow morning," Patrick offered.

"I'd heard that. A Pave Hawk going in?"

Patrick nodded. "Two."

"Good." Whittenhall looked anything but happy. Beneath his eyes were deep shadows and his skin had developed a sallow color. He was restless. He paced and ran his hands over Patrick's radio equipment and maps.

Through enlightened eyes, Patrick watched the marshal. Now that he had an inkling of what he was involved in, the nervous energy made more sense. Whittenhall had been a bundle of twitchy and fidgety movements since Patrick first met him.

If Kinton was right, Whittenhall had every reason to be anxious.

Whittenhall was scum. The worst kind. Someone who'd abused his position and power for his personal gain. And possibly tried to help a murderer walk.

Patrick wanted to be there when the arrogant man toppled.

Paul Whittenhall slammed the RV door as he stepped down the metal stairs.

Goddamn it.

He couldn't stand the pretentious look that'd been in the sheriff's eyes. Collins knew something but wasn't sharing. Paul's stomach clenched, and he reached in his pocket for his antacid roll. His third roll of the day.

What does Collins know? What the fuck is going on in that forest?

He hadn't heard from his team. Gary had sworn not to tell Boyles the secondary mission objective, but now it didn't matter.

That morning one of his marshals had casually mentioned that Matt Boyles had been in Kinton's wedding years before.

Shit. He'd stupidly sent Kinton's best friend in to kill him.

That would never work. Boyles was going to balk when it came to taking out Kinton, no matter how Gary spun the situation. He'd told Gary to play up Kinton's nervous breakdown to Boyles. That was the rumor Paul had fed into the marshals' gossip train. In the right ears in the office, he'd planted the story that Kinton was suicidal, seeing a psychiatrist, and heavily medicated.

Every agent remembered Kinton's meltdown in his office. Jumping to the assumption that he was mentally unbalanced shouldn't take too much effort.

Kinton *was* unbalanced.

Paul knew the man had become an isolated loner. Kinton had always been a private man, but after he was fired he'd turned into a hermit. The part about the psychiatrist was true. Paul had stayed updated on the former agent's movements. Undoubtedly he'd been placed on some sort of medication. All those psychiatrists throw drugs at their mental patients.

Paul had been rattled to the core when he realized Kinton was on the rescue team.

How did Kinton find out the plane had gone down?

Paul had been waiting at home, expecting a call from Linus. Waiting to hear that Besand was on his way to Mexico. They'd worked out a perfect plan. Linus was going to take the fall as the agent who let him get away, but he'd felt it was worth it to have Paul bail him out financially. The agent had been so over his head in debt, he'd been willing to do whatever Paul had needed. What Paul hadn't foreseen was a plane crash.

His gut churned painfully again. He went through antacids like they were M&M's. And that was in conjunction with pre-scription meds for his ulcer.

He was going to need a vacation when this was over. He ran a hand across his sweating forehead. Twenty degrees out and he was sweating like he was in the south during a heat wave.

Gary had to succeed. Besand and Kinton couldn't both walk out of the woods.

Paul couldn't face the alternative.

Tomorrow. Tomorrow those helicopters would go in, and then he'd know his future.

CHAPTER NINETEEN

Brynn blew out a breath and let her eyes drift closed again, listening to the medley of male snores. Did any of them not snore? This should be the last night. Today they should be evacuated by helicopter. Thank God. She didn't want to face the long, icy hike out to civilization. When she got out, she was going to spend a day at a spa. Doing girlie things. A facial, a massage, salt scrub. Anything to counterbalance the testosterone she'd been living with for days.

Last night she'd nearly choked on the air in the plane, it was so thick with alpha male hormones. When it had come time to sleep, Liam had stretched out next to his brother and glared at her, waiting for her to join him. She'd ignored him, talking in hushed tones with Jim in the seats, putting off the decision of where she wanted to sleep. The chairs weren't a possibility. As comfortable as they were, she couldn't sleep sitting up.

Alex had laid down in the cargo area, putting a little distance between himself and Liam. On the plane there was no place that was truly distant from anyone else. When Brynn was tired of men all she could do was close her eyes.

She'd continued talking to Jim, but suddenly grew aware of an angry whispered conversation in the cargo bay. Her head had swung in that direction, picking up hissed tones, but the only words she caught were "too old" in Liam's voice. He and Alex had each risen up on one elbow, glowering at each other. Even Jim had stopped speaking at the heavy tension that suddenly filled the plane. She'd stared between the two men. What were they arguing about? Her? Was that it? Liam had been throwing dark looks at Alex since the ex-marshal had stepped foot on the plane. When she'd nearly cried in relief at the sight of Alex after hearing those gunshots, Liam had known. And he couldn't let it go.

They'd looked ready to start swinging fists. She'd grabbed a thin blanket and stepped into the space between the two angry men. Alex's face had immediately gone blank, hiding behind that mask she'd seen too many times. Liam's eyes had burned as he watched her, but his mouth had stayed shut. She'd split a glance between the two men. "Are you going to keep me awake? Because I'm exhausted, and right now all I want to do is sleep so it gets closer to the time of those helicopters." Both men had shaken their heads. She'd laid down between them, touching neither, and immediately fallen asleep.

Now she realized she'd moved into Alex's heat during the night. She pressed her cheek against his sleeve. The man was a furnace and it felt heavenly, but if she wanted to keep the peace on the plane, she couldn't let Liam wake to find her snuggled against Alex. She reluctantly rolled over, instantly missing his heat.

Liam wasn't on her other side.

She sat up, blinking at Tyrone, and then scanned the plane, counting heads. Four seats had bodies. She quietly stood and stepped in the aisle. No Liam. Panic dried her mouth. Where'd he go?

Her spine instantly relaxed. He must have stepped out to go to the bathroom. That was it. She rolled her eyes at herself. *Idiot.*

"What's wrong?"

Thomas's eyes met hers in the dark. She startled at his whisper.

"Nothing. Liam went outside, I guess. I was surprised to wake up and find him gone. I wasn't thinking clearly."

Thomas nodded, but his sharp eyes didn't leave her face. "How long has he been gone?"

"I don't know. I'm sure he'll be right back."

She perched on an empty seat and squinted at her watch. Almost 5:00 a.m. She sat in silence with Thomas as she watched six minutes tick by. She rubbed at her face, her stomach tightening as each minute went by.

"It's been too long." Thomas stood and stepped resolutely toward the door He pushed it open and stared motionless at the snow. Brynn moved to peer around him.

No footprints. The snow was a perfect white icing.

"Oh, God." Her hands clenched into fists. "Where is he?" She backed up to a chair and sat, feeling her sense of balance vanish.

"Fuck." Thomas slammed the door shut. Jim and Matt Boyles jumped in their seats at the sound, both leaping to their feet nearly before their eyes opened. Both men had their hands on their weapons as they blinked at Brynn and Thomas.

Jim spoke first, his eyes narrowing on Brynn's face. "What is it? What's happened?"

"Liam's missing," Brynn whispered. Jim's gaze flew to Thomas, his eyes questioning. The big man nodded.

"No tracks."

"How can there be no tracks?"

All four turned in the direction of Alex's voice. He was on his feet, crouched in the cargo bay, his SIG in his hand. Brynn hadn't heard him stir. His eyes were penetrating shots of steel in the dim light.

No one answered. His question was rhetorical.

"Fuck." Tyrone's quiet curse rattled from the cargo area, and Brynn's heart cracked for him.

Jim leaned over a seat and shook Ryan awake. He stirred, waking slowly, pushing Jim's hand off his shoulder with a mumbled complaint. Brynn wanted to check his forehead but forced herself not to move. Ryan wouldn't appreciate the mothering in front of the other men. Her fingertips dug into the edge of her seat.

"What do we do?" Her words were barely audible. Was he lost? Had he gotten turned around in the forest? Had a bear found him? *Had Besand found him?*

"We go look for him," Alex stated calmly.

Brynn met his silver eyes, letting his confidence flow over her. Hope started to form in her heart.

"We'll break up into teams and search. There's got to be a sign of him somewhere." Alex's gaze lingered on Ryan's flushed face. "Ryan stays here with Tyrone." Ryan didn't protest, silently telling Brynn how horrid he felt.

Jim spoke first. "Matt and I together. Alex, you go with Thomas." He paused, meeting Brynn's eyes.

She looked down at Tyrone, ignoring the wet trails from his eyes. "I'll stay."

"Can you use the gun?" Jim asked.

Brynn swallowed and nodded. Ryan's blurry gaze met hers, and she knew he couldn't shoot if they had a surprise visitor. Someone needed to stay.

"I'll do whatever needs to be done." *Please, God, let nothing happen.*

"Get dressed," Jim ordered. "Matt and I'll head west, and you guys head east."

Alex and Thomas nodded, pulling on their jackets.

"Fire twice if you find him."

"When we find him," Alex muttered as he checked both his guns. Fear clenched Brynn's gut. The last time Alex had left he'd nearly been shot.

A hand slipped into hers and squeezed. Tyrone looked up at her in sympathy. "He'll be all right. They'll all be back."

Brynn gave an automatic smile and glanced back just in time to meet Alex's gaze before he stepped out of the plane. Silver eyes bore through her and touched her heart, warming it. Then he was gone, and she was empty.

"One, two, three, four. Yes! All of them." Using his binoculars, Darrin counted as he watched the searchers leave the plane. Alex in his bright-blue coat stuck out from the little group. So did the big dude who never wore a hood. The other two bodies looked and moved the same; he couldn't even tell which one was the woman.

Darrin needed a GPS to get out of this cursed forest.

And now the plane was empty.

It'd been a stroke of luck last night when the young guy had snuck out to piss. His pants had literally been down when Darrin slammed him in the head with a rock.

His luck was holding. Now all of them were going out to search for their fifth companion.

He tucked away the binoculars and moved toward the plane.

"One hour."

Alex nodded at Thomas's third reminder. Jim had ordered that they meet back at the plane after two hours of searching. Alex followed in the big man's footsteps, eyes constantly scanning for anything unusual in the snow. Any color, any movement. Anything. Every few minutes they'd stop and yell Liam's name only to be answered with silence. At least the weather was breaking. Blue sky was trying to peek between the clouds. The choppers could come soon, but they couldn't leave a man short. Pessimism was starting to make his feet drag.

What had happened to Liam?

If they hadn't been in the middle of the forest, Alex might have thought Liam left to put space between the two of them. A small wave of guilt washed through him. Last night he'd wanted to ram his fist into the younger man's mouth. The man had done his best to push Alex's buttons.

Liam must have left to take a piss. There was no other reason to leave. Liam knew the choppers were due today, and he would never leave Tyrone. Even though Liam might be a colossal pain in the ass, Alex understood his devotion to his brother.

Thomas broke into an awkward half run. "There. Over there."

Commanding his exhausted muscles to move, Alex jogged through the fluff. Ahead, at the base of a fir was a motionless red mound. *Fuck! Are we too late?*

Thomas darted under the branches and knelt by the still figure, uncovering Liam's face, and placing two fingers at his neck. Alex caught up and collapsed next to Thomas.

"Is he dead?" Alex huffed. Liam's face was white, almost a blue-white, and the man was way too still.

"He's got a pulse, a weak one," Thomas answered. "We've got to get him heated up. At least he's dry. Give me your hand warmers."

Alex handed over the warmers and froze at the sound of the gunshot.

"What the—" Thomas started.

And another gunshot.

Brynn. Alex's heart jumped into his throat. Adrenaline pumping, he leaped to his feet and took a step in the direction of the plane. He stopped, whirled around, and moved a step back toward Liam. He stood immobile, his heart and mind racing. *Who to help?*

"Could be the other team," Thomas said without conviction. His gaze met Alex's and then returned to Liam as he deftly packed the warmers under Liam's armpits.

"No." Alex knew in his gut the shots had come from the plane.

Thomas pulled his cell from his pocket. "I've got a signal. I'll try to reach Jim. Get him over here. You get back to the plane. But keep an eye out."

Relief flooded through Alex. "You sure?"

"Yes. Now get moving," Thomas ordered.

Alex didn't need to be told twice.

CHAPTER TWENTY

He was going to die.

Alex's lungs burned to the point he thought they were about to give out. He'd pushed hard through the snow, following the trail he and Thomas had broken during their search. Thirty minutes had passed since the shots. The forest had been silent since then.

Is she OK? Dear Lord, please keep her safe.

The plane came into view. All was quiet. Thirty yards away, Alex stopped at the top of a small rise and rested his hands on his knees, panting hard.

"Brynn! Ryan!" he shouted.

Still quiet.

He squinted at the snow by the plane door. *Is that blood?* His mouth dried up.

"Brynn!" His voice cracked and he sucked in another burning breath to yell again.

The door opened a few inches. "Alex?" Ryan yelled.

Alex fell to his knees, eyes watering. *Thank God. They are OK.*

"Alex? That you?" Ryan's call wavered, and Alex heard his fear.

Sparks of panic shot through his spine as he fought for breath.

"Ryan! It's me." Alex pushed to his feet and started to stumble down the slope. "What happened?"

Ryan stuck his head out. "He's got her! He's fucking got her!"

Noooo! Alex's heart split cleanly in half.

Darrin was a dead man.

Ryan pushed the door open as Alex staggered closer. There was blood on the snow. And it made a trail away from the plane. *Brynn?* His gaze followed the red-smeared path.

"Oh, God. Is that her blood?" Alex whispered. He fought down the bile in his throat.

"No." Ryan said. "That's Kiana's."

"Kiana's?"

"He fucking shot the dog. Kiana attacked him, and he shot her." Ryan's voice faltered. "He walked right in...no warning or nothing. Scared the shit out of me when he grabbed Brynn...I thought he was gonna shoot her. He held a fucking gun to her head and demanded a GPS. He was shocked that we were here. He'd counted how many people left the plane and expected it to be empty. He didn't know Tyrone, Liam, and Matt had joined us."

"A GPS?" Alex repeated. His brain spun wildly. He stared at Ryan, who held a rag to his bloody mouth. The kid looked ready to collapse. "Where's Tyrone?"

Ryan jerked his head toward the back of the plane. "He's lying down. Got kicked in the head."

"Oh, shit. With his injury..."

"I know," Ryan said. "He's thrown up twice since then. Not good."

Alex stepped inside. The sharp odor of vomit hit him in the face. He swallowed hard and squatted next to Tyrone. "How you doing?"

"I'm good," the hurt man croaked.

Like hell.

"Fucker took her." Tyrone winced. "Walked right in the door. Ryan and I were asleep back here. He caught Brynn off guard."

Anger flowed through Alex's veins. "I'm going to kill him."

"He took Ryan's gun...Brynn had it. She got off one shot... missed."

"Then Darrin punched her," Ryan added. "Right in the side of the head. Took the gun from her and got her in a headlock."

Tyrone pointed at Ryan. "This idiot tried to rush him and got nailed in the mouth with the gun...fucking lucky he didn't shoot him..."

"You shouldn't have grabbed at his boot!" Ryan argued.

"Jesus Christ! How long ago did they leave?" Alex couldn't sit still. He had to go after her.

"Twenty minutes maybe," Ryan said. "Damned dog went after them. He shot at Kiana when she lunged at him...thought she was dead." He shook his head as he met Alex's gaze. "Man. Brynn's scream..."

Furious, Alex ran a hand through his hair. *Shit.* The image of Brynn in Darrin's insane arms…

"I gotta go." Alex strode to the door and hesitated, looking back. "The other guys… Shit!…Thomas and I found Liam! He's alive, but barely."

Tyrone let out a loud breath. "Thank God."

"I left Thomas with him when we heard the shots. He was gonna try to get a hold of Jim."

"Just go, Alex!" Ryan urged. "Get her back."

Powered by rage, Alex stepped outside and followed the bloody trail.

"Hurry the fuck up!" Darrin roared in her ear.

Brynn stumbled in the snow. Pain shot through her shoulders as Darrin yanked her up by her hands that were tied behind her back.

"I could move faster if you untied—"

"Shut up!" He shoved at her back.

Brynn concentrated on keeping her balance. *Asshole.* She wiped a wet cheek on her shoulder. Darrin had yelled and pushed the whole way. She couldn't count the number of times she'd tripped. At least walking along the river was a little easier. The snow wasn't nearly as deep. She just had to watch out for slick rocks with her snowshoes or else she'd slip and fall down the steep slope into the water.

"I don't know how far it is to the train trestle," she told him again. "We could be walking for a week."

He let out a crack of sharp laughter. "I'll find it eventually. I'll move faster once I don't need you."

What? "Need me for what?" Her stomach twisted woozily. "I'm slowing you down, you just said so."

"You're bait."

"Bait?"

"Man bait." He laughed again.

Alex. The lunatic is trying to draw him out. Fresh tears prickled at her eyes. *First he killed Kiana and now he'll kill Alex.*

Darrin roughly yanked her to a stop. "Sit." He motioned at a fallen tree. Brynn gratefully sat and immediately continued her subtle fingering of the bungee cord he'd wrapped around her wrists. If she could only figure out where it hooked…

He pulled a short rope from a pocket and started to wrap it around her ankles. Brynn started. Apparently, she was done walking. He fumbled with the rope and then abruptly spun around, pulling her down from the log and close to him, slapping a hand over her mouth. "Quiet!" he whispered in her ear. Goose bumps rose on her arms, and Brynn shuddered.

Darrin peered over the fallen tree. A wide grin crossed his face.

"Alex," he breathed.

Brynn jerked in Darrin's arms, dread filling her stomach. *Alex.*

At the river he lost the trail. Along the water, the snow was choppy and uneven below the trees and the blood had slowed to the occasional drop. Scanning for the next drop, Alex stopped at the top of a ten-foot drop-off and eyed the icy, rushing water. Pure snow runoff.

"Morning, A-man."

Alex's throat closed as he slowly turned.

Brynn. His heart warming, Alex looked into her terrified brown eyes and held her gaze, ignoring Darrin, who had an arm around her neck and a gun at her head. She stood motionless in the man's tight hold, gasping with short breaths, her cheeks flushed.

"Beautiful girl, isn't she?" Darrin smirked.

I'll get you out of here, Brynn.

From twenty feet away, Darrin didn't look too tired for a man who'd been sleeping in a freezing forest. Alex had expected him to look as exhausted as he felt. Worse, even. Instead, Darrin looked downright pumped. Energetic. The killer's gun hand shook slightly, and Alex knew it was from excitement, not fear.

"Drop the gun, A-man." Darrin grinned.

Alex fixed his gaze on the killer and tossed his gun between them. He slowly raised his hands. *Damn.* He'd brought only one gun.

Alex's heart rate had nearly reached its limit, but he held himself calmly, eyes steady on Darrin's. Alex imagined knocking him down, wrapping his hands around his neck and squeezing. Using all his strength as Darrin's eyes bulged and he struggled for air, watching the light fade in his gaze as the evil exited his shell.

Alex saw himself standing up in victory, a corpse at his feet.

But why didn't he feel the satisfaction?

Darrin stepped closer and noticed Alex's gaze flick to his snowshoes and back again. "Surprised? I was when I stumbled across a backpack chock-full of just what I needed to make it out here. Thanks for leaving me the gift."

"You found Thomas's pack."

Darrin nodded, eyes gleaming. "The clothes were a little big. Not too bad."

"Who changed the flight plan? Whittenhall?"

Darrin sneered and gave Brynn's neck a tighter squeeze. Her eyes briefly flared in pain.

Alex took that as a "yes."

"How did you get on the rescue team?" Darrin asked. "Whittenhall would never send you out here."

"I was waiting at the airport in Hillsdale. When you didn't land as scheduled I made some calls. They told me the flight plan had been closed. Then I figured out your flight hadn't landed anywhere else. When I called the tower at Aurora to see if your flight had rerouted there, he told me about the small charter plane going down in the Cascades. I decided it was a definite possibility that the plane was yours."

"So the locater *was* working. That's how you found my plane."

Alex shook his head. "Gotta be in line of sight to pick up its signal. They weren't able to get any search planes in the air because of the storm and wind. Someone on the ground saw your plane in trouble and called it in. We had to guess where you went down."

Breathe in and out. Keep it even. His arms started to ache from their elevated position. Brynn's gaze never dropped from his. She was his lifeline. *Focus on her.* "What have you got on Whittenhall? Why would he change the flight plan for you?"

One side of Darrin's mouth twisted up, but he didn't answer.

Alex could tell the man wanted to answer. Darrin liked to talk. Especially when he thought he held the upper hand. Alex pushed harder. "I knew Whittenhall was dirty, and he pulled Linus into it with him."

Darrin smirked. "Idiot. Linus couldn't handle his addiction. Put that lovely family at risk because he was too spineless to handle a little gambling."

Rage ripped through Alex's nerves. *Don't think of Linus's kids.* He loosened his locked knees.

"What happened to Linus?"

Darrin shrugged. "He was dead when I woke up."

"The pilots weren't."

"One pilot was. The other was on his way."

Brynn struggled at Darrin's words, her eyes narrowing.

"You could have done something," Alex shot back.

Darrin's eyes widened. "Like what? Hold his hand? He called me an asshole. I was more than happy to let him watch the blood slowly drain from his body. I didn't owe him anything." His eyes darted about as he snorted.

"What did Whittenhall owe you? What was big enough to make him set up a chance for you to walk away, disappear?"

Darrin tilted his head as if debating an answer. "He's my cousin."

Alex blinked. "Family ties? He's breaking you out of prison because you're related? I don't believe it." *That can't be all.* If Darrin were *his* cousin, he'd put as much distance between them as possible.

Darrin shook his head, a grin splitting his face. "No. It's much more than that. Cousin Paul and I were very close while growing up. Even if he was ten years older."

"So you were close. How close?" Alex gave a smirk and raised a brow. He'd learned early on that Darrin got agitated if Alex hinted he thought Darrin had homosexual tendencies. It was one of the ways he could get Darrin to talk more, spill more secrets. Anger seemed to loosen the filter between Darrin's mouth and brain.

"Fuck you!" Darrin's knuckles whitened on the gun. "I'm not a faggot! It wasn't like that!"

"Then what are you talking about? You're not making sense. You're just talking in circles."

"He was there! He was there for my first!"

"Your first faggot blow job?"

"My first kill! He was there! He watched and did nothing to help her!" Darrin's grip tightened on Brynn's neck again. She shuffled with her bound feet, fighting to keep her balance.

"Who? Brenda?" Brenda Jeal had been Darrin's first victim twenty years ago. Her lovely face flashed through Alex's mind, followed by a dozen others.

Darrin laughed, anger evaporating, and waved a dismissing hand. "God no, way before that. Shit. We were still kids."

Fury bubbled up Alex's spine. Kids? He'd killed as a child? And Whittenhall had been there? "Kids?"

"Paul's younger sister." Darrin said the words like they tasted like the finest chocolate. Rich and delicious.

"What?" Bile curdled in his stomach. Darrin was lying. No one would…

"She drowned and we watched."

"You couldn't get to her?" *Please, God.*

"No, we were there in the pool with her. She couldn't swim. We watched." He gave a slow smile.

Pool. Drowning. Samuel. Alex physically deflated, his arms dropping. A wave of Darrin's gun had him lifting them back in the icy air.

Darrin laughed. "Oh, sorry. Remind you of someone?"

Alex blinked to get Samuel's innocent face out of his mind. He mentally steeled his determination.

"I'm not armed. Let's see you try to take me down. You've always said you could kick my ass if you weren't sitting in a jail cell. Here's your chance to prove it."

Darrin rolled his eyes, but Alex saw the interest flicker. "Yeah, right. I'm the one with a gun. Try to talk me into putting it down." He turned the gun on Alex. "I've thought a lot about how I would kill you if I had the chance. I've had lots of time to think. A bullet in the brain would end things too quickly. I wouldn't like that. I've heard kneecaps are nice and painful, but I don't trust my aim to be accurate enough to hit your skinny legs."

Alex closed his eyes. *Better the gun on me than Brynn.*

"Open your eyes!" Darrin shrieked.

Alex obeyed. Darrin looked overstimulated, crazed, like a kid who'd been sucking down sugar and caffeine all day.

"Gut shot. I should be able to do that. You don't die right away unless I rip your aorta or something. I've heard people can suffer for days after being shot in the stomach. You'll be begging me to shoot you in the head."

Darrin's eyes lit up, and his gun lowered slightly to line up with Alex's stomach. Brynn thrashed in his grip. "No! Don't!"

Darrin gave her neck a rough twist. "Shut up!"

A gray blur lunged at the killer. Kiana's teeth clamped around Darrin's hand, and he shrieked as he dropped the gun. He flung Brynn to one side and kicked at the dog. Alex tuned out Kiana's howl as he sprinted and tackled Darrin at the waist.

CHAPTER TWENTY-ONE

Brynn landed face-first in the snow, unable to catch herself with her tied hands. She flipped over and scooted away from the thrashing men. Alex was on Darrin's chest, his hands around the murderer's throat. Where was the gun? Brynn wildly scanned the snow and couldn't see it. The cord at her wrists gave an inch and she yanked harder.

Darrin's fist connected with Alex's jaw, jolting him off balance. The men rolled, and Darrin ended up on top. Until Alex's knee connected with his crotch. Darrin grunted, lost his grip, and Alex scuttled out from under him. From a crouch, Darrin sprang at Alex and knocked him on his back.

Brynn gasped. "Alex!"

Alex's foot hung over the cliff's edge. He thrust with his other foot and heaved away from the drop-off. Fists and snow flew. Curses and grunts filled the air.

Brynn saw Kiana raise her head. *Thank God!* The dog had been immobile since Darrin's kick. Brynn struggled with her hands and felt the cord slide another inch.

"I'm gonna drown you like I drowned your retard brother!"

Brynn looked up and her heart stopped. Darrin had maneuvered the struggle back to the cliff's edge. On his back, Alex's shoulder dangerously bordered the rim.

"Fuck!" Flinging his legs up and shoving with his arms, Alex propelled Darrin headfirst over the edge toward the river. The killer screamed.

"Alex!" Brynn shrieked as Alex flopped on his stomach and grasped at the snow to keep from tumbling off the edge. He caught his balance and twisted to look over the ledge at the water. Alex lay transfixed for three seconds. He shot to his feet and his silver gaze appraised her. "Are you OK?"

Brynn nodded, her heart racing.

"I'll be back." Alex dashed downstream.

Alex fixated on the bobbing head in the river as he floundered along the bank. Darrin vanished and reappeared. Alex pushed hard, his lungs straining for air. Ahead, a tree had fallen partway into the river. If Darrin could catch it…

The rough water swept the man under the trunk.

"Damn it!"

Alex slid to a stop. Why'd he run after the man? Panting, he rested his hands on his knees. Because he was better than Besand. He couldn't be a cold-blooded killer; it wouldn't bring his brother back. And death was too easy for the murderer. He deserved a lifetime behind bars.

Color flashed on the other side of the tree trunk in the water. Alex squinted.

Darrin had caught a branch.

Alex jogged to the tree, pulled off his snowshoes and coat, and climbed onto the trunk. Darrin clung to a thin branch, his legs pointing downstream, his eyes wide. On frozen hands and knees Alex crawled out over the river. The tree sloped down at a thirty-degree angle into the water. He felt like he was about to tumble headfirst. It was like crawling on a narrow, rounded sheet of ice covered in snow. The tree vibrated with the pounding of the river and shook as debris caught in its underwater branches.

Holy Christ.

He inched forward, and his right knee slid. He sucked in a fast breath then righted, found a solid grip, and continued to creep forward inch by inch.

He stopped above Darrin's branch and straddled the tree. He leaned forward, laying his chest on the trunk, and stretched out his right hand, anchoring himself with a branch in his left hand. Darrin clung to the branch with both hands, immersed in the water up to his armpits, and stared at Alex's hand.

"Grab it, damn it! I'll pull you in." His knees tightened on the trunk like he was riding a horse. "Grab my hand!" His left hand slid a millimeter, and he tightened his hold. Darrin's white fingers moved stiffly on his branch. His face was pale, his lips blue. He was running out of time. His limbs would soon be useless.

If they weren't already.

"Now!" With a jerk, he stretched out his hand another half inch, feeling his shoulder protest. One of Darrin's hands unclawed from the branch and pawed uselessly. Alex grabbed it. It was like grabbing ice. Slick, wet, and frozen.

"Now, hang on! Pull yourself up the branch while I pull!" Alex gave a steady long heave. Darrin tried to get some leverage on the branch to drag himself closer. The water pulled at his body, weaving him from side to side, trying to drag him away. Agony struck Alex's right shoulder and his arm ripped from its socket. "Fuck!" Pain shot nails down to his hand. "Pull up! Pull yourself up!"

Darrin focused on Alex's shoulder. Alex followed his gaze and saw the outline of his right deltoid muscle showed a deep notch where it should arc. The arm was useless. A gleam narrowed the killer's eyes. He sucked in a breath, let go of his branch, and hauled on Alex's arm with all his weight.

Alex's anchoring hand slipped off its branch. He flailed about for a grip as Darrin shrieked with laughter.

Strong arms wrapped around Alex's waist. "Shake him off," Brynn shouted in his ear. Alex shook his head.

"I can't move my arm!"

From behind, Brynn shifted him and Alex grabbed a secure branch. He exhaled, his heart ready to pound its way out of his chest. He felt Brynn slide toward Darrin. "Brynn! What are—"

Brynn swung her boot down on the killer's grip. At the impact, pain ripped through Alex's arm and he bit down on his lip.

Darrin let go.

The water ripped the killer downstream. Alex held his breath and watched Darrin vanish under the surface. He counted to ten. *Come up, you bastard!* Darrin didn't reappear.

Brynn tightened her arms around Alex and rested her head against his back. "It's OK, you tried."

Damn it.

Slowly Brynn inched backward, keeping one arm around Alex's waist. She tuned out the rush of the water, concentrating on the man in front of her.

She took a shuddering breath. She'd almost lost him.

"Are you all right?" Alex asked over his shoulder.

She nodded. "Yes."

"You came out over the water."

Quivers rattled down her spine. "You needed me. Now, careful, I'm gonna hop off onto the bank. I'll help you down. Watch your arm." His arm dangled uselessly, looking longer than the other. *Shit.* She couldn't reset it alone.

Alex awkwardly climbed off the tree and pulled her close with his good arm. "I thought you were dead. I didn't think I'd get to you in time." He pressed his face into her hair.

Brynn leaned into his chest, her arms sliding up around his neck, the horrors of the past hours melting away. Nothing else mattered. She was safe. Darrin was gone.

"He was going to pull you into the water," her voice cracked.

She felt a rumble in his chest. "I thought I was a goner. Thank God…"

He lifted his head and ran a hand down her face, pushing back her hair, gazing ferociously into her eyes. "I didn't think we were going to have a chance."

Warmth spread through her. "We do now."

He smiled, and her heart contracted at the sight. His smiles were so rare. *I want to see more of them, a lot more.* Her arms tightened about his neck. He winced. She stepped back. "Your arm. I forgot."

"I don't care. Touch me again," he begged, eyes sparkling.

She reached up and held his face, the stubble rough to her hands. Gently she tugged his face to hers and kissed him.

His mouth was soft and warm, and she wanted more of his heat. She moved closer, and he deepened the kiss. This was what she wanted, what she needed. He stopped to catch his breath and leaned his forehead against hers, his eyes closed. "Brynn," he whispered. Tears pricked at tenderness in his voice.

"Helloooo! Alex! Brynn!"

"That's Jim!" Brynn turned at the shouts and Alex mumbled a low curse. "Over here!" she yelled back.

Alex pulled her back to face him. "We're not done here. Agreed?"

Happiness sparked through her, and she gave him a wide smile. "Not by a long shot."

"Brynn!" Jim hollered again as he and Thomas stepped into view. Thomas had Kiana in his arms. Brynn met them halfway, burying Jim in a long, deep hug. "Thank God you're OK," he said. She turned to Thomas and rubbed Kiana's head.

"Is she all right?"

Thomas nodded. "Bullet grazed her. She's lost some blood, but I think she'll be fine. Not real happy about me carrying her." Kiana thrashed in his arms, and he gently set her down. Brynn threw her arms around him, and he patted her awkwardly on the back.

"Thank you," she whispered.

Jim and Alex were speaking in low tones as Jim assessed his shoulder.

"Where's Besand?" Thomas asked.

"Dead. He went under in the water." Brynn shuddered at the memory of the insane man's eyes as he floated away.

"Good," Thomas said ominously. His face brightened slightly. "And Liam's gonna be fine. Has a big knot on the back of his head and was pretty chilled, but he'll live. Matt's playing nursemaid to all three guys."

"Thank goodness," Brynn breathed guiltily. How had she forgotten about Liam? "Alex's shoulder is out of joint. Can you help me put it back?" The big man nodded.

She met Alex's powerful gaze as they joined him and Jim. Her limbs went weak. How would she have lived without him?

Thomas spread his parka on the ground. "Lie down," he ordered Alex.

Alex eyed the coat. "This is gonna hurt, isn't it?"

"Just for a second."

"Fuck." Alex obeyed.

"Use his jacket to make a U around his ribs," Thomas instructed her. "Pull both sleeves toward you. It's got to keep him from moving while I pull on his right arm." Brynn nodded. She knew the drill.

"Never seen this done before," Alex muttered. "Except in *Lethal Weapon*, when Mel slams his shoulder against the wall."

"Just hang on for a minute," Brynn soothed him.

Thomas gently bent Alex's elbow so that his fingers pointed at the sky. He pulled out firmly on his elbow then rotated his arm like he was guiding him to throw a baseball. Alex gasped and clenched his jaw. The notch at the shoulder didn't change. Behind Brynn, Jim swore softly.

"Gotta do it again," Thomas muttered. He wiped a hand across his forehead.

Brynn nodded, pulling firmly on the sleeves to keep Alex from sliding toward Thomas's pull on his arm. Thomas did the

overhand pitching movement again and Brynn heard a *thunk* as
the bone slid into the socket. A gruesome sound.

"Ahh," Alex exhaled, his face relaxing. "God! That's better."

"You're gonna hurt tonight." Thomas repositioned Alex's
arm across his chest. "I need something to rig him a sling."

Jim ripped open his jacket. "I've got on an extra shirt." He
dropped his jacket and pulled a long-sleeved thermal over his
head. Brynn slid the parka out from under Alex while Thomas
tied the shirt around his arm and fastened it at his neck.

"That'll do."

"Thanks, man." Alex held out a hand, and Thomas pulled
him up to his feet.

Brynn wrapped Alex's coat around him and rested her head
on his chest. "Ready to head back?"

Alex kissed the top of her head. "I'm ready for anything as
long as you're with me."

Brynn fought back tears. Happy tears.

Jim spoke up, "Anyone else hear a chopper?"

CHAPTER TWENTY-TWO

Two Pave Hawk helicopters briefly hovered over the base camp, and Alex stared in awe at the mass of people, cameras, and microphones. The copters landed, blowing the hoods and hats off the spectators and media. Other Madison County Search and Rescue members used their bodies to set up a protective alley from the copters to waiting ambulances, which immediately sped Liam and Tyrone to the hospital. After a short argument, Alex and Ryan refused to get in the ambulance. Alex accepted some painkillers and a sling, and then he brushed off the EMT's help.

Reporters shouted their questions at the small group. Brynn stuck close to Alex, alternating between glaring at him for refusing care and glaring at the reporters. Sheriff Collins and two other deputies hustled the tired group into the Madison County RV. Collins shooed out the deputies and slammed the door. Alex inhaled the smell of hot coffee; his mouth watered. Someone had cranked up the heat to heavenly. Alex yearned to lie down on the cheap mattress in the back of the RV and sleep for a week. He noticed Matt casting longing looks in the direction of the beds too.

Collins poured six huge cups of coffee, and everyone sighed as they sipped. He filled a bowl with water and set it down for Kiana. The RV was crowded with seven bodies and a large dog, but it felt like a palace after the plane.

"OK." Collins leaned his bulk against the tiny sink, took a sip of coffee, and ran a hand across his forehead. "You're sure Darrin Besand didn't survive? You thoroughly checked the area?"

Everyone nodded.

"No one could survive in that water," Jim added.

Collins's gaze rested on Matt and he lifted a brow. He turned to Alex. "You didn't tell me yesterday that you'd found the team of marshals. What happened to the other marshal?"

"Gary Stewart. He took a shot at Alex. I tackled him and he pulled a gun on me." Matt looked directly at Collins as he spoke.

"I shot Stewart." Every set of eyes turned to Alex. "He was about to shoot Matt in the head."

"Stewart had orders to kill you, didn't he?" Collins asked flatly.

Alex nodded.

"Because Whittenhall was worried Darrin would tell you his dirty history if you caught up with him out there," Collins added.

"Darrin did talk. He claimed Whittenhall stood with him and purposefully watched his younger sister drown in a pool years ago." Alex spoke evenly as Brynn nodded. He felt her hand slip into his.

"What?" The men reacted at his words, bodies stiffening, eyes widening.

"That's fucking sick," Matt said.

"When they were kids?" Ryan paled.

"Your tip on Paul Whittenhall has opened a big can of stinking worms," Collins said to Alex. "You were right about him."

Alex's gaze shot to Collins. "You found a reporter to run with the story? One who figured it out?"

"Who? Who figured out what?" Ryan spoke.

"Regan Simmons, reporter for Channel 5 in Portland, found the money trail that led from Whittenhall's dirty pockets to an offshore account in Darrin's name. She dug deeper and found a dozen prisoners who'd been moved to cushier prisons or released abnormally early. She's got families willing to testify they paid Whittenhall to give their imprisoned relative all sorts of illegal breaks.

"And she's set up a media blitz that's informed every citizen in Oregon and probably in the United States what the scumbag was up to. I had three deputies following every move Whittenhall made since yesterday morning when Alex called me with his suspicions that Whittenhall was on the take. I didn't want Whittenhall heading for the border when the news broke. When Regan's proof started pouring in, I had him arrested."

"He couldn't have managed those favors alone. There's got to be more people involved. Dozens, maybe," Alex muttered. *Linus.*

Collins nodded. "They're coming out of the woodwork. Darrin had been blackmailing Whittenhall with the information. Apparently, Darrin's attorney had a file to open if Darrin died under unusual circumstances. A file Darrin used to keep Whittenhall under his thumb. And guess what? This plane crash was unusual enough for the attorney to open the file." Collins shook his head. "In there was proof that Whittenhall was involved in receiving monies from families of his prisoners and that he committed murders when he and Darrin were kids."

"His sister," mumbled Alex, feeling the contents in his stomach spin.

Collins nodded. "And more. At least three more between the two of them."

Alex's hands ached to punch Whittenhall in his blowhard mouth. At least he'd managed to stab him once. *How had the agent become such a powerful man in law enforcement? How had he fooled people for so many years? Obviously, the man had serious mental issues.*

The room fell silent, and Brynn squeezed his hand. Collins's brown gaze pinned him. "One more thing. I'm not going to charge you with impersonating a federal agent. I understand why you did what you did, and I'm going to do everything I can to keep your name out of this mess, because, frankly, I don't know how to explain it." Collins's look extended to the others. "As far as you're concerned, it was just the regular four-man SAR team out there until you met up with Boyles and Stewart."

Relief rolled through Alex like a storm.

"What about Stewart?" Alex asked. "There has to be a reason he ended up dead."

"I shot him when he pulled a gun on me," Matt stated.

"I witnessed the whole thing," Thomas spoke for the first time.

They can't do this.

"No. This isn't right." Alex straightened. "My shots, I take the consequences."

Collins ignored him and looked at his watch. "I've got a press conference to handle." He pointed at a tiny TV as he stepped out of the RV. "Take a listen."

Alex slumped. His hand shook as he lifted the coffee cop to his lips. Matt turned on the TV.

Fifteen seconds later the group watched Collins on the small screen; the harsh camera lights made his face appear more tired than in the RV. Collins looked over his audience and waited, his solemn countenance bringing silence to the press. Admiration for the tough man welled up in Alex's throat. Collins was the kind of man he would like to work for.

Collins spoke, "All the men on board the US Marshals' transport perished in the crash. Two pilots, a marshal, and serial killer Darrin Besand." A quiet ripple sounded from the crowd.

"My search and rescue team camped at the crash site because one member became ill and couldn't hike out. Due to adverse weather conditions, we couldn't go in and get them. Day before yesterday, the team split up. Two men had intended to hike out for help when they crossed the path of a chopper wreck. Without my knowledge or approval, this civilian chopper had been searching for the downed plane. The pilot was severely injured, and the team returned to the crash site with the two men from the chopper."

Collins paused and studied the silent crowd who hung on his every word. "The US Marshals' office sent in their own two-man team to search for the plane. When one of the marshals turned on the other, he was killed in return fire. The second marshal came out with my team just now."

A murmur rolled across the crowd. Reporters started to shout questions, but Collins held up his hands for silence. "There were two head injuries, a team member with a dislocated shoulder, and another member with the flu. You all saw them walk to the ambulances, and I'm told they'll be just fine. Now I'll take a few questions." The crowd erupted. Collins singled out one reporter in front.

"Why did one marshal shoot at the other?"

Collins paused. "The shooting marshal was acting under direct orders from Paul Whittenhall. I know you've all heard about the corruption at the upper level of the Oregon Marshals' office. The second marshal is lucky to be alive. Paul Whittenhall has a lot to answer for. And he'll be doing it from a prison cell."

A blurry mass of questions rose from the crowd. Collins pointed at a woman.

"Sheriff, how long have you known no one survived the plane crash?"

Collins looked grim. "I knew about three of the deaths early on and spoke privately with their families. One body wasn't found with the plane. The plane had split into two pieces and the searchers didn't locate the last body until yesterday. I was waiting for news of the fourth death before releasing the news of all the deaths. That'll be all for now."

Matt turned off the TV.

A knock sounded on the door, and one of the deputies stuck his head in. "Who wants to go to McDonald's? Then a hotel with real beds?"

CHAPTER TWENTY-THREE

Alex ate two Big Macs, a supersize fries, and a Coke. Then fell promptly to sleep in the Suburban on the way to the hotel.

Brynn shook him awake as the deputy pulled to a stop. People in the lobby stared at the dirty and disheveled group. In a stupor, Alex checked in and said good night to Ryan, Jim, and Matt at the elevator. He held on to Brynn's hand, unable to let her go.

They stumbled into his room. Alex immediately showered while Brynn called the hospital to check on Tyrone and Liam. He considered shaving, but there wasn't a razor in the little kit from the hotel, just a toothbrush and toothpaste. He brushed for ten minutes. No razor was a good thing, because he might accidentally cut his throat in exhaustion.

Alex stared at his pile of filthy clothes on the floor in the bathroom and shrugged at his lack of clean clothes. He slipped his arm back into the sling, grabbed a robe off the back of the door, and stepped out of the steamy bliss into the warm room. Brynn had cranked up the thermostat.

"Liam's gonna be OK," she announced. "Tyrone too. The hospital's gonna keep Tyrone for a couple of nights but will release Liam in the morning." She gave him a quick kiss, pushed past him, and closed the door to the bathroom.

Alex looked at the closed door. Then looked at the bed. He dropped his robe and slid under the covers naked.

Fuck, yes.

Crisp, clean sheets. Four pillows. And lots of blankets. Heaven. Groggy with fatigue, he instantly fell asleep.

He woke as Brynn slipped into bed beside him. She smelled of fresh soap, damp hair, and woman.

She was in his bed.

That thought was enough to bring him fully awake.

He turned her to him, just as he had that night in the airplane, and she nestled her head into his chest with a sigh. He brushed the hair off her cheek and ran his hand down her back, in shock that she was next to him.

And man, oh man. She was *naked* next to him.

He pressed his lips against hers, running his tongue along her top lip and then catching her lower lip between his teeth, eager to get closer. She leaned into the kiss, responding fervently. He kissed her deeply then moved up her cheek, tracing the path his eyes had followed a dozen times. He felt her lips press against his neck, and she gave a tiny jerk, then giggled.

"You need a shave. It's soft but tickles my lips like crazy."

"No razor." He gave a slow grin, holding her gaze. "No clothes, either."

"Is that a problem right now?"

"God, no." He moved back to her mouth, and her hips moved against him. She shifted closer, lifting her leg to run her bare foot up his calf. The sensation raced up his leg to his spine, and hot desire shot through his nerves.

Her hand moved to his stomach. And bumped his right arm.

"Ah!" He froze. Stars danced before his eyes.

"Oh! I'm sorry. Crap."

"This isn't going to work, is it?" He pulled his good arm over his eyes.

"Don't even think about stopping!" She pushed up on one arm. "I've been waiting three days for this, and I'm not going to let that shoulder put it off any longer. We'll make it work."

Alex uncovered his eyes and studied her. "Three days?"

She sniffed. "The first day I thought you were an aloof, cold fed."

"And after that?" His ears perked up, eager for her reply.

"I thought you were interesting." She rolled onto her back, copying his position, looking at the ceiling.

"Interesting," he echoed.

"And kinda good-looking."

"Kinda?" He raised one brow.

"With a hard, incredible body." She glanced at him out of the corner of her eye and gave a sly grin.

"How could you tell through four layers of clothing?" Pleased, he rolled her on top of him, loving the feel of her naked skin on his. She carefully avoided his shoulder, placing her hands on the bed by his neck, as his erection pressed at her. Her pupils dilated and her hair swept across his chest. His gaze locked on those gorgeous lips.

"Through what?" Her breaths came faster.

He ran a hand through her hair and pulled her face to his, lightly pressing her lips to his. "I forget what I said." He settled in to kiss her harder, not giving her a chance to come up for air. His hand traced down her back, following smooth skin, and then around to touch the side of her breast. Her nipples hardened against him. Alex moaned at the sensation.

"Make love to me, Alex. Please. Right now." She spoke against his lips. "I just need to feel you inside me now."

"But..." He wanted to explore, investigate every inch of this body that he'd been dreaming of for four days.

"Now, Alex. We can take our time later. Next time." Her hips rotated slowly against him.

She didn't need to ask him twice. He ran a hand to her center; his cock hardened at the slick wetness.

Her nails traced up his chest, over the sling, to graze his nipples. His body jerked at the contact as fire spread from her simple touch. Her lips curved against his, and she did it again. His back arched off the bed.

His finger circled her clit and he felt her grow wetter, her body softening at his touch. He repeated the movement, drank in her answering moan, and sunk two fingers deep inside her, pressing upward.

"Ah! Alex!" She arched her spine, pressing down, drawing him deeper.

Lifting up, his mouth moved to the side of her neck, grazing his teeth up to her ear. His fingers slid out, moved around her clit again, and she shuddered. He ran his tongue along the edge of her ear, and she rose up on her knees. Taking his cock in hand,

346 • KENDRA ELLIOT

she guided him to her entrance. Her breath came in short gasps, and she tilted to ease his way. So hot, so slick. With one hand he grasped her shoulder, pulling her securely to him, lightly sinking his teeth into her ear and ramming home.

She inhaled, nails sinking into his chest. The little stabs of pain helped him find a measure of control. He held still for three seconds until she started to move on top of him, settling into a rhythm. A fire built at the back of his spine, and he clenched his jaw to keep from exploding into her. He slid a hand down her stomach to touch her again, tease her. Her knees dug into the mattress as she sucked for air.

"Alex." His name was a soft gasp as her contractions clamped around his cock. He plunged deep, letting go and filling her as he hoarsely uttered her name in prayer.

Brynn opened her eyes and found Alex's steel gaze watching her. She blinked, surprised she wasn't startled to wake up next to him. Warmth flowed over her as she remembered last night's activities.

"What time is it?" She stretched. *A real bed.*

"Six in the morning."

"Have you slept?"

"Off and on. Each time I wake up, you're still here. I tried to stay awake to simply look at you and enjoy having you next to me." His lips curved into a smile that touched her heart.

Alex rolled onto his back and reached for a mug on the nightstand.

Brynn shot up. "Is that coffee?" She leaned over him, inhaling deeply through her nose, her stomach growling at the rich scent. It was black, she noted. *He likes his coffee black.*

"Want some?" His eyes were innocent.

She narrowed her eyes at him. "You need to learn to not get between me and my first cup of coffee each morning."

He stilled, his eyes widening a fraction. "I will?" he asked quietly.

"You will what?"

"Each morning. Not get between you and your coffee."

She swallowed, her mouth suddenly dry. "I'd like you to," she whispered, knowing they weren't talking about coffee.

"You barely know me."

She shook her head. "I know plenty. You're a man who cares about others, risks his life for people he barely knows and fights to find truth when he knows something isn't right." She held his gaze, pulling the words from her heart. "I know your brother's death hurt you deeply, but I swear you came to peace with it while we were out in the woods. You had the chance to kill the man who killed your brother. Instead, you risked your life to save him. You joined our group for your own purpose, but you became a part of our tight-knit little family. Even Thomas likes you. Thomas doesn't like anybody."

Alex coughed and grinned. "You think so?"

She nodded.

"You've given this some serious thought."

"I have. I had to figure out why I fell for you within days, when I'd been with Liam for years and never felt as I did in the woods. Locked in that tiny plane with seven other men, you were the one who attracted every sensor in my body."

Alex looked at her, transfixed.

She blinked hard.

He gave a slow smile as he sat up, put his coffee back on the table, pulled her head close, and kissed her softly.

"The first time I saw you in that dripping rain, a fire lit inside me. Something flared that'd been cold since Samuel's death. You made me feel alive, and I didn't recognize the feeling. It'd been too long."

He ran a finger down her cheek, following it with wondering eyes. "I was so focused on that killer, I'd shut out everything good in my life. I couldn't remember what it'd felt like to be happy or content. You made me want to be the man I'd been years ago. The man I thought I'd never be again." He pressed against her, and arousal flared in her veins.

She rested her hand over his heart and marveled at the powerful, rapid beats. "I don't want you to be empty again," she whispered.

"I'm only looking forward," he promised. His gaze held hers in its steel grip. "I see myself bringing you coffee every morning for a very long time."

She swallowed hard, happiness tightening her throat. "That sounds perfect."

His grin widened. "And I've always wanted a dog…"

ACKNOWLEDGMENTS

A fantastic team of generous people helped shaped this book. Thank you to Jennifer S. for her stories about search and rescue, for her experiences as a forensic nurse investigator, and for being the type of woman who made me think, "She'd be a fabulous heroine." Thank you to my brother Blake Caudle, a pilot, for being patient with all my airplane questions. Thank you to my girls who ate soooo much frozen pizza and who loved to tell their friends, "My mommy writes books." I owe thanks to my agent, Jennifer Schober, and my editors Lindsay Guzzardo and Charlotte Herscher, who made *Chilled* a wonderful book. And the biggest thanks goes to my husband, Dan, who read this book and flatly informed me the final action scene sucked. He was right. Together we made it better, and I hope my readers enjoy the story.

ABOUT THE AUTHOR

Born and raised in the Pacific Northwest, Kendra Elliot has always been a voracious reader, cutting her teeth on classic female sleuths and heroines like Nancy Drew, Trixie Belden, and Laura Ingalls before proceeding to devour the works of Stephen King, Diana Gabaldon, and Nora Roberts. She graduated with a degree in journalism but went on to become a licensed dental hygienist. Now a Golden Heart, Daphne du Maurier, and Linda Howard Award of Excellence finalist, Elliot shares her love of suspense in her second novel, *Chilled*. She still lives in the Pacific Northwest with her husband and three daughters.

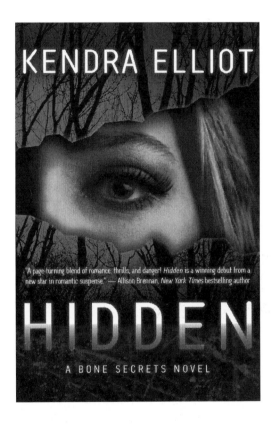

Made in the USA
Charleston, SC
15 September 2012